A
TASTE

of
BLOOD
WINE

BOOK ONE
of the
BLOOD WINE SEQUENCE

A TASTE of BLOOD WINE

BOOK ONE
of the
BLOOD WINE SEQUENCE

FREDA WARRINGTON

TITAN BOOKS

A Taste of Blood Wine
Print edition ISBN: 9781781167052
E-book edition ISBN: 9781781167250

Published by Titan Books
A division of Titan Publishing Group Ltd
144 Southwark Street, London SE1 0UP
www.titanbooks.com

First edition: October 2013

10 9 8 7 6 5 4 3 2 1

A CIP catalogue record for this title is available from the British Library.

Printed and bound in the United States.

CONTENTS

This book is dedicated with love to my mother, Ida Warrington, who let me watch vampire films at an impressionable age...

RIDE TO HELL

Oh! hateful shadow!
Oh! pallid companion!
Why mockest thou my grief and woe?

HEINE, "DER DOPPELGÄNGER"

The battlefield was deserted now. The fighting swept onwards, leaving an uneasy lull that lay as thick as fog, shuddering with distant explosions. As he moved across the devastated plain, the vampire paused to look up at the sky.

Shellfire punctured the skin of night. A mile away, scarlet spheres of light rose against blackness; sparks fountained and fell in showers. The vampire was arrested by yellow fire-trails and the soundless fall of smoke. Beauty, even here. A rocket, drifting down on a silk parachute, lit up the landscape. The freezing light filled shell-holes with phantom movement.

Underneath the fire of the sky lay craters, ruined trenches and lines of barbed wire trodden into the mud; and everywhere, the dead and dying.

The vampire walked through no man's land where men had been buried by explosions, thrown out of their rough graves, half buried again; where the wounded were left to die because their comrades could not reach them. He walked unhurriedly: an impossible apparition to anyone left alive. The thud of shell-bursts that drove men mad did not trouble him. Several bullets had passed through him, but his flesh healed swiftly in their wake. The carnage could not touch him physically, yet his eyes were clouded.

The dying: he sensed them all around him. Through the stink of mud and smoke rolled the smell of blood, heavy and sweetly enticing. His thirst rose, independent of his horror. Thirst and revulsion. The powerful tang of death and blood congealed in the back of his throat.

No human could hear the cries of the injured above the barrage, but the vampire could not shut them out. Screams and sobs, the last dry groans of those who were past calling for help. One voice, plaintive and piercing, cried in German for his mother.

No one would come to help them. No one could.

Deep in a crater, the vampire found a soldier submerged in mud. His uniform was plastered to his body, his face black with dirt, but his eyes flickered white with each burst of false daylight. An English soldier, this one. Viscera gleamed through a great hole in his abdomen. To the vampire's enhanced sight, the reds and purples of raw flesh were vivid. Blood seeped into an oily pool in the floor of the shell-hole.

The man was in agony almost beyond speech, but he reached out to claw at the vampire's legs. A grimace broke like a wound across his face.

"Knew you'd come if I hung on. It's this ruddy 'elmet. Can't get comfortable."

The vampire knelt beside him, supported his head and removed the tin helmet. The hair beneath was baby blond, the face under the grime so young; too young... yet old enough to die in war.

"Thanks, mate," said the soldier. "Where's Harry, did they find Harry?"

"I don't know," the vampire replied softly. He bent down, looking at the pulse beating in the boy's throat; avoiding his eyes. *God, so young.*

"They coming with a stretcher?" The young man swallowed drily. "Gawd, it hurts. Will it be long?"

"No," said the vampire. "Not long."

The skin of the boy's neck tasted foul, bitter with ingrained filth. The hot pulse of blood laced the foulness, drawing the vampire on until the skin broke and fluid burst onto his tongue.

Crystal sweetness. A ruby light that out-dazzled the battle flares, the two-edged ecstasy of feeding: a compulsion so strong that it almost sickened. Wrong to take pleasure in this death, impossible not to... The vampire closed his eyes in bliss as he drank, but the bitter taste remained.

Only once the boy cried out, more in shock than pain. Then he sank into unconsciousness. His heart rolled on tenaciously like the endless rumble of guns, each throb softer and heavier than the last, clinging to life... until there was stillness. One moment of utter silence and peace.

As the vampire let the boy go, the reality of battle came down like a booming tarpaulin. He felt warm, on fire, but the young soldier's skin was icy and his head hung to one side. Free of pain, at least.

The vampire raised his head. He wanted to move on, but something made him pause: an unmistakable tightening of the ether.

The air crystallised in the image of a stained glass angel, stark black and white. Stepping from a hidden dimension, this apparition became flesh and blood: an immense, forbidding man with dark hair and waxen skin. The face, too angular to be handsome, radiated the solid conviction of a born leader. There was a mole on his left cheek, a black singularity against the whiteness.

The newcomer looked down at the vampire, his eyebrows a severe dark line.

"I find you in the strangest places, Karl," he said. His voice was deep and resonant. A priest's voice.

The vampire Karl sat back on his heels. The intrusion wearied and alarmed him equally.

"I didn't ask you to look for me, Kristian. I don't want you here," he replied.

"You don't want me?" There was keen, sweet menace in the intruder's voice. "You can't deny me, any more than you can deny the existence of air! Not the air, nor God, nor myself. You shouldn't be here, beloved. I am your master, and I want you back."

An explosion shook the air. Kristian looked up, distracted, even shocked. His profile was harsh against the red glow.

Karl waited for the noise to fade. Then he said, "It's four years since we last had this argument. I hoped you had let me go. Why confront me here, now?"

"I'm trying to save you from yourself."

Kristian squatted down, eyeing the corpse that lay between them.

"Did the boy die fast, or slowly?" he murmured. "Did he suffer?"

Karl, repulsed, didn't answer.

Kristian spoke in a harder tone. "There's no need for you to be here. There are cities where lights glitter and living people throng the streets, the war no more than newsprint. You could feed among them and return to the comfort of Schloss Holdenstein, with the rest of my flock. Why immerse yourself in this horror?"

"Why not?" said Karl.

"Because it's nothing to do with us, this human mess!" Kristian struck the ground. "We are above it!"

"Are we?" Karl feared Kristian, but would never let the fear win. "Why shy away from evil, when our kind personifies evil? You dismiss it now – but later you'll want every detail. Vicarious thrills from afar. Perhaps the war horrifies you because it is a greater evil even than you."

"Do not speak of evil, Karl." Kristian's dark eyes gleamed. "The only Devil is mankind. This is the very folly for which we must punish them. What should I do but watch and laugh as they destroy each other? Yet you immerse yourself in it. You're no better than a boy poking a dead rat with a stick. Do you think you are doing any good here?"

Karl stood up slowly. He was caked with filth, but the dirt was nothing to him. He felt divorced from the squalor. He and Kristian were spectres glimpsed only by the dying.

"No," he said quietly. "What I do is wrong. But some of them... they're only children."

"Do you think I don't know what you feel?" Kristian moved beside him and rested a heavy hand on his shoulder. "You cannot die, yet you're still obsessed by death. The more you pursue it, the further it recedes. So why torment yourself, when I've given you the answers a thousand times?"

"You think you know everything," Karl said wearily. "How can you stay so arrogant, after seeing this?"

"There's nothing arrogant about the truth." Kristian's grip tightened. "I could pass along those wretched lines of soldiers like a hurricane, an angel of death worse than any shellfire. I'll show them war, I *am* war!" His lips drew back from long white teeth. "Still, I choose to remain apart because it's nothing to us, merely insects battling in an ant-hill. We have the whole sky, the Crystal Ring. Why obsess over the petty concerns of men? Come back with me, Karl." Kristian's voice became fatherly, persuasive. He ran a finger along Karl's cheekbone. "Still such a beauty. You shine like a star in this filth. It can't touch you."

The other vampire was silent.

"I can *make* you come back."

"I know," said Karl. "But you won't."

Kristian's smile was poison. "I'm waiting for the happy day when you return of your own free will."

"Do you have infinite patience?" As always, Karl felt trapped by Kristian's domineering power, but he pushed the feeling away. Rashly, he spoke his mind. "I look at you and see no answers. Only hollowness. God and the Devil... they're just words, attempts to give shape to the unknowable. Yet they evaporate even as you speak them and the world is still here, unchanged. Cling to your beliefs, if you must. Don't impose them on me. They give no meaning to this madness."

"Blasphemy!" roared Kristian. With one hand he held Karl's arm hard enough to crush the muscles; with the other he thrust a sharp fingernail deep into the flesh of his throat.

Gasping at the savage pain, Karl tried to break his grip. But Kristian was as unyielding as rock. He kept his fingernail in the wound as Karl's swift-healing, unhuman skin closed around it.

"I could tear your heart from your chest!" cried Kristian. "How will it feel, to be bodily pulled apart when you cannot lose consciousness? To be torn and heal, over and over? I've done worse to others less wayward than you!"

He ripped his fingernail out of Karl's throat. The wound reopened in a jagged flower of agony. By instinct Karl stepped sideways into the dimension from which Kristian had first appeared, a world aslant that only vampires could enter: the Crystal Ring. Kristian dived after him.

To mortal eyes they became invisible. To their own sight, the battlefield lost perspective, as if compressed into two dimensions. Instead, the sky unfolded into a new and miraculous realm: a vista of infinite depth, rolling with fiery colours. The lower air currents solidified into bronze and violet hills. Higher still, mountains towered like thunderheads, gleaming black and deep blue. Crimson light from above washed over the slopes. These formations were translucent and changed shape like clouds in their majestic drift across the heavens.

Karl fled towards the lower hills, felt Kristian's claws snagging him. As world and sky changed, so their bodies transformed to slender ebony creatures cloaked in lacy wings. Angel-demons, fighting in their own realm, a dream-terrain flowing like liquid glass. On cold slopes of cloud they struggled, Kristian lunging with bared fangs, Karl thrusting him away with all his strength.

"You owe me everything!" Kristian's voice echoed like thunder. "I made you. You are mine! Without me you'd be dust. How can you look on your creator, saviour, master and not adore me?"

Karl broke his grip by dropping out of the Crystal Ring and back to Earth. He emerged twenty feet up in the sky and fell hard onto the ground. Kristian landed beside him.

Back in human shape, the two vampires rose from the battlefield mud and stood apart. Kristian radiated anger like a furnace, but Karl stared past him, feeling empty, only wishing to be left alone.

"Speak, Karl," Kristian snarled. "To fight so hard, you must be full of rage."

"Is that what you want from me? A reaction?"

"Yes! Anything!"

"I owe you nothing," Karl said coldly. "I didn't ask for this existence."

"Does a child ask to be born? I made you a feather in God's dark wings. In His name, I gave you eternal life!"

"How long have you lived? A few hundred years? You cannot conceive what 'eternal' could possibly mean. No one can."

Kristian only blinked, and for a moment Karl thought that he had won.

"I'll never come back, Kristian, because I feel nothing for you. Why can't you accept that? All I ask is to be left alone."

Kristian moved closer, his voice low. "I have the power to destroy those I create. You would not be the first to enter the *Weisskalt*. Don't think yourself so special."

"Oh, I believe you. I no longer care, that's all."

Kristian's savage face relaxed. "You are a liar, beloved. You care." He came close enough for Karl to feel the soft, scentless breath on his cheek. "You may not fear for yourself, but what of those you love? The sins of the fathers…" He opened his hands, his skin gleaming through the dirt in bone-white lines.

"There is no one left."

"What of Ilona? Don't pretend she means nothing!" Kristian exclaimed. "There, I have only to mention her name to see the pain in your eyes."

Karl kept his anxiety out of his voice with a struggle.

"You love her. You wouldn't harm her."

"Would I not?" Kristian retorted. "How else to make you understand that I would make any sacrifice to bring you back?"

Karl turned to him in shock, giving Kristian his moment of triumph.

"Kristian, in God's name –"

"Ah, now the heretic calls on God? I'll give you time to think." Kristian began to scrape Karl's dried blood from under his fingernails. "But don't be too long. A pity, if Ilona has to pay for your defiance."

Before Karl could respond, Kristian stepped away, palms open in malediction. His body elongated to a dark streak as he arced away and vanished back into the Crystal Ring. An after-image of his face – pale granite, etched with the severe brows, the dark pits of his eyes, the single black mole – lingered for a second.

Kristian was gone, but his threat hung like gun-smoke in the air. Karl began to feel cold. The noise of battle seemed muffled, but the voices of the dying were as clear as bugles calling him.

He had to stay. A painful decision, dangerous – but the only one he could make. To heed the threat was to let Kristian win.

There is no God here. No revelations to explain any of this, he thought. *Science, then? What might that tell a vampire, who by the laws of nature should not exist?*

One voice in particular drew him; a German crying pitifully, "*Mutti... Mutti, hilf mir...*"

He went towards the sound. A strange mist was drifting across the battlefield, like a vampire of another kind, sucking the last warmth from the dead. It crept down into the shell-hole where the young English soldier lay drained of life. Not the first of the wounded to whom the vampire had brought swift oblivion, nor the last.

This night would be endless.

PART ONE

I lived alone without you
Shadows on my wall
Ghosts in my looking glass
Voices in the hall
At first I didn't understand
I had nothing left to sell
And although I played with fire
My life was cold as hell

HORSLIPS, "GHOSTS"

CHAPTER ONE

OUTSIDE THE RAIN

Fear was an irrational predator.

Charlotte Neville stood on the edge of the crowd, blinking at the glitter of beads on evening dresses, lights blurring in a haze of smoke. The gramophone's cheerful rasp pierced the babble of voices. The whole room seemed to shimmer in time with her heartbeat.

This fear had stalked Charlotte all her life, but the more she tried to reason it away, the deeper it dug its claws. Shyness, others called it, but that soft word did not begin to encompass the dread that lay clotted inside her, ready to flame up in any social situation.

This is only Fleur's house, not some grand affair, she told herself firmly. But logic couldn't break her phobia. She sidled to an empty armchair in a corner and sank into it, trying not be noticed. *It's not that I don't want to be friendly. Why do I always feel out of place and tongue-tied? Even my own sisters think I'm a fool.*

It had been her Aunt Elizabeth's idea to launch her into society, an attempt to kill or cure. And, like trying to learn to swim by leaping into the depths of the Arctic Ocean, it was killing her. The whole London Season had been a nightmare. *If only Anne were here, I'd have an ally...* Her friend Anne, though, had more sense than to waste time in what she scorned as "the marriage market". *I wish Anne's good sense would rub off on me*, she thought, *then none of this would matter.*

Charlotte couldn't account for her fear of socialising, but it was very real and filled her with shame. It was ridiculous, especially compared with the genuine terrors that her brother David and his friend Edward had faced in the Great War. For their sake, she must put on a brave face.

She watched her slender, copper-haired sisters circulating among the guests: Fleur, tall and fashionable in her long pearls, always smiling a little as if she knew the latest gossip. And Madeleine, pretty and animated. With a cigarette in a long holder, she looked far more sophisticated than her almost-eighteen years. *And I'm nearly two years older*, Charlotte thought. *I so wish their poise hadn't passed me by.*

She closed her eyes, imagining she was at home in Cambridge. The closed, quiet world of her father's laboratory... the bulky curve of his back as he leaned over a piece of equipment, while she sat with her notebook making sense of his commentary. The cellar walls were dank and bare, yet safe and familiar. There was little sound, beyond the dull hum of a generator and the gurgle of water pipes. No one there but herself, Father and their assistant Henry, a large, untidy young man with a brilliant mind too focused on physics to care about his grooming or social skills. Henry she could tolerate, because she was used to him. He demanded nothing of her, unlike these society people who expected her to sparkle and parade like a circus horse, who disdained her when she failed.

Her chair sagged under the weight of someone sitting on the arm. She opened her eyes and found Madeleine beside her, the beads on her oyster silk dress straining the frail fabric as she leaned down in a waft of smoke and perfume.

"Charli, when's Father giving his lecture to the Royal Society?"

"Oh – next Friday evening." Charlotte was startled. Madeleine had never shown interest in their father's lectures before.

"What's it about?"

"The Electrical Structure of Matter."

"The electric – what? Never mind. I'll tell him it's terribly interesting."

"Tell who?" Charlotte asked.

Madeleine swung one foot, all nervous energy. "I've met the most delicious young man. He's from Vienna, his name's Karl von Wultendorf, and he's fascinated by science. That's why he's in

England, to study. When I told him our father is Dr George Neville, Karl had heard of him!" She mimicked an Austrian accent, badly. "'Ah, the famous physicist. I should so love to meet him.' So I've been telling Karl that he simply must come to Cambridge, that's where all the exciting discoveries are taking place. Isn't that true? You know better than me."

"Well, yes, but –"

"But what? He's the most wonderful man I've ever met. If he comes to the lecture, I can introduce him to Father, who will invite him to Cambridge…"

Charlotte's stomach tightened. She hated strangers visiting the house. She was clinging to thoughts of home to get her through each wretched party, so the thought of her refuge being invaded was unbearable.

She said, "When did you ever attend one of Father's lectures?"

"I'll make an exception for Karl von Wultendorf." Madeleine's eyes elongated like a cat's. "I'd make an exception to *anything* for him."

"Where is he?"

Madeleine leaned closer and whispered, "Over there by the window, talking to Clive. Don't stare."

Discreetly Charlotte glanced at the stranger, who was with a small group framed against the red velvet curtains. Fleur's husband Clive was beside him, blocking her view, so she saw only that he was slightly over six feet tall and slim, his hair dark with a reddish glow. It was enough, though, to reveal him as an attractive, imposing man. A threat. She looked away quickly.

Charlotte usually suppressed her feelings until they choked her, but this time her misgivings won.

"No," she said sharply.

Madeleine's face fell. "What d'you mean, no?"

"You can't invite complete strangers to Father's lectures, let alone to our house."

"I can do what I like." Madeleine's mouth became a sulky rosebud.

"You'd better not."

"What's the matter with you, Charli? You're being ridiculous – No, I'm not going to argue, it would be too undignified."

Madeleine slipped gracefully to her feet and walked away to rejoin her friends, her face radiant again as if nothing had happened.

Charlotte was trembling. Much as she loved Madeleine, her love was too often spiked with envy of her younger sister's easy confidence. Unworthy, but she couldn't help it.

Charlotte hadn't gone to school with her sisters. Instead she'd been educated at home by her father. Their mother was long dead, and he had been her constant companion, training her to work with him. Reclusive by nature, she'd taken willingly to the role, but it meant a sheltered life in the dry, donnish atmosphere of his circle. She avoided the social side of Cambridge life, happy to be a quiet presence at her father's side, respected both as his daughter and his assistant.

And yet... she must want something more, or she would not have surrendered to her aunt's wishes.

"Charlotte will suffocate," Aunt Elizabeth had said. "It's essential for a girl to enter society, especially with the shortage of eligible men after the War. Look what a good marriage Fleur made. You must let me bring her and Madeleine out together – or do you want her growing into a dried-up old spinster, George?"

Her father had responded with a lot of huffing, but hadn't tried to stop Charlotte giving herself over to her aunt to be presented at Court, and all the palaver that followed.

Charlotte, however, was no debutante. She longed to be charming and confident, to make friends and attract admirers, but the cold reality was that she hated it. She felt nothing in common with these bright, brittle people: young rich folk who all knew each other, who scorned anyone who did not fit in. Away from her own safe world, she'd fallen apart.

So much for Elizabeth's hopes of matchmaking. If a man showed more than a passing interest, Charlotte would freeze with involuntary dread that turned her eyes to ice and her tongue to stone. However polite her words, everything in her demeanour growled, "Don't come near me!"

Then she would overhear comments that crushed the little self-esteem she possessed. "Madeleine and Fleur are grand girls; it's a shame their sister's so stand-offish. Pretty, I know, but I shouldn't bother, old chap; she's as miserable as sin."

So the more she suffered, the more she withdrew. Only her dread of Aunt Elizabeth's wrath had kept her from fleeing back to Cambridge. Her aunt and sisters made a great show of "despairing" of her, not realising she found their disappointment the most painful blow of all.

Alongside her shyness, she harboured a streak of contempt for this social circus. Perhaps these people were wonderful beneath the glitter, but they seemed shallow compared to those she truly loved: her father, her brother David, and Anne.

The thought of home was all that sustained her, but if Madeleine began dragging her new friends back to Cambridge – nowhere was sacred.

I've had enough, she thought. *My aunt's not here. I can slip off to bed. I'd rather be scolded by Fleur in the morning than sit here another moment.* She rose and hurried to the open door. No one noticed, until she made the mistake of glancing back to make sure.

The stranger, Karl von Wultendorf, was staring straight at her.

In that moment, everything changed. The world ceased to exist for a heartbeat, then recreated itself: the same yet indefinably askew. A shadow was whispering to her.

The attention of any man alarmed her, whether he was handsome and brash like Clive, or as awkwardly dull as herself. This man, though, was more than handsome. He had an aura of dark beauty that magnetised the whole room in the most sinister way; indifferent to potential admirers, as a candle-flame is indifferent to a moth. Yet it was not so much his beauty that arrested her as his air of self-containment. That, and the way his gaze cut into her like a light beam – cold and dispassionate, straight into her soul.

The look flatly terrified her. She fled up the stairs, praying that she would never see Karl von Wultendorf again.

"Who is he?" Madeleine asked at breakfast, wilting over a plate of toast. Even tired, she had the charm of a sleepy kitten, her copper-red bob aglow in the dull morning light.

Fleur wasn't really listening to Madeleine's chatter, Charlotte observed, but gazing distractedly into the conservatory where her easels stood amid tangles of greenery. Fleur had always been creative, painting landscapes, flower studies, and portraits in oils or delicate watercolours. Her husband Clive sometimes belittled her talent, a foolish habit that infuriated Charlotte.

Now Clive sat behind a newspaper as if in silent disapproval of her sisters. Madeleine didn't care, of course, but his presence made Charlotte uneasy.

"Who is who?" said Fleur.

"Karl von Wultendorf, of course."

"I don't know. A friend of a friend… all sorts of odd people get dragged to my parties, I never know who half of them are."

"They're brought along for their novelty value," Clive said from behind *The Times*. "Anyone strange or foreign, preferably with a title, and we're supposed to find them entertaining… bloody ridiculous."

"Don't be such a misery, dear," Fleur said mildly. "Even if he gate-crashed, he was too lovely to turn away. I should love to paint him."

"Oh, ask him to sit for you!" exclaimed Madeleine.

Clive gave a disapproving grunt. Fleur didn't react. She was so uncharacteristically listless that Charlotte began to worry. Was it more than tiredness and the after-effects of drink?

"Well, I'm in love," Madeleine declared. "If I find out he's married, I shall die. He isn't, is he?"

"For goodness' sake, Maddy, I don't know!" said Fleur.

"Don't snap at me! Is your morning head that bad? I expect Charlotte to be dull and unsociable, but not you."

Charlotte toyed with a boiled egg. Maddy's remarks were more thoughtless than malicious. They were also accurate. She loved her sisters, yet from childhood – to her perpetual regret – she'd had little in common with them.

Fleur sighed. "Sorry, Maddy. The truth is, I had a wonderful idea for a painting last night and I can't wait to start."

"Wonderful idea?" Madeleine said archly. "You should keep away from substances brought by your strange friends."

"You should try them, dear." Fleur stretched, the sleeves of her robe sliding down her lily-white slender arms. "Makes one feel so marvellously creative."

Charlotte swallowed a mouthful of egg whole, almost choking. She assumed they meant cocaine. Their father would be outraged at Fleur for trying to corrupt their baby sister. She tried to hide her shock, but failed.

"Oh, don't give me that old-fashioned look, Charli," said Fleur.

"But it's illegal."

"All the best things are," Fleur said dismissively. "To be honest, I rather wish you chaps would go home. You are darlings, but you know I can't bear distractions when I'm painting. You don't mind, do you?"

"Well, I do rather," said Madeleine. "I was hoping to stay a few more days."

"You can go back to Auntie's house."

"You know Aunt Lizzie left town last week. She's gone back to Parkland Hall to organise my birthday party."

Fleur was unmoved. "Go home, then. You don't mind, Charli, do you?"

"Of course not," said Charlotte, too fervently.

"Oh well, Charlotte wouldn't mind," said Madeleine. "She's hardly the life and soul of any party, is she?"

"Do be grown up about it, Maddy. It's really important that I work. I'll telephone Father and ask him to send Maple to fetch you."

"God, home. What a bore," said Madeleine.

"Buck up, Mads. It's not long to your party, is it?" Fleur stood up and moved to the conservatory as she spoke, turning in the doorway.

"Two whole weeks," Madeleine groaned. Then her face brightened. "Oh, I hope Karl will come to Father's lecture. I *must* know who he is."

In the car on the way home, it was Madeleine who sat in silence, while Charlotte made conversation with Maple, her father's chauffeur and valet. He was a sweet man, not an atom of unkindness in him. The familiarity of his long, white-whiskered face comforted her. On the back seat of the Rolls Royce, a smoky leather scent wrapped around her like a blanket and she began to relax. Eventually she fell asleep.

When she woke they were in Cambridge and almost home. Her

head ached and her throat felt dry and sore. Rain was sheeting along the tree-lined street as Maple guided the long bonnet of the Rolls through the gateway to their house.

"Are you all right, Charli?" said Maddy. "You're deathly white."

"It's nothing, I think I've a cold coming on," Charlotte replied, coughing.

Madeleine shrank away theatrically. "Well, don't come near me with it."

The Nevilles' house was a graceful villa of creamy grey stone, sheltered by trees and a high wall. Charlotte drank in the sight as Maple opened the car doors. There was Sally, the maid, waiting in the porch, her thinness accentuated by her long black uniform, her hair in untidy wisps around her kindly face. With her was Maple's wife Mary, a prim little hen of a woman who mothered everyone. Both hurried to welcome the Neville sisters home.

As Charlotte stepped inside and shook rain off her coat, the homely scent of ingrained beeswax and tobacco greeted her. The walls were panelled in dark wood, the rooms crowded with Victorian furniture. On rainy days, the gloom was oppressive, but at this moment the house spoke to Charlotte of peace and solitude.

Since their mother died, Mary Maple had presided over the household, aided by Sally and a cook; not a large staff by some standards, but George Neville preferred simplicity. He would probably have been happiest if he and Charlotte had lived there alone.

"Oh, I hate this house," Madeleine said with feeling, shivering as Sally took their coats and hats.

"Maddy!" Charlotte exclaimed.

"Well, it's so dark. Living here doesn't mean I have to like it."

Their father came into the hall to welcome them. He was wearing a shabby tweed suit over a shirt with an old-fashioned stand-up collar. His grey hair – once as red as Maddy's – was thinning, and his white moustache was stained yellow by tobacco. Charlotte, who loved, respected and feared him, was shocked that Madeleine could be so downright impertinent. Yet it was Maddy who ran to kiss him, not Charlotte. She'd never been demonstrative.

"Had enough of London at last?" he said, awkwardly patting her shoulder.

"No, never," said Madeleine. "Marvellous party last night."

"H'm? Was your aunt at this party?"

"No, she went home to Parkland last week. You know that."

He shook his head, torn between pleasure at their return and disapproval of their gallivanting in London. "She's supposed to be chaperoning you."

"Oh, Father, don't be so conventional. We were at Fleur's last night, not an opium den."

He glowered, but Madeleine took no notice.

"I didn't want to come home, but Fleur chucked us out because she wants to paint. Can you believe it?"

"Oh, well, the Season's over, isn't it?" He glanced meaningfully at Charlotte. "Time to resume useful work."

They entered the drawing room, a dimly lit space of brown, crimson and ivory. The air was busy with the ticking of a dozen clocks, their father's collection.

"Not me," said Madeleine, stretching out on a sofa. "I've been invited to lots of weekends in the country."

"Have you indeed? Let me consider that. You are not going on your own."

"Well, I'm sure Charlotte's not coming with me." Madeleine removed her shoes and flexed her silk-stockinged feet. Oblivious to her father's stern tone, she contrived to evade his discipline like a fish sliding through wet hands. In contrast, Charlotte was enmeshed by his authority, couldn't bear to incur his disapproval. "Don't be grumpy as soon as we're home."

"I'm not in the least bit grumpy, young lady. We'll discuss it after lunch." He looked at Charlotte. "And how did you enjoy all this debutante nonsense?"

What to say? He must guess that she'd loathed it, but she couldn't admit as much in front of Madeleine. Before she'd composed an innocuous reply, her sister was talking again.

"Father, I've a favour to ask." Her tone became earnest and respectful. "Charli and I met an Austrian visitor last night, a most charming gentleman, who is interested in studying at Cambridge. I suggested he come to your London lecture next week so I may introduce him to you. He'd be so thrilled. He says you're famous!"

George Neville huffed a bit, pretending not to be flattered.

"Oh, well, I dare say it won't hurt to invite him up, show him around. I presume he knows my field is experimental physics? Is that his area of interest? Famous, h'm."

Charlotte didn't hear her sister's reply. Her head was spinning. However irrational her feelings, she couldn't endure the idea of a stranger in the house. It was a sense of foreboding: that once invited, he might never leave.

She interrupted, "I didn't meet him. We know nothing about him, Father, and you're far too busy. Maddy shouldn't have –"

"Charli, what's wrong with you?" Madeleine said, exasperated. "He's only a man, not a sabre-tooth tiger."

"Still, I'm the one who works with Father, not you."

Madeleine's brown eyes narrowed. "What right have you to tell me who I can invite to a lecture, or to our home? You've been impossible, the whole Season. In fact, you nearly ruined it for me."

"What?" Charlotte gasped.

Their father tried to interrupt but Madeleine wouldn't stop.

"My first Season should have been a whirl of sheer fun from start to finish. Instead you're there like a ghost at a feast, vanishing like a scared mouse if anyone dares look at you, people asking, 'What's wrong with your sister?' and me making excuses for you, 'Oh, she's shy, only happy with her books.' Well, I don't think you're shy at all, Charlotte. I think you're an utter, selfish misery!"

Numb, Charlotte walked out of the room. Their raised voices followed her.

"Madeleine, please, that was uncalled for. If your mother was alive..."

"Well, it's true, Father. A girl's Season should be about *her*, not about jollying along a hopeless older sister. Why did she even bother?"

Charlotte went upstairs to her bedroom, sat at her dressing table, and put her head in her hands. Madeleine was right. She'd been too wrapped up in her own fears to see that her behaviour might hurt her sister. Maddy might be self-centered, impetuous, and full of herself – but still, she was young. She deserved some gaiety before adult life began.

Suddenly Charlotte saw her own life as a dark vortex: her father's home not a refuge but a prison, because she couldn't face the bright coldness of the world. Failure loomed like a cloud, and at the centre was Karl von Wultendorf: the gaze that had flooded her with terror. Maddy's rage was the last straw.

All this is my own fault. There's something wrong with me.

Charlotte felt choked with guilt. She would do anything to heal the rift with Madeleine, but she couldn't change the past, nor repair her flawed self.

Why am I so terrified of life? Maddy's right, I shouldn't have gone to London, but I did so to prove I could be normal, and all I've proved is that I'm not.

Someone tapped on her door, turning the knob. She turned round, hoping to see her sister there. Maddy rarely stayed angry for long.

Instead, her friend Anne Saunders peered cheerfully around the door. Not waiting for an invitation she strode in, slim and long-legged in a white shirt and riding breeches. Her cropped dark hair framed a strong face with dark eyebrows, a warm and lively expression. She'd known the Nevilles since childhood; her father was their doctor, and recently Anne had got engaged to their brother David. Also she was Charlotte's only close friend, a feat she'd achieved by sheer persistence, meeting aloofness with warmth until Charlotte finally lowered her guard.

"The Prof says you're not well," said Anne. She gave Charlotte's father that nickname, although he wasn't officially a professor. "Was London that exciting?"

"Hardly." Charlotte smiled, glad to see her. "Don't come too close, I think I've caught the flu."

"Oh, I never catch things like that," Anne said dismissively. "Well, what sort of time did you have? Find a string of suitors? Potential rich husband?" She sat on the edge of the bed.

"God, no." Charlotte shuddered. "I don't want one, thank you."

"Come on, this is me you're talking to. There's a dreadful atmosphere downstairs, while you're lurking in your bedroom. What's happening?"

Charlotte took a breath so deep it hurt. Her lungs were on fire.

"I'm being foolish. I hated London, so Maddy's furious with me, and I feel terrible."

"Maddy's angry because you didn't enjoy yourself?"

"It's my own fault." Charlotte gave a brief explanation.

"It sounds as if she's being childish, not you," said Anne. "Why do you always blame yourself?"

"I…" She paused. "Really, there's no use in going over it."

"That's your trouble," Anne said gently. "All these years I've known you, Charli, and you still can't confide in me?"

"It's nothing, truly. I hope Maddy will forgive me. I'm much more worried about Fleur. I think she's dosing herself with… something."

"Cocaine?" Anne didn't sound surprised. "It's probably the fashionable thing among her set, not that I'd know. I'm sure she's sensible enough to stop. You worry too much."

"And Maddy's taken up with some awful stranger."

"Oh, why's he awful?" Anne leaned forward, fascinated.

"Because he's a stranger!"

Anne started to laugh.

Charlotte said, "Yes, I know it's ridiculous, but I felt – oh, I don't know. I'm under the weather. You should go away until I'm more rational, and less infectious."

"Well, if you say so." Anne stood up, looking sadly at her. "Go to bed with a hot drink and some aspirin; that's advice from the doctor's daughter. And don't forget David will be back for Madeleine's fancy-dress do. He'll cheer you up, if I can't. Have you decided on your costume, or is it secret?"

"Lord, I haven't given it a thought." She gave a groan of exasperation. "I'm sorry, Anne. It's Maddy's eighteenth birthday, and all I can do is moan! I'm just not – I'm sorry."

Anne placed a hand on her shoulder. "I'm concerned about you, Charli. You have to talk to someone eventually, you know."

Anne let herself out, leaving Charlotte feeling worse than ever. Anne was only trying to help, but Charlotte couldn't bear to be seen as weak, hopeless and needy. *Brave front*, she told herself. *I'm not made to be a party girl. I'm a cold scientist. Cold cold cold. That's who I am.*

Madeleine stayed away but her father came to her, felt her hot forehead and shook his head.

"Get yourself into bed, m'dear," he said with bossy affection. "You're no use to man nor beast in this state, spreading germs. Go on, I'll send Mrs Maple with a hot drink."

This is really quite funny, she thought later, as she lay sweating and shivering in bed, staring at the dark ceiling. *Only I could be glad to catch the flu. Now I'll miss Father's lecture to the Royal Society, but I wanted an excuse because I'm too much of a coward to meet Maddy's gentleman friend. Despicable, but I do not want him here!*

When she fell asleep, fever extended horrifying tendrils into her dreams.

A weird, rhythmic noise approached her from a great distance. She stood on a brooding, desolate shore; a sooty beach and an iron-grey ocean. She felt tiny under the inky sweep of the sky, helpless before the waves' crashing power. Birds were flying towards her with a steady *whump-whump-whump* of wings: featherless, primeval creatures with long teeth like razors. The only specks of colour were their blood-red tongues, each one slithering and hissing in a cage of fangs. Slow and malign, they flew towards her. The anticipation of their approach was unbearable.

Then David was beside her. The beach was a battlefield, and as they waited for the birds to attack, he was giving cheerful instructions: "Don't shoot until you see the whites of their eyes, old girl."

Looking around, she saw behind them a bright green meadow sheened red with poppies. "David, I've found a way out!" she cried, and began to run towards the brilliance.

He wasn't with her. She tried to turn back but couldn't. A vast trench lay in front of her and he was on the far side, with Anne, Fleur, Madeleine and Father. They were stranded. Charlotte was helpless. She couldn't save them from the dark birds that soared inexorably closer on vast black wings – yet she wouldn't desert them. She stopped and faced the creatures. The agony of waiting was an electric heaviness in her stomach. It felt strangely thrilling, as if she dreaded the raptors and desired them at the same time. Their mouth-beaks opened and the steaming red coils of their tongues came lashing out...

Every cell of her body tightened and she woke, gagging with fear. Yet mingled with the nightmare she experienced a pleasure so intense that it left her breathless.

The darkness was a warm breathing weight on top of her...

Drenched in sweat, she found herself lurching up in bed, switching on her bedside lamp before she was properly awake. She sat gasping for breath, her whole body a mass of pins and needles. Gradually the racing of her heart began to ease.

Lamplight shone dim and warm on panelled walls. Hers was a moody room, at times comforting, at others full of dark, frightening corners. Charlotte was desperate to break the veil of her night terrors. She glanced at the clock: three in the morning. Picking up the photograph of her mother from her bedside table, she lay back and focused on the beautiful face.

Charlotte could barely remember her, but sometimes she sensed her mother actually beside her, placing a cool hand on her forehead. *It's all right, darling. Go to sleep.*

The portrait was more an icon than a memory; so far away was the slender, stately woman in Edwardian clothes. She had an unusual face, its length balanced by large, deep-lidded eyes and a full-lipped mouth. The nose was short and delicate. Although her expression was solemn, a slight lack of symmetry in the features made her look girlish, exquisitely pretty under a mass of shining hair. The faded sepia had been hand-tinted with coloured inks. Her eyes were a rich violet-grey, her hair warm brown frosted with golden-blonde.

Charlotte knew the colours were true, because she was the image of her mother.

Annette Neville had died soon after Madeleine's birth. Charlotte had been less than two years old, too small to remember more than fleeting impressions: a swish of long skirts, cool white hands. Her father and mother laughing together. Then an endless night of screams muffled behind closed doors... The horror replayed in her mind's archive, first the screams and then the silence that rang forever with echoes of her mother's pain.

Charlotte believed in ghosts. She believed them to be tangible phenomena with a scientific explanation, unknown as yet. An interaction between places where the dead had lived and the minds of the living? She knew that ghosts were real to people who saw them. She often felt her mother beside her, like a friend, radiating all the calm wisdom that Charlotte lacked.

Her father had never recovered from Annette's death. But at least he had Charlotte, who was so like her. That was why she could never leave him. It was her duty to replace her mother in his heart... She was the photograph come to life, the image that must stay the same forever.

Charlotte left her bed and went to the window to stare out at rain-drenched darkness. She felt oppressed, webbed into the pattern of her life. Her head was full of images. A glowing, sparking laboratory in a cellar. Dark oak rooms through which the living moved like ghosts and the voices of the dead still echoed. A pale face with amber eyes that gazed straight through her...

And the sky... was she seeing things, going mad? She could *see* the wind, and it was solid: a hill of liquid glass that turned slowly over on itself like a wave. On its slopes were black shapes. The dark birds of her fever? Not flying, these creatures, but running. Running towards her through the sky.

CHAPTER TWO

COILS OF ICE

The beauty of Kristian's castle, Schloss Holdenstein, gave nothing away. A mass of brown turrets, dark-tiled roofs, arched windows and balconies thick with ivy, it seemed a natural outgrowth of the sheer wooded gorge on which it stood, framed against the sky. The river Rhine was a cloudy mirror far below.

Always alive, this river. Kristian leaned on a wooden rail and looked into the broken reflection of the gorge, discerning subtle hues and detail that no human eye could perceive. The Rhine endured forever. Its moods changed, but in the end it was always the same, always there.

"Like me," he said to himself. "Like us."

When Kristian spoke of "us" and "we", he meant himself and God.

Inside the castle lay a web of corridors, cells and chapels through which his vampire flock moved as softly as monks. Only a few dozen. There had been more in the past, but Kristian had destroyed many who were imperfect. Those who remained were obedient. They went away to feed, but always returned to their master, carrying on them a dark aura that, over centuries, had seeped into the stone walls. Delicious, blood-dark power.

Ilona was in the castle. Kristian sensed her presence the moment she arrived. She was like quicksilver, elusive. Humans were furnaces, scattering their auras wastefully around them. Vampires, however, were as cool as diamond; some, like Ilona, so transparent as to be invisible. Nevertheless, she couldn't hide.

Kristian did not go to meet her. She must find him. As he waited, he brooded on Karl.

It was five years since he'd confronted Karl in the infernal landscape of the War. A painful decision, to let Karl follow his own misguided path, but for the best. Let him learn by his mistakes.

"My children all come back to me in the end," Kristian said aloud. Five years... so little time in the fiery arc of eternity across which he sailed like an ever-rising sun. "My patience is boundless." Kristian looked up at the clouds. "*Our* patience, Lord, endures forever."

Yet the thought of Karl was a stitch in his heart. Each pull filled him with rage. And when anger rolled away, the emptiness of Karl's absence was still there.

Kristian gripped the rail, wood fibres fraying under his fingers.

"You presume too much on my mercy, Karl," he whispered to the air. "If I'm forced to harm my angel Ilona, you are to blame. You have driven me to it. You were warned."

"*Grüss Gott*, Kristian," said a crisp female voice.

He looked round to see Ilona in the balcony doorway, gypsy-brilliant against the castle interior. She'd adopted a Bohemian style with embroidered silks and a tasselled shawl, and she had dyed her hair again – no natural shade, but bright scarlet.

Her appearance displeased him. She grinned, all rebellion and bravado.

"Kristian?" she said. "Are you going to stare at me all day?"

"What have you done to your hair?"

"Don't you like it?" She stepped into the light, daring him to be angry.

"This is vanity, Ilona. It's a mortal weakness, to paint and colour yourself. We should be above such folly."

"It's not vanity, it's camouflage," she retorted. Her rose-red lips thinned. She shook the offending hair free to flow over her shawl like arterial blood. Whatever her guise, her face remained perfect. A milk-white oval: the features of a statue with dark unhuman eyes, all the more shocking when the marble expression came to life. Like Kristian's own face. Like Karl's. "How do you expect me to move among humans without blending in?"

"I don't believe there is a fashion for scarlet hair."

His scorn made her defensive.

"Since the War, Kristian, anything goes, the more outrageous the better. If you weren't a recluse you would know that. Do you expect me to dress like a nun?" She laughed, revealing small neat teeth; no visible fangs. "Actually, why don't I? It would be perfect."

"You think your irreverence shocks me, but the trappings of religion are a mortal delusion. They imagine that layers of cloth bring them nearer to God, when in truth they can't hope to know Him. They use clothing to disguise their spiritual emptiness. Your attempt to goad me means nothing, my beloved. It is shallow."

Her smile vanished. Her eyes turned glass-sharp.

"Don't call me shallow, *Vater*. Don't ever call me that."

He let his mouth relax into a smile. He could afford to be indulgent. Ilona always tested him, but his power over her was complete. She couldn't help but adore him.

"Then be your courageous self," he said.

He moved towards her. She folded her arms.

"You don't frighten me," she said. "Nothing does. Why should it, when you're always reminding us that we're immortal?"

Ignoring the barrier of her forearms, he locked his arms around her. She resisted him stiffly for a moment. Then she sighed with a mix of resentment and pleasure, and freed her hands to return the embrace.

Kristian rested his lips lightly on her neck, felt her shiver as he whispered, "You will need your courage." He opened his mouth, pressed his teeth into flesh, felt the canines lengthen and pierce the sweet cool skin. Vampire flesh healed swiftly, so he had to keep his fangs in the wounds, sucking until the slow blood turned liquid.

Kristian never drank from humans. Everything about them disgusted him – their heavy, hot blood, laced with smoky mortal odours. Vampire blood alone was pure, the divine exhalation of rubies.

Only a taste, like champagne in his mouth. Just a reminder, a gesture of affection.

Ilona tensed, making the faintest sound in her throat.

Retracting the stabbing teeth into their sockets, he held her at arm's length.

"What kept you away for so long, my lamb?"

"Only some foolish young man who was in love with me."
Her brown eyes had softened and her voice was lazy. "Are you
jealous? Oh, I forgot, human emotions are beneath you."

He nodded, but her mockery grated. "Where is he now?"

She shrugged. "Dead. I grew bored. That's the trouble, they all
bore me in the end."

"All except me," said Kristian. "Did you miss me?"

"With all my heart." She drew her fingertips across her throat
and held them up, smeared with blood. The marks of his fangs
had already vanished. "As much as I would miss this."

Sucking her fingers clean, Ilona sat on the balcony rail, leaning
against a pillar. This looked dangerous: the stone was crumbling
and the wood rotten, but if she fell she would simply land like a
cat, or glide into the Crystal Ring. Cupping her elbows, she stared
at the river curving far below.

She asked, "Why did you send for me?"

"I need you."

"I'm flattered, but if you're lonely it's your own fault. You choose
to spend your time here, waiting for the world to come to you."

He leaned on the edge beside her.

"But they do come, don't they?"

She looked at him with a touch of haughtiness, almost a sneer.

"To the Court of King Kristian. Oh yes."

He smiled, taking her jibe as a compliment.

"Not the Court, but the Temple. The unseen Church. I ordered
you home for a purpose."

He saw tension flicker through her. He hadn't expected her to
guess his meaning, and her hair-trigger reaction irritated him. His
tone hardened.

"I last saw Karl during the Great War."

"Really," she said flatly.

"He was beyond the reach of reason. I decided to let him come
to his senses in his own time."

"A good decision. And final?"

"No, not final."

Her sweet face became pinched. "I knew that was too much
to ask."

"He's had his freedom. I want him back now."

"He won't come."

"Oh, this time he will. Do you know where he is?"

Ilona tilted her head at his urgent tone. "No."

"Then you will help me to lure him here, Ilona."

She leapt up, her hair and clothes a swirl of coloured flame.

"Oh, no I won't. Do your own dirty work! Every vampire in this damned world is subject to you. Can't you bear to let even a single one go?" She released her breath. "No. Of course you can't. That's the point, isn't it? Not a single one."

Kristian's own rage was a steady cold wind.

"Now that is blasphemy, beloved. Karl wronged me. He cannot escape vengeance. And you hate him. So why are you fighting me?"

Ilona looked away. Her eyes narrowed.

"Because I don't want him back with you. I never want to see him again. Never, ever. How can you ask this of me?"

Kristian felt the coil of ice tightening.

"You'll help me… because you love me, and hate him."

Ilona turned on him. "I hate you too at this moment, my lord. If he returns, I shall leave. You think you control everyone, but you cannot have us both."

Kristian's large hand encircled her slender upper arm, an iron shackle. The more she protested, the less he cared. His heart was a swollen thundercloud.

"It will be as I command. You'll lure him back."

"What am I now, bait?" She drew back her lips in scorn. "You don't imagine my presence could snare him? My God, such optimism."

"You are slow, my beloved." Kristian released her so suddenly that she almost went over the balcony. "It's what will happen to *you* that will sway him."

"Blackmail!" She laughed, hard and angry. "Kristian, how can you live so long and still not understand? Karl loathes me in return. Your threats will mean nothing. He'll laugh."

"Ah, there you are wrong. There you misjudge him completely. He still loves you, Ilona. He adores you with all his soul."

Her expression froze. "With what are you threatening me?" she whispered, staring at him. Knowing.

"Karl is stubborn. The only way to reach him is to carry out the deed. If he wants to save you, he had better come to heel."

"No. You wouldn't."

Her fury and fear were enticing. Kristian felt dark excitement thread through him. She was fire and blood. He reached for her.

Ilona reacted swiftly, almost too fast for him. The instant she realised the danger, she arched backwards over the balcony rail and vanished.

Kristian was after her in a split second. He caught her as she flashed into the Crystal Ring. Together they fell through the unseen dimension.

She fought violently, but their altered, rarefied bodies tangled like lace on barbed wire. No escape. The world below turned flat and dark, while the sky became a tiered landscape of light. A soft golden ridge arrested their fall. Kristian clutched Ilona and began to climb relentlessly.

The warm lower layers of air condensed into a chain of hills, gleaming bronze, rising and falling in slow waves. The cloud-hills sailed on air, their substance honey-thick: dense enough to bear weight, but treacherous. They flowed as far as Kristian could see, in constant motion like ocean tides.

Against the dappled slopes, the two vampires were delicate ink sketches: birdlike, demonic. Dragonflies spun from black crystal.

Ilona's struggles hindered Kristian, but she couldn't stop him. He carried her to a ridge from which a vapour-wisp formed a pathway towards the higher levels. Contour-lines of light curved through everything, guiding him; a magnetic field made visible, some claimed.

Kristian scorned science.

Karl, an unbeliever, said it was impossible to explain the Crystal Ring. Why should immortals be privileged to enter another dimension, weird beyond human dreams? Its geography corresponded to that of Earth, enabling them to travel unseen from place to place. Like the sky, it enveloped the world. Its beauty was ineffable. Half swimming, half flying through its atmosphere was a dizzying rapture. Yet the Crystal Ring was far more. Unable to sleep on Earth, vampires must come here to rest. And although the Crystal Ring held dangers, it was essential to their existence.

Science should explain this, but can't, argued Karl. *Yet.*

Kristian, however, knew precisely what the Crystal Ring was. The mind of God. And God naturally allowed only His chosen dark messengers to enter His mind; this savage heaven.

He rose to a colder, wilder region where vast mountains soared like purple-black thunderheads. A rich fiery glow spilled down their flanks. Kristian ascended a floorless canyon, light flowing violet and amber around him. The climb was hard. The Crystal Ring's substance was viscous, now holding him like a fly in treacle, now dissolving so that he slid back.

Ilona beat his shoulders and cursed him all the way.

At last he gained a mountain peak, dizzied by the depthless void all around him. The atmosphere was dense and cold, heaving like a sea. Even as he paused, the peak began to roll over on itself, threatening to plunge him down again. The next layer, a sapphire plain, seemed miles above. He swam upwards through the semi-fluid air, guided by glowing lines of magnetism.

"Damn you. Take me back," Ilona cried. Her voice was faint. She'd stopped fighting and clung to him.

Kristian began to shiver. The Crystal Ring exacted a toll from those who climbed too high. Even Kristian was not immune.

He needed warmth. Although their bodies were different here, he could still feel the swell of Ilona's veins. Reaching the sapphire plain, he slid his fangs into her throat and sucked until the sluggish fluid became a stream of fire on his tongue.

The strength he gained was short-lived but fierce, intoxicating. He drank to strengthen himself and to weaken her.

When he lifted his head, her gaze fixed on his in disbelief, full of pain and betrayal.

"Let me go." Desperation stole her voice. "Don't do this to me."

Kristian felt a pang of pity. "It's only for a while, my lamb, I promise. Just until Karl comes back."

"You know he won't come back!"

"He will."

"You bastard. You will be sorry."

"I think not, my love." He stroked her head. "I said you would need your courage."

She fell silent, weak from blood-loss, as he rose through haloes of indigo light. The Crystal Ring was soundless, a sweeping realm of unbearable beauty. As Kristian neared its upper limits he felt warm again. Euphoric. Still it took all his strength to go on.

The light paled. A silver-blue sea rippled above him, mysterious and delicate. As he broke through its surface, sudden iciness bit into his bones.

Ice crystals formed a swirling staircase by which he ascended to his destination: a vast plateau forty miles above the Earth's surface, lonelier than the heights of Mount Everest, hurtling endlessly through nothingness. The *Weisskalt*.

Bitter cold sang through him. The *Weisskalt*'s beauty was sharp as a knife-edge, lit by thin raw sunlight, dazzling white. He saw the rich blue curve of the Earth and the blackness of space, scattered with stars and galaxies like tiny whorls of fire. Still Earth, and yet... another realm entirely. The very mind of the Creator.

How could Karl not believe in God?

Ilona's blood would sustain him long enough for his purpose. He only had to hold her a little while, until she fell asleep.

Kristian drank again. She moaned faintly and he stroked her hair. God, how she loved him, this one. He would make amends to her.

She became still in his arms and he thought she was gone, until he saw a faint scintillation in her eyes.

Her lips parted stiffly and she said, "Ask Pierre."

He leaned close to hear her. "Ask him what?"

Her expression was etched clearly on her shadow-face: the sour pleasure of a small triumph in defeat.

"Ask Pierre where Karl is. He's known all this time." She gave a painful laugh, then the smile froze on her face.

"No, that's impossible. He would have told me. Ilona!"

He shook her. No response. She'd waited until the very last moment to deliver this tormenting information. Now nothing would drag further answers from her.

"Why did you not tell me?" he roared.

He cursed, but there was nothing he could do. If he took her back to Earth and reawakened her, then she wouldn't serve as a lure to trap Karl... As a minor act of revenge, it was effective.

Clutching her weightless form, Kristian walked on until he

reached rows of folded black shapes against the whiteness. He kept them all together, so that he would never lose anyone. They were like cocoons, or mummified creatures. Pitiful. Yet he remembered each one by name, and their individual beauty. Here were Katerina and Andreas, whom he'd punished for showing deeper loyalty to Karl than to Kristian, their master.

He stared at Katerina's frost-pearled face. Her body was like a fold of black parchment, paper-delicate yet frozen hard, a fossil. He trawled his fingernails down the length of her form, lost in a well of memory. How she'd hurt him. How they all did.

This was the paradox of the Crystal Ring. It gave vampires life and freedom, but any who lingered risked being overcome by cold and exhaustion. If they lost the strength to escape, they sank into hibernation.

Immortals could be killed with difficulty, but Kristian believed that death was God's choice alone. Placing deviants into an icy coma was far preferable. This way, Kristian held the power of life or oblivion over his flock forever.

Some had lain in the *Weisskalt* for centuries, others only a few years. They were the ones who'd disappointed or betrayed him, or broken his heart. Some he might wake one day, when he felt they'd learned their lesson; others must sleep for eternity.

Tenderly, he laid Ilona alongside them.

"Mind your step, Herr von Wultendorf," said George Neville. "The stairs are steep."

"Please, use my first name," said Karl, following him down into darkness. Behind him came the assistant, Henry Millward, and Dr Neville's daughter Madeleine. Her heels clicked lightly on the brick treads. "I so enjoyed your lecture last week."

"Ah, but did you understand it?"

"I believe so," said Karl. "If not, it's a failure of my intellect, not of your exposition. You made a complex subject very clear."

"You speak such beautiful English!" said Madeleine.

At the base of the steps, Dr Neville flicked a switch. Light fell coldly on bare walls and water pipes, gleaming on glass and metal structures, and on tangles of wire that hung from the ceiling like jungle creeper. The cellar was a cave of mysteries. The new and unexplored still had power to fascinate Karl.

"Well, erhm – Karl, here we are. The Neville laboratory." The scientist cleared his throat. "Not quite the Cavendish, but we've achieved some fine results here."

Henry, a large, dishevelled youngish man with spectacles and springy brown hair, crossed the room to adjust a piece of apparatus – more out of nervousness than necessity, Karl thought. Madeleine stayed close to Karl, almost touching him.

"Grim, isn't it?" she said with a mock shiver. "I never come down here normally. It's a wonder Henry, Father and Charlotte don't take root, like mushrooms."

Karl smiled a little. She was a lovely girl, very confident. Her radiance, the blood-glow through her translucent skin and red highlights shifting on her hair, all held his gaze as might a work of art. Even the straight, loose modern fashions had elegance on her form: a freshness and freedom. He couldn't help but watch Madeleine, and she basked in his attention.

"No luxuries, but it's perfectly serviceable," said Dr Neville. "The reason I set up my own laboratory is that they're positively fighting for bench space in the Cavendish. You wouldn't believe how small a budget we survive on. So I equipped my own cellar to free space for someone else – not to mention taking Henry out of their hair." He chuckled. "Anyway, do look around."

Karl breathed mingled odours of strange gases and metals. A generator hummed in the background. There were sturdy wooden tables forested with clamp stands and vessels, glass-fronted cupboards crammed with bottles, tubing and flasks. Shelves and a filing cabinet were piled high with books. On a desk, scattered with paper, the only objects placed with any care were three framed photographs.

Karl paused. One, the caption informed him, was of a scientific conference before the War; George Neville was part of an illustrious group including Rutherford, Thomson, the Curies, Einstein. Another was of the Neville children, three small girls and a fair-haired boy. The third showed a lovely Edwardian woman with a toddler on her knee, both clear-skinned and wide-eyed, fixed forever in shades of grey. Across the corner of the frame hung a cross made of tightly woven hair.

"It's dreadfully untidy, Father," said Madeleine. "How can you work in this mess?"

"I know exactly where everything is."

Henry looked up from his work. "Oh no, this is what happens when Charlotte isn't here." He seemed shy, a touch bovine. "She keeps us in order. We really can't cope without her."

Karl had seen Charlotte briefly at the party where he'd met Madeleine; a gazelle who had caught his attention for a moment before she fled.

He said, "I trust she's not unwell."

"Had the blasted flu, so I packed her off to my sister's in Hertfordshire to convalesce," said Dr Neville. "If it was the flu."

"Oh?"

"Well, her aunt insisted on dragging her around palaces, parties and balls all spring, but she's a quiet girl, hates all that nonsense. It was bound to make her ill. I shouldn't have allowed it. Anyway, Charlotte's the academic one. Fleur and Madeleine are the socialites, aren't you, m'dear? And my son David is the outdoor, military type. So Charlotte's indispensable." He indicated the photograph of mother and baby. "That's her with my late wife Annette. Grown up the image of her mother. H'm, my brains and Annette's looks."

There was a faint shifting of the air. Karl looked round to find that Madeleine had gone.

"Oh, don't mind her." George Neville apparently construed nothing from her departure. "Henry, light the Bunsen and put some water to boil, there's a good chap."

"Right-o, Professor." Henry went obediently to the sink, filled a metal beaker and placed it on a tripod over a blue jet of flame.

Neville gave a dismissive chuckle. "He will insist on calling me that. You must understand it's only a nickname. I'm not a professor."

"Yet," said Henry.

"Well, I was nearly elected to the physics chair in 1919; dashed influenza epidemic got me." He tapped his chest. "Never been quite right since. Anyway, Trinity made me a lifetime research fellow, so I do as much lecturing and coaching as I wish, and the rest of my time's my own to play with atoms and numbers."

He led Karl around the laboratory, explaining the equipment; a vacuum pump, a gold-leaf electroscope, a liquid air machine, a Wilson cloud chamber, a scintillation counter. The devices with which wondrous discoveries were made looked smaller and more primitive than Karl had imagined.

"And this is the mass spectrograph." Dr Neville rested his hand on a black cylinder, mounted on a wooden stand and connected to the thick coiled arc of an electromagnet. "For separating isotopes. This is what we're working on, the structure of radioactive elements. From studying the tiniest components of matter we hope to understand the processes taking place inside stars. The ultimate aim is to uncover the laws that govern the universe itself." He gazed into the air, then his attention snapped back to Karl. "Ambitious, eh? What our work mainly consists of is lots of infuriating fiddling about and infinite patience, which I lack. I'm a bad experimenter, really. That's why I need Henry and Charlotte to carry on with things if I want to go off in a flight of speculation. Still interested?"

"Naturally," said Karl. "More than I can say."

"I gather you're a musician."

"I was."

"Never studied science at all?"

"Yes, but only as a layman. Like you, I simply want to understand the universe."

George Neville looked appraisingly at Karl. His irises were milky silver.

"You see, you could apply to one of the colleges and start with the mathematical tripos, but…"

"I should like to learn from you, Dr Neville," said Karl. "If I could work alongside you, share your discoveries as you make them, there could be no better path to knowledge."

The request was presumptuous, Karl knew. He might be refused, but doubted it. Although some people reacted uneasily to him, most were drawn in without knowing why. He could sense Dr Neville developing a baseless but unquestioning trust in him. The ease of it made him feel a little sad.

Even as Karl made conversation, he was conscious of Henry

and Dr Neville, not only as men, but as potential prey. Their breathing, salty warmth wreathed through the tang of the cellar. Karl was aware of his own fangs, sharp canines that appeared normal while retracted. Even if he let them slide to full length – bared them as if to say *see, this is what I am!* – they were only a superficial sign of the chasm that lay between him and mortals.

He would not touch these people. It was their knowledge he needed, not their blood. The temptation was still there, however: a dark organic pull that he must suppress.

Then Dr Neville said, "How are you at glass-blowing?"

Karl smiled. "I don't know, I've never tried."

"You may laugh, but we have to make all our own equipment. Shaping a good cardboard strut for a photographic plate is just as important as intricate mathematical reasoning. And a damn sight more useful. Isn't it, Henry?"

"Or the stamina to sit up all night counting alpha-particles until your eyes fall out," said Henry. Karl sensed hostility towards interlopers.

"I should be happy to do whatever was required of me."

"I can't pay you anything."

"I was not asking for a job, Dr Neville. On the contrary, if you need resources for your laboratory…"

Neville looked startled. "Well, I couldn't possibly accept money, but I dare say the Cavendish would be grateful for any new equipment." His gaze switched to the Bunsen burner. The water was boiling vigorously, Henry apparently having forgotten it. "Oh, rescue that water, would you, Karl? You're nearest."

Karl folded one hand around the beaker and stood holding it as the physicist went on. "Normally I wouldn't dream of taking on someone with no formal learning, Karl, but to encourage a person with such thirst for knowledge would be a delight. And there's the most important factor of all."

"Which is what?"

"The ability to make a good cup of tea. There's a teapot around here somewhere. We often brew up down here; saves bothering the staff, y'see, especially since Sally sprained her ankle on the stairs once. Adds a nice schoolboyish touch, I think. Henry, sort out the teapot, will you? What are you staring at?"

Then Dr Neville stopped and opened his mouth. Karl realised why they were staring. He'd picked up a vessel of boiling water in his bare hand and was still holding it. He disregarded the heat, knowing it couldn't harm him, and forgetting how extraordinary this must look.

"Your hand!" Neville exclaimed.

Karl set the vessel down. Both men hurried to him, flustered.

"My God, I forgot to say, use tongs!"

Karl gave his hand a perfunctory inspection. "There's no harm."

Dr Neville touched the beaker, snatched his hand away.

"Ouch! That must have scalded. I'm most dreadfully sorry. Quickly, run it under the cold tap to be sure."

Karl went to the sink and did so, only to avoid an argument. This was the danger: that some small sign would give him away. Yet it was little danger, really. No rational person would interpret the incident as anything sinister.

Henry grunted. "Welcome to the laboratory, sir. Dr Neville neglected to mention that we're forever cutting, burning or otherwise damaging ourselves in the noble course of our work."

"I'll look on it as my initiation, then," Karl replied mildly.

"Are you sure the hand's all right?" asked George Neville.

"Perfectly."

He frowned. "Excellent. But…"

"I have tough skin," said Karl, "from playing the cello."

Charlotte was running away.

Flu had ambushed her for two weeks. Normally she would soldier on, but this time she surrendered to the kingdom of fever-dreams as if sinking into the arms of a lover. Illness became a veil to hide her from the world.

She had mixed feelings about staying at Parkland Hall – she loved the house and gardens, feared her aunt – but this time she'd welcomed the opportunity, for it meant missing Karl's visit to Cambridge. She hoped that the longer she delayed, the better the chance she'd never have to meet him at all.

She knew her anxieties were irrational, but there was a dark web on her that she could not shake off.

Why, when my life is so blessed, do I feel so empty?
Convalescence gave her too much time to think. In her bedroom
– a large chamber resplendent in blue and gold with a four-poster
bed – she leaned on a windowsill and stared at the view. A summer
haze shimmered over the trees, drifting like silver gauze over a
distant lake, blurring the horizon into the sky. The landscape
looked as she felt: lethargic.

Her window overlooked a broad lawn that was edged by a
stone balustrade on which roses and wisteria twined, shaded
by a vast plane tree. On the far side, one hundred steps swept
down through a belt of silver birch, laburnum, conifers and
rhododendrons to a further lawn, this one of Italianate layout
with formal flowerbeds and a fountain. Beyond lay a steep drop
into semi-wild woodland. To either side were water gardens, rose
arbours, mazes; and then the wild gardens that she loved the best
because they were shadowy and mysterious, set with statues and
follies that had been gathering lichen since the eighteenth century.

As a child, her happiest moments had been spent exploring
those gardens. Still were, in fact. It was like stepping into another
time where she could forget everything, even herself.

Right now Charlotte felt like a fugitive fleeing an unseen beast.
However fast she ran, it kept gaining on her with heavy, slow
footsteps. And the beast was real life.

A marquee was being erected on a side lawn. She could see the
white walls flapping, men hauling on ropes, members of the Hall
staff rushing to and fro. The butler, Newland, was supervising.
Tomorrow was Madeleine's great day, her eighteenth birthday
party. The world – so it felt – would be descending on Charlotte's
refuge.

She would endure the socialising for Madeleine's sake. At least
Anne and David would be here.

"I dare say you'll survive," she scolded herself. "This time,
think *only* about Maddy, not your foolish fears."

A noise made her start.

"Talking to yourself? I wonder about you, dear, really I do."

Aunt Elizabeth entered, angular and elegant in gold silk voile,
a sash around her hips and a wide-sleeved jacket of the same tone
on her shoulders. Five years younger than Charlotte's father, she

had a strong-boned face that never seemed to age. She wore her hair in a youthful, dark bob.

"I hope you're feeling better," Elizabeth began ominously.

"Yes, Auntie, I'm well again, thank you."

"Good, because I insist you enjoy yourself tomorrow, or at least, *feign* delight. You can't use the excuse of flu to hide in your room. I won't have Maddy upset by *anything*."

"I wouldn't dream of it." Charlotte tried to sound positive.

"Not intentionally, but you don't seem able to help yourself. Whatever shall we do with you?"

"There's no need for you to do anything," she said quietly. "I'm quite happy working with Father. I should never have tried…"

"Yes, well, don't let's dwell on it. Not everyone is cut out for society, obviously."

"I suppose not," Charlotte said, shrivelling inside. Elizabeth needled her constantly. She saw Charlotte's ineptitude as an embarrassing reflection on herself. The only project in which Elizabeth had ever failed, apparently, was her attempt to mould her niece.

Lady Elizabeth Reynolds' absent husband was a baronet and an ambassador to the Far East. It was a curious marriage: he was usually abroad, while Elizabeth preferred her life in England, reigning over Parkland and maintaining her status in high society. They had no offspring. Neither seemed to mind how rarely they saw each other. Charlotte had heard it whispered that their union was one of "convenience".

"All is not lost." Elizabeth's tone became gentler. "You still ought to think about the future, dear."

She meant marriage, Charlotte realised. She hadn't expected this turn in the conversation.

"I don't see much point, Auntie. I'm not likely to marry and I don't want to."

"You don't wish to be alone and impoverished, surely?"

"I shan't be alone. I'll be with Father."

"But be practical, dear. George won't live forever."

Charlotte was shocked by Elizabeth's bald statement about her own brother.

"Lots of women are alone these days."

"Yes, the War changed everything. You don't need to tell me. Some girls must make their own way, but there's no need if you don't have to."

"Auntie, I'm sorry I let you down. You made it plain that my social incompetence was so extreme that even the most dim-witted, dull male on the planet wouldn't want a wet blanket like me."

Elizabeth sighed through her nose. "My dear, certain things were said in the heat of the moment. You'd have a string of decent suitors now, if you hadn't frozen them all out. But perhaps, all along, we should have been looking closer to home." Elizabeth's lips formed a cupid's bow. The smile erased all hardness from her face and made her radiantly pretty, like an older, darker-haired Fleur. "Think about it." She patted Charlotte's arm, and left.

Charlotte dared not think what her aunt was implying. It was hard enough to let her family near her. The thought of some man invading her life in a far more intimate way was repellent. But to marry someone you rarely saw, for the sake of a title, lands and status? That was worse.

Then Charlotte understood the source of her pain. She wanted love, like any human, but some fatal internal flaw had locked her heart in ice. Something deeper than fear. It would never release her. Her eyes widened and her fingernails dug into the painted windowsill. *I'm doing this to myself, but I can't stop.*

So strong was her sense of foreboding that it was no surprise when two blows fell on her before the party, one after the other, like the soft double thump of a trap.

CHAPTER THREE

SEEING THROUGH THE VEIL

"So glad you invited me, old man. Find it hard to get out and socialise these days... well, you know."

"Edward, you should get out more, and I'm going to make damned sure you do from now on." David Neville steered his green open-topped Bentley through the gates of Parkland Hall. The sight of the estate always raised his spirits. On each side of the driveway, sunlight shone between chestnut trees, oaks and copper beeches. Sheep grazed under the broad level spread of branches. At the top of the hill stood the Hall, a structure of straight Georgian lines and mottled grey walls: simple yet magnificent.

David glanced at the thin, pale man in the passenger seat. Edward was the same age as him, twenty-six, although he looked older. His mousy hair was prematurely thin, and his blue eyes were never still. That alertness, the complete inability to relax, was the legacy of the trenches.

"Soon, all this will be mine," David said drily.

Edward laughed. "Sounds as if you're planning to bump off your aunt."

"That wouldn't get me far; the heir is some other nephew of my uncle's. No, I shall have the responsibility without the privilege of ownership, but that's fine by me. Aunt Elizabeth promised me a free hand to administer the estate, and I'll thoroughly enjoy the job."

"Will you be living at the Hall itself?"

"No." David looked eastwards, but woodland obscured his line of vision. "You can't see it from here, but there's an old manor about a mile off. Dilapidated, but a splendid house, good thick walls. Anne and I plan to do the place up. It'll be perfect for us."

Edward gazed thoughtfully out of the side window, hands clasped on the walking stick that rested between his knees.

"You seem to have it all worked out. I envy you."

David brought the Bentley to a halt.

"Listen, old man, I wasn't going to speak until later, but now's as good a moment as any. My sister's party was a pretext to get you here. I want to see how you like the place. When I become estate manager, I'll need a right-hand man. What do you say?"

"You want me to work for you?"

"*With* me, Edward. Can't think of a better man for the job."

Edward was silent for a moment.

"You don't need a shell-shocked wreck like me, David. I don't want pity."

"It's pragmatism, not pity," David said brusquely. "You can do the job, I need you, and I won't take no for an answer."

A hesitant smile. "Then I'd like nothing better."

"That's the spirit." David clapped him on the shoulder and drove on. "And while you're at it, propose to one of my sisters, will you? Charlotte would suit you perfectly. Yes, she's shy, but a lovely girl underneath."

"Actually, it's Madeleine I'm rather sweet on."

"Oh, that's what they all say. Why not be original?"

They laughed together. Edward shook his head.

"However many times I've said you owe me nothing, I confess I'm grateful."

"Good God, man, stop making it sound as if I'm doing you a favour," David retorted. "You saved my life. I'm in absolute bloody awe of you."

An hour to go before the guests would begin to arrive. In the lull – after the frantic business of dressing up – Charlotte stood with Fleur and Madeleine on the terrace, breathing in the garden's sweet air. In white shifts and long black wigs, their eyes striped with kohl and bracelets on their bare arms, they might have stepped from the walls of an Egyptian tomb. Madeleine had chosen to be Cleopatra, with her sisters as handmaidens.

Charlotte had mixed feelings about fancy dress. In one way she felt ridiculous, but in another she welcomed the disguise. Even elegant Fleur looked slightly silly for a change.

The late summer evening was warm but overcast, darkening early. Standing on the long sweep of the terrace, with the house rising on one side and the gardens falling away on the other, Charlotte experienced a wonderful feeling of peace. Past and future dissolved into mist. There was only now. It was so pleasant to be with her sisters, simply listening to their voices.

Fleur was enthusing about the painting she'd begun. Madeleine listened and nodded, her eyes shining with impatience.

Then Fleur asked, "Did you see him again, your wonderful Austrian?"

"He came to the house yesterday." Madeleine gripped Fleur's arm. "It was unbelievable. My plan worked all too well. Father was so taken with Karl that he's asked him to come and work in the laboratory."

Charlotte turned rigid. This was exactly what she'd dreaded.

"Which one? The Cavendish?" Fleur said.

"No! Aren't you listening? Karl is going to work in *our* laboratory, at home!"

"Fancy," said Fleur, raising her eyebrows.

Madeleine glanced at Charlotte as if to judge her reaction. Charlotte kept her face neutral, thinking, *Whatever I say, it will be the wrong thing and I refuse to cause an argument.* Maddy bit her lower lip, frowning.

"Aren't you pleased?" said Fleur.

"Yes, but... I didn't think this far," Madeleine said quietly. "Thing is, I had so many plans: new friends to see, house parties, wild adventures, and now I shan't want to go, because Karl will be in Cambridge."

Fleur stroked Madeleine's arm. "Can't you take Karl with you?"

"He'll be *working*. And Father won't let a strange man go with me, even with a chaperone."

"I'm sure there are ways around it. Clive and I – well, let's say

Aunt Lizzie didn't know the half of what we got away with. So, I hardly need ask if he's taken a fancy to you?"

"I believe he has." Madeleine's expression brightened. "The way he looks at me... You're right, Fleur. Everything will be perfect." She turned to Charlotte. "Oh, you're not miserable about it, are you, Charli? Please don't be. Not on the best birthday of my life."

Charlotte smiled and murmured her blessing, but her heart felt thick and cold. She felt ashamed of ill-wishing Maddy's dreams. While her sisters lived deep in the stream of life, Charlotte remained on the riverbank, watching life flow past, fleeing from anything new. And she envied them.

A French window opened, and Elizabeth – a passable imitation of Queen Marie Antoinette – swept onto the terrace.

"Charlotte, would you come inside? Your father's arrived. He wants a word," she called.

I'd like a word with him, too, she thought. *I suppose he's going to break the news gently about Karl joining us.*

Her father was in the blue drawing room, named for its delicate Wedgwood-blue colour scheme. A chandelier hung from an elaborate ceiling rose, its light glinting on gilded furniture. On one side of the room, glass doors opened onto a flight of stone stairs that curved down into the attached orangery. Charlotte heard the fountains pattering beneath exotic foliage.

Her father, unsurprisingly, had shunned fancy dress for a well-worn evening suit.

"Good evening, m'dear," he said. "How's the flu?"

"Oh, I'm better now, Father, thank you. Did you have a good journey?" They sat together on a gold-coloured chaise longue, Elizabeth in a chair facing them, and made small talk. Her father seemed ill at ease. His expression was grave and he kept glancing at Elizabeth.

Eventually Charlotte said, "Father, I know what you're going to say."

"Oh, do you?"

"Madeleine told me." She sounded calmer than she felt. "About you inviting the Austrian scientist to work with us. Is it true?"

He looked guilty and awkward. "Oh lord. My dear, it's a temporary arrangement and he's a very pleasant young man, nothing for you to worry about. Treat him as an undergraduate. You never mind helping out with teaching, do you?"

"Yes, but..." She couldn't express why this was different. She could cope with her father's students on a strictly professional, scientific level, but Karl was no ordinary student.

"In fact," Elizabeth interrupted, "that's not what we need to discuss, is it, George?"

Now Charlotte was bewildered. What else could there be? And yet, logically, the tension between her aunt and father was unlikely to be about Karl. Elizabeth lit a cigarette in a long holder and blew a cloud of smoke into the air.

"Do you remember the little talk we had yesterday, about marriage?" she asked Charlotte.

"I remember, but I didn't understand."

"Oh dear, haven't you worked it out?" Elizabeth was on the verge of mirth; her father's face was stormy. "I had a telephone call, you see. Someone wishes to propose."

"To me?" said Charlotte, going dizzy.

"Of course to you. Your father's upset because your suitor spoke to me first. To ask my opinion, as if he couldn't make up his own mind, the fool."

"But who is it?"

"If your eyes open any wider, my dear, they'll fall out. Henry, of course. Who else? Henry telephoned me, and then he asked your father. Very sweet and old fashioned of him, I'd say."

"He *what*?" Charlotte gasped.

"Well, you are a dark horse. I had no idea you and Henry were keen on each other," Elizabeth added with a touch of spite.

Charlotte was horrified. "We're not. I mean, I had no idea..."

"It's perfectly simple," Dr Neville said gruffly. "Henry wants to marry you, but the silly ass daren't say anything, so he begged us to ask on his behalf."

"Good God," Charlotte whispered. She looked around wildly. "He's not here, is he?"

"He's safely in Cambridge, dear," said Elizabeth.

Dr Neville looked narrowly at his daughter, as if she'd conducted a clandestine romance under his nose.

"I swear, I gave him no encouragement," she said. "Tell him

no! Oh, this is too embarrassing – I had no idea Henry had such feelings. How can I go on working with him after this?"

"Wait a moment, dear." Elizabeth leaned over to tap Charlotte's hand with bony fingers. "Naturally your father doesn't want you to marry and leave him, but I think he's being a little selfish in this instance."

"Nonsense," he growled. "Charlotte doesn't want to get married. She said as much without any prompting from me."

Charlotte's vision blurred with the rhythm of her pulse. *God, they've been sitting here arguing over this, over my life!*

"Give her time to think." Elizabeth looked firmly into Charlotte's eyes. "This is a good offer; the best you're likely to get, considering you wrecked my efforts to find you a decent match. He's a steady young man, his family is well-off, and you are temperamentally suited. What's more, as he's set to be George's shadow for life, your father won't lose you. It's the perfect solution." She sat back triumphantly.

"Solution to what?" Charlotte felt like a fly bouncing on a web.

"Don't be silly. It's common sense, isn't it, George?"

Dr Neville made a growling noise, deep in his throat. Charlotte recognised it as assent. Then she understood.

"You – you've already decided, haven't you? You agreed on this before you sent for me!"

Her father exhaled. "The trouble is, your aunt's right. A girl needs a husband. At least I know Henry, he's a decent sort, and we can all live in the house together."

They both gazed intently at her. She loathed being the focus of attention, and felt she'd been backed into a cage. She couldn't fault their logic. Nor could she rally an argument.

She thought, *It is the answer. If I'm married, it will stop me wishing for a life I can't have. Everyone will be satisfied and they'll leave me alone.*

While part of her stood aghast, she heard herself saying, "Very well, I'll marry Henry, if it's what you want."

"You've made the right decision, dear." Aunt Elizabeth picked up the telephone from a side table. "Why not call him now, to tell him the good news?"

That was deliberate cruelty. Charlotte hated her fiercely at that moment, but only gave a quick shake of her head.

"No. If he doesn't telephone me, I'll speak to him when I go home."

Elizabeth smiled and replaced the mouthpiece. "Quite right, dear. The poor boy must speak sooner or later, unless he means to conduct the entire marriage by proxy." She laughed. "How about a bicycle for your wedding gift? Never were two flat tyres better suited!"

Charlotte ignored her aunt's cruel wit as the enormity of the commitment hit her. Struggling to breathe, she clung to her dignity.

"If you'll excuse me, I should... rejoin my sisters."

She hurried through the open French doors, down the steps into the orangery, and out into the garden. She was almost running, the black plaits of her wig swinging around her shoulders.

Here she could hide. The rippling sea of foliage drew her in, making no judgments, asking nothing of her. Down through the belt of shrubs and birches she went, across long lawns past towering monkey-puzzle trees, until she reached the balustrade that separated the gardens from the woods.

Charlotte sat on a stone bench at the edge of the Italianate garden. Coldness bled through the thin material of her costume, calming her. And there she remained as dusk gathered and the world moved on without her.

Now the guests would be arriving... Now the party would be in full swing. The marquee walls would be taut and glowing. She imagined rising heat, the scent of crushed grass. Skeins of music and laughter drifted to her. But she stayed away. *Away, by my own choice. I refuse to feel sorry for myself. I choose not to be part of it.*

Across the grey flat of the lawn, a fountain danced, reflecting firefly colours from Chinese lanterns strung in the trees. At the summit of the one hundred steps, she saw a few guests walking in the shadow of climbing roses and plane trees, distant, oblivious to her. Beyond, the Hall was lit up like a palace of ice.

She tried to forget her aunt, her father and Henry. She had no thoughts, and only one desire: to dissolve into the cool balm of the night. To find peace...

Her reverie was interrupted.

A silhouette flowed towards her, topped with ringlets and swaying feathers. A regal seventeenth-century lady in stiff green satin and silver lace.

It was Anne. Thank goodness.

"Charli. I've been looking everywhere. Here, drink this." She placed a glass of champagne in Charlotte's hand. "Aren't you freezing in that thin shift?"

"Not at all," she said untruthfully. "Did my aunt send you?"

"I would have come anyway, but yes, she said something."

"Oh, God." Charlotte drank. Her throat was dry and the champagne was delicious. "Is she very annoyed with me?"

"Not really. Irritated that the birthday girl had only one hand-maiden, that's all. Maddy's having the time of her life, but people are asking where you are."

"Oh." Charlotte sighed. "I truly didn't mean to let Maddy down, but... it's all about appearances, that's what I can't bear. How embarrassing, to have a hopeless sister like me! She needs to be accepted and adored by her new crowd, I understand that. And I want to do all the right things, for her sake, but I always seem to trip up."

Anne's hand warmed her goosepimply arm.

"It's not your fault she's so precious. Maddy and Fleur think the universe revolves around them. Everything must be perfect, or it's the end of the world!" She rolled her eyes. "I could never be part of their set. But David and Edward are here, and my mother and father. They want to see you."

That made it worse. Friends *en masse* became a different entity, an audience of strangers. She swallowed the rest of the champagne and said nothing.

Anne looked keenly at her. "Is it true that you and Henry are engaged?"

Charlotte groaned. "I suppose Elizabeth's told everyone."

"Only the family. It was quite a shock, I can tell you!"

"Not half as much as it was to me." Charlotte closed her eyes. "Oh, Anne, what am I going to do?"

"Talk to me," Anne said gently. "Tell me why you're unhappy."

Her kindness brought Charlotte close to tears. As the champagne reached her head, the cloud of pain spilled out.

"It's as if I belong nowhere. I'm a misfit, even in my own family. You don't feel like that, do you?"

"Only because I couldn't care less what people think of me."

"But I *do* care!" Charlotte exclaimed. "I'd do anything to be like Maddy and Fleur, full of life, always knowing the right thing to say. I'd give my soul simply to be *friends* with them, just to be accepted."

"They do accept you."

"Yes – as their shy dull sister. They don't know how I feel inside. They don't know the real me."

"But whose fault is that, Charli? You never let anyone near you."

"I know. I wish I could change my nature, but the more I try, the harder it seems. The trouble is, Father chose me as his favourite – only because I'm so like our mother – and Fleur and Maddy resented me for it. I don't blame them. They punished me, I suppose."

"In what way?" Anne sounded shocked.

The confession felt disloyal, so Charlotte understated the pain of her childhood. "Oh, you know how children can be. They belittled me, excluded me from their circle. I learned to withdraw into myself, and now I can't unlearn it."

"The little beasts! Didn't David protect you?"

"David didn't notice. No one did. You're the first person I've told, actually. Of course they grew out of their nastiness, but our roles were set by then. I can't complain at being Father's right-hand girl – that's where I belong – but part of me still wishes I could fly alongside them." She laughed. "I'd love to be seen as a soaring eagle, instead of a mouse in a hole."

Anne was frowning. "Your sisters play a cruel game with you, Charli. I've seen it. They goad you into changing, then scorn you when you can't. You should learn to hold your chin up, and ignore them!"

"I do try," Charlotte let out another sigh. "Still... I so longed to be part of their world. That's why I let my aunt take me to London. Anne, it was like drowning. Crowds of people staring, judging... Even if someone was nice to me, I was so nervous I would freeze and make an excuse to escape. You could see their eyes clouding over... A 'flat tyre', my aunt called me. That's why I can't refuse Henry."

"I don't see the connection."

"Who else will ask me? As a married woman, I'll become acceptable and people won't think I'm odd and pester me."

"Oh, Charli," said Anne. "Who cares what they think? No wonder you're miserable. You let your family walk all over you! You must tell your aunt you've made a mistake. Be firm."

"I can't, it's too late."

"Rubbish! Why can't you stand up for yourself? I could shake you!" She put her arm round Charlotte's shoulders and said more gently, "If you go on like this, they'll destroy you. They've done a pretty effective job already."

"It's easy for you. You're brave. I'm frightened to get married, frightened to say no. What can I do?"

"Let me help you. It's like talking to a brick wall." Anne's tone was affectionate. She hugged Charlotte, kissed her cheek. Charlotte felt an unaccustomed sense of warmth and release. *We're friends, we are real friends!*

She returned the embrace awkwardly.

"What would I do without you, Anne?"

"That's better. One step at a time, you *will* learn to be proud of who you are! Now, I'm going to ensure you enjoy this evening, if it's the last thing I do. Look, there's David." Anne pointed across the lawn. "Who's he talking to?"

Charlotte saw her brother beyond the fountain: a splendid musketeer in a feathered hat. With him was a tall slim man who looked familiar…

Then she realised, and her heart leapt up to choke her. It hadn't occurred to her that Madeleine would invite Karl to the party. The moment she saw him, a feeling of wrongness drenched the world, as if reality itself had taken a darker shape.

He was slightly taller than David, slender and elegant in an eighteenth-century costume of black velvet; long legs outlined by close-fitting breeches, a tailored coat with white lace at the throat and cuffs. His hair was full and dark, almost black but for reddish highlights. His face was beautiful. Wholly masculine, yet the mere word "handsome" could not be applied to him, any more than it described a Renaissance angel. His beauty took away her breath completely.

Now what's happening to me? she thought wildly. Panic swelled in her heart. She could only define the feeling as... *recognition.* She'd sensed danger the first time she'd seen him at Fleur's, but had the wit to flee before his spell ensnared her. Now it was too late. She wanted to run, but was transfixed.

Karl had a quality of stillness that drew her, like a clear, deep lake. Something out of the ordinary, too enthralling to be human, both fascinating and dangerous. His long white hands looked luminous, and as he turned to glance at her, only his eyes seemed alive in his carved visage – amber jewels lit by fire.

And it should have been impossible to discern his eye colour at such a distance...

Anne said, "Oh, it's Maddy's new beau, isn't it?"

The words hit Charlotte like gloved fists. They spoke of possession. *Madeleine possesses him as Henry now possesses me...*

The spell was broken. The stranger was walking away and David was striding towards them, sweeping his feathered hat from his head in extravagant greeting. He was blonder than Charlotte, with a friendly, open face lent character by a once-broken nose that had set crookedly. She was glad to see him. Somehow he made the world safe again.

"Come on, let's brave the party." Anne slid a hand through her arm. "David and I will look after you. You know, not everyone's a snob like Elizabeth; there are lots of people who think kindly of you, if you'd give them a chance to be friends."

Safe between David and Anne, Charlotte found the party bearable.

The marquee was huge; no expense had been spared for Madeleine. A dance band played jaunty songs amid a jungle of potted palms. Despite the servants' efforts to keep the chaos under control, the party was the worse for wear: tables in disarray, their crisp white cloths piled with plates and glasses. The smell of crushed grass and stale wine rose with the heat of dancing bodies. Maddy and Fleur were in the thick of it. Smoke wreathed the canvas ceiling. Guests in Roman togas danced with harlequins, medieval princesses with gypsies and giant bears.

The three of them joined a table with Anne's parents and

David's friend Edward Lees: a flamboyant group in costumes inspired by the Dumas novel, *The Three Musketeers*. Charlotte had never dreamt that in all her life she would see Dr Saunders dressed in bright scarlet as Cardinal Richelieu. She smiled, and her self-consciousness began to slide away. She'd known Anne's family since childhood, while Edward, whom she'd met occasionally, was as shy as Charlotte in his way.

He was gentle and polite, but she sensed an underlying mood. David had explained that Edward had been in low spirits since the War. They had said little about their ordeal in the trenches, but she knew that it had been terrible. Her imagination could paint frightening pictures. She felt unspoken empathy with Edward.

Protected in her circle, not required to make conversation, Charlotte drank too much champagne and watched the party drift around her in a pleasant haze. Edward apologised for not asking her to dance, as he couldn't walk without his stick. Charlotte smiled and said she preferred to watch, anyway.

She relaxed, wondering what she'd been afraid of... until Anne nudged her, and said, "The Prof's heading this way."

Her father looked out of place in his evening suit, as one of the few who'd refused to make a "damned fool of himself" by dressing up. Beside him came Madeleine and Elizabeth, with Karl between them like a prize.

Sudden tension sobered Charlotte. Heads turned as Karl walked by. While other guests looked self-conscious or comical in costume, Karl's black velvet seemed part of him, as if he would have been perfectly at home in the eighteenth century. His hair was very deep auburn, not quite black; a rich colour that flooded her eyes. Although he drew attention, like a live panther in their midst, he seemed untouched by their reactions. He was the dark still centre of a whirlpool.

"Ah, Charlotte, there you are at last," said her father. His tone was cheerful, holding no recrimination for her absence. "I think I've introduced Karl to everyone except you. So, may I present Karl Alexander von Wultendorf; Karl, my daughter Charlotte, who, as I'm sure you're tired of hearing, is utterly invaluable to me."

Charlotte stood up and found Karl's intense, beautiful amber eyes gazing into hers. She felt herself dissolving in their crystal light.

He said, "I am delighted to make your acquaintance, Miss Neville. We seemed to keep missing one another."

His voice was low and clear, with only the gentlest trace of an Austrian accent. He took her hand, and the touch of his long cool fingers sent a weird sensation through her like a slow electric shock.

She was almost too nervous to open her mouth, yet it seemed vitally important that she say the right thing. This moment meant something. His eyes held her, cutting through her fear. His beauty went right through her core like a hot sword.

He added, "I am so looking forward to working with you."

Then Charlotte rebelled at the way his gaze captivated her, resented his glamour. She pulled her hand out of his and said coldly, "I'm afraid the laboratory will be rather too cramped with four of us there."

Karl's reaction to her rudeness was infinitesimal, she couldn't tell whether he was offended, surprised or unmoved. Still intent on her, he said, "I'm sure we shall manage."

Madeleine spoke, and his attention flicked away from Charlotte, swift as a dragonfly. She sat down and stared at the table. Irrationally and fiercely she rejected him for the way he'd transfixed her, making her feel she was someone special and interesting – only to turn away as if she were nothing.

"…and naturally, we're very proud of David," George Neville was telling Karl, resting a hand on his son's shoulder. "So many families lost their sons, you know. We're so very lucky that he came back. And it's all thanks to this young man here." He waved a hand at Edward. "They were in the same regiment, you know."

"Father –" David interrupted.

"Oh, let your old pater tell the story. Edward saved David's life. David was injured by a mortar. Edward sat with him all night in a shell-hole full of water until the bombardment died down, then carried him back behind the lines. Took a bullet in the leg on the way, but still kept going. Got a medal for it, a knighthood would have been more in order, but there you are. Heroes, both of them." Dr Neville nodded emphatically, ignoring Edward's embarrassment.

Karl's eyes widened almost imperceptibly under dark eyebrows.

"There was a great deal of bravery in the War," he said.

Edward shuffled on his seat. "Oh, nothing brave on my part, I can assure you. One did what one had to. But I expect you know…" He looked up at Karl, and his face froze.

"Yes, which front did you serve on?" David asked conversationally.

There was a brief, heavy silence. What Karl's reply would have been, they never knew; Madeleine rescued them.

"Oh, don't talk about the War," she said. "In my capacity as Queen of Egypt – Queen of this party, at any rate – I absolutely forbid it." She slid her hand through Karl's arm; he didn't resist. "I can't imagine why you want to hide in a stuffy old laboratory with my father. You must be frightfully dedicated."

"I would like to uncover the secrets of the universe," said Karl. "Is there anyone who would not?"

Madeleine said, "I think the only secret is to have fun."

They looked at each other, their conversation excluding the others.

"Do you have no curiosity?" he said.

"Mm!" Her kohl-lined eyes sparkled. "I'm very curious about finding new ways to enjoy myself. You can't work all the time. The only sensible way to exhaust oneself is by dancing…" She was leading him towards the dance floor as she spoke.

"Maddy's making very sure no one else gets near him," Anne commented. "Attractive, isn't he? If he were a woman, men would be fighting duels over him."

"Men probably fight duels over him anyway," Elizabeth said drily.

Charlotte's father was talking to Dr and Mrs Saunders, pulling out a chair to sit down with them. She wished she could corner him and demand, "Don't I have any say in who works with us? How could you agree to this? I don't trust him!" Of course, she would not. She forced down her confused feelings, buried them.

Unspeaking, she listened to the murmur of conversation: Anne's voice, David's voice, rising and falling, making no sense. The air felt heavy and stale in her lungs. Her head ached and she was trembling.

Around her the party whirled on. She watched Madeleine and

Karl threading graceful curves through the crowd of dancers; she saw women watching Karl, men watching her sister, jealous. Then she looked at Edward and he too was staring at Madeleine as he fumbled with a silver cigarette case.

He's in love with Maddy, too, she thought, feeling desperate sympathy.

The dance ended: Madeleine and Karl were coming back. Edward's stare moved with them, blatant enough to be bad mannered. Then Charlotte saw Edward's face turning ghastly, blanching beyond white to greyish-blue. His eyes were round, bulging, irises circled by white. The silver case fell from his fingers, scattering cigarettes everywhere. His lips were parted, his breath quick and shallow.

Alarmed, Charlotte leaned towards him. "Edward? Are you all right? You don't look well."

He didn't respond. When she touched his arm, he leapt right out of his seat, his chair flying backwards and his stick toppling to the ground. Everyone turned to stare at him. Then he started to scream.

Charlotte leapt away from him in panic. It was a terrible sound, a man screaming, deep and tearing. Drops of spittle flew from his mouth and he was pointing at Karl, backing away until he collided with a tent pole and the whole marquee shook. Karl stopped where he was and stared back at Edward with an expression of slight surprise.

"Take him out!" Edward yelled, his voice thick and hoarse. "Get him away, get him out of here. Vampire." The word was a rasp on his last thread of breath. "*Vampire.*"

CHAPTER FOUR

SHADOW AGAINST THE WALL

Waves of astonishment rippled across the marquee. Conversations stopped, heads turned, dancing couples stumbled to a halt. The music fizzled out, one instrument after another. Over the undercurrent of murmured exclamations, Edward went on screaming and screaming.

"I see what he is! Death! Get him out!"

David watched his friend in shock and dismay. Everyone seemed paralysed, as if Edward's frenzy created an invisible wall around him.

It wasn't the first time David had had to brave the flailing limbs and hold onto his rigid shoulders until he calmed down.

"It's all right, old chap. I'm here. Steady," he said gently.

Edward fought blindly, foam gathering in the corners of his mouth. The stocky, imperturbable butler, Newland, hurried forward to help, followed by two of David's friends, also former soldiers. Their expressions were grim. *It's taken them back to the trenches, too*, David thought. *This raw fear… God, will it ever let go?* As they struggled to hold Edward, Dr Saunders came to them, pushing up the sleeves of his scarlet robe.

"We'll take him into the house," said the doctor. "I'll fetch my medical bag."

David let the others take Edward and hung behind. It took three of them to manhandle him out of the tent, and he fought all the way; white-eyed, grey-faced, with soul-chilling cries tearing out of his lungs. David was shaken to the core, yet he felt obliged to say something before he went after his friend.

I refuse to be embarrassed or apologetic on Edward's behalf, he thought. *I owe him better than that.*

The screaming faded. Like air rushing into a vacuum, the hubbub of conversation rose swiftly. With Edward gone, everyone's attention focused on Karl. Of them all, he looked the least perturbed. His face was almost expressionless; a touch of surprise, then a slight drawing down of his eyebrows, but otherwise he was composed.

"I hardly know what to say," David said gravely to the Austrian. "This is a regrettable situation, but please don't blame Edward. He's been unwell for some time. If you'll excuse me, I must go and see how he is."

"Of course," Karl said, inclining his head. He seemed to understand, but Madeleine's eyes were glittering and her cheeks were red.

"It's an absolute disgrace," she said. "What possessed him to make such a scene, and how dare he say such dreadful things to one of my guests?"

"Madeleine," said David, "shut up."

Edward lay on the bed with one arm over his face, quiet but shattered. Dr Saunders, his costume half dismantled, sat on the edge of the bed placing instruments back into his medical bag. His broad, kind face was serious.

"I've given him a sedative, David. He should be all right now, but I'd get him some expert help, if I were you."

"He's seen a psychiatrist," David sighed. "He's been so much better lately, I really hoped these breakdowns were behind him."

Edward looked out from under his arm. His eyes were bloodshot.

"But he's a vampire," he said. "The man's a vampire."

"Come on, old man." David put a hand on his shoulder. "You're overwrought. Is it because he fought on the other side? Look, the War's over. An Austrian's just an ordinary chap like anyone else."

"I know. It's not that. I can't make you understand. I see things no one else can see. Please listen…" His voice was growing slurred.

David looked at Dr Saunders, who shook his head.

"Try to get some sleep, there's a good chap," said David, patting Edward's arm. "I have to go, but I'll be here when you wake up, don't worry."

With a heavy heart, David returned to the marquee. The dance band was playing again, the party continuing as if nothing had happened. He was glad.

Charlotte and Anne came to him, and asked how Edward was. He hugged them, then wove through the crowd until he reached Karl. He sat down in a chair opposite him. The Austrian acknowledged him with a friendly enough look. David sat forward, aware that others were listening, but wanting them to hear.

"Look, Herr von Wultendorf, I'm most awfully sorry," he began. "I don't know how to apologise – not for Edward's behaviour, which isn't his fault, but for the embarrassment caused. You must have found it distressing, but I can assure you it was far more distressing for Edward. I must explain, although he won't thank me for it."

"I could see he was disturbed," said Karl. "There's no need to apologise or explain."

"But I must. Edward suffers from neurasthenia. He was badly shell-shocked during the War and it destroyed his nerves completely. He has terrible bouts of depression, and sometimes these fits of hysteria. He can't help it."

Karl nodded. His eyelids were lowered. "I guessed as much."

"But that's why I can't abandon him. If not for him, I wouldn't be alive. People who weren't there can't imagine how deep such comradeship goes. It makes me furious when ignorant people write him off as an embarrassment. I shall always stick by him, whatever he does. I want you to understand that."

"David, it's quite all right." Karl looked up, his expression receptive. "The incident caused me no embarrassment, and the only thing that matters is Edward's health."

David let out a breath of relief. "Thank you for understanding. I know he'll feel bad when he recovers, but it will help him to know you've been so decent."

Elizabeth, who was sitting nearby, leaned across to Karl and rested her hand along his velvet sleeve, unashamedly flirtatious.

"If only our governments could sort things out in such a civil manner. I do hope this won't prevent you feeling perfectly at ease and welcome among us. We are all quite harmless, really!"

They're lucky, being able to laugh it off so easily, David thought bitterly.

Passing along the Hall's main corridor on his way back to Edward, he glanced through the doorway of the large drawing room and was surprised to see Charlotte there. She stood in darkness at the window. In her Egyptian costume, she seemed a ghost from another time. A faint glow from outside dappled the room and painted her bare arms with silver.

"Hello," he said. "Had enough of the party?"

She turned like a startled thief. "Oh, David, you made me jump. It's so hot and noisy in there. And after... what happened, it all seemed a bit much."

He went to her and they stood side by side, looking out at the garden.

"I've rather lost the taste for enjoying myself, too."

"How is Edward?"

"Resting." David gave a slight shake of his head. "I'm worried. When he has these bouts, they're usually triggered by a loud noise – a reminder of gunfire – and I can calm him quite easily. I've never known him react to another chap like that. What was it about Karl? Strange, but sometimes, when Edward meets a person, he seems to know all about them without being told. I'm not saying it's some supernatural hokum, but there are definitely things going on in Edward's head that I don't understand."

"Perhaps he's just highly perceptive," said Charlotte. "Karl – Karl seemed to take it well."

"Yes, thank God, he was very understanding. Others might not have been."

She looked sideways at him.

"What do you think of Karl?"

"Oh, I hardly know. Usually I can weigh up a fellow straight off, but with von Wultendorf it's not so easy. He doesn't give much away. Seems decent enough, but..."

"You don't like him?" She sounded anxious.

"I've no feelings either way. Father's obviously taken to him. The way Maddy, Aunt Lizzie and their cronies were fawning over him – taking hospitality a bit too far, but not his fault, I suppose."

Charlotte laughed. He took her hand and tucked it through his arm.

"Thank goodness there's one female in this family who isn't mooning over him. You've got more sense, haven't you, sis?"

"There's more to a man than a handsome face."

"Well, that must be so, if what I hear about you and Henry is true."

"Oh, that." She winced.

"For a newly engaged woman, you don't seem overjoyed. Are you sure you're doing the right thing?"

David loved Charlotte, but didn't understand her. She was like a shy forest creature seen at a distance between the trees: hunted, doelike, following some secret path of her own. Even as he stood with her, he sensed she was not really there, as if her real self was slipping away through the green caves of the forest, elusive.

"It's only that I don't want any fuss," she said with a forced smile. "It's not official yet. It's for the best, David, honestly. If I don't marry Henry, I shan't marry anyone. We'll be comfortable together, and even Father's happy about it."

I don't altogether believe you, sis, he thought, *but I know you won't talk to me.*

"Well, if you're sure. I had hoped you and Edward... but no, how could I expect you to take on a fellow with his problems? It's a shame, though. You would have been good for each other."

She rested her head against his arm, and said nothing.

Kristian found Pierre in Vienna, ironically enough. The city that Karl so loved; might Karl be here after all?

Pierre was always easy to find. He was a creature of habit and Kristian knew his haunts, the elegant European cities where he felt at home. Besides he was ordered never to stray too far, in case Kristian needed him.

A halo surrounded the moon. Its light penetrated the Crystal Ring, falling blue and glassy on the otherworld as Kristian moved through it. Vienna still existed, but was only semi-tangible, distorted. Buildings crowded together, skewing at impossible angles, their walls built of air. Kristian passed through brick and stone as if through shadow, the buildings' occupants never suspecting his presence. One might shiver as he passed by, but none guessed that God's dark wing had brushed them.

And as he was invisible to mortals, so were they to him – except for their auras. Human-shaped gaps were delineated by needles of blue, red and gold fire. They moved as swiftly as moths and their voices were thin, like harpsichords heard through closed doors. The Ring deformed the rooms through which he moved, turning them to grey, static spaces in which the fiery outlines of mortals fluttered and buzzed.

Once or twice Kristian paused to drink a human aura.

Although he abhorred human blood, he still needed their energy. This way he could suck out pure life force without touching their hot gritty flesh. Needles of light slid into his pores and he breathed warmth, bathed in pure energy.

However young and strong the victim, they would fade fast. Their companions would watch them sink and die of some trivial infection, protesting, "But he was always so healthy, so strong!"

None of this concerned Kristian. He felt satisfaction that he had dispatched one more sinner to face God's justice. The flame went out, the wick smouldered in the darkness, and he moved on.

Drifting through the blue-black twilight of Schönbrunn Park, he sensed another vampire. A cool aura like a diamond pressed into his forehead: cold, sharp, faintly radiant. Soundless, Kristian stepped out of the Crystal Ring.

There was disorientation as the real world unfolded, like a fan flicked open, or a vast painted canvas springing into three dimensions. The change was profound, as if the Earth had been created anew just for him. Moonlight slanted across the park, full of subtle colours that only his immortal eyes could see. Through this soft and shining landscape Kristian walked between tree shadows towards the other presence.

By a hedge wall, he paused. A few yards away, in a clipped archway, he saw the vampire with a potential victim. They were talking, the vampire pretending to ask directions. Moon-pale, he loomed over the man, edging him backwards, making no attempt to hide his nature.

Kristian recognised Pierre's tall figure in an expensive dark coat. His prey was short and solid, middle-aged, slightly drunk. Kristian observed the man's sudden shift from nonchalance to unease. Abruptly sober, he tried to break away – then Pierre's arms shot out like two black cobras to press him into the hedge.

The vampire's face was hard and gleaming, his eyes ghostly blue, his hands like bleached, gnarled wood. In an instant of dazzling horror, the man realised what was happening. His mouth fell open but no cry came out; he wriggled like an impaled maggot, while Pierre merely looked down with amused condescension. He pulled back his lips, let the man see the shining ivory thorns of his canines. In no hurry. Gloating, as if about to bite into a delicious fruit...

Eyes wide, Pierre leaned towards his prey, relishing the man's terror. The scarlet tip of his tongue touched his own lips, then the man's neck. He paused, taut with anticipation, his icy breath flowing over the victim's throat. Then he struck.

The man's body convulsed as the fangs went in. Kristian felt an empathic surge of excitement, which turned as swiftly to revulsion. If only all vampires would sip auras instead of blood; if only they *wanted* to. Kristian despaired of breaking his flock's sinful lust for contact with human flesh.

To drink from other immortals was different. Not lust, but a show of love and power.

The man's hands were white against Pierre's sable coat, outstretched fingers waving, imploring. Their movement grew feebler as the vampire sucked out his strength. Now they clutched pathetically as the man slid to the ground, eyes rolling back, jaw hanging. Pierre leaned against the hedge in a stupor of pleasure, his face flushed and a lock of curly brown hair hanging on his forehead.

Kristian strode to him and seized his coat lapels.

"Fool!" he hissed. "Do you want to be discovered? I could see you a mile away."

Judging by Pierre's shock, he'd had no idea that Kristian was watching, like a huge, all-seeing dark god.

"So?" His red mouth curved. "If I took someone in broad

daylight by St Stefan's Cathedral, what could anyone do about it?"

"Every time a vampire is seen or a victim found, rumours run wild," Kristian replied. "Less so in this sceptical century, perhaps, but it still happens. I can't tolerate their superstition, the way they invoke their pathetic religion against us, who are closer to God than they'll ever be! The dark wings of heaven should be silent and invisible."

"I fear," said Pierre, "that my own spirit is too mean to encompass your ideals, beloved master." He shook free of Kristian's grasp and smoothed his coat. Although Pierre chose expensive clothes, he still had an untidy look that betrayed the poverty he'd known in life. A spirit burning with injustice, Kristian remembered. Ripe, just after the French Revolution, for initiation.

"All the more reason to strive for perfection. You should have been alert."

"I was occupied," Pierre said, unabashed. "And you frightened me to death... so to speak." He grinned, but Kristian kept a dour expression. He poked the victim with his foot.

"You are careless. If he dies..."

"Oh, he'll go home, have bad dreams... then he'll forget. But what if I'd killed him? Why is it acceptable to kill in your way, but not in mine?"

Kristian was in no mood for his flippancy.

"A thousand times I have warned you. If you can't kill invisibly, do not kill at all!"

Seizing Pierre, he tore his left sleeve open and ran a sharp fingernail down the inner forearm.

Pierre yelped. A string of claret beads seeped out of the wound. Kristian drew the arm to his mouth and licked the blood away. A new line oozed out.

"You cannot die but you can still feel pain... and how sensitive vampire flesh can be," he said.

An old fear clouded Pierre's blue eyes.

Kristian made a second slash beside the first, vicious and ragged.

"What the hell have I done to you, Kristian?" Pierre burst out furiously. "Haven't I always been loyal? Let me go!"

"Loyal, you?" Anger boiled like tar within him. He tore open Pierre's wrist with his nails. "Don't lie to me."

"I swear to God, I don't know what you're talking about."

"I *am* your God! Tell me where he is."

"Who?"

"Karl. Tell me."

"Oh. So that's what this is about." The French vampire's eyes narrowed. "You're wrong. I haven't seen Karl for years."

Kristian tightened his grip.

"Stop lying. Ilona told me you know where he is. It's hard to understand why you failed to tell me."

"No – you've got it wrong. For God's sake, let go and listen to me!"

Kristian held on for a moment longer and then released him. Pierre relaxed, gasping and holding his injured arm, the wounds already beginning to heal.

"It's Ilona who's lying. *She* knows, not me! Damn it, I wish you'd leave me out of your games."

"This is no game. Explain."

Pierre steadied himself. "Ilona makes it her business to know where Karl is. Always. So why don't you ask her?"

It was a horrible revelation, the idea that Ilona might deceive Kristian.

"How dare she!"

Pierre shrugged. "She's perverse. She hates Karl but can't leave him alone… and I wish to God she wouldn't involve me."

Kristian's hands snaked out and forced Pierre against the hedge. The stiff branches yielded to his weight.

"Well, it's time for Karl to come back, and you are going to find him for me."

"Do your own dirty work!" Pierre snapped back, struggling as uselessly as his recent victim. "You presume too much on love. You say you chose us because we are spirited, yet when we desire a little freedom, you seek to crush us! Find Karl yourself!"

Pierre's throat moved as he spoke, pale and gleaming in the folds of his shirt and coat. Kristian felt himself enter a higher state of deadly calm rage.

"Not this time," said Kristian. "I will have loyalty, Pierre. I will have obedience." Then he stabbed his fangs into Pierre's neck.

He drew the dense, ice-bright vampire blood into his mouth

and began to swallow, striving to drain Pierre's defiance with his blood; to suck him dry and leave him humiliated, terrified, pleading forgiveness.

At last he let go and Pierre slumped, catching at Kristian's stiff black clothing. His head drooped, brown curls dishevelled.

"Yes," he gasped. "Anything for you."

Kristian felt almost tender towards him then. This was the way of power: a vampire who could drink another's blood proved himself the stronger. Kristian had done this countless times to vampires who defied him. He always won. Always.

"I know, beloved one," he said. "I know."

"I'm thirsty. You must let me..." Pierre strained towards the mortal who still lay collapsed at their feet, but Kristian held him back.

"Wait," he said. "I must make sure you understand why I had to punish you."

Pierre looked up. His face was dead white and his eyes shone feverishly.

"Kristian, I'd never do anything to harm you. I swear I don't know where Karl is, but I'll find him, if it's what you want. Trust me, as I love you."

"I do, my dearest friend."

"But it would save us both trouble if you just asked Ilona."

Kristian thought of Ilona, asleep in the highest circle of the Crystal Ring. Again he saw her eyelids closing, her stiff lips uttering a last tantalising lie, *"Pierre knows..."*

"Impossible, at present. When you find Karl, don't approach him. Just come straight back to me. Then I'll tell you how to proceed."

"You are a hard master," said Pierre, with a gleam of his former defiance. "But how can I refuse you?"

Ah, how he loves me. "Regain your strength quickly. You'll need it." Kristian kissed him on both cheeks and dropped him. With affectionate disdain he watched Pierre crawl to his unconscious victim and begin to suck back the strength that his master had stolen.

Now the man would die, for certain.

* * *

Charlotte slept badly. When morning came she lay in a restless doze, haunted by her ridiculous yet unpleasant dreams. She was married to Henry, but Henry was actually a teddy bear who sat brooding and moth-eaten in the corner of a huge medieval hall. And at the far end of the hall hung a portrait of Karl, a luminous Pre-Raphaelite portrait with every detail painfully sharp. The eyes seemed alive, shining under the dark brows. Her breath quickened and a strange hot fear pulled at her.

"I tried to tell you he was just a painting," said Edward, pointing with his stick, "but no one would listen."

She woke. Someone in her room opened the curtains and light spilled in, dazzling.

"I surely hope you aren't suffering from too much champagne," said Anne, "because it's a perfect morning to go riding."

Charlotte felt delicious relief at escaping the dream – until memories of the previous day flowed back, a patchwork of disasters. Yes, it would be good to avoid the ordeal of breakfast... having to face Karl, or think about Henry. One good thing had come from the party: her deepening friendship with Anne, which held her steady like a talisman against her fears.

The park slanted before them, shining with watered-gold sunlight and green shadow. They trotted beneath the rustling branches of copper beeches and ash trees, Charlotte on a chestnut mare, Anne on a headstrong bay hunter. Birds broke upwards through the leaves as they passed: showers of birds, wheeling in a wave.

In the back of Charlotte's mind was the inescapable thought, *Tonight I'll return to Cambridge with Father; tomorrow, I shall have to face Henry.* Now, instead of a refuge, the lab would be like being trapped in a cage with two lions running loose.

At this moment, though, nothing could touch her.

"I can't wait to get home," said Anne. "I miss riding my own horse desperately."

Charlotte smiled. "I suppose Elizabeth's horses aren't the same."

"Of course not. I can't go a day without riding, but I came out with an ulterior motive. I want to look at the old manor house where David and I will live once we're married. I heard they've started the renovations, and I want a good look around without her ladyship talking my head off."

"Wouldn't you rather go with David?"

Green-speckled tunnels of woodland drew them in. Hoof-beats thudded softly on the path.

"It would have been nice if he'd come too," Anne replied. "But the Prof asked him to show Karl around the estate."

"Oh – to keep Karl away from Edward?"

"And away from Madeleine, I think. I gather your father's none too pleased at her flirting with him last night."

Charlotte sighed. "That doesn't surprise me. But if Maddy's set her heart on something, it's not in Father's power to stop her."

"What did you make of Karl, now you've met him properly?" Anne said, teasing. "Isn't he outrageously handsome?"

"I want nothing to do with him," Charlotte stated with vehemence.

Anne was taken aback. Then she said thoughtfully, "*Too* attractive, perhaps. You're right, I wouldn't trust him, either."

"I wish Maddy had never met him. Why was he at Fleur's party, anyway? It's as if we've invited some stranger off the street into the lab – Father simply wouldn't do it. I can't think what possessed him."

"Charli, there's no sense in upsetting yourself about Karl. He might be nice, when you get to know him."

"You're right." Charlotte tried to shake off her unease. "I'm being an idiot."

"Well, keeping in mind the slight possibility that Karl may become your brother-in-law, you may have to get used to him. Though I have a feeling…"

"What?"

"Men like Karl can be very charming, but they leave trails of broken hearts behind them. I'm afraid he might hurt Madeleine."

"He'd better not!" Charlotte said fiercely. "I should kill him!"

A mile along the woodland path, they saw the manor house. Its walls rose stern and grey through a clearing in the trees, shouldering up through a covering of ivy and moss. Brambles massed around its flanks, spilling into drifts of willow herb. Charlotte and Anne halted the horses and looked up at its leaded windows.

"Pretty grim, isn't it?" said Anne. "At least they've cleared the path. It's a start."

Piles of scaffolding, bricks and pipes lay ready for the estate workmen. Anne and Charlotte dismounted and tethered the horses. They walked up four steps to the iron-clad front door, which swung open to Anne's touch. An exhalation of damp sighed out to meet them.

"It's years since I came here," said Charlotte.

In the hallway, the flagstones echoed under their riding boots.

"You know the place, then?" Anne asked.

"When we stayed with Aunt Lizzie, we often played here."

"Weren't you frightened?" Anne shivered.

"Not really. I loved the ancient atmosphere. Strange, isn't it? It must have been the only time Fleur and Maddy were scared, and I wasn't."

Charlotte looked around the lofty hall of pale stone and dark wood, a medieval manor crystallised in time. A broad staircase swept up to the landing, lit by wedges of gossamer daylight. Dust lay thick on the sills, cobwebs curtained banisters and candelabras. The huge firegrate was full of ashes and shadows. The atmosphere lay heavy as if it had not been disturbed for centuries.

"It seems such a shame to modernise," said Charlotte, moving through the hall.

Anne hung behind. "I have a confession. This place rather gives me the creeps."

"You? I didn't think anything scared you."

"I'm not scared," Anne said crisply. "Just... well, spooky is putting it mildly. I'll be glad to have electric lights and all that. We shan't ruin it, Charli; the idea is to preserve the house rather than let it fall down."

"I heard it dates from the Wars of the Roses or before." Charlotte climbed the stairs as she spoke. "You'll find Elizabethan and Georgian alterations. Last inhabited in the 1790s, my aunt told us."

"I believe her," said Anne, following.

From the landing, Charlotte looked at the hall below and the ceiling arching above. The black, ornate beams gave the feel of an ancient church; slightly sinister, intruding from a lost time.

She remembered her sisters trying to terrify her with tales of hauntings, but failing, because the house intrigued her.

Anne went through a door to a solar.

"There's a bed in here that must date from the sixteenth century. Extraordinary tapestry cover, but it's absolutely thick with dust..." There was the sound of flapping cloth. A cloud billowed out and Anne emerged, coughing.

"Ugh, smell the mildew. It will take an army to clean this place! I'm going to have the chimneys swept and a fire laid in every grate to dry out the damp."

Downstairs, they entered a dim kitchen with iron-grilled windows and store rooms choked with the debris of centuries. Anne was uncharacteristically quiet.

Presently Charlotte asked, "Are you sure you want to live here?"

"Of course! It's a challenge." Anne struggled with the latch of a cracked, age-darkened door. "Where does this lead?"

"It's the cellar," said Charlotte. "Not nice down there."

"Unless you're a rat or a spider." The door came open and a stagnant scent rolled up. Faint gauzy light spilled down the steps, forming oblongs barred with shadow, and across one of these oblongs Charlotte clearly saw the silhouette of a cat.

The shape padded across the light and was gone.

Anne said, "Did you see that?"

"A cat?" said Charlotte.

Anne nodded. "How could it have got down there?"

"I don't know, but we can't leave it." Charlotte started down the steps. She remembered doing this as a child, caught between delicious terror and excitement. Now the feeling caught her again, electric.

There is no cat, she thought.

At the bottom lay a dark space like the crypt of a church. Peering into blackness, she saw nothing, but sensed the weight of the cellar walls and ceiling. The air was chilly, thick with the stench of damp stone and mould.

"Charlotte!" Anne's voice came from halfway down the stairs. "If we leave the door open, the daft animal will find its own way out. Give me a dog any day."

But Charlotte moved deeper into the cellar. It was a compulsion.

Wintry cold penetrated her riding clothes and she hugged herself. The darkness contained layers and layers of age, lost lives and energies weighing down the air with echoes. She listened. There was a vibration in the air, like the ghost-resonance of a door clanging shut... centuries ago.

"Charlotte? Don't blame me if you break your leg!" Anne called. A pause. Then, more anxious, "Oh, do come out. What are you doing?"

"Yes, I'm coming." Her fingers brushed a pillar as cold as a stalagmite. The touch released more vibrations into the air, felt rather than heard. Gooseflesh tingled over her. "It's the same," she murmured. "You're still here..."

A circle of light played across the wall in front of her. Anne was descending the steps with a lamp. And where the light fell, she saw the feline shadow again.

As the light brightened, glistening on barrels and crusty wine jars, the cat vanished.

"There is no cat, Anne," she said. "It's a ghost. I used to see her as a child. I wanted to see if she was still here."

Then Charlotte turned round and found, not Anne behind her, but Karl. She jumped violently and stepped away, heart pounding with shock.

"I'm sorry, I didn't mean to startle you," he said. Lamplight lit red sparks in his dark mass of hair. His eyes were amber glass flecked with gold.

"You frightened the life out of me!" she exclaimed.

"I apologise. I thought you knew I was there." His lips elongated with a trace of amusement and she thought he was mocking her. She held herself rigid. It was strange to see Karl in everyday clothes, a suit beneath an unbuttoned dark coat, though he looked no less elegant. He would be at ease in any clothing, like a slender hand in a black silk glove.

"Where's Anne?" she asked, trying to sound matter-of-fact.

"In the kitchen," he said, as if to say, *It's all right, I have not murdered her.* "David has been showing me the estate. We saw your horses outside. Anne seemed concerned that you'd ventured down here in the dark, and David knew the workmen had left fresh oil-lamps here, so..."

She became aware of voices upstairs: Anne and David. She released her breath.

"Oh, I see. Thank you." *How do I escape?*

"What were you saying about ghosts?" He offered her the lamp, and as she took it his fingertips brushed her palm, cool as satin. The touch sent shocks racing along her nerves. She recoiled inwardly. Karl raised more fear in her than any ghost. Before she turned into a complete stammering fool, she reminded herself sharply of what they were to each other: colleagues in research.

"Did you see the cat?" she asked.

"Yes."

"Then you can't tell me ghosts don't exist." She went to the far wall, picking her way through debris and scampering shadows.

"I was not going to. I believe people see things."

"But have you wondered what a ghost might be?" She spread her fingers on the cold, rough wall. "Not a soul who can't rest, but an image we can call back. This stone is full of quartz. Some crystals have electrical fields, and they vibrate in response to a stimulus. What if they could absorb certain wavelengths and produce them again when disturbed – by light, for example? When photons fall in here, each crystal bounces them back in a particular pattern – and we think we see a cat."

Karl was gazing at her as if he had never seen her before.

"A cat that prowled here centuries ago? It is an interesting theory," he said. "But why should crystals pick up that image and not another? Why no nervous rats?"

She smiled, suddenly forgetting to be self-conscious.

"Perhaps it's just our eyes making shapes out of shadows. Or only certain events produce enough energy to imprint the crystal structure. Or I'm talking nonsense, because ghosts are more than visual."

"Yes, they are emotional," said Karl. "Do you see others?"

"My mother, but that's different, I feel her more than see her…" She stopped. This was too personal. "I mean, there's a reaction between the human mind and certain places. Thoughts are a kind of energy. Do you think that sounds unscientific?"

"I think," said Karl, "that we should go upstairs." His expression brought her unease crawling back. His gaze was intent upon her yet distracted, as if she'd said something to disturb him. "I should like to talk about this, but it is very cold. You're shivering. Would you like my coat around your shoulders?"

Karl was used to women – men, too – becoming drawn to him, infatuated. He thought little of it, because they were not seeing *him* but an outward shape, an arrangement of lines and planes that for some reason struck the eye as beauty. And more, they were touched by vampire glamour, a subconscious recognition of something intangibly alien. That was the lure that snared his prey, even if he chose not to take advantage of it. The vivacity of Madeleine and Elizabeth was pleasant, even mesmerising, yet he could easily detach himself from their rapt attention.

Charlotte was different. She rarely met his eye. She was abrupt and withdrawn, a pale creature hiding within a shell, camouflaged. Intriguing, because she tried so hard not to be noticed.

Yet when she said, "Have you thought what a ghost might be?" Karl began to pay closer attention. She had the beguiling look of an actress on film: a striking contrast between the darkness that rimmed her large eyes and the pallor of her skin, an expression of solemn vulnerability. Her hair, a mixture of russet and gold, was long and coiled at the nape of her neck, as if she was unconscious of fashion or deliberately defiant of it.

She was a paradox. She shied away from people, yet walked boldly through a dark cellar that would make most sensible folk hesitate. She spoke of ghosts not with a shiver but with analytical curiosity.

Only once she smiled, there in the darkness. And the smile transformed her face into pearl and gold, as if she'd turned her face to the sun.

Karl was in no position to dismiss the supernatural. He felt the heavy chill of the cellar and consciously desired to leave. Charlotte refused the offer of his coat. Like a sea creature drawing in its tentacles, she folded herself away, saying nothing as they mounted the stairs. In the kitchen she went straight to Anne and David, almost physically hiding behind them.

They talked about the spectral cat, laughing now. Karl liked the way the English made a joke of everything. Then David took out his pocket watch and said, "Good Lord, is that the time? I have to drive Edward back to London; his family are expecting him. Annie, you and Charlotte finish your hack while I take Karl back to the Hall. I'll telephone later."

Anne pulled a face at him. "I hope I'll see more of you than this when we're married!"

David embraced her and whispered in her ear, making her laugh. Charlotte stood apart, self-contained, uneasy. Karl could put most people at ease with friendly questions, but all he drew from her now were monosyllables. She had withdrawn the fragile tendrils of communication. Her eyes, her voice, her self; she would give him nothing. He let her be, and a moment later she was gone from him physically as well.

Edward was subdued but listless in the Bentley. His face was wax grey with exhaustion and he chain-smoked nervously throughout the journey, compressing the cigarettes between shaking fingers.

"Those damned sedatives leave you with a hell of a hangover," he said, trying to make light of it. "It's a swine, having the morning after without the night before."

"I'm sorry you had such a rotten time," said David.

"No, I should apologise. Didn't mean to embarrass you, but I couldn't –" He squeezed his eyes shut and pinched his colourless forehead.

"It's all right, old man. It's forgotten. But you should see your doctor as soon as you get home. In fact I'll make sure you do."

"There's no need."

"It's not optional."

"I don't need the bloody head-doctor, damn you!" Edward sighed and slumped back in his seat. "Sorry. Sorry."

"I'm doing it for purely selfish reasons," David said, pretending to be off-hand. "I need you fit for work as soon as possible."

"I won't let you down." Edward lit a new cigarette, wound down the window and let the dead stub tumble away on the wind. "I'm not mad, David."

"I know that."

"But you don't! You're like all the others, 'Poor Edward, such a tragedy, be kind to him because he was a hero but now he's quite barmy.' But I'm not. Last night isn't forgotten, and I can't take back what I said."

David glanced at him, mildly alarmed.

"Steady on."

"No." Edward's voice was tight but calm. "You know I have these intuitions. I don't want them, I can't explain them, but don't they always prove right? I'm not hysterical. Look." He lifted a hand off his knee and held it level. "Trembling a bit, but I'm as normal as I'll ever be. In the cold light of day, I will say it again. It's nothing to do with the War or my... troubles. Karl von Wultendorf is –" He gave a shake of his head. "It does sound too crazy, doesn't it? But I'm deadly serious, old man. Whatever Karl is, he's dangerous. Please watch out for your family, David, before it's too late."

CHAPTER FIVE

TOUCHING THE LIGHT

Karl could step into a dimension that lay aslant from the corporeal world and move through a whirling landscape in which light was solid and rock ran like liquid. Through the Crystal Ring, he travelled to distant parts of the country to step out of nowhere and feed on some stranger whose face and life meant nothing to him. Then he would vanish and return to Cambridge, to masquerade as human before the kindly, unsuspecting Nevilles.

He hadn't anticipated the pleasure he found in working with them. He absorbed knowledge and ideas with a thirst as intense as his need for blood. Another kind of vampirism. And they gave so much, so willingly.

Soon after Karl arrived in Cambridge, Dr Neville showed him around. Karl drank in the city's grandeur with a delight that felt like love. In Trinity College Chapel, Karl stood gazing at great statues of Newton, Tennyson and Bacon, timeless in the sombre grey light.

You are dead, yet your effigies preserve you forever, larger than life, he thought. *My flesh is as unyielding as your marble, but I still move and see and think... Different kinds of immortality. Yet acid would eat you, cold would crack your substance...*

"We come to chapel regularly," Dr Neville was saying. "You're welcome to join us, naturally."

"Thank you," Karl replied, "but I don't attend church."

Dr Neville raised his eyebrows. "Oh. Well, no obligation."

"Do scientists still believe in God these days?"

"I can't speak for the others, but I don't see a conflict. There's more in this universe than science can account for, believe me."

"That is certainly true," said Karl.

"The very fact that nature works according to the laws of mathematics, and that our brains are capable of understanding those laws, indicates that there must be a *mind* behind everything. As Einstein puts it, the only incomprehensible thing about the universe is that it is comprehensible."

"But perhaps we comprehend the world as it is, because if it were any different we would not be here to see it."

Dr Neville gave Karl a shrewd look.

"Not a blasted atheist, are you?"

"I was brought up as a Catholic," said Karl, "but now I could only describe myself as agnostic."

"Can't make your mind up, eh?"

"Let's say I keep an open mind." Karl smiled. "And do you also believe in the Devil, sir?"

George Neville snorted. "Not the sort with horns and a tail. But yes, I definitely believe in the power of evil."

Karl moved away to look through the screens into the main body of the chapel. Its stately, hushed dignity moved him.

No unseen barrier bars me from a sacred place, he thought. *I could walk up the aisle and lay my hands on the altar without harm. I walk in daylight. What kind of God would create a being such as me? If I prayed, would it be Kristian's dark God who heard me? I think not. A true God would not tolerate such a demon in a holy place... and since I am tolerated, it follows that God does not exist. And Kristian's vengeful deity, who visits vampires on mankind as punishment? How can I worship a God who exists only in Kristian's warped mind?*

They emerged into Trinity's Great Court, where sunlight gleamed on golden-beige stone and wide expanses of grass.

"Even if science finds all the answers," Dr Neville went on as they walked, "it wouldn't disprove God's existence. In my view, the main achievement of physics so far is not relativity or quantum theory, but the recognition that we are still very far from discovering a grand unifying theory of everything. Now that's the Holy Grail."

Dr Neville's ambition was vast, Karl reflected, yet blinkered. He knew nothing of the Crystal Ring.

"How could a unifying principle explain creatures that defy the laws of nature?" he asked.

"What creatures?"

"Suppose there were beings that could see normally invisible phenomena, such as the atmosphere, or magnetic fields…"

Dr Neville rose to the challenge. "There may be animals that see beyond the visible spectrum. When we see the wind, we're actually noticing indicators: clouds moving, trees leaning, debris flying through the air. Likewise, iron filings show us lines of magnetic force very plainly."

"That's the human viewpoint," said Karl. "Imagine a creature outside your experience, who perceived the atmosphere as dense enough to walk on, as a man climbs a hill. Suppose the Earth's magnetic field was tangible enough to guide me as I travelled on the wind. Could physics explain such a change in nature?"

"You've described a bird."

"No. Something other. Let us say an angel, since you believe in God."

Neville frowned. "H'm, trying to catch me out? Very well. I'd question whether the world itself had changed, or your perception of it. An observer on the ground might notice that *you* had changed, your body so rarefied that air seemed solid to you. And perhaps this light form is deflected by magnetism, as atomic particles are."

Karl was pleasantly surprised by Dr Neville's response to his bizarre question.

"Yet imagine I don't see the observer as dense and solid, but as a body of light and heat. Pure energy, like myself."

Dr Neville was filling his pipe as they walked.

"Well, that's akin to the paradox of relativity. A pilot flying his plane at close to the speed of light, lying flat in the line of flight, would appear to stationary observers to have become a dwarf. Yet if he looks in a mirror in the cockpit, he sees no change. To him, it's the people on the ground who look flattened out."

Karl was amused. "So, this impossible situation could be explained by relativity."

"My dear fellow, *everything* is a question of relativity. There's nothing in the universe that is not moving in relation to everything else." Dr Neville paused to light the pipe, puffing out haloes of smoke. "We're hanging by our feet from a globe that falls around the sun at twenty miles a second. Meanwhile the sun is moving away from its fellow stars, while the entire solar system is rushing all of a piece through empty space. It's enough to make one reach for the brandy... Why are you smiling?"

"Because you answered my question, strange as it was."

"I'm not sure if that's a virtue or a weakness," said Dr Neville. "The more bizarre the problem, the more it engages my imagination. I haven't answered it, by the way. Doubtless the more I pondered the situation, the farther I'd be from an answer."

Karl said quietly, "My experience, exactly."

Within weeks of returning to Cambridge, Charlotte feared she was going mad.

Whatever she believed about ghosts, she was not gullible: she knew that the presences she sensed might be only a product of her mind. But there was no explanation for the apparition she saw one bright autumn morning.

Glad to escape the house, she had delivered some paperwork from her father to the Cavendish Laboratory. As she emerged from the stern building into Free School Lane, she saw a man standing by the monastic walls of Corpus Christi College. The stranger had a quality of unnatural stillness that caught her attention, reminding her of Karl. His looks were less pleasing: although handsome in his way, his eyes were a little too large and wide-set, giving him a sinister cast. For some reason he was glaring straight at her with a look of malevolent amusement. Chilled, she stared back for a second or two – and then he *vanished*. Flicked out of existence, as if he'd never been there.

Charlotte reeled away, half running along the lane to King's Parade. There she walked in a daze, surrounded by the hiss of bicycles and the flapping of black gowns. The bustle eased her back to reality. Opposite were the spires and arched windows of King's College, solid and yet honeycomb-delicate, as if tethered lightly to the ground. Risking injury as she wove between cyclists, she hurried across the road and into King's Chapel.

There was no one inside. She sat down, folded her hands, and prayed.

Corpus Christi was said to be haunted, but by a ghost of the seventeenth century, not of the twentieth. The modern, cruel-eyed young man had been so vivid, down to the folds of his scarf and the tilt of his hat... yet he had *disappeared*.

The chapel calmed her. Slender lines of stone soared up to the intricately fanned ceiling. The windows pierced her with jewel-bright colours. Was it God she felt here, or only the sublime golden light within the branching vault; the echo of all the souls who'd worshipped here, of the kings who had built the chapel? She didn't know. To sit in glowing silence was enough.

Her father's laboratory no longer felt comfortable and safe. Charlotte tried to continue as if nothing had changed, but the effort was wearing her thin.

Outwardly, Henry was the same unthreatening figure: bulky, untidy, forever pushing his spectacles up the bridge of his nose as he worked. The idea of him becoming her husband was unreal. Previously they'd been at ease with each other, but now she felt awkward, as if beholden to him in some way. Whatever this feeling was, she couldn't define it as love.

It wasn't as if Henry had made things difficult by being emotional. In fact he'd been sweet, which made her feel worse. When she'd arrived home from Parkland Hall he had been waiting, breathless and pink-faced with nerves, clutching a diamond ring in a box.

"You must think I'm such a fool," he'd said, "but I simply didn't know how to ask you. I'm so glad, Charlotte. Um – I'm not awfully good at this romantic stuff, so we'll just, er, carry on as normal, shall we?"

He kissed her cheek, as if she were a maiden aunt. Charlotte was taken too much by surprise to say, "No, it's a mistake, I can't marry you!" – and now it was too late. The trap had closed. Henry being what he was, life went on as before; except for the awful prospect of marriage looming over her. She couldn't back out, because even her father was pleased now.

"Never imagined my little girl getting married," he'd said, patting her shoulder. "But now I think about it, it's perfect. Henry and you. Of course."

Henry, and me, and Father... Henry was ten years older than Charlotte, having worked with her father as student and postgraduate. In fact, Dr Neville was closer to Henry than he was to David, his own son. For Charlotte to marry him was the bonding of a magic circle.

She should be happy, yet all she felt was trapped. But with Karl... with Karl it was worse.

When he and Henry were in the laboratory, heads bent together over an experiment, the contrast between the two men could not have been more startling.

Karl possessed a quality that she could only call *presence*. He had beauty and personality combined with an inexplicable aura, a luminosity that held the attention – almost like an actor on film, silver light and shadow, hypnotic. While Henry was all bustle, it was Karl's dark, still grace that filled the room.

Charlotte had decided in advance how to treat Karl. Keeping firmly to her own rules, she was distant, polite and professional; it was the only way to cope. She tried to accept him, but her unease grew worse each day. Small consolation that her father had secured him lodgings in town, rather than offer him a guest room – possibly with Madeleine's virtue in mind.

Yet Karl could do no wrong. Her father was delighted with his intense concentration, faultless observation, swift absorption of knowledge. Charlotte looked on with suspicion. Sometimes he and her father had philosophical debates in which Karl said the strangest things, as if probing for some arcane revelation that would unleash a nightmare if it were ever spoken.

Madeleine apparently saw nothing threatening in Karl. Every afternoon they took tea in the drawing room and she would bounce in, as fresh as spring, talking about everything under the sun except science. How could Karl not find her enchanting? He was different with Maddy, no longer serious but warm and charming. Madeleine was happy. Charlotte was pleased for her, ashamed of her own negative feelings... but every morning, she woke dreading the day ahead.

She sat, head bowed, twisting her gloves between her fingers. *I could leave... but where would I go? I can never leave Father. Dear Lord...* As she looked up, the chapel's grandeur flooded her with guilt. *How dare I pray? If I go mad, it serves me right. There's something dark in my soul... It's no good excusing myself as "shy". I fear the truth is far worse: that I'm cold, twisted and cowardly. Do I want to run away from other people – or from myself?*

"I saw someone... vanish. Do you think I'm going mad, Anne?"

"I think you're in danger of making yourself ill. I'd so like to shake you out of it!"

They sat on the long green bank of the Cam, watching punts slide through curtains of willow that kissed their own reflections in the water. College buildings rose in golden-grey beauty on the far side. The sun's warmth had a clarity and softness that came only in late September.

Anne leaned back on her elbows. "Come riding with me, instead of staying cooped up in the lab. The fresh air would help you put things into perspective."

"I have to work," said Charlotte.

"You speak as if you've no control over your life, as if your father, Henry, Karl, everyone else makes the rules and you have no say. Why not take matters into your own hands?"

"It's not that easy."

Anne touched Charlotte's arm. "I don't mean to be unsympathetic, but I've never suffered this sense of helplessness. No one controls *me*."

"I wish I was like you," Charlotte said wistfully. "Sympathy's the last thing I want. I need your good sense."

"Well, I try," said Anne. "Is it having any effect?" She started laughing. "Sorry, I know it isn't funny – but between you and Edward, I think the world's gone crazy."

Charlotte smiled, despite herself.

Anne went on, "Talking of Edward, apparently he still insists that Karl is... well, not all he seems. Not that I believe Edward's psychic, but David respects him too highly to dismiss his concerns. So, David's investigating Karl's background. Did he tell you?"

As her brother divided his time between London, Cambridge and Parkland Hall, Charlotte saw little of him.

"No, he hasn't mentioned it."

"He's being discreet, obviously, but I thought you should know. It's odd: David hasn't found out a thing so far. Fleur can't remember who brought Karl to her party, and all the guests denied knowing him."

This disclosure made Charlotte uneasy.

"It's too bad of David to snoop around, as if Father's own judgment isn't sound."

"But look at it from David's point of view. His sister's fallen for a stranger. What if they got married, and Karl turned out to be... a criminal of some kind? He might be a bigamist, a spy, a murderer, anything. All David can say is, 'Edward tried to warn me and I didn't listen!' Mind you, I wouldn't envy Maddy marrying a man who has women swooning at his feet all over the place. I wonder how often he takes advantage?"

She spoke flippantly, but Charlotte felt a physical jolt that drained the blood out of her head.

"Oh, don't. What a horrible thought."

Anne sat up, looking curiously at her. "Not jealous of Maddy, are you?"

"Jealous?"

"You say you dislike Karl, but perhaps you're protesting too much. Would he be on your mind if you weren't just a tiny bit attracted to him?"

"That's preposterous!" Charlotte was dizzy with indignation.

Anne shrugged, grinning. "Why? Because the Prof's daughter isn't supposed to have such base urges? But it's perfectly normal to have feelings. Perhaps if you admitted as much and were kinder to yourself, you wouldn't be so unhappy and you wouldn't be seeing weird apparitions."

"We're spending a few days at Parkland at the end of October," said Madeleine, one evening when the day's work in the laboratory was over. "You must come with us, Karl. There's lots to do, riding and shooting and so forth, and Aunt Elizabeth's holding a musical evening. It would be so lovely if you'd play a duet with me, piano and cello."

Karl said, "I don't know if your father can spare me."

"I'm not a slave driver," Dr Neville responded gruffly. "I intend to shut the lab and have a few days' rest myself."

"Oh, please come, Karl," said Madeleine, so sweetly that Charlotte wondered why he was so reluctant. "The musical evening's for charity. Everyone who can do a turn simply must join in."

"In that case, I should be delighted," Karl said graciously. Then he looked at Charlotte. "And will you take part as well?"

Charlotte felt her face turn hot.

Madeleine said, "Oh, don't ask for miracles. Actually, she has a lovely voice, but ask her to sing for an audience and she runs a mile. She's only happy hiding with her books – aren't you, Charli?"

Charlotte tried to smile, wincing inwardly at the sting of Madeleine's words.

She went to bed early, but couldn't sleep. Her father was dining in college, Madeleine had gone to a dance with friends, and the servants to a music hall show. No one would be home until late. She was alone. The house was shrouded in rain and she felt eerily isolated, as if on an island with nothing beyond but grey veils of water. She felt like a dream figure, a formless ghost. Only the rain was real.

Anne had helped, but there was only so far Charlotte could presume on her friendship. Her deepest fears lay inside her and no amount of talking would exorcise them. Like twin spectres they haunted her: unwanted marriage, and unattainable freedom.

The thought of kissing Henry repulsed her. The idea of lying in the same bed, of his hands on her body – she cringed and curled up under her bed covers. Did other women have these fears? Not Fleur, who'd returned from honeymoon with a smug and knowing air. The difference was that she and Clive adored each other.

I ought to love Henry but I feel nothing. It's not fair on him.

Then, unbidden, an image slid into her mind of herself with Karl. Kissing, lying together... Shock took her breath away. Dark excitement, blackened with terror... In denial she pushed away the image, but it crept back. In near-panic she sat up, turned on a bedside light, and saw her mother's face in the photograph. Shame suffused her. *God, how can I think of such things?*

She sighed. Hopeless trying to sleep. Rising, she slipped her dressing gown on over her nightdress and made her way downstairs to the study, shaking her hair loose as she went.

The house was quiet, bathed in a steady rush of rain. Strange, the door to the study was open. She crossed to the desk and switched on a lamp. Warm radiance fanned across book-lined shelves and the heavy oak desk, where her typewriter stood between neat piles of paper.

She sat down, stifling a yawn. Her father was writing a book based on his lectures, and her task was to type the manuscript. This was a soothing occupation, even wrestling with his illegible handwriting. A distraction from her dark thoughts. She inserted a fresh sheet of paper into the machine and found her place in the notes.

As she set her fingertips to the keys, she knew with paralysing terror that she was not alone.

Clasping the back of her chair like a shield, she turned very slowly to stare at the small couch behind the door. The shock of finding someone there almost stopped her heart. When she saw it was Karl, she entirely lost the power to move or speak.

He was regarding her with equal surprise. Remaining seated – as if he thought the courtesy of standing up would frighten her away – he said gently, "Charlotte, I seem to make a habit of startling you. Forgive me. I thought if I spoke, I would alarm you even more."

Her tongue and lips worked, but no sound emerged. She was acutely aware of being dressed only in her nightclothes. Her pulse was thundering.

Karl indicated a book that lay open beside him and added, "There were some works I wanted to consult, and Dr Neville was kind enough to suggest I come this evening to read at my leisure."

"But you were sitting in the dark," Charlotte managed to say.

"I was thinking more than reading," said Karl.

"Er – Father should be home at any moment." She looked desperately at the door. "He's rather late."

Karl's eyebrows lifted. "Please don't let me interrupt you. Do you always work at night?"

"No, I – I couldn't sleep, that's all." She glanced at the typewriter and knew she stood no chance of concentrating with Karl in the room. She gave a quick shake of her head. "It doesn't matter."

"In that case, won't you come and sit beside me?"

He extended a hand towards her. She froze, caught between the urge to flee and the requirements of good manners. One awkward encounter, and her barrier of professional distance was ripped away like rotten silk. Horrifying, to discover how fragile those defences were.

Yet his hand – luminous and rimmed with red light – was compelling. She took a breath and somehow found herself pushing back the chair and walking towards him. As his pale, slender fingers touched hers a shockwave went through her body. Strangely, it was a wave of coolness, soothing. She sat down, suspended like dew on a web.

"I was as startled as you when you came in," he said. "I'm sorry I gave you a fright."

"It doesn't matter, truly." She tried to moisten her dry mouth. "I didn't know there was anyone in the house – obviously."

"Your appearance is perfectly modest and charming," he said with a slight smile. His fingers were entwined with hers, and she didn't know how to pull free. On his right hand he wore a gold ring with a blood-dark, polished garnet. He was looking at her, but she could not meet his eyes. Instead she stared at the ring.

"Charlotte, are you afraid of me?"

The question was a shock. So direct. It hung in the air between them, unanswerable yet demanding a reply.

"Er – I – of course not. What makes you think that?"

"Well, we've worked together for weeks, yet you still never speak to me unless you have to. Is there a reason?"

"No, really – if I've been unfriendly, I apologise, I never intended…"

"Won't you tell me what you do intend?" he said softly. Sharply aware of his gaze, she was compelled to look up, and the radiance of his eyes, close to hers, instantly swallowed her. Irises of deep amber sparkled with gold and red fire, the pupils large and depthless…

"I don't know that I can."

"Charlotte." The beauty of his voice was like a kiss. "There's nothing you can say that could possibly offend me, as long as it is the truth. Even if you admit that you hate my presence here."

"Of course I don't!" Whatever she felt, it was not hatred. Why not tell him the truth? "If you must know – yes, I am sometimes… nervous of you."

"Why?"

Her lips parted. She shook her head slightly. *So many reasons.*

"I know it's foolish, but I wasn't blessed with courage. I fear everything new."

He lowered his eyelids. She noticed how very long his eyelashes were, curved darkly against his cheek.

"I think you do yourself an injustice. You are shy, and not happy; anyone can see that. Do you think I'm cruel, asking you to be honest?"

"It's difficult for me," she whispered.

"I don't wish to distress you, but fears need to be challenged. And I give my word that you have no cause to be afraid of me. Can you believe me?"

He met her eyes again and she felt her tension bleeding away in the warmth of his gaze; melting.

"Yes," she said sincerely. "Yes."

"I am serious, Charlotte. I wish you to feel at ease, to see me as a friend. To know you can say anything you like; simply to be yourself."

"I wish I could." *To be like Maddy and Fleur!* "It would be wonderful."

"I'm telling you that you can."

He means it, she realised. It was a revelation, like bursting out of a chrysalis. Almost physically she felt a great burden of anxiety sliding away. She'd tried to dismiss her fears as imaginary, but only now, for the first time, could she accept this as true.

Such warmth lay in Karl's expression. There was no need to say anything. They both laughed. She wasn't sure why, but the moment was magical. His eyes instilled her with tranquillity, the feeling that it would be heaven simply to sit here forever, while outside the rain fell soothingly, unceasingly.

Karl was not the cold-hearted charmer of Anne's warnings. He actually cared for her... and the knowledge dismantled her armour, left her basking in the moment without realising how vulnerable she'd become. The touch of his fingers was divine. She'd never before been so conscious of him physically. Their thighs were touching, yet her usual instinct to recoil vanished. Instead she dared to enjoy the firmness of his long leg against hers. Karl had a clean, enticing scent of newly washed hair, fresh clothes. So perfectly graceful, his slim body and everything about him...

Then he lifted her hand, and said, "You are not wearing your engagement ring."

Ice-cold reality hit her.

"I don't, at night."

"You don't imagine," he said, "that if you are unhappy, a loveless marriage will make you any happier?"

She pulled herself free and sat forward, hands pressed between her knees.

"That's nothing to do with you."

Karl was silent for a moment.

"Ah. Forgive me."

"No, I didn't mean to be abrupt." She took a breath, mastering herself. "Henry and I are well suited. I don't expect marriage to be ecstatically happy. People who do are usually disappointed, so my aunt says."

"It's good to be realistic, but not bitter. Do you love someone else?"

A wave of pain caught her throat. His words were so gentle, yet like knives they slid through her defences. *Does he want blood?* she thought.

"No," she said at last. "There is no one else."

"There should be." Karl took her wrist, and stroked the fine skin with his thumb. The sensations aroused by his touch went right through her core. She longed to clasp his hand, but dared not, and the very act of resisting was an unbearable ache. If he had kissed her then she would have submitted, allowed anything.

Instead he was looking past her, and the stroking of her wrist was almost unconscious.

"You should live your life, Charlotte. Think what is best for yourself, not for others. You deserve better."

Then she realised. He was being *kind* to her. Nothing more. Yet with her disappointment came a rush of relief. In reality, a declaration of love or an attempt at seduction would have terrified her. This, at least, meant she was genuinely safe with him, that he truly was a friend.

"I don't need or want pity," she said quietly.

"This is not pity, Charlotte." He leaned forward, his shoulder warm against hers. "Never think that. I'm distressed to see you unhappy, that's all. However, you do have courage. For one thing, to keep your hair long in defiance of fashion shows admirable independence."

She smiled. "My mother had long hair. That's why I won't cut mine."

"As long as it is your choice," he said. "You should sing at the musical evening, if only to dispel your anxieties. Would you do so, for me?"

His eyes lifted all the breath out of her. There was wordless communication between them, and she knew that if she took one more step, she would fall over the edge and be swallowed.

"Yes," she answered. "If you like."

Then there was only the rush of rain in the silence... and she would have given her soul for those few moments to last forever. Did it matter that his expression was changing, the pull between them darkening? The change was so subtle that she sensed no danger. Too trusting. His attention was completely on her now, but his warm gaze turned fervent, and he leaned closer as shivers of anticipation cascaded down her spine.

His lips parted and she saw the whiteness of his teeth. He said, "You had best go back to bed, before it is too late." His fingers tightened on her wrist and she was pinned there, with no desire to escape. Wanting...

"Too late for what?" she gasped.

"For you to get any sleep." As he spoke there was a swish of car tyres, headlight beams slicing between the curtains. "Your father is home. In time." He drew back and released her wrist. The spell was broken.

Charlotte didn't respond at once. Then she leapt off the couch as if she'd been scalded.

"Oh my God – he'll kill me if he finds us alone together."

"Of course he won't. He thinks you are perfect." Karl smiled calmly. "If he finds me reading a book and you sitting at your typewriter, what can he say?"

"In my nightclothes? Oh no, I must go."

She hurried to the doorway then stopped, compelled to turn back. She gazed at Karl, knowing that every second brought her father nearer to the front door, yet unable to tear herself away. Karl was no longer looking at her, and his expression had become immeasurably sad and distant, as if a vast gulf lay between them that could never be spanned.

"Karl, is something wrong? What is it?" she whispered.

"Nothing, Charlotte," he said. "Go quickly, it's dangerous to linger."

A key rattled in the lock. She turned and fled upstairs.

CHAPTER SIX

PALLID COMPANION

"Karl is in England," said Pierre. "He appears to be living in Cambridge."

Kristian received Pierre in the depths of Schloss Holdenstein, in a windowless chamber lit by torches flaming along the walls. Their light turned the air smoky gold. Kristian sat in a tall carved chair like a bishop enthroned on a dais. The effect was one of austere and absolute power.

Two identical blond male vampires sat on the edge of the dais, looking impassively at Pierre. Stefan and Niklas: Kristian's pets. Their radiance contrasted with Kristian's stark paleness and the priestly black of his robe.

Pierre distrusted their knowing aloofness.

"What," Kristian said, "is he doing in Cambridge?"

"He's taken rooms in the town, and most days he visits the house of an eminent scientist."

Kristian leaned forward, absently stroking Niklas's golden-white hair.

"Why?"

"Knowing Karl as I do, I'd guess he is studying science."

Kristian's thick brows drew together.

"Science is the witchcraft of mankind." His tone alerted Pierre to trouble. "It is a source of evil. Karl knows this, so how dare he sully himself?"

Pierre marked a gleam of peasantlike terror behind the

formidable face, a reminder that Kristian had been born in an age of ignorance. Fear made Kristian dangerous.

"Tell me what else you found out."

Pierre resented Kristian for treating him as an uncompromising father would his errant son.

"There was a limit to what I could discover without being noticed, but I observed that the scientist has a beautiful family, a number of lovely daughters..."

"Whom you will not touch," said Kristian. "The object is to find Karl, not to indulge yourself. And Karl must be punished."

"For seeking knowledge?"

"For turning his back on God and embracing the works of man!" Kristian sat back, drumming his large fingers on the arm of his throne. He was lost in thought for so long that at last Pierre spoke hesitantly.

"Beloved master..." *How I hate calling him that!* "What do you wish me to do?"

The vulturine eyes refocused on him.

"Go to him, Pierre. Tell him that if he wishes to see his adored Ilona again, he had better return to me."

Ilona was a frequent, vivid presence in the castle, as bright as splintered glass. How empty the rooms seemed without her, Pierre realised.

"Have you sent her away?" he asked.

"Yes, she is gone forever – unless Karl returns. She is in the Crystal Ring. In the *Weisskalt*, sleeping."

One of the blond vampires, Stefan, jerked up his head in shock. Pierre met his blue eyes, saw his own feelings reflected there. Any mention of the *Weisskalt* filled him with dread: the biting, endless cold, the utter silence... Being torn from life into oblivion, not knowing if you'd ever wake again. That was the power Kristian held over them all. If he could do it to Ilona, he was capable of doing the same to anyone.

"*Mon Dieu,*" Pierre said. "Even her. Is no one sacred to you?"

Kristian reached forward and caressed Pierre's cheek.

"You are all sacred to me, my friend. That is the whole point. You are all sacred."

* * *

Karl sat alone in the laboratory, an hour before Dr Neville was due to appear. He was at a side bench, gazing into a small glass dish of clear liquid. In it, there floated a sliver of his own flesh, sliced from a finger. The cut had already healed, but the sliver lay without dissolving in concentrated sulphuric acid, as if in water.

So far he'd found no chemical that affected vampire flesh. Even radium failed to burn.

"I must impress upon you the risks of the radioactive materials with which we work," Dr Neville had said. "If I send you to the Cavendish to collect any radioactive substance you must follow the safety procedures: use gloves, change your jacket, wash thoroughly. The talk in the papers about the dangers of radioactivity and X-rays may be exaggerated, but still, we must all have regular blood counts to set our minds at rest. It's quite safe, as long as we're careful."

Yet Karl could be as careless as he liked. Radioactivity did not affect him. He was careful to evade the blood tests, however.

He'd thought that if nothing in nature could destroy a vampire, there might be a lab-produced substance that could. Apparently it wasn't so.

Something must kill us, he thought, prodding at the skin fragment. *Acid and fire do not burn us... cold only forces us to sleep. There must be a way, other than beheading... a method that would take Kristian completely by stealth, because there is no other way to defeat him...*

Or are we truly immortal? What if the severed head lives on? Even Kristian can't tell me what immortality means.

Karl was in Cambridge to seek answers, but was beginning to believe that even here, he would find none.

Meanwhile, he knew he was becoming too involved with the Nevilles. They intrigued him. Madeleine's vivacity, David's good nature and innate decency, Dr Neville's enquiring mind, Charlotte's mystery... He hadn't let himself draw so close to humans for years. That was the danger, their seductiveness. Personality and flesh formed a single entity, multi-layered, intricately jewelled... and could he entirely detach himself from the desire to take his preoccupation to its natural conclusion? To feel their flesh under his fingers and consummate his need for blood... But to what end? To see them disintegrate into madness, or even die?

No. The prospect was enough to freeze his thirst. He would not touch them. He must not.

He'd come perilously close with Charlotte, that night in the study. He only meant to offer friendship, and yet, despite his resolve, her sweetness had ensnared him... drawing him into a spiral from which only Dr Neville's arrival had saved them both. Worst of all was admitting to himself that he wanted more from her than blood, and much more than friendship... for that, too, was wrong.

He would not let it happen again.

Disturbing, that Edward had recognised what he was, but the age of scepticism was on Karl's side. Inevitably, Edward was the one regarded as strange, not Karl. The memory brought an ironic smile to his lips.

He sensed a human presence moving above before he heard light footsteps on the stairs: Charlotte. The prospect of her company was pleasant – too much so. *I am human, and I am her friend, nothing more*, he reminded himself. *Let us both believe it.*

"Oh! Good morning, Karl," she said. "You're early."

"You also."

"Father asked me to replace the gold leaf in the electroscope. It's so fiddly, I seem to be the only one who can do it." Instead of muttering an excuse and fleeing, she leaned on the bench beside him. This was great progress. "What are you doing?"

He knew it was unfair to have soothed her fears with a touch of the tranquillising glamour he used on his victims; yet his motives were sincere. Karl didn't want her to be miserable or afraid. She was still nervous, but now she held her ground with him, testing herself.

"Nothing interesting," he said. "I was examining the effects of various chemicals on skin."

"Human skin?" She stared into the dish. "But whose is it?"

"Mine, of course." He half smiled. "It's only a sliver, Charlotte. I could hardly cut a piece out of your father or Henry, could I?"

"Well, no, but..."

"So many substances affect the body in terrible ways."

Charlotte nodded. "I've seen awful burns from people being careless in the lab, but there are worse things."

"Oh?"

"Like the chlorine and mustard gas they used in the trenches... Too horrible to believe, but I saw men dying from it. My father did government work during the War, so my sisters and I stayed with Aunt Elizabeth in her London house. She took in wounded soldiers and we helped nurse them."

Karl frowned. "You must have been so young."

"We were, but perfectly able to run around fetching and carrying. I'll never forget the ones who were gassed. Like watching someone drowning very slowly. I wished I could breathe for them... It was such a strange and frightening time, yet when I look back I remember how *real* it seemed. Nothing since then has ever seemed so real." Her eyes were downcast. "David hardly talks of the War, but from the little he says, you realise how terrible things were. I don't think people understand. Not yet. It must have been far worse than anyone can imagine."

"It was," Karl said quietly.

Charlotte flushed. "Oh, I'm so tactless; of course, you would have fought on the other side, but – I'm sorry, if you have painful memories I didn't mean to –"

"No, Charlotte." He could hardly explain that he'd been on no side but his own. He put his hand over hers for a second. "A vicarious pain, if anything. You are right: no one knows who was not there. Still, the silence will be broken eventually."

Her grey-violet eyes were full of amethyst shades that only vampire sight could perceive; her expression an intriguing mix of passion and seriousness. Unlike Madeleine, who was all sparkling surface, Charlotte kept her inner self hidden behind filigree doors and veils. Karl wanted to see her smile.

He said, "Tomorrow we go to your aunt's beautiful house again. I hope you haven't changed your mind about singing."

"I gave my word, didn't I?" Light came to her face, and the soul-link flowed between them like a shared secret. "I've practised a song with Maddy. Anyway, I can't escape now."

"Why not?"

"Henry has arranged to visit his parents, and he wanted them to meet me. I had to tell him I can't let Maddy down."

"You refused to let him show you off to his family? Isn't that rather cruel?" said Karl.

He hoped his teasing would not upset her. She only lifted her shoulders, half smiling and half sad.

"I don't think Henry really minds what I do," she said.

Charlotte leaned her head back and gave herself up to the clean wind blowing into her face. She let sensation replace thought until there was nothing but the noise and motion of the car as it sped along leaf-strewn lanes. Trees rushed by in a glory of tangerine, bronze and plum-red. Hopeless to keep thinking, *I must not want what I can't have.*

Normally, Maple would have driven Dr Neville and his daughters to Hertfordshire. Maddy, however, had contrived for them to be given a lift in Karl's elegant dark-red Hispano-Suiza. She sat in the front beside Karl, talking non-stop as he drove. Charlotte was in the rear seat: an unwelcome chaperon. Her companion was a cello in its case, borrowed from a music society for Karl to play.

She didn't wish that Henry was with them. She only wished that Madeleine was not – and then felt guilty.

Charlotte could not have explained why one conversation with Karl had changed everything. That night in the study – only three weeks ago – he'd ceased to terrify her and become a friend. Strange and wonderful transformation. Now, in the resulting euphoria, she wanted to be near him constantly, as if to reassure herself that the change was real. Still nervous, yes, but alight with a new, delicious excitement. It felt right that they were friends, *only* friends – so why did she resent Maddy's insistent presence?

The lanes grew narrow, forcing Karl to slow down. At the gates of Parkland Hall, he stopped to let a farm cart pass across the entrance. The shaggy white horse rolled its eyes at the vehicle; the farmer, muffled in scarf and cap, called a cheerful, "Mornin', sir. Thank you!" Then Karl steered the Hispano-Suiza onto the drive, which lay like a grey ribbon across the lush estate.

Charlotte was pleased to see David's Bentley already in front of the Hall. A footman was unloading his luggage. The front doors stood open and Newland was waiting, a broad, grey-haired figure impeccable in black. He was the perfect butler, Charlotte knew, fiercely loyal to Aunt Elizabeth.

He came out to welcome them, telling Karl, "If you'd care to leave the motor car here, sir, Charles will unload your belongings and park the vehicle for you. I shall inform Lady Reynolds of your arrival."

It was pleasant to be at Parkland again, Charlotte thought as she stepped inside. The invigorating autumn air made her feel light and optimistic.

From the entrance a red-carpeted staircase, flanked by pillars of tawny marble, rose from the lower hall to the family living rooms on the first floor. At the top was a spacious upper hall, where sunlight slanted across aquamarine carpets, flared gold on the frames of oil paintings, and burnished antique furniture to chestnut-red. Charlotte felt she was entering an older, safer time. Even the prospect of singing to an audience was less horrifying in the glow of Karl's friendship.

In the upper hall, David, Anne and Aunt Elizabeth came to greet them with hugs and kisses. Elizabeth looked as sophisticated and modern as Madeleine. When she saw Karl – elegant in a dark overcoat and white cashmere scarf – her face lit up and she made such a fuss of him that Maddy began to look affronted.

Charlotte sensed the game at once. Elizabeth and Madeleine were no longer aunt and niece, but rivals. Glances flashed between them like swords. She saw that Karl noticed too, and he looked at Charlotte in amused dismay.

"It's so lovely to see you, my dears," said Elizabeth, finally taking notice of the rest of them. "Isn't your father with you?"

"He stopped off to play golf at Royston with some friends," said Charlotte. "He'll be along later."

"Fleur and Clive aren't coming, unfortunately," said Elizabeth. "Clive couldn't get away from the bank."

Madeleine pulled a face. "What a bore. Fleur could have come without him – unless it's an excuse to carry on with her precious painting. Never mind, we'll cope. Karl and I have rehearsed a lovely duet, haven't we? And I'm accompanying Charlotte, too."

Elizabeth's perfect eyebrows lifted in surprise.

"Oh, you've been persuaded to sing at last?"

"We live in hope," said Maddy, "but there's plenty of time for her to lose her nerve."

Karl turned to Charlotte.

"You are not nervous, are you?" he said, smiling. He took her hand and held it up so her palm rested lightly over his fingers. "No, your hands are perfectly steady. You are not going to let me down."

"I wouldn't dare!" Charlotte laughed, completely forgetting herself. Elizabeth and Madeleine looked at her as if she'd grown an extra head. She stepped back hurriedly and looked at the carpet, her face hot.

Elizabeth slid her hand casually through Karl's arm.

"You must think me a frightful hostess, standing about in the hall. Come into the drawing room, where we'll be comfortable."

"Thank you, Lady Reynolds," said Karl.

"Don't be so formal! Call me Elizabeth."

Charlotte suppressed a hollow feeling as her aunt led Karl away, with Madeleine on their heels. Then she smiled as she recalled the amused look he'd given her.

Anne kissed her cheek and said, "It's nice to see you looking happier. Things improving?"

It was so good to be with David and Anne again. They exchanged news as a footman took their hats and coats.

"How's Edward?" asked Charlotte.

"Very well, actually," David replied. "He seems as right as rain, except for the one problem."

"He's not still calling Karl a vampire, is he?" Anne said bluntly.

"No, but he's edgy." David pushed a hand through his fair hair. "That's why I didn't invite him, as Maddy was so insistent on Karl being here. But Edward hasn't used the *word* again, which is an encouraging sign. I don't know. Father's full of praise for Karl. I can't fault his behaviour or manners, and to my knowledge he hasn't laid a finger on Maddy, despite her flaunting herself shamelessly under his nose."

"Even Charli gets on with him now – don't you?" said Anne.

"Well – well, slightly," said Charlotte.

"Oh, come on, Charli, it's obvious he thinks the world of you too. So, can we chalk it down to Edward's overactive imagination?" Anne stood on tiptoe to kiss David's nose. "Never mind, old thing, you had to be sure."

"Wish I could convince Edward," said David.

Charlotte said, "I can't understand why I ever disliked Karl." She looked at Anne and smiled. "I think I might enjoy myself this time."

Pierre trod softly through the grounds of the Georgian mansion, looking up at lighted windows. He felt like an orphan in a fairy tale, observing from a distance the enchanted lives of the rich. Should he press his face against the glass? What a shock that would give them all – especially Karl.

This was delicious, knowing he had the choice of watching from outside or walking into their midst.

The darkness had a silver bloom and the air was soft, stirring ivy and wisteria along the terrace. A pair of French doors stood open, spilling a slice of light. He heard the velvet-deep tones of a cello threading through the bright notes of the piano. Recognising Karl's touch, he smiled. How delightful it would be to appear through the windows now: how dramatic. Pierre envisioned the humans inside, the air dreamy and golden with their warmth, and thirst drew demanding fingernails down his throat.

Pierre paused, watching the curtained light.

Do not touch the family, Kristian had ordered. But Kristian was not here. Mortals were faceless to him. How would he ever know?

In the music room, with its white and gold decor and curtains of powder-blue velvet, Charlotte stood clutching the edge of the Blüthner grand piano. Women in sparkling evening dresses and feathered bandeaux, men in evening suits; Elizabeth's guests were a shifting blur. David and Anne were in the front row with her father, Elizabeth ensconced next to Karl. Charlotte could not look at her audience. She tried to pretend that she and her sister were alone at home, practising.

Madeleine played the introduction and Charlotte began to sing. Her voice trembled at first, but the room fell quiet as the clear, mournful notes echoed.

Calm is the night;
The streets all are silent;
This house she dwelt in,
She, I lov'd dear;
'Tis long ago since she hath left it,
So long, long ago
Yet the house is here!
Here, too, stands a man who skyward is gazing
His hands he's wringing in woe and despair;
Oh! horror!
For when I mark his features,
The moon revealeth mine own visage there!
Oh! hateful shadow!
Oh! pallid companion!
Why mockest thou my grief and woe?
The anguish all by love begotten
On summer nights so long ago!

As the last note rang away, a sensation struck clear and sharp through the haze of faces. Karl was staring at her. Even from the corner of her eye she felt the intense light of his gaze. He was utterly still, like the moon shining through scudding clouds. And he watched her with the complete attention of a cat on its prey, his eyes clear and unwavering. The look turned her hot and cold all over.

Too melancholy, she thought. *I should have chosen something else. Why is he looking at me like that?* Then the moment was over. Applause and voices washed over her to break the tension.

Charlotte found herself shaking from head to foot. She and Madeleine went back to their seats as people crowded round to praise them, but the smiling faces were too close, the voices too loud. Her old phobia resurfaced, and she had to escape.

While Elizabeth was calling the guests to supper, Charlotte slipped out through the French windows and onto the terrace.

She leaned on the stone balustrade, taking deep breaths. The gardens lay in moon-washed gloom beneath her, tranquil and soothing. Although the air was mild for autumn, her silk voile dress – printed with pale roses, inset with gold lace – gave no warmth. Gooseflesh sprang up on her bare arms.

She heard soft, slow footsteps behind her. A cool draught blew across her back, and without looking round, she knew it was Karl there. Silky material slid across her arms, wonderfully warm on her bare skin; he took his time arranging the shawl, then his hands remained on her shoulders.

"I thought you might be cold," he said.

"Thank you. It was so hot indoors." Without thinking, she added, "How did you escape from my aunt?"

He laughed. "How could you tell I wanted to escape?" Then, moving to look into her eyes, he said, "Your sister was right, you do have a beautiful voice. But that song – why did you choose it?"

His intensity unnerved her. "Didn't you like it? Perhaps it was too slow and mournful, but everyone chooses happy songs; I like sad ones. It was 'The Shadow' by Schubert."

"'Der Doppelgänger'," said Karl. "With words by Heine. I remember, though I haven't heard it for a long time. The way you sang was haunting."

"I should have chosen something more cheerful," she said.

"No. Never be afraid to be different. Everyone loved it, and they wanted to tell you so. I didn't realise quite how you dislike being the centre of attention."

"I hate it," she said with a shiver.

"So you came outside?"

"Partly that." She glanced up at him. "And the way you were looking at me."

He drew a soft breath. "Your voice, and the words… they made me aware of so many things."

"What do you mean?" She looked sideways at him. Light from the French windows illuminated his skin, caught tiny gold highlights on his dark brows and lashes. His jewel-like eyes were intense, unblinking, seductively beautiful. Perhaps she should have felt fear but instead there was a sense of the inevitable, like falling. Thrilling danger.

He took her hand and said, "Will you walk around the garden with me, Charlotte?"

They went the length of the terrace, past the orangery, and along a path that wound between arches of soft foliage. The leaves were dry and poised to fall, but moonlight transmuted them into a mass of silver and crystal. Karl's arm was around her shoulders now, his touch felt heavenly. No desire to pull away, only to press closer to him. No need to speak. Charlotte was caught up in floating excitement, a blur of thoughts. When did the change begin? She didn't know, but the transition seemed so natural that she felt no doubts – only wonder that she'd ever been afraid of loving him. *Yes, let us walk together in the garden, deeper and deeper until the leaves cover us and no one can find us, no one judge us...*

They came to the water garden, a shrouded secret place where a pool lay beneath a tree-covered mass of rock. Karl led her onto the little bridge that spanned the pool, and they leaned side by side on the wooden rail. The water was obsidian-dark. Their shoulders were pressed together, and she felt an ache of anticipation so deep that it hurt.

"What did you mean about the song?" she asked. "You didn't explain."

"Yes, the song, Charlotte," Karl said softly. His eyelids swept down. He was not looking at her eyes but at her mouth, and he looked sad, so sad. He slid an arm across her shoulders, fingers stroking her neck. Then he leaned towards her and kissed her, very gently, but for a very long time.

Charlotte found herself arching towards him, strung taut with an exquisite mixture of desire and relief. Their mouths joined like moist, opening roses. A strange heat was pulsing inside her. Oh, the taste of him...

Could there be any other moment to compare? A fragile burning, frost vaporising into the sun, an ache more poignant than any deeper intimacy... and it was everything. Surely nothing could surpass the simple, bone-deep relief of touching, when touching had been forbidden for so long. She pressed her palms into his shoulders, as if to feel his flesh, his hidden self, through his clothes. She couldn't let go.

Oh, God. All this time I thought I felt nothing, that I couldn't love

*and didn't care... and I was so wrong... God, yes, he is beautiful.
I've fallen just like everyone else. I thought nothing mattered when
all the while I was in despair – the lies I told myself – I didn't know.
This can't be happening – but it is and I'm glad, so glad...*

Then Karl folded his arms around her, rested his cheek on her
hair, and said, "Forgive me."

"What for?" she asked, breathless.

"I vowed not to intrude on your life. Now I have broken the
vow."

She was too spellbound to question his words.

"Karl, I hardly had a life until I met you! There's nothing to
forgive, and even if there were, I'm sure I'd forgive you anything."

"Anything?" He held her away from him, firm hands clasping
her arms. His eyes were lynx-bright, his face shaded with sorrow.
"Be careful what you promise. Some things cannot be forgiven."

"What do you mean?"

"That I am bound to hurt you. Your sister, too, though I never
meant to."

Then she felt a trickle of anxiety, a reminder that his inner life
was completely unknown to her. A glimpse of hidden darkness...
*Why is he saying these things? Oh no, if he's going to tell me
he's already married, I don't want to hear it!* Yet his eyes were
so tender... and it seemed perfect that they left the bridge and
walked on slowly through the bowers of the wild garden, arms
around each other. Charlotte was too euphoric with hope to
believe he was capable of wrong. He must have good reasons... A
cascade of emotions filled her, paradise and torment mixed. *Oh,
don't let this end, ever!*

After a while she asked quietly, "What did you mean – about
hurting Maddy?"

Pierre stood beneath a huge plane tree at the edge of the lawn,
listening to the skeins of music flowing out of the windows,
applause following like rain pattering on dry leaves.

He saw a young woman stepping out onto the terrace, one
of the daughters. She had russet-brown hair that burned gold in
the slightest gleam of light, violet-grey eyes radiating irresistible

innocence, like a fawn. Wasn't she the one he'd frightened half to death in Cambridge?

Damn Kristian's rules.

Pierre drifted forward, then drew back. Karl had joined her. They talked for a while, walked away together like lovers... *Oh, this I must see!* Pierre paused, meaning to follow at a safe distance, but then another of the daughters appeared. This one lacked the vulnerable charm of her sister, but with her self-assurance and her bobbed Titian hair she was just as alluring. The glowing end of her cigarette arced through the air like a firefly.

She came to the balustrade and called into the darkness, "Karl? Are you there?"

"Here I am," Pierre answered, smiling. He moved to the edge of the plane tree's shadow, so she could see his form but not his face. She was uncertain, but she trotted down the terrace steps and came to him quickly enough. *Oh dear, hoping for romance. Shall I tell her Karl's with her sister? I am not so cruel.*

As she reached him, Pierre stepped out of the shadows and let moonlight fall across his face. The girl stopped, the red cigarette end hovering in mid-air.

"Who the hell are you?" she demanded. Her eyes widened, glazed.

"Be a little more friendly, *chérie*," said Pierre. He grinned, letting the white fangs slide out over his lower teeth. She looked more puzzled than afraid. Only when he seized her by the shoulders did her mouth drop open in shock. He knew how he must look to her: the white, staring face of death. She twisted and her feet skidded from under her, but he held her firm.

"Don't be afraid," he said, lips brushing her ear. "It's only a dream."

How delicately pearl-pink were the contours of her throat. Untouched. Doubtful that any man had even kissed this soft skin, let alone closed his teeth on it... like this. Nor stabbed bone-sharp fangs through the virgin surface into the swollen red vessels beneath, felt the rich fluid fountaining into his mouth. Like this. *Ah, this...*

She moaned faintly as she started to swoon, and it sounded like a moan of pleasure.

His violation of her seemed far deeper than merely that of the flesh, and the feeling sharpened his rapture to an almost unbearable height. Too sweet, to feel her energy burning into him, while she went limp and heavy in his grasp.

At last he laid her down onto the ground and curved her neatly over the roots of the tree, a drained and broken flower. He didn't want them to find her too quickly.

He paused for a moment, regarding her with dreamy satisfaction. Then he turned away and went in search of Karl, the taste of the girl lingering deliciously in his mouth. Smoke, perfume and blood.

With luck, Karl would be too taken up with his victim to realise another vampire was nearby.

He caught sight of them walking beneath silver birches and laburnums. Pierre kept a careful distance, but with preternatural senses he could hear and see them through the cloud of leaves.

Pierre sighed with longing. *Oh, she is a beauty, Karl. How have you waited this long?* Such a charming tableau: the vampire and his victim. Him lean and predatory, a panther in human form; a gentleman poet, with those brooding eyes and his shining dark auburn hair shadowing his forehead. *Can't they ever see it? We're too perfect, all mortal dross seared away. No human male could be that beautiful, or possess an allure so powerful. There should be a warning, like the bright colours of an animal signalling, "Don't come near me, I'm poison!" But no, they never see. They fall every time.*

And she, with her wide eyes, peeping out of that shimmering halo of hair – so vulnerable, so hopelessly trusting.

Yet what is he doing? Talking *to her?*

"What did you mean about hurting Maddy?" the girl was saying. "You know she's in love with you."

Karl said, "She thinks she is."

"And what – what do you feel for her?"

How anxious the poor child looks. Such divine pain.

"If you trusted your own judgment, Charlotte, you would know the answer. I am fond of her, as I'm fond of your father, no more than that. But she can't see it, and I fear she will take it badly when she does. This sounds like vanity, but it's not.

Sometimes people see something in me… I wish to God it were not so."

She looked uncomprehending. Pierre thought, *If only she realised how out of her depth she is!*

"Why?" she asked.

Karl turned to her, clasping her hands.

"Because it is for the wrong reasons. The worst of reasons. And is it any different for you, Charlotte? I can't tell. How do I look to you? Fascinating, not quite human, perhaps? Can you explain why you feel drawn to me?"

Pierre stopped dead, one hand resting against the rough spongy bark of a sequoia. *My God, he's going to tell her the truth! Karl, you sentimental fool, please don't tell me you imagine you're in love with her!*

"I don't understand," she said.

You don't want to, thought Pierre.

But Karl only said, "I'm sorry." He held his hand to her cheek. "You are the last person I wish to hurt. If only I felt as little for you as I do for Madeleine, I would not have let this happen. I thought I was strong enough to treat you only as a friend; I was wrong."

Charlotte looked completely astonished. *Poor child, is this the first time she's imagined herself in love? No wonder she looks so confused. A complete innocent…*

She said, "You speak as if you care for me."

"Oh, Charlotte, is it so unbelievable? You must not place so little value on yourself. If you could see yourself with my eyes… I can't say I'm sorry that I kissed you, but it was wrong of me, all the same."

"Then why did you?"

"'*Der Doppelgänger*'… It reminded me how very short life is. Those you love are there, and then they are gone. Such images still have power over me." Only Pierre perceived the irony in his words. "Sometimes it takes very little." And he kissed her again, holding her gently, as if she were made of porcelain.

How can he ignore the soft warm rush of blood under the rose-petal skin? Pierre wondered, recalling the still-lingering sweetness of Charlotte's sister.

"Don't be sorry," said Charlotte. "I'm not."

"What use are words, anyway?" Karl murmured. "They don't matter. Just to be with you..."

Oh, Karl, you are too easy to love. No wonder you frustrate Kristian so. But you know your nature will win in the end, and that's why you look so sad when she opens up to you like a rose. Touching. Nauseating. Only don't pretend that, when you finally lose control, you won't enjoy it!

Grinning to himself, Pierre twisted away from the mortal world and speared through the Crystal Ring. By the time they made a certain discovery, Pierre would be long gone.

No need to look for me, my friend, he thought, pleased with the evening's work. *I shall come to you soon enough.*

For Charlotte the garden became an enchanted realm; silvery and tree-dappled, lined with gold and stretching forever under the sky. One moment she had been wrapped in numb isolation; no love, a future with Henry, Karl only a friend. The next moment, a revelation. *Karl chose to be with me. Not with my sister or my aunt, not with anyone else. With me!* Such a relief to shed the coldness, to realise, *This is what I've been missing. I was dying for lack of passion...* They walked along wild paths, past stone cherubs on overgrown fountains, as if moving through another world in which only they existed. Arms around each other, hands entwined. Both carefully holding back, denying the temptation to do more. This was enough; it was everything.

Neither wanted this to end.

Eventually Karl said with reluctance, "We should go back."

She felt light-headed as they returned through the luminescent dusk of the lower gardens, up the one hundred steps towards the top lawn. She didn't care what Karl's strange words meant, nor what might happen next. There was only now.

Then Karl stopped and said, "There's someone... Charlotte, look."

He was pointing at the plane tree on the left border of the lawn. Puzzled, she saw nothing in the shadows. But as they went closer she made out a pale shape curved on the ground, a slender female figure. The grass around her glittered as if with tiny stars...

Charlotte saw they were glass beads, broken and spilled from the dress.

Reality thundered down like a waterfall, drenching her.

"Oh my God, Madeleine!" she cried. "What's happened?" She bent over her sister, touching her shoulder. "Maddy?" The skin felt icy; there was no response. Gently rolling her over, Charlotte cradled Madeleine's head, but her eyes were closed and her face pale and slack. "Karl, help her…"

Karl knelt down and touched his fingers to Madeleine's throat. Charlotte saw a pair of bluish crescent-marks, perhaps a trick of the starlight. Then he stood up and stared into the darkness.

Charlotte went rigid with disbelief and terror that Maddy might be dead. When she felt a faint, warm breath on her cheek, she almost wept with relief.

"She's breathing. Help me take her inside, quickly."

Karl bent down and gathered Maddy in his arms. She groaned as he lifted her, her head resting limply in the crook of his shoulder.

"She must have fainted," Charlotte said, shaking with anxiety. "Perhaps she hit her head. I don't understand, she had hardly anything to drink because she was playing the piano all evening."

Karl did not reply. They went up the steps onto the terrace and through the French windows into dazzling light and warmth. Within seconds, people were crowding round in concern, Newland and Aunt Elizabeth taking Madeleine from Karl's arms.

As they carried her away, Karl said quietly to Charlotte, "Call a doctor. Secure the doors after me and don't go outside again."

She was alarmed. "You don't think there's an intruder in the grounds?"

"I'm sure there's no need to worry." He clasped her arm gently and went back onto the terrace before she could stop him.

She locked the French doors as he'd asked, then ran along the corridor to find the others.

Madeleine lay on the chaise longue in the blue room, her face white against the striped satin. Anne shepherded the guests into another room, while David and their father watched anxiously over Madeleine.

"I've telephoned the village doctor," said Elizabeth, following Charlotte into the room. "He'll be here in ten minutes. A fine doctor you are, George. What use is a Ph.D. in philosophy at a time like this?"

Neville made a harrumphing sound. "And a fine aunt you are, feeding lethal cocktails to children."

"She's a grown woman, and she only had a glass of champagne," Elizabeth retorted. "How is she?"

"I think she's coming round," said Charlotte.

Madeleine heaved in a huge breath of air. She blinked and made an effort to lift her head, which lolled as if weighted with lead.

"Come on, Maddy, there's a good girl," said Elizabeth, massaging her hands. "What happened to her, Charlotte?"

"I don't know. Karl and I found her lying on the top lawn."

"What d'you mean, found her?" said her father, looking at his pocket watch. "It's at least an hour since the three of you disappeared. Weren't you all together?"

Before Charlotte could answer, Maddy spoke. "Someone in the garden." Her words were slurred. She rubbed at her neck. "It hurts."

"What does, darling?" said Elizabeth. She lifted Madeleine's hand away, but there were only two tiny blemishes on her neck that might be the imprints of her own fingernails.

"He bit me," said Madeleine.

Elizabeth looked at David. "She's confused. Maddy, try to think, did you faint or did someone hurt you?"

Madeleine's chest rose and fell convulsively under the glitter of beige and pink beads.

"Karl," she said.

Charlotte's anxiety knotted into foreboding.

"What about Karl?" David asked gently.

Maddy frowned. "I don't know."

"She can't have seen Karl outside," said Charlotte. "He and I... He was with me all the time. Talking."

Suddenly they were all looking at her. Her father wore the puzzled scowl she dreaded.

Elizabeth said, "So, you've been in the garden with Karl all this time?"

"Yes." Charlotte almost lost her voice.

"But not with Madeleine. So she might have been lying out there for a whole hour, for all we know."

Charlotte was too distressed to speak. The thought of Maddy lying unconscious and neglected was horrible.

Elizabeth turned her attention back to Madeleine.

"Do try to remember what happened, dear. If someone did hurt you, it's very serious."

"I can't remember, Auntie. I went outside to find Karl... to call him for supper, I mean... then I was lying on the ground and it was cold. There were eyes." Madeleine pressed a hand to her forehead. "I'm dizzy... Pins and needles."

"This is upsetting her," said David.

Elizabeth brushed strands of hair from her niece's forehead.

"Don't think about it now, dear. Try to rest."

When the doctor arrived, he diagnosed anaemia and low blood pressure. Without committing himself to a cause, he prescribed rest and plenty of liquids, hinting vaguely at "women's troubles".

Once he'd gone, they took Madeleine to her bedroom. Charlotte sat with her while Elizabeth went to talk with David and their father. Madeleine clung to Charlotte's wrist with white, frail hands. It was dreadful to see her distraught, so unlike herself.

"Charli, where's Karl?" she said. "I want to see him. This isn't fair."

"What's not fair?" Charlotte said gently.

"You all want to take him away from me, but I'm the one who loves him." To Charlotte's dismay, Madeleine began to weep. "Karl..." All Charlotte could do was to hold her, stroking her hair, murmuring words of comfort; while inside she was aghast at her own hypocrisy. *I let him kiss me and speak those tender words, and now Maddy's breaking her heart over him. I never meant this to happen.*

That miraculous time with Karl must have its price... and she was beginning to pay already.

Madeleine had cried herself to sleep by the time Elizabeth came back.

"I'll sit with her now, Charlotte. However, a word before you go to bed..." Her aunt gripped her arm and propelled her into the corridor, closing the door behind them.

"I don't know what's got into you, dear, but you'll find yourself in serious trouble if you continue with this behaviour," she hissed.

"What behaviour?" Charlotte gasped.

"Disappearing alone with a man in complete darkness for an hour! I can't imagine what you were thinking. It's not that *I* care, but what is your father to make of it? I should think he's furious, and as for your fiancé – you know how rumours spread, so don't imagine Henry won't hear about this. You've never had a clue how to behave; you go from one extreme to another. I despair."

"It was only a walk." She blushed. "We lost track..."

"Knowing you as I do, I would normally believe you. But you've always been hopeless at lying, Charlotte. You shouldn't even attempt it. Go to bed, before you cause any more trouble."

Before Charlotte could defend herself, her aunt was gone and she was left staring at a closed door. Devastated, she retreated to her own bedroom. How could Elizabeth care about her being alone with Karl, when Madeleine was ill? Surely it couldn't be jealousy that made her aunt so angry?

Yet the reason was obvious. Elizabeth regarded Madeleine as a fair rival for Karl's attention. Charlotte was not meant to be in the arena; she'd dared to break the bonds of her role, and that was forbidden. She couldn't forget the way they'd looked at her: David's disapproval, her father's puzzled anger, Madeleine's tears... as if she'd committed some nameless crime.

If they only knew it, they were right, of course. She was engaged to Henry, and her walk with Karl had not been innocent. Elizabeth's philosophy – more sophisticated, if rather less moral – was that the crime lay in being found out.

Where's Karl? Charlotte wondered. *Has anyone gone to look for him?*

She wanted to go downstairs and find out, but Elizabeth's spiteful words held her back. For a while she sat on the bed in her evening dress, heartsick with worry.

Already the walk was taking on a mythical aspect, too vivid to be real, every detail etched into her soul with diamond and fire. Only now did the shockwaves strike her. *This can't have happened, not to me. Did Karl say he loved me, did he actually say it? No, but words don't matter. I knew. We both knew.*

She'd stepped into heaven for a short while... but her bliss had met a harsh end. Now there was a veil of darkness over the house, and Karl was gone.

The clock chimed two a.m. No good, she couldn't rest until she knew Karl was safe. Soundlessly she let herself out, and tiptoed along the broad corridor past a number of other bedchambers until she reached his room.

There was no answer to her soft knock. Pulse thudding, she turned the handle. Instinct told her that the room was empty – so her heart almost failed when she saw Karl sitting by the window, in shirt sleeves, his profile pearly against the indigo sweep of the sky. He was so pale, so utterly still, that for a second she had the horrible impression he was not alive.

"Karl? Thank goodness you're back! Are you all right?"

He stirred from his reverie and turned to face her.

"Of course. What is it, Charlotte?"

She would have rushed to him, but the look in his eyes stopped her. The usual tranquillity that drew her to him had been replaced by something fervid and disturbing.

"You were gone for such a long time," she said, foolishly nervous. "I was worried."

His mouth softened a little. "There's never any need to worry about me, *liebchen*. I can take care of myself."

She hugged herself, shivering. "But did you find anyone?"

Karl paused. "No."

"So Madeleine can't have been attacked. It would be too awful to think there was a criminal wandering in the grounds! She doesn't remember much. The doctor was certain she simply passed out. Aunt Elizabeth's sitting up with her..."

She trailed off. Karl was looking at her strangely, as if he'd completely forgotten about Madeleine.

"Ah. Good. You know you should not..." His eyes were embers. He moistened his lips. "You should not have come here, Charlotte."

She should have left then, but hesitated for a fatal few seconds. She felt the voiceless magnetism again. His beauty cut the ground from under her, more than ever now they had kissed and touched.

But the blameless warmth they'd shared in the garden was darkening into a compulsion. And although she thought herself a stranger to such feelings, she recognised them – from dreams, from the secret heart of her subconscious. When he said, "You should not have come here," she didn't need to ask why.

Molten panic ran through her. The darkness in Karl's expression lay on the whole room, ensnaring her. Charlotte knew what would happen if she stayed. She knew it was wrong, sinful, dangerous; and even knowing, she began to walk towards him. All sense of self-preservation vanished. She felt like a child wading through a warm lake, stepping over an unseen shelf and sinking into deep water.

Karl stood and came to meet her. He took her hand and lifted it, his forearm twisting around hers, as if to hold her and keep her away at the same time.

"I should make you leave," he said. "I should not have come back at all."

She couldn't move. She closed her eyes, felt his hand tighten on her fingers, while waves of dread and excitement fell as heavy as honey through her. *This must not happen.* The words hung there in the darkness, like guilt, but they were nothing to do with her.

"Please don't," she whispered. "Don't make me leave."

Then his hands curved into her hair, and he was kissing her temples, her cheeks, her mouth. Just for a moment his lips rested warm and silken on her throat, and she felt her own pulse beating against them. Then he leaned his head against hers.

"Oh God," he said. "Charlotte."

After that, they did not speak for a long time. There was wordless communication, as if their eyes were not lenses but tunnels of light leading directly from one mind to another. Karl was no more in control than she was as they moved to the curtained bed.

She felt only one pang of fear as they shed their clothes, an echo of the images she'd conjured about Henry – but it was distant, only there to show how far removed her doubts were from this reality. Karl peeled layers of silk from her with reverence, stroking trails of heat over her skin. And then she felt the astonishing sensation of his hair brushing her breasts, and his mouth on the buds of her nipples… As his arms slid around her, as their limbs entwined pearl-white against the cover, she knew there was nothing to fear. Her lover was gentle, compelling, hypnotic. Karl caressed every curve of her with rapt amazement, as if she were a goddess.

And his body, too, was breathtaking: creamy and flawless. She'd never dreamed of such masculine glory, sculpted from moonlight; still less that she would dare to touch and stroke him everywhere, nervously at first then with growing boldness; even the dark hair between his thighs and the forbidden dark fruit that she'd never dared to imagine. Even that was beautiful, and terrible.

We should not... The thought became a meaningless chant, fading away. *This is wrong...* But no, that was in another world, a desiccated world to which she and Karl no longer belonged. They swam together in a realm where morality and constraint had no place. Had never existed.

Wondrous, that he was stroking her soft skin and the secret places that no one else had ever seen or touched. Heat swelled and dew gathered against the warmth of his palm. Wondrous that she could allow this and feel no guilt, only rapture. Delirium. The mask of the ice-cool angel fell away and he was a demon, all fire and appetite. A serpent, piercing her. A sword of flame, spilling waves of crimson pleasure. She felt only a brief flare of pain and then she was swallowed up in fever, wild hunger, amazement that they were doing this... ah, doing *this*...

Now she found the truth that lay at the heart of everything: all the fears, veiled warnings, knowing smiles, restrictions; the blood-red stamen at the centre of society's tightly folded flower. The paradox of an ecstasy that was fretted with danger.

And she found breathless, instant addiction. *The Crystal Ring...* had Karl murmured those words? Yes, like crystal it was, a blazing circle of diamond, beating outwards in waves of light. And it was like blood; hot, flowing, pulsing, animal. He smiled down at her cries and then she felt him falling with her, sharing the sweetness, the astonishing sweetness so intense it verged on agony...

Only as the waves faded there was a moment of discord when she felt his mouth pressing like a circle of darkness on her neck... as if the release of physical desire unleashed a more sinister passion in him.

It happened too fast for her to react. She anticipated pain and arched to meet it, not caring... but the sting never came. Instead he turned his face away with a groan. His hair lay like silk across her throat, but his arms were rigid, as if he was struggling to push himself away from her.

Then she felt him relax. When he turned towards her again, there was unreadable distress in his eyes.

"I will not," he whispered. "God help me, I never shall."

She had hardly enough breath left to speak.

"What's wrong?"

"Nothing, *liebling*." His face was tranquil again, his eyes amber veils over his soul. He smiled at her and stroked her cheek.

"I hope you aren't sorry."

With ecstasy still trickling over her like sweat, she said, "No. I could never be sorry."

CHAPTER SEVEN

NO SPOKEN WORD

When Madeleine woke, she knew she was dead.

The oak posts of her bed had turned to stone. So had the canopy and the curtains, their folds rigidly sculpted and ingrained with dirt. Crypt walls rose cold and shadowy around her. The chest of drawers was an altar, stained with blood-red light. She was an effigy on a tomb, and she would be here forever amid dust and spiders.

Something moved at the foot of her tomb. She saw two life-size puppets with painted wooden heads, swivelling their jagged black-and-white faces towards her and away again as they chattered. They moved in jerks, wooden jaws snapping. Their speech sounded like flies buzzing. Madeleine watched from a state of bewildered paralysis.

One of the heads turned to her and spoke clearly.

"Are you awake, dear? How are you?"

As the puppets approached her, they changed. Their outlines softened and she recognised her father and aunt.

She cried out, "I'm sorry!"

"Whatever for?" Her father leaned down towards her, his features clearly human and familiar. Pale grey eyes, creamy moustache, a scent of pipe tobacco.

"For dying. I didn't mean to."

He looked sideways at Elizabeth. "Dying, you say? Nonsense."

"Death is eternal. You mustn't visit me."

Her thoughts seemed clear as she spoke. *I've lived my life in a cloud of light, I never thought of the future… never dreamed I wasn't infallible. Immortal.* Now the delusion had been whipped aside to reveal an ugly reality. She thought, *Why have they come to visit my tomb? Is it right for the living to mock the dead, to caper like marionettes, flaunting their life?*

She felt her aunt's bony hand around her fingers.

"You'd hardly be talking to us if you were dead, dear. You were having a nasty dream."

"Come along," said her father with forced jollity. "Sit up and have some breakfast, eh? You'll soon be right as rain."

Madeleine laughed inwardly. How could an effigy be made "right as rain" by food? It would crumble against her stone lips. A ludicrous image. Everything was ludicrous and alien.

Yet she remembered human eyes. *Human?* Auburn-golden eyes that looked into hers and warmed her… *Yes, he could bring me back to life, only him – like the Prince kissing the Sleeping Beauty.*

"Karl," said Madeleine. "Where's Karl? Please let me see him."

Her aunt said, "George, I think you'd better leave us alone."

Her father hesitated, frowning. "But…"

"You know you're hopeless with invalids. Run along, this is women's talk."

Grumbling, he left. As the door closed, the crypt shook itself back into a bedroom. Madeleine was confused. With every breath, the world shifted, now bright, now dark. No longer safe. Her only anchor was Karl, the memory of his eyes holding her steady.

"Sit up and drink your tea." Elizabeth propped pillows behind her, put a cup in her hands. "Plenty of fluids, the doctor said. Are you feeling any better?"

There was a game to be played. Madeleine must pretend to be alive, to get what she needed.

"I would, if I could see Karl."

"Oh dear, is that what your fainting fit was about? It's no good making yourself ill over him. No man is worth that."

"He's different."

Elizabeth pursed her lips. "He is a very charming young man, too much so. I'm beginning to think it's unhealthy, the way everyone's losing their reason over him."

Memories of the previous day returned, fever-bright.

"Even you were trying to take him from me, Auntie!"

"Oh, Maddy, I was only flirting. Quite frankly, I thought it would do you good to realise you can't always have what you want."

"I love him. No one else does."

Clasping her hand, Elizabeth said, "My dear, I didn't realise how strongly you felt. I wouldn't hurt you for the world. I'd forgotten how painful love can be when you're young. I know this is hard to accept, but don't you think, if he felt the same, that he would have said something by now?"

"He loves me too. I know he does."

Elizabeth went quiet, then said, "Well, for the sake of your poor heart, I hope you're right. But don't you think it's strange, the way he vanished into the garden with Charlotte last night?"

"Did he?" All Madeleine recalled was going onto the terrace... noticing the tall figure she'd thought was Karl, until she saw blue eyes in a hard white face... then the aching dizziness... *Yes, and then Karl and Charlotte bending over me!* Fear shot through her, but she pushed it away. "That's impossible."

"I think it's quite incredible. Even in the unlikely event that Karl *has* taken a romantic interest in Charlotte, I thought she was too terrified of men to let one anywhere near her. Yet the fact is, they *were* together, and looking so sheepish about it, I can't believe they were only discussing science." Aunt Elizabeth's mouth was a grim line. "Of course, I've always suspected that Charlotte's 'shyness' is an excuse to do as she pleases. There's a streak of contrariness in that young lady that's almost wicked."

Madeleine couldn't listen. "No, Karl wouldn't want Charlotte. She has Henry."

"Indeed so. And if she has some idea of chasing Karl, I'll knock it straight out of her. Don't worry, darling."

Madeleine nodded, but her aunt's voice was distant, echoing off the crypt walls. Everything was decaying; time was crumbling the stone itself to dust. She had to breathe very deep and blink hard to hold the world in place.

"I must see Karl," she said.

"Later. You're not well enough to see anyone just yet."

"Then I shall get well as fast as I can," said Madeleine.

* * *

"I could never be sorry," Charlotte had said, yet by the following morning, remorse was threading icy tendrils through her.

As she sat at breakfast, she felt as if her iniquity was branded on her forehead. Surely it must be blindingly obvious what had happened – yet everyone carried on as if they noticed nothing. There was no sign of Karl. David and Anne sat talking business with Elizabeth. Other house guests drifted in and out of the breakfast room, reading newspapers and making idle chat.

Madeleine appeared, pale but smiling bravely. She said nothing to Charlotte. Her friends, cracking jokes about one too many White Ladies, took her away to be cosseted in one of the drawing rooms.

No one mentioned the previous night's events, life had already returned to normal. But not for Charlotte.

She'd left Karl in the early hours, not wanting to risk discovery when a maid or footman came in with tea, but alone in her room she'd gone into a state of shock. *Gods, what have I done?*

And where was Karl? He often made courteous, plausible excuses to avoid mealtimes with the Nevilles – perhaps he disliked English food – but she'd thought he would at least make an appearance to be sociable. Now she was possessed by unreasoning terror that she might never see him again.

Could he have deceived her? Was he in fact a hypnotically charming rake whose only aim had been to violate her and flee?

No, she refused to believe it.

What had seemed enchanted the previous night was heinous in the light of day. She felt as if a wall of glass had slammed between them, the instant she left him. If Karl walked in now, what on earth would they say to each other? However off-handedly they tried to behave, Elizabeth was too sharp not to read the signs.

Yet the memory of that other-world remained clear and shining. How could she regret it? The experience had changed her forever. In a dream Charlotte wandered out of the breakfast room and along the corridor; unconsciously searching for Karl, frightened of finding him, terrified that she would not.

As she stopped to look through the letters on the upper hall table, Anne appeared dressed in riding kit.

"Charli, I've hardly had a chance to speak to you since last night. You're almost as pale as the invalid. Are you all right?"

"Yes, but I – I'm rather worried about Maddy."

"Oh, if she's out of bed already, she'll be fine. I thought I should warn you about this morning's gossip before you hear it elsewhere. They're all speculating about you and Karl."

Charlotte's eyes widened. "What about me and Karl?"

"Oh, come on! Disappearing into the depths of the garden."

"Oh, that." She leaned on the table, uttering a sigh.

"Isn't that enough? What else have you been up to?" Anne said teasingly.

"No one said a word at breakfast."

"Well, they can't talk in front of you, can they? I know you hate it, but take no notice. Gossip is the lifeblood of these people, and no one escapes forever. It was like that for David and me, until we got engaged."

Charlotte spread the letters into a fan on the polished surface.

"All the same, I wish they wouldn't. I shan't dare show my face again."

"Nonsense. The good news is that your family have decided not to interrogate you."

Charlotte bit her lip. "I wish people wouldn't talk behind each others' backs!"

"I don't like it either. That's why I'm telling you. It's too much for the Prof and David to believe the worst, so they're giving you the benefit of the doubt. You're still a pure white lamb in their eyes." Anne looked steadily at her. "But you can tell *me* the truth, Charli. Is there something between you and Karl?"

Charlotte didn't know what to say, even to her best friend. She felt an urge to confess, but the words wouldn't come. She couldn't bear the experience to be confined and lessened by someone else's judgment… not even Anne's.

"There might be," she whispered eventually.

"Oh dear," Anne said softly. "Can you talk about it?"

"Not yet. I'm sorry. I need to collect my thoughts."

"Nothing like being on horseback for clearing the mind. I'll wait for you to change, if you like."

The idea of escaping into the fresh air was tempting – but

what if Karl reappeared and she missed him?

"I'd like to – but really, I'm too tired. Sorry."

"No stamina! I'll see you later, then." Anne began to walk away, then turned back. "You ought to think carefully about Henry, you know. This could turn into an awful mess."

It already is, thought Charlotte. Heaven and hell.

She was beginning to think she'd imagined everything, that Karl had vanished like a ghost at dawn. Then, as she passed the library, she glanced in and saw him sitting on the brown leather couch. There was a book open on his knee, but he was gazing out at the garden.

Her head spun with shock. She almost walked straight past the doorway, but it was too late, he had turned and was looking at her. The graceful way he stood to greet her as she approached was enough to reawaken sensations that melted all through her, from her throat to the soles of her feet. Everything about him was more poignant now for being so sweetly familiar.

"Where have you been?" she said.

"I had to go out for a while." He lifted her hand and turned it over to kiss the inside of her wrist. "I'm being so unfair to you, dearest heart."

Ominous words. "How?"

"Sit down." They sat easily, resting against each other with no awkwardness at all.

Charlotte relaxed. They belonged together, that was how she'd felt from the beginning, if only she'd realised.

"Last night…" he began slowly. "I know it was wrong, but you must not feel guilty, Charlotte. The blame was all mine."

"No it wasn't!" She was startled to feel so indignant. "Do you think I have no will of my own?"

His eyebrows lifted. He almost smiled, but his eyes remained serious.

"Your will is stronger than you know, but that's not what I mean. I don't believe you could give yourself to someone unless you trusted them completely, could you?"

"No. But I do trust you completely."

Karl sighed. "Ah. I know that, you see. I knowingly betrayed your trust. That's why I say the blame is mine."

The seed of dread grew heavier.

"What on earth do you mean?"

"That I can make no promises to you. I would if I could, but it's impossible."

All at once her foreboding became a fearful coldness. She'd had no thoughts of the future and the idea of marrying Karl hadn't entered her head. Now he said "impossible", disturbing visions began to settle like crows within her. She tried to chase them away but in black flurries they returned. *Did I hope...?*

"I wouldn't presume to ask or expect any such thing," she said faintly.

"But you have every right to do so. This is a society in which marriage and virtue mean everything. They mean nothing to me, but you're the one who has to live in this world, Charlotte, not I. You are the one who will suffer. I knew this, but I am selfish and I let it happen anyway."

She hung onto his hand, searching for rationality while all her hopes streamed away.

"If you'd proposed marriage in order to seduce me, that would be different. But you never promised anything."

"And I cannot," he said gently. "I am in no position to marry anyone, beloved. I should have told you before. I should have told you *instead*."

She did not want to ask, but couldn't stop herself. She was falling again, this time into painful confusion.

"Do you have a wife in Vienna?" Her voice sounded dry, distant. "There's someone else, isn't there?"

"No," he said, eyelids lowered. "I am not married, there is no one else."

"Why, then? Have you taken a religious vow?"

He actually laughed at that, very softly. "No, nothing like that. I won't lie, so it's better I don't say anything. You've a right to know the reason, but I can't tell you. I know it's unfair, but I cannot."

"Very well, I won't ask. I'm sure it's a good reason."

"It could hardly be worse," he murmured.

"I don't know what you want me to think, Karl! Were you a spy in the War, or something? If you're trying to tell me you're what David would call a 'cad', that you only pretended to care

for me – I'm sorry, I just don't believe you are that good an actor."
She forced herself to speak with dignity, though the tears ached
behind her eyes.

He was right; they had committed a sin that could only be
rectified by marriage. Never had she felt so spiritually remote
from her family, yet so morally bound to them. Imagining her
father's devastation if ever he found out, she went deathly cold.

Karl stroked her hair, quiet. Then he said, "The only way to
stop this happening was to avoid it in the first place. Now I don't
know what we are going to do. Charlotte, you must *never* doubt
the strength of my feelings for you."

"God, no." Her voice caught in her throat. "I don't doubt that.
You would only hurt me if you left. You're not going to leave,
are you?"

"I should," he said, eyes sorrowful. "But I can't – even though
I can see no way for this to end, except in anguish."

"I don't care! This is worth the pain, whatever it is."

Anyone might have walked in, or seen them from the terrace,
but he drew her to him, kissed her, held her tight with his head
bowed against her hair.

"What *are* we going to do?" said Charlotte. She felt as if she'd
grown up very suddenly, broken through a barrier of naive fear,
and found herself no longer an observer of life but right there in
the middle of it, for the first time, passionately *living*. "I'll have to
break my engagement."

"Not for my sake."

She looked at him, shocked.

"You don't think I could still marry Henry after this, do you?"

"You must do whatever you feel is right. But don't
misunderstand me, whether you are married or not is irrelevant
to what I feel for you."

The words flew out before she could cage them.

"You mean you can't marry me, but you'd be quite happy to
commit *adultery*?"

"Only if you consented, beloved."

"I don't think you have any morals at all!"

"Not a single one. I thought that must be clear by now."

She tried to feel offended, but couldn't. His eyes were swallowing her into mesmeric darkness. He placed his long delicate hand against her cheek.

"Look into your heart, Charlotte. We sit here arguing about right and wrong, when all the time we both know that the conventions of society have nothing to do with us. Haven't we always known it?"

That night, it was Karl who went to her room, and again the night after.

During the day they behaved as if nothing had changed – Charlotte with difficulty, Karl with invisible ease – but after midnight she would sit waiting for him, watching the ever-swaying movement of the trees from the darkness of her room.

And when they were together, there was only the voluptuous tide of their obsession. No concept of sin, because there could be none in the exquisite tenderness they shared. No thought of the future, that uncertainty remained unspoken behind Karl's eyes. Charlotte dared not ask who he really was, or what was going to happen to them. She feared that if she did, the spell would break and he would vanish. They barely spoke at all; there seemed nothing left that needed expression in words.

Is this what being in love is like? she thought on the third morning. She was alone in the library, staring out at the rain. *This loss of control, this madness? Now I know why I was so frightened.* But the affectionate partnership of Anne and David seemed a world away from the fever of her relationship with Karl. It couldn't be healthy, this bewitchment...

An addiction, yes. An opium-poppy lushness, heavy as laudanum, purple as night... and at the centre of the darkness, the burst of joy, the blazing ring of crystal. *It must be wrong. Why else must it be kept secret?*

She thought of Karl's words, "How do I look to you? Fascinating, not quite human, perhaps? Can you explain why you feel drawn to me?" She didn't understand, but it *wasn't* human, the way he could become as still as frozen starlight or as fluid as shadow. A changeling beauty. A dew-silvered web on which she threw herself, willingly, again and again.

She felt like a courtesan of old, abandoning herself to wild delicious lust with no care for the consequences. Charlotte Neville did not do this sort of thing. Strait-laced, timid and moral, Charlotte was a good girl.

Only she was not.

Still, her turmoil was jewelled with exquisite moments. Snatched secret meetings in the wild places of the garden, on the rare occasions they could escape the house without arousing suspicion. The wicked pleasure of pretending nothing was happening in front of the others. Karl's cool angelic mask, his gracious indifference to Elizabeth's and Maddy's flirting; the speaking looks he gave Charlotte, and the secrets they shared. There was a thrill in knowing her family would never dream their shy lamb had tasted such forbidden pleasures; even in imagining their outrage if they found out.

And above all, there was Karl, naked in the moonlight, as passionate, beautiful and amoral as Lucifer himself...

"You must have had many lovers," she whispered on the third night in her bed.

"Not many," he answered with a sad smile, "and not for a very long time."

She laughed. "It can't be that long. You're no more than five or six years older than me, at most."

"Nevertheless," he sighed, "it seems an immeasurably long time ago."

"I'm jealous of them," she said, soft and intense.

"Charlotte." He turned to her, eyes shining with fire, his fingertips caressing her breast. "Don't be. There's no need. They are... long in the past. I'm with you now. And I have never felt for anyone as I feel for you."

His gaze was so fierce that it disturbed her more than reassured her. He never forbade her to ask questions, but he never answered them, either. All she could trust was his passion for her. It was only when they were apart that the glow faded and doubts dripped coldly into Charlotte's mind.

What if I found I was expecting a child? I should die of shame. I'm being such a fool, but I can't stop.

There was always a moment in their love-making when

he seemed to want more from her, and had to struggle against himself, as if afraid he would hurt her in some way. Once the moment was over, he became his tender, loving self again. Still, the struggle seemed harder each time. Worse, this alarmed and excited her to such an extent that she knew she'd truly fallen from grace. Did this happen with all men? She had no comparison and there was no one she could ask.

Worst of all was the guilt she felt about Madeleine. However spoilt Maddy could be at times, Charlotte felt protective towards her. Maddy came first and must always have what she desired. It was her natural due for being the prettiest, the youngest – and compensation, perhaps, for not being their father's favourite. The fact that Karl had no feelings for her was irrelevant, Charlotte couldn't shake off the idea that she'd "stolen" him from her sister.

Poor Maddy, to feel about Karl as I do but without return... but does she? How could she? She's never strayed into that dark country... She would have held out for formal courtship and a wedding ring. And what does that make me, to risk everything for nothing?

If Karl loves me, we should marry. All my life that's what they've told us, that marriage is the righteous path and anything else is a sin. Even Elizabeth says so, though I'm quite sure she doesn't practise what she preaches. Yet I don't know, I don't care...

Seduction. *This is what it means: to be drawn into something wicked, not because it seems evil, but because you're deceived into believing it's right.*

I'm drowning. I feel as if I'm the first person this has ever happened to, but I'm not. It's been the same cry down the ages. How can something so beautiful be wrong? The cry that precedes ruin...

In a few days they would return to Cambridge. Elizabeth's only remaining guests were David and Anne, Charlotte and Madeleine, Dr Neville and Karl. A pleasant family gathering... except for an atmosphere thickening like winter around them. Perhaps it existed only in Charlotte's mind, but Maddy's illness and her own secrets seemed to darken everything.

This can't go on, but I can't bear it to end...

Outside, the wind was lashing leaves from the trees and scattering them across rain-soaked grass. All the lovely autumn foliage beneath which she'd walked with Karl became tattered rags.

The library door opened and her aunt's voice startled her.

"Charlotte, dear, will you come into the blue room? You have a visitor."

Charlotte felt no suspicion at first. Contrary to her threats, her aunt had said no more about her walk with Karl, or their suspected affinity.

"Oh, who is it?" she asked.

"I'm surprised you even ask." Elizabeth's manner was brisk. "I did warn you I'd correct your behaviour before you ruin your life and give your father heart failure."

How foolish of her, to imagine her aunt would let the matter rest.

Henry was waiting in the blue room, with a serious expression she had never seen before. Charlotte was dismayed. Her father was beside him and they looked like lawyers about to announce the death of a relative.

Her lips parted, and she managed to say, "Hello, Henry, I – I wasn't expecting you."

Henry was such an awkward, lumpen figure compared to Karl. He seemed a total stranger. That she'd ever agreed to marry him was incredible.

"Lady Reynolds sent for me. Apparently there are one or two things we ought to clear up." He stammered a little, but the passion in his voice took her by surprise. "She said there had been – um, certain rumours about you and Karl, and while I'm sure they're completely unfounded, I won't tolerate such things being said about my fiancée. If you'd come to my parents as I asked, this would never have happened, and it's too bad of you. My mother agrees. So far you've put no effort into this engagement whatsoever, and every time I try to pin you down to a date, you make excuses. Well, enough is enough; we are going to sit down and discuss this and I am not going away until we've sorted out the whole thing and set a day for the wedding."

Shocked, Charlotte found her aunt looking squarely at her with raised eyebrows, as if to say, *"Don't appeal to me, this is exactly what you deserve!"*

I'm trapped, thought Charlotte. Then, *No. Why should I be?*

The feeling of panic fell away and she felt sorry for Henry. Behind his crooked wire glasses was a look she'd never noticed before, but which she now recognised. *Oh Lord, he's in love with me! He's probably felt this for years and I never even knew. And I'm going to hurt him.*

Trembling, she said, "It's no good, Henry, I can't go through with it."

He blinked at her. "I beg your pardon?"

"I can't marry you! I'm sorry." She stepped forward and gave him back the ring. Bewildered, he stared at the diamond glitter in the palm of his hand.

"I don't understand, Charlotte. Why? What have I done wrong?"

This was Henry's trouble: he thought life went in a straight line, he never looked to left or right. So hard to divert his one-track intelligence, it was like being cruel to a faithful dog.

"You've done nothing wrong," she said. "It's my fault. I – I don't love you, and I should never have said yes in the first place."

"Is there someone else?" he said wildly. "It's Karl, isn't it? I don't believe it, how could you be so deceitful?"

His words cut, but she couldn't defend herself. She wished the floor would swallow her.

Henry looked helplessly at her, then at her father.

"I see," he said eventually. He thrust the ring into his pocket. His face was rigid. "Well, in that case, er… I think, sir, it would be best in the circumstances if I left your employment and found a position elsewhere."

Her father's face fell. "What?"

"Miss Neville and I can hardly go on working together without deep embarrassment on both sides, therefore it would be best for everyone if I left."

"No!" Charlotte exclaimed. "There's no need for that, we'll be just as we were before."

"No, we won't, Charlotte." Henry's harsh tone shocked her. "How I could stay, knowing you regard me with such contempt?"

"I don't—" she gasped, but he spoke over her.

"No, my mind is made up." He turned to her father. "I'm sorry, sir," he said, stepping away with a self-conscious, dipping motion. "Sorry."

As he went out awkwardly, closing the door with a quiet click behind him, Charlotte's father turned on her.

"Do you see what you've done? Is this what you wanted to achieve with your selfishness? I can't think what's got into you, young lady."

She had broken the magic circle. Unforgivable. His anger crushed her.

"But you can't have wanted me to marry someone I don't love? You were against it to start with," she protested.

"Love be damned! You've just lost me the best assistant I've ever had!"

Before she could start to apologise, Elizabeth said, "Don't blame Charlotte, it was you who employed Karl in the first place."

Dr Neville was outraged. "Don't be ridiculous! To suggest Charlotte had some nefarious motive for walking around the garden with Karl is deplorable. D'you think I don't know my own daughter?"

"Really, George, if you'd take off your blinkers for five minutes you might notice that she is a grown woman and he is a man. These things do happen, even to Charlotte, unlikely as it may seem."

Charlotte felt her face colouring. She knew her aunt's game. Elizabeth didn't want to believe that Karl was genuinely attracted to her, but she *did* want to punish her.

"Nonsense!" her father declared. "If anything untoward *has* taken place, I would hold you to blame, Elizabeth. You are supposed to be chaperoning my daughters."

"Oh, you are so old fashioned," said his sister, folding her arms. "I can't watch them every minute of the day. You've kept Charlotte so cloistered, what chance has she against a wolf if she meets one? These Continentals make a pass at anything that moves."

"That's a dreadful thing to say, and it's not true!" Charlotte cried. "Karl's a perfect gentleman, one of the kindest people I've ever met, and I won't hear such things said about him!"

She broke off. They were both staring at her, judge and jury, as if she had condemned herself with her own voice.

Her father's expression was grave and formidable. His rage filled the room.

"Don't you think you owe rather more respect to Henry and me than to him? If ever I find out there's an iota of truth in this – What would your mother have said?"

Always the comparison with her perfect mother that needled straight to her heart. Charlotte hung her head, then felt his hand on her arm.

"I'm returning to Cambridge tomorrow," he said portentously. "I trust you'll be coming with me."

Later, as they all sat in the main drawing room after dinner, Charlotte looked around at her family; her father straight-faced and quiet, Elizabeth smug, David and Anne their unaffected cheerful selves. They veiled their feelings in the English way and went on as if nothing had happened, making small talk as the butler and maid served coffee. No one said anything to anyone... Yet the atmosphere was fragile. They all knew Charlotte was in disgrace. Henry had gone back to Cambridge, and tomorrow her father would take her home like a child expelled from school.

And what of Karl? Would her father turn against him, send him away? *And all this for a walk!* she thought. *Ye gods, if they knew the truth, the sky itself would fall.*

Karl had been out all day, and now they were in the same room there was no chance for them to speak privately. Apparently nothing had been said to him about Henry. Charlotte was the scapegoat; he was still the revered guest, incapable of wrong. He'd stayed in the dining room with David and her father for their port and cigars ritual; now he sat with Madeleine on the sofa as she asked questions about Vienna, responding with easy charm while his untouched coffee turned cold.

Maddy was trying to put on a brave face, but still wasn't her normal self. She seemed tired and vulnerable; restless if Karl wasn't there, as bright as a candle flame in his company. More determined than ever to snare Karl's attention, she was visibly growing desperate as his friendly manner remained impersonal. Only when he met Charlotte's gaze did warmth fill his eyes, a secret communication that left her in no doubt of his feelings.

At the same time it was agony to see her sister suffering.

Charlotte could see no way to get Karl alone, without being obvious. Even if she could, what good would it do? While they'd been friends, she had talked to him easily. Now they were lovers, it seemed too much went unspoken.

Anne glanced at her once or twice, and she thought, *Oh, Anne, I know you want to help and I'd do anything to tell you the truth, but even you would condemn me.*

The room was bright and warm, with a fire crackling in the red marble fireplace. The curtains were open, the windows holding two worlds in one shiny black plane: the reflection of a bright domestic scene, and silver raindrops lashing the glass. Charlotte's gaze drifted to Madeleine's face and she noticed her sister staring at the French doors even while Karl was speaking to her. *How cosy and safe it seems in here*, Charlotte thought with irony, and as she did so, she saw Madeleine's expression change. Her eyes enlarged, her mouth opened, and she cried out, "He's there!"

All within a split second, Charlotte glanced at the windows, saw something dash across the terrace, and then there was a tremendous *boom* as a figure flung itself against the glass doors like a crashing bird. Everyone leapt up, exclaiming with shock.

There was a man pressing himself flat against the glass, arms outstretched, staring into the room with a wild grin and wide, mocking blue eyes, leering at them.

David was moving to the window, her father pulling a bell rope to summon servants, Elizabeth rushing to comfort the distraught Madeleine.

Anne came to Charlotte, saying, "Who is that lunatic?"

Charlotte stood petrified because she recognised the face: it was the man she'd seen near the Cavendish Laboratory in Cambridge, whom she'd taken for a ghost. He seemed to be watching their panic, laughing at them.

"What's your game, sir?" David shouted through the glass. "Infernal bloody cheek!"

He grasped the handle, and Elizabeth said, "Oh, don't open the door, David, for heaven's sake! Make sure it's locked!"

"I've no intention of letting this madman in," David replied. "Where's Newland? Father, when he comes, have him send some men into the garden. I'm not letting this beggar get away."

In the midst of this, Karl stood still and quiet in the centre of the room.

"There's no need, David," he said.

"What?"

Karl paused. "It's someone I know."

Elizabeth laughed in disbelief. "What strange friends you have, Karl. Couldn't he use the front door, like everyone else?"

Madeleine would usually have been the first to make a joke, but now she only sat round-eyed as if too stunned to speak.

Karl moved to the French window. Although outwardly self-contained, Charlotte realised with shock that he was furious. She'd never seen him angry before. The stranger put his head on one side and blinked at Karl through the glass.

"Excuse me, please, David," said Karl, reaching past him to unlock the doors.

"What the devil are you doing? Don't let him in!" David cried.

"There appears to be no choice." Karl opened the glass doors. The stranger thrust himself into the room, still grinning, but Karl caught his arm and stopped him. They all backed away, and Karl said, "I must apologise."

The stranger said loudly, "Why, what have you done, Karl? This is no way to greet a friend, trying to break his arm. Aren't you pleased to see me?"

He spoke with a French accent, but his English, like Karl's, was near perfect. He was a tall man in his late twenties, clad in an expensive dark coat and cashmere scarf. He had angular features, with full lips and a cleft chin. His hair fell brown and curly across his forehead. He was handsome, Charlotte thought, but for his eyes: intensely blue, they were too large and heavily lidded, with a cold humour that repelled her. Yet he had a quality that reminded her of Karl: a power of presence that eclipsed the whole room. *It's him, the man I saw in Cambridge, the one who vanished!*

"Good heavens, Karl, do you really know this person?" said Elizabeth.

"I'm afraid so," Karl replied.

Undaunted, the Frenchman kissed Karl on both cheeks.

"My dear fellow, how well you look! The English air must suit you. And the English food, eh?" He winked at Elizabeth, who looked astonished. "You must excuse the unusual manner of my arrival but it is such fun teasing Karl. He's so terribly conventional, don't you find? I would do anything to drag a reaction from him."

Karl's face remained expressionless.

"What are you doing here?"

"At the moment, I am waiting to be introduced to this charming company."

Karl smiled, but his eyes were red ice.

"I am hardly going to do that, Pierre."

Pierre beamed around with a white smile, as if he found Karl's attitude mildly exasperating. His gaze rested on Madeleine. She stared back, blank-faced, as if about to faint. Then he looked at Charlotte, and she had the terrible impression that he knew all the secrets of her soul and found them amusing.

Newland was in the doorway, whispering to Dr Neville.

"Oh, but you must forgive me for intruding on your party," said Pierre. "I was so eager to see my long-lost friend, my manners have deserted me – as his sense of humour seems to have deserted him."

David said coldly, "I don't think any of us found it funny that you frightened my family half to death. Karl, I don't care if this fellow is a friend of yours or not. He must leave immediately."

"Of course," said Karl. He tightened his grip on Pierre's arm. "If you will first allow us to talk privately." David tried to object, but Karl went on, "I've known Pierre a long time, but you see, he is rather to me as Edward is to you. Unpredictable, volatile – yet I cannot disown him."

"Oh." David looked taken aback.

"You patronising devil!" said Pierre to Karl. "Are you suggesting I'm some kind of maniac?"

"You make it obvious, without any suggestion from me." Karl looked at Elizabeth. "You will excuse us?"

Pierre objected extravagantly. "Oh, Karl, how can you drag me away from these charming people, when we have only just met? You are too cruel." He looked pleadingly at Elizabeth. "He is always dreadfully cruel to me, Madame, the tales I could tell you…"

"Goodness, I'm sure we'd all be fascinated!" Elizabeth said, raising her eyebrows. "You can take your friend into the library, Karl. Er – would he like a drink?"

"Oh, you are too kind!" the Frenchman exclaimed. "But I fear my taste would prove very expensive for you –"

Karl interrupted, his voice soft yet sharp, like a razor. "You have forfeited any claim to hospitality, Pierre. I'm sure you have much to tell me that's of no interest to anyone else." He gripped Pierre's elbow and guided him to the door, past the astonished butler.

"Do you wish me to escort the gentleman off the premises, madam?" he asked.

"No, it's all right, Newland," said Elizabeth. "Everything's under control. But the rest of us need a drink, after all that. Whisky, anyone?"

Trembling, Charlotte sat down by Madeleine, who was quiet now but listless, her eyes dull.

"Are you all right?" Charlotte asked.

"Yes... perfectly," Madeleine replied, but she seemed miles away, unreachable.

David and her father were discussing the intruder, verging on an argument. Charlotte looked round for Anne and realised her friend was no longer in the room.

"I didn't see Anne go out, did you?" she said.

"Don't go after her," Madeleine said in the same flat tone. "Stay with me, Charli."

Anne slipped through the French window a few moments after Karl and Pierre left, while the others were too busy talking to notice. She went along the terrace until she reached a grainy lozenge of light falling from the library windows. There she stopped, peering through a tangle of wisteria tendrils to the lighted interior. Voices drifted through an open vent.

She intended to eavesdrop and felt no conscience about it. Charlotte's interests were her priority.

Pierre was browsing idly along the bookshelves, all languid animation. Karl sat on the arm of a chair, motionless like a cat watching a bird. His face was serene, a china mask, but his lack of expression held menace.

"Why are you here, Pierre?" Karl's voice was calm, almost conversational, hiding a paper-thin blade of ice.

"That's an unfriendly way to greet an old friend, especially after all these years," said the Frenchman. "Show me a little warmth, at least."

"After the way you announced your presence? I knew it was you, when we found Madeleine."

What the hell does he mean? Anne thought.

Pierre put back his head and laughed.

"Don't look so grim. I did her no lasting harm. You know it was only a joke."

"Your sense of humour and mine are a world apart," said Karl.

"I know. That makes it even more amusing. It would be no fun to torment you, otherwise."

Karl paused, glancing towards the window. Nothing in everyday life frightened Anne, but now gooseflesh tingled down her back. *He can't know I'm here!*

Then Karl whispered something to Pierre she couldn't hear.

His companion laughed and exclaimed loudly, "So what if anyone is listening? Do you have something to hide? Let them listen!"

Anne drew back, shocked. A thread of angry determination went through her. *Right, if you don't care, I'll stay where I am!*

"He sent you, I suppose," said Karl.

Pierre selected a volume and reclined on the couch as if he owned the place.

"Come now, did you expect to escape forever? He's given you years already; all good things must end. And this, I must say, is a very good thing. How did you find this beautiful family? All under the pretext of studying science, too! *Mon Dieu*, Karl, I have to hand it to you, you certainly have style."

Karl's eyes turned even colder.

"You're wrong, Pierre. Quite wrong."

Pierre dropped the book aside.

"Oh no, don't give me that! They are too beautiful. Isn't it thrilling to know that with one look, one word from you, they'd all forget each other and fall into your embrace? I wish I had half your charm."

"And I, half your imagination. I do not touch those I know."

"Hypocrite."

"It may well be hypocritical, but it's the rule I live by."

Pierre sneered. "Then you must get some perverted pleasure from tormenting yourself."

"No, but neither do I relish tormenting others."

"Unlike myself, I suppose. But I say you are lying, Karl. Not to me, perhaps, but to yourself."

"Meaning?"

Pierre rose and paced. His tone was taunting. "I saw you with your arms around Charlotte, having such a very interesting conversation – when you could keep your lips from hers. My God, how long do you think you can hold out? Is this some scientific experiment to test the limits of your will power? If you start feeling *other* desires for her, she had really better beware, but who's going to warn her?" He laughed.

Karl's eyelids swept up, light caught his irises like tiny flames igniting.

"You know nothing about it," he said softly.

For the first time Anne saw something truly dangerous in Karl. Behind his beauty and gentility, a cold and menacing darkness lurked that was far more chilling than Pierre's surface spite. She was horrified, but not for her own sake. *Oh, Charlotte, do you know anything about this man?*

"If you were sincere, you'd have gone nowhere near her," said Pierre. "If she really means so much to you. It proves you enjoy playing with fire, so don't pretend otherwise."

"You had better stop this, Pierre."

"Why? I like embarrassing you." The Frenchman stared at the window. "So what if they hear too much? They can always be silenced."

Anne drew back, and found herself retreating along the terrace almost at a run. *I won't let them frighten me*, she told herself fiercely. *I can't use what I've overheard to prove anything.*

But she was going to tell David, before it was too late.

Karl sensed the human presence moving away. It was Anne, he knew. He daren't guess what she'd made of their conversation. But he couldn't concern himself with that until he'd dealt with Pierre. No witnesses now.

"Ah, *mon cher*," Pierre went on, "you can't be ruled by human sentiment. For God's sake, Karl, accept your nature!"

"I'm sure God would be the last to appreciate the effort," said Karl with a brief sardonic smile.

"Spare me the theological quips, will you? I have enough of that from Kristian."

"I suppose he sent you to fetch me."

"Not exactly." Pierre leaned on the rolled leather arm of the couch. "He knows you won't come for the asking."

"And he's right. How did you find me?"

"Sheer persistence. But I have something funny to recount; the one person who always knows where you are is Ilona. She has shadowed you for years."

Karl was caught off-guard as emotions flamed through him.

"That's impossible. I would have known."

"Why should you? She can creep up right behind me and I don't know she's there, even Kristian can't sense her presence easily. We may be sensitive, but we are not psychic, more's the pity."

Karl paused, brooding. Then he said, "I suppose Kristian sent her. I'd be foolish to think she sought me of her own free will. But where is she now?"

"Ah well, that brings me to Kristian's message. All this talk of, 'Karl must come back of his own accord' and then he resorts to the basest emotional blackmail..."

"What do you mean?"

Pierre held up his hands, as if to say, *"Don't blame me!"*

"Kristian took her into the Crystal Ring. Up into the *Weisskalt*. He says she'll remain there until you go back to him... I think he's reached the end of his tether, as the English say... as I think you are about to do also."

Pain hit Karl, so raw he couldn't speak. Ilona, frozen in deathlike sleep... He could have torn apart the message-bearer with fangs and bare hands, but that would solve nothing. He waited until the feeling pooled into deadly silence inside him.

Eventually he was able to speak calmly. "I should not be surprised. I shouldn't ask, 'How could he?' but, 'Why has he waited so long?' Kristian has never had a principle to his name."

"And what have principles to do with us?" Pierre said with

sudden passion. "What use have wolves for principles – or angels, for that matter? If you dropped your foolish morality, Kristian wouldn't be able to use it against you!"

"Since when have love and morality been the same thing? So I should just leave her there? How good of you to give me this advice, Kristian's errand boy."

Pierre's mobile face became vindictive.

"What am I? Only one of the arms of the octopus. As we all are. Even you."

"But wouldn't you prefer to be free?" Karl thought he'd escaped the weary despair induced by Kristian's possessiveness. *I knew this would come... I should have been ready.*

"My dear, I *am* free. I worship Kristian's strength of my own free will, as I'd worship the perfection of a Michelangelo sculpture. It's a work of art."

"You talk nonsense, Pierre. You drift with every wind that blows, then try to justify yourself."

"I do his will because it pleases me, but I don't obey slavishly." Pierre's lips drew back in an unpleasant smile. "Kristian ordered me not to touch this luscious family, but I chose to disobey and I intend to do so again. How will he know, unless you tell him? Better run to him and beg for his help, Karl, for only he can stop me."

Enough. Pierre had taken a step too far. Karl had hoped to send him away unharmed, but in the space of a breath he saw that it was impossible. Without hesitation, without anger, he moved like light to seize Pierre and pull him to his feet.

"We'll see, shall we?" Karl said, very softly.

For a few seconds they struggled, not violently but in stasis like arm-wrestlers. Karl slid his hand into Pierre's hair and slowly dragged back his head. Pierre's mouth opened. His blue eyes pleaded silently with the ceiling. Then Karl closed his mouth on the cool smooth skin of his neck.

Karl had not fed that evening and suddenly he was ravenous. Vampire blood was not rich like that of humans, but held a different compulsion, a fiercer fire blazing through his body and mind... and that was why he failed to sense another human nearby until the red veil subsided, and it was too late.

CHAPTER EIGHT

CRYSTAL VISIONS

When David reached the library window he stopped, transfixed. He saw Karl with his back to the window, embracing Pierre, his face buried in his neck. Not kissing; something worse. In that horrible attitude they stood motionless, except for the twitching of Pierre's stiffly outstretched arms. Presently a trickle of blood appeared from his sleeve, made a red rivulet over his hand, and dripped to the floor.

What the devil are they up to? David thought. *Anne said there was something strange going on, but this?*

Eventually Karl raised his head. His grip slackened; Pierre's knees buckled and Karl let him down gently onto the couch, where he lay with his long limbs in disarray and hair tousled around his slack face. There was a crimson stain on the collar of his shirt.

Pierre uttered an obscenity in French. Then he said, "I hate you," as if he were actually saying, "I love you."

Karl turned his profile towards the window. His expression was cool and there was no blood on his mouth, but David thought he looked different, glowing, intangibly in control.

"You will not lay a finger on any member of this family," he said softly. "Is that clear?"

Pierre lifted his head. His blue eyes looked sleepy, unfocused.

"Miserable bastard," he said. "Dog in the manger, I think that's the phrase."

"It's a simple command," said Karl. "You will not touch them."

Touch us? For God's sake, what does he mean?

Pierre said, "You drain me, then expect me to starve to death?"

"I don't care what you do once you leave this house."

"How do you expect me to leave?" Pierre exclaimed. "I can't move from this seat, let alone do anything else."

"Don't be a fool," Karl said coldly. "You can walk to the door. I will drive you somewhere. I want you far away from this house as fast as possible." He clasped Pierre's upper arm and pulled him up like a rag doll.

Pierre stood swaying in his grip.

"Your charming hosts will think me terribly rude."

Karl laughed, a soft, mellifluous sound that chilled David.

As they walked to the door, Pierre said, "What about Ilona?"

David did not hear Karl's reply. They were gone.

The library had a frozen look, like an empty stage, but the plum-red drops of blood on the carpet glistened with significance.

Karl spoke as if he's trying to protect us from Pierre, thought David, *yet Karl's own behaviour is inexplicable. "Dog in the manger," Pierre called him – as if Karl has some vested interest in us... But what? Christ.*

David's first instinct was to stop the men and demand answers. He sprinted down the terrace steps, around the side of the Hall, past the kitchens, but he had to scale a gate to reach the front drive and he was too late. Karl's Hispano-Suiza had gone from the open garages. He heard the swiftly receding growl of its engine.

David swore. No point in chasing them. Better to go back and see if Anne could shed any light. He was thinking of Edward's warnings. *What I saw and heard might make sense if they literally were – No, it's too preposterous!*

While David was outside, Anne took Charlotte into the orangery. Light filtered through the glass doors from the blue room, and the gleaming twilight was eerie, filled with the patter of fountains. They sat in wicker chairs under orange trees and other exotic plants. Foliage massed across the roof like a jungle.

Anne told Charlotte what she'd overheard: that the Frenchman claimed to have seen her with Karl in the garden. That all she'd witnessed had made her uncomfortably suspicious of Karl.

"And they knew I was there," Anne said. "I kept out of sight, but they *knew*."

Charlotte listened with her head bowed. Eventually she said, "You shouldn't have been spying on them, Anne."

"Maybe not, but there were extenuating circumstances. If there's... a problem, it's best we know."

Charlotte looked up, her face frozen.

"Remember I saw a man outside Corpus Christi College who vanished, and I thought I was seeing things? It was that man, Karl's friend Pierre."

"Are you sure?"

"Positive."

Before Anne could pursue the matter, David came running down the steps from the blue room and flung himself into a chair opposite, breathless.

"What happened, did you see anything?" said Anne.

"Let me get my breath back. Yes, I saw a damn sight more than I wanted to," David said grimly. "Look, Charli, it would really be best if I spoke to Anne alone."

"No," Anne said firmly. "She has a right to hear this, however difficult. It's about time you started treating Charlotte as an adult."

David pushed back his hair, sighed.

"I thought I did. Actually, I was trying to spare my own blushes, but – all right, then – I saw, er—" He cleared his throat. "I saw Karl in some sort of embrace with Pierre. Arms around him, his face in Pierre's neck. Don't know how to describe it, really."

"Are you suggesting something... homosexual?" said Anne. "Oh, don't look like that, I do know about these things!"

David frowned at her, then his expression cleared and he shook his head.

"I'm not that prudish. I feel I should pretend to be – that's Father's influence. Yes, it's possible, but it didn't look like affection, Anne. It's more usual for chaps to sock each other on the jaw in a fight, but what Karl was doing to Pierre looked positively nasty. Pierre stood there like this –" David held out his arms in a stiff posture "– and when Karl stopped, he'd drawn blood."

"What, out of Pierre's neck?" said Anne.

"That's how it looked. He practically had to carry Pierre out of the room afterwards."

"It's impossible!" cried Charlotte. "You must be mistaken, both of you!"

"No need to get worked up about it, sis," said David, apparently surprised at her reaction.

"Oh, David," said Anne, thinking, *Hasn't he guessed why she's upset?* Although she'd tactfully left out Pierre's comments about Karl kissing Charlotte, surely David must have an idea. "Let's try to be calm and rational, shall we?"

"None of this makes sense," he said. "It sounds as if Pierre has ill intentions towards us and so, by implication, does Karl. The question is, what kind of intentions? God, it doesn't bear thinking about. Suppose Maddy *was* attacked, and it was Pierre who attacked her?"

"There must be an explanation," Charlotte said helplessly. "Karl was trying to protect us from Pierre."

"And from the way it sounded, protect us so that he could do something unspeakable to us himself!" David stared at his fists, clenching and unclenching them. "Don't forget, Karl claims this madman as his friend. I don't pretend to understand what's going on, but until I do, I don't want any member of my family anywhere near Karl. God, I wish I'd taken Edward seriously!"

"I hope no one's going to say the word 'vampire'," Anne said drily. "Edward must have meant it as a metaphor for whatever he saw in Karl, but…"

Charlotte broke in. "When Edward made a scene at Maddy's party, you said it was because he was ill."

"So I thought," said David. "However, since then he's kept warning me against Karl, and he is a perceptive judge of people."

"But you're sitting there suggesting Karl is some sort of perverted maniac!" Charlotte said. "I don't believe it. He would never hurt anyone."

David looked gravely at Charlotte, as if he was wondering why she was defending Karl so vehemently. *Has the penny dropped at last?* Anne thought.

He said, "Anyway, they've both gone now."

"Gone?" Charlotte looked horrified. "Where?"

"I've no idea, old thing. I went after them but they disappeared over the horizon in Karl's motor. Anyone's guess if Karl even intends to come back."

"No, he must!" Charlotte said, stricken.

David leaned forward and patted her entwined hands.

"Charli, what is this? I couldn't believe the gossip about you and Karl, but I'm beginning to think... No one's angry with you, but you must tell the truth."

"What do you want me to say? I love him."

"Does Karl know?"

She nodded. "He feels the same for me."

David sat back with a sigh. "Oh, Lord," he murmured. "So that's why you gave Henry the elbow. It's got to stop, old girl, you see that, don't you? Perhaps this is a massive misunderstanding, but the point is that we don't know. We know nothing about him at all, really, do we? Father took him on trust. God knows what risks you were taking, spending time alone with him."

"But I've known him for ages. We work together. He's always been so kind... He would never do anything to hurt me!" Charlotte's voice was fierce, her eyes moist.

Anne looked at David and said, "Would you be a good sport and clear off for a while? I want to talk to Charli alone."

"Of course." He stood up, straightening his dinner jacket, looking solemnly at them. "You're the best one to sort this out. I'm going to have a word with Maddy, see if she recognised Pierre. And then I'm going to keep a look-out for von Wultendorf. If he dares to come back, I'm going to have this out, man to man."

"Do be careful," said Anne.

"I shan't do anything rash. The thing is to behave normally, pretend nothing's happened, and worm the truth out of him. If that fails, there's always the gun room."

"David!"

"Only joking. Look after my sister."

He kissed Anne's cheek and walked to the stone steps that led up into the house. When he'd gone, Anne drew her chair close to Charlotte's and put an arm around her shoulders.

"Goodness, you're shaking. I didn't realise how much this has upset you."

"Those terrible things you and David said... I don't believe them."

"It's not a matter of belief. We saw with our own eyes. Karl isn't what he seems, there's something dangerous in him."

Charlotte let out a single sob. Anne held her tighter.

"Oh, my dear, this must be awful for you. But look, if he *isn't* quite the gentleman he appears, isn't it lucky you found out before it's too late?"

Charlotte's head drooped. Her hair fell forward in a frosted-gold curve, hiding her face.

"It is too late."

"How? You don't mean..."

"I love him so desperately. I couldn't help myself."

"Oh my God," said Anne.

She was utterly shocked, and couldn't hide it. She prided herself on a modern outlook, and heaven knew, her relationship with David was not as virtuous as it should have been – but that was different, they were at least engaged. The truth was, she simply couldn't believe it of Charlotte. Not shy, naive Charlotte. Anne released a breath. Perhaps her naivety was her downfall.

"When did this happen?" she asked.

"After the musical evening," Charlotte said wretchedly. "And every night since. Swear you won't tell anyone, it would be the end of everything."

"I wouldn't dream of it. I assume there's no prospect of marriage or you wouldn't be in such a state..." Anne remembered the coldness in Karl's eyes, and shuddered. "Oh, Charli, how could you be so foolish? I never dreamed his intentions were so dishonourable!"

"It wasn't foolish! You don't know anything about it."

"I know," Anne said more gently. She drew Charlotte's head onto her shoulder, stroked her hair as the tears came. "Didn't I say, he's the sort of man who breaks everyone's hearts?"

Charlotte sat alone in her room, watching trees swaying against a slate sky. She was so cold that she'd stopped shivering and now sat numb, leaning against the windowpane without energy or inclination to warm herself. Rain drummed the glass like thousands of tiny fingernails.

Karl had not come back.

One moment she would think, *But he's bound to come to me, why shouldn't he? As far as he's concerned things are no different, he can't know what David saw – can he? He'll come back soon – then, oh Lord, what do I say to him? Do I ask him straight out what it means, or do I pretend nothing happened? Should I be afraid?*

The next moment, *He won't come back. I know he won't.* And the nervous leaping of her heart would swell into overwhelming despair.

She felt alienated. She was in disgrace with her father and aunt; Madeleine was lost in some dark world where Charlotte couldn't reach her. Only Anne knew the worst of it, and although sympathetic, she made no secret of her disapproval. David had already turned against Karl; how much worse, if he learned his guileless sister had willingly let herself be seduced...

But what does it matter what they think? They could never understand, not in a thousand years...

This was like the time she'd been feverish with flu and in dread of meeting Karl... she laughed without mirth. *Do I wish I'd never met him? No, oh no.* She felt swamped by the same heavy, nightmarish atmosphere. And again, she had a fevered illusion of fluid purple mountains in the sky. The clouds became tattered angels, ephemeral jet-black beings released from a netherworld to chase each other along the wind.

I'm going mad, thought Charlotte. *If Karl doesn't come to me, I shall go mad.*

The night swept on until she fell asleep where she sat, and still Karl did not return.

Once he'd disposed of Pierre in a remote stretch of countryside, Karl drove halfway back to Parkland Hall, left the car at the edge of a wood, and entered the Crystal Ring.

The trees around him warped and melted to crystal spines. A spiral of wind solidified, becoming a deep blue pathway that ascended through the tree tops to vast banks of bronze cloud. Karl began to climb. Everything changed: his body became dark and attenuated, cloaked with lacy webs too delicate and tattered to be called wings. He stretched his thin hard limbs and ran on all fours, like a hound.

One thing Kristian would not expect him to do was to go to the *Weisskalt* himself. He had never tried before. As far as he knew only Kristian had the power to go there without succumbing to frozen sleep; only he could return, or bring other vampires back with him. But Karl had no choice. He wouldn't give in to Kristian, and couldn't leave Ilona near death. The only answer was to rescue her himself.

The stolen warmth of Pierre's blood filled him with fire. He prayed it would be enough to sustain him. He felt no apprehension, only single-minded intent, swift and fierce as the flight of an arrow.

The hillside steepened. Karl was in a gully with walls rising ever higher around him like tidal waves of ink. He was falling. The Crystal Ring was in constant motion, and sometimes he had to run simply to stay in place. There were no maps of a region that was never still; only the map in a vampire's mind, and the gleaming lines of magnetism.

The Crystal Ring was vast, each layer greater than the last, like the rings of an onion. Where, on the outermost skin that kissed the stars, did Ilona lie?

A thermal caught him, bearing him like a magic carpet to a higher level. Glints of gold broke through the darkness. Karl felt like a wolf, running silent and alone through winter pine forests. The first breath of cold touched him.

As he ran, he had time to think.

He'd left Pierre seriously weakened. In that state, he would be starving, dangerous; wherever Karl left him, Pierre would feed. That was not Karl's concern. Pierre could do what he liked – as long as the Nevilles were not harmed.

Yet Karl couldn't forget Pierre's vicious words as he had bundled him out of the car.

"You think you can live two lives, human and vampire? You think you can live among them and not bring them any harm?"

"I can. I have," Karl had replied, soft as snow.

"You are fooling no one except yourself, my friend." The Frenchman's face had been stretched taut, his eyes huge and burning with starvation. "As soon as I am strong again, I shall return. I want them now."

His face had receded, like a lamp bobbing on water, as Karl drove away, but the words stayed with him, thin and piercing with hunger. "*I want them.*"

Karl had desired nothing from Dr Neville but knowledge. Why prey upon and destroy that source of knowledge when he could feed elsewhere, upon strangers in distant towns? It had seemed simple. It would have remained so, if not for Pierre's interference...

But no, he couldn't blame Pierre or even Kristian. By entering the Nevilles' household, by letting himself be captivated, Karl was the one who'd put them in danger. He had led Pierre to them. Madeleine was suffering already. Perhaps he would bring Kristian, too.

And then there was Charlotte...

Dear God, what am I doing to her? He'd drawn her into the vampiric circle of fascination, when true kindness would have been to leave her alone. She had an allure that obsessed him as no other human ever had. That was no excuse; it was selfishness. He'd known exactly what would happen if they came to love each other, yet he had let it happen anyway.

Every time they made love, the craving to feed on her blood – to possess her completely – grew harder to resist. Yet the more he resisted, the stronger his need became. She was in greater danger every time and remained unaware... And the tension between his desire, and knowledge that consummation would destroy her, was agony.

What kind of love is it, that can only destroy?

He should leave, while the damage could be limited to a broken heart. *She would forget me, eventually... and I should miss her forever. Everything Pierre said is true. If I stay, my nature will win.* Yet now he could not leave. He had to remain with the Nevilles to protect them from Pierre.

He laughed noiselessly as he ran, but the laugh died in a silent howl. He saw Charlotte dying in Pierre's embrace, or in his own. And if he managed to resist, and went on and on resisting... He saw Charlotte dying of old age, leaving only a memory to haunt Karl. An unseen hand on his arm, when he turned, no one there. He heard Heine's words in her clear voice… "This house she dwelt in, she I lov'd dear…" Then there would be only the ice-wind of an existence that went on forever.

Karl arrowed upwards. Mountains of violet quartz, glittering as they rolled through the firmament, bore him to their summit, and thence onto pale blue pathways to the next layer.

Ilona… Where are you? He stretched his senses wide, searching for the black-diamond coolness of another vampire. He felt nothing, but a thought came to him.

Germany.

Would not Kristian have taken the shortest route, climbing directly from Schloss Holdenstein into the Ring? Karl let the magnetic field draw him southwards, keeping his bearings like a bird. The lines rippled from blue to green to gold like an aurora.

A long way… the light grew pale. Mountains gave way to mare's-tail wisps. Coldness drenched him. Now he focused wholly on his journey through this clear, aching beauty, the lucent surfaces on which he struggled to gain height. Once or twice he lost his footing and fell in slow motion through the viscid atmosphere. No harm done, except the steady leaching of his strength.

He broke through a paper-thin layer of mist and saw a plateau rising under the blue-black vault of space. He was unprepared for the *Weisskalt*'s ineffable beauty: a vast ice cap gliding on a silent ocean of cloud. The stars were like flowers. In their light the plateau shone a luminous, eerie blue-white.

The temperature, far below freezing, entombed his limbs as he crawled onto the blinding-bright surface. At least the fabric of the *Weisskalt* seemed stable. Although as fragile as a snow-crust, it didn't flow or dissolve beneath him.

Karl's body burned and ached with cold. He felt leaden, but the shifting light filled his mind with brilliance, with unheard music. The wonder and the pain… *Is this God's joke on us?*

He sensed them now. They pricked his mind, like pieces of coal thrown into the snow, like a field of stars in negative. The sleeping vampires.

In the eerie whiteness he walked among them. *Liebe Gott.*

They were dead, weren't they? So small, like crumpled black sails. A wave of grief washed over him. Were they aware of anything? Pasted on the edge of eternity, did they still hunger for blood and life, and endure the slow passing of time?

God, if this is all we can hope for...

They all looked the same, yet he knew Ilona at once. She lay on the end of a neat row, slightly apart. Hers was a deceptive presence, like a glass sliver, invisible until light caught a blood-red flash from its edge. That was how her spirit felt to him: unseen but sharply embedded within him.

There were others, too, who'd been his friends, Andreas and Katerina not least among them. Karl would not look for them, couldn't bear it. He thought, *If I can do this for Ilona, could I not have saved you, Katti, Andrei?* Yet it was not that simple. He wasn't sure he even had strength enough for Ilona.

Her skin crackled with ice as he knelt and lifted her weightless form in his arms. She felt brittle, as if the pressure of his finger and thumb might break her. False wings folded around her. Her eyelids were closed in her unhuman face. Diabolically lovely. *What are we?*

He wept.

"Ilona," he murmured through his tears. He didn't know how to revive her. His own joints were stiffening and fatigue was clouding his mind. He stumbled, and felt white frost begin to cover him.

A surge of will forced him awake. Ilona... and Charlotte. Fighting paralysis, he crawled towards the path that led down to warmer layers, with Ilona clasped in one arm. He paused to bite his own wrist and sucked until blood began to flow.

He held the wound to her lips. After a few moments he felt her mouth tighten and her tongue working roughly against his skin.

She seemed to grow heavier in his arms. His head began throbbing from blood loss, and he had to pull his hand free, but it was enough, she was alive.

The cloud-ocean below, so chilly on the way up, now warmed him like a tropical lagoon.

"Kristian?" murmured Ilona, like a child half asleep. "Kristian... you came back. I knew you would."

"Ilona," Karl said softly.

She opened her eyes and stared.

"You!" she gasped.

Her hatred cut through him, as always. Every time like the first. Even here, even though he'd rescued her, her loathing surfaced by reflex. She began to struggle, although she was pitifully easy to hold.

"What the hell are you doing?" she said furiously. "Why couldn't you leave me alone?"

"Look around you," Karl said impassively. "Where do you think we are?"

"In the Crystal Ring. I know where I am!"

"And you wanted to remain near death rather than be saved by me?"

"Yes!" she hissed. "Damn you. Kristian would have come back for me, I know he would."

Fierce currents tugged at them. The cloudscape darkened. Against swollen hills, a black shape came flitting towards them.

"But he imprisoned you," Karl said, watching the shape. "That's how much he cares for you. Don't tell me you still love him, after this."

Ilona laughed harshly. "And am I expected to love you, for rescuing me? You can't win my love by putting me in debt."

The venom in her tone still hurt, even after all this time. He didn't reply. He gazed at the creature swooping straight towards them, a nightmare wraith.

Kristian.

Karl waited, holding Ilona to him.

The master vampire seemed surprised that Karl didn't flee. On a billow of iron-grey cloud they faced each other.

Kristian said in German, "I should destroy you for this, Karl."

"For saving someone we both love?" said Karl.

"You always think you can outwit me." Kristian's voice was low with fury. "How dare you take her from the *Weisskalt*? You could have frozen there before you could escape!"

"Your God must have favoured me," Karl said sardonically.

Kristian's anger deepened. "You almost killed yourself, and for nothing! I can take her and put her back in a moment!"

"What would be the point?" Karl felt unspeakably weary. "We could go on like this forever."

"So what do you suggest?"

"That you leave us both alone. Why is that so hard? You have power and you have your God, so why do you need us?"

"It's you who needs me, if you'd only acknowledge it," said Kristian. "Why should you escape retribution? Give her back."

"Ilona, have you nothing to say?" said Karl. "Are you really content to be a pawn between him and me? Don't you want to be free?"

Ilona came to life at his words and pulled away, her dark figure gleaming with red and purple fire, the lacy false-wings fluttering like a cloak.

"Don't talk to me about freedom!" she snapped at Karl. "What freedom did you give me? What choice? Love! There's no such thing! You make me sick, both of you."

Then she turned and raced away along a thunder-grey slope. The slope rolled and swallowed her into a glowing chasm.

Kristian started after her but Karl leapt and caught him. They tumbled through nothingness.

Karl fought hard, but he was drained and Kristian's strength was overwhelming. The other vampire's skin felt like snake-leather as he wound his arms around Karl, suffocating. Kristian's power flowed like a snowstorm. Karl lost his grip, all sensation left his limbs, and he felt the stabbing ache of fangs in his throat.

Whiteness spread through him. His eyes closed and he felt the heaviness of sleep, bone-biting cold, and beneath that, very distant, something nagging like a pebble to be noticed...

Ah, terror. That was it.

"So... you're leaving me to the *Weisskalt*, at last," Karl mumbled through stiffening lips. "Whom will you persecute after me? I never thought you'd admit defeat so easily."

The fangs came out of his neck like daggers, chased by a sickening uprush of pain.

"Defeat?" Kristian's face swam hideously in Karl's vision. "Ah no. You're mistaken. The game will continue a while yet, and the conditions are the same. You'll come to me in the end, one way or another."

Then Kristian dropped him.

As Karl fell, he entered a state of disorientation lasting moments or hours. He felt no impact, only gradually became aware of lying face down on damp soft ground, the scent of leaf mould thick in his nose.

Karl was on Earth again. He saw red fungi nestling under ferns, and a huge spider edged with light swinging between the fronds inches from his face. He stretched, staring at the whiteness of his hands against the soil, at his shirt cuffs and the dark sleeves of his coat. Human again – in appearance, at least.

He'd saved himself... simply by reminding Kristian that it was a psychological victory he needed, not a physical one.

With difficulty he pulled himself onto his knees. He was horrifyingly weak. Thirst possessed him, throbbing like a heartbeat. Dawn glimmered through woodland, and a hundred yards away he saw the glint of a sleek burgundy car.

Despite Kristian flinging him carelessly away, Karl's subconscious had guided him to the right place. He couldn't return to Parkland Hall with this desperate hunger on him, but if he could reach the car...

Leaning on a tree, he hauled himself to his feet and shook leaves from his coat. Some creature was leaping through the undergrowth. A dog. In a flash of black and white, it bounded towards him, then stopped dead, barking hysterically.

Animal blood was no use. He looked up, saw a human standing by the Hispano-Suiza, the dog's owner, presumably. Karl reached down, let the dog catch his sleeve in its teeth, ran his other hand over its forehead. The beast fell quiet and lay down at his feet.

Karl stepped over it and walked between the trees, his sight shimmering. The man looked like a gamekeeper, dressed in rough tweeds, a rifle under his arm. His face was ruddy and weather-beaten.

"Don't mind Sammy, sir," said the man. "He only bites poachers. Sam, come here!" The dog ignored the command. "Don't know what's got into him. This your motor car, sir?"

"Yes," said Karl. A red aroma of heat flowed from the gamekeeper in waves. Karl could think of nothing else. He moved closer to the man, wholly caught in the enticing net of warmth.

"Odd place to park. Can't imagine anyone abandoning such a beauty…" The man turned, found Karl leaning over him, and started backwards. "You all right, sir?"

He must have looked horrifying to the gamekeeper. A bloodless, mindless creature, rising from a grave in the mists of dawn. But the man had little time to reflect on this before Karl struck.

A brief scent of tweed and sweat, then the flesh broke and blood flowed into his open mouth. The relief was so acute that he almost cried out. Heat to thaw the ice, glittering rain on parched earth. And life. Rich sensual energy filling every cell.

As the flow slackened, he came back to himself, let the man slide out of his hands to the ground. Karl had drunk him dry. He hadn't killed outright for years; a wave of disgust went through him. He'd been unable to stop, and even now the thirst was not fully assuaged.

It could take days, even weeks, to recover from Kristian's attack. Until then he would be too weak to enter the Crystal Ring, so he was effectively trapped on Earth. The thought was uncomfortable.

He dragged the stocky body into the undergrowth. The dog watched, drooling, all instinct to defend its master gone. Karl glanced back, then climbed into the car, taking his trilby hat from the passenger seat and pulling it low over his eyes.

Given a choice, he would have driven to the nearest port and taken a ferry to the Continent. But he dared not leave the Nevilles, in case Pierre came back. And there was Charlotte… How would she feel if he simply left without explanation?

Yet it would be better, in the end. *If I don't leave her…*

Karl started the engine and steered the car onto the rain-damp lane.

He knew Anne and David had witnessed some strange things. Awkward, but he could form a plausible explanation. As a rule, vampires could make humans believe anything. Perhaps, if he salvaged the situation, he could continue his studies in Cambridge as if nothing had happened.

Until Kristian's patience ran out again.

The thought depressed him. He felt exhausted, as if no amount of blood could revive him. Perhaps he should feed again, but the prospect held no allure. Charlotte was a shimmering presence in his mind. He wanted to see her, wanted no one else.

When Karl brought the car to a halt on the gravel half-moon in front of Parkland Hall, David Neville was standing in the portico. He raised a hand in greeting, but his open, honest face was serious, and his attempt to act casually was unconvincing. *But let us play the game*, thought Karl as he stepped from the car.

"Good morning, David."

"Morning!" David replied. "We thought you'd gone for good, old man. Where on earth have you been? My aunt's been worried."

Karl smiled. "My friend had to return to London so I offered to drive him. I'm sorry to have caused any anxiety. In view of his excitable state of mind, I thought it wise to take him off the premises as quickly as possible."

"Well, I suppose you did the right thing." David stood looking at him. "Must have been dashed embarrassing for you…"

"Quite."

Karl began to move towards the house, but David stopped him.

"I know you must be tired, but I've a favour to ask."

"Of course. Anything."

"Well, you know that Anne and I are having the old manor house renovated. I have some decisions to make and I'd appreciate someone casting an objective eye over the place. Would you mind coming up there to take a look?"

"David, if you have something to say about last night, there's no need for a pretext. I am quite happy to talk about it."

David looked startled, but Karl's apparent openness disarmed him.

"Well – I did have in mind to mention it, but I'm on my way to see the workmen now and I'd appreciate your company. Chance to talk in private, clear up one or two things."

In other words, you don't want me back in the Hall.

"In that case, I shall be delighted to come with you," Karl said graciously. He moved towards the portico. "However, I have had a long drive, so if you'd excuse me for a few minutes…"

David looked unhappy about him entering the mansion, but there was nothing he could say without seeming ill mannered. *Oh, this English etiquette.*

"I'll wait for you," David said ominously, leaning on the side of the Hispano-Suiza, hands in his coat pockets.

"I shall not be long," said Karl. *How fiercely you love your family, David*, he thought. *Mistrust is written all over you. Strange that you can be so wrong about me... and yet, so right.*

CHAPTER NINE

INTO THE DARKEST HEART

Charlotte stared at her reflection in the mirror: eyes rimmed with tired shadow, lips too dark against her drained skin. She pressed powder on her cheeks in the hope of disguising her paleness, but she felt desolate.

Over her slip and stockings she put on a beige dress sashed across her hips, a long matching sweater, a rope of pearls. She brushed her hair until it was a crackling mass of gold around her shoulders, then did her best to smooth the ripples, pinning them at the nape of her neck and trying to tame the wisps that escaped around her forehead and ears. She was shocked to see how normal she looked. No outward sign of turmoil, no marks of shame. She felt fragile, though, as if the slightest blow would shatter her.

Taking a deep breath she left the room, went along the corridor and knocked on Madeleine's door. She expected to find her sister still in bed, but she was at her dressing table, half dressed, brushing her bobbed hair with vigour.

"How are you?" Charlotte asked gently.

"I'm perfectly well, thank you." She sounded surprised. "Why shouldn't I be?"

"You were so pale and quiet last night, after that man broke in…"

"He didn't break in. Karl let him in," Madeleine said briskly.

Charlotte cautiously went nearer, feeling a mixture of protective tenderness and guilt.

"Had you seen Pierre before? On that evening you fainted in the garden?"

Madeleine put down the hairbrush and exhaled. Her forced brightness could not mask the gloom in her eyes.

"I don't know, Charli. Perhaps... but I had such awful dreams afterwards. Everything's muddled. David would go on about it, but I couldn't tell him anything. Don't you start."

"You ought to stay in bed," said Charlotte. "Perhaps see the doctor again."

"No."

She shut Charlotte out, wouldn't be helped. In that, they were more alike than Charlotte had ever realised.

"I only feel ill if people make a fuss. I'm quite all right and I don't want Karl thinking otherwise." She turned and clutched Charlotte's right forearm with both hands, seemingly oblivious to the rumours about her sister and Karl. "He'll come back this morning."

"What if he doesn't?"

"He must." Madeleine's eyes were feverish.

She looks obsessed, Charlotte thought with alarm. *Like me?*

"And as soon as he does, I'll let him declare his feelings. He's been such a gentleman, hiding his affection for me, so as not to upset Father. It's time for the world to know!"

Dismay weighted Charlotte's heart. "Oh, Maddy, I don't think you should."

"What do you know about it, Charli?" Madeleine retorted. "You've never been in love."

By the end of breakfast, Elizabeth was not in the best of moods. Her whole family was out of sorts, and it all came back to Karl. Beautiful Karl, who caused such trouble and then walked away smiling as if butter wouldn't melt in his mouth. Not that she could be angry with him. On the contrary, an affair would not have gone amiss, if only he'd been responsive. Since he was not, she thanked God she was too worldly-wise to lose her head over him. But these young girls, how they suffered.

At least she'd quashed the flirtation between him and Charlotte... If there'd been anything to it in the first place, which, on reflection, she doubted. Just a brief, gauche infatuation on Charlotte's part, she suspected, and Karl too polite to reject her. *If he's indifferent to* me, Elizabeth thought, *he must prefer his own sex.* The problem now was to make poor Maddy accept that he had no interest in her, either.

Crossing the upper hall, Elizabeth was startled to see Karl walking up the long red staircase from the front door. She'd never doubted he would return, yet the sight of him arrested her. The graceful way he ascended the steps, peeling off his driving gloves; the way his expressive gaze met hers.

He said, "Good morning, Lady Reynolds. Please accept my apologies for last night. I shall explain later but I'm in a hurry and I need to see Charlotte."

She stiffened. Why would he want to see *Charlotte*?

"Surely I could be of more help to you, my dear?"

"Not in this instance."

She fished for an acceptable explanation. "Ah, scientific business?"

He didn't answer. His manner was courteous, but his eyes hardened perceptibly.

"Where may I find her?"

She meant to challenge him further, instead found herself replying, "In the orangery." He thanked her, walking away before she gathered her wits enough to wonder what had compelled her to tell him.

Elizabeth waited a few moments, then followed. Hearing conversation in the blue drawing room, she paused, recognising Madeleine's voice. A minute later, Maddy ran out into the corridor, white-faced and blind with tears.

Elizabeth caught hold of her.

"Maddy, what is it?"

"Oh, Auntie, Karl – Karl – I tried to talk to him but he said –"

"Hush, dear." Elizabeth gently pulled her niece back into the blue room. "Tell me later. There's something odd going on."

Through the glass doors, they looked down into the orangery. Charlotte was sitting alone, a newspaper lying unread on her knee. Karl was on his way towards her. As he crossed the tiled floor, she looked up and came to life. Her face transformed, she leapt out of the chair and all but threw herself at him. Karl received her in his arms and held her tight.

Madeleine made a faint, disbelieving noise in her throat.

"Not a sound," whispered Elizabeth. Her lips thinning, she moved through the doorway to the top of the stone steps, keeping Madeleine firmly at her side. They watched from above, concealed by foliage. If Karl and Charlotte knew they were being spied upon, they showed no sign.

"I waited for you all night," said Charlotte. "I thought you weren't coming back."

"I'm so sorry, beloved, but I had to take Pierre away."

"Everyone was saying awful things last night. I didn't know what to think."

"It's easy for people to misinterpret events they don't understand," Karl said gently. "I regret causing you anxiety. Unfortunately, I've offended Madeleine too, quite without intention."

"How?"

"I can't explain now, I've promised to go to the manor house with David and he's waiting for me."

"It's an excuse to ask you about last night," she said.

"I know. So the sooner I set his mind at rest, the better."

"Could I come with you?"

"It's best if you don't."

"But Father and I are driving back to Cambridge this morning. What if we're gone before you come back? He's so angry about Henry, I'm afraid he won't let you work with us any more."

"Charlotte, don't worry." Karl stroked her cheek with a tenderness that gave Elizabeth an unexpected pang. "I hate to see you distressed. Believe me, I am coming back. Here, and to Cambridge."

Then he bent and kissed her mouth. Charlotte responded, not with surprise, but with sensual eagerness. His hand cradled her head and she pressed herself against him, no stranger to his touch. A long, deep kiss between two people who knew each other far more intimately than anyone had guessed; two people who had recently become lovers.

It took a lot to shock Elizabeth. If this had been Fleur or

Madeleine she would simply have taken them to one side and given some stern advice. However, seeing Charlotte in Karl's arms roused her to disproportionate wrath. Charlotte was a creature she'd never been able to control. She despised the girl's timid bookishness, almost feared the strange, stubborn soul that lay beneath: closed away by shyness yet wayward, unmalleable. The only consolation was that she lacked the spirit – so Elizabeth thought – to break out of her narrow life. Now to see her stepping so wildly out of line filled Elizabeth with resentment, the desire to crush her completely.

Elizabeth felt Madeleine's body stiffen and tremble. Karl drew away reluctantly from Charlotte, kissing her hand as he left. As he came lightly up the steps, he showed no surprise at seeing Elizabeth and only glanced at her in passing: an insouciant look, cold. He walked on without a word.

"Karl?" Madeleine started after him, but Elizabeth held her back.

"Hush, dear." She guided Maddy back into the blue room. "This is a shock to me too, but let's be calm. I'm sorry you had to find out like this, but you wouldn't have believed me unless you'd seen with your own eyes. I certainly didn't."

"He can't love Charlotte!" Madeleine was fierce with grief. "I – I tried to talk to him, but he said he doesn't love me, he *couldn't* court me because he was in no position to get married. Not to *anyone*."

"Did he, indeed?" Elizabeth said grimly, hugging her.

"Was he lying to me or to her?"

Charlotte was on her way up the orangery steps. Entering the drawing room, she saw Elizabeth and stopped, turning rose red. Before Elizabeth could say anything, Madeleine marched up to her sister and slapped her hard across the face.

"You viper!"

Charlotte reeled away, her eyes filling with water.

"What was that for?" she gasped.

"Karl is mine, not yours! How dare you try to take him from me! You *traitor*!"

Charlotte looked so devastated that Elizabeth almost felt sorry for her. Yet she didn't defend herself, which made Elizabeth want to slide the knife in.

With an arm around Madeleine to quieten her, she said coolly, "Maddy, you've behaved with great dignity so far; don't spoil it. Remember you're blameless in this. Well, Charlotte, should we congratulate you?"

"Why?"

"Well, obviously the only correct thing for Karl to do is marry you, so has he proposed?"

Charlotte was wild-eyed, impaled by her aunt's cruel perceptiveness. Her mouth opened but no answer emerged.

Heavens above, she hasn't even the guile to bluff it out. "No," Elizabeth went on. "Apparently – so he informs Madeleine – he cannot. Did he lie to you, make false promises?"

"No!" A touch of spirit at last. "He told me he can't marry. He wouldn't say why – but he never lied to me."

"Well, how noble of him," Elizabeth said witheringly. "He probably already has a wife, you little fool! No decent girl allows herself to be made love to until she has a ring on her finger; certainly not to discard all her morals like some kitchen slut. Haven't you listened to a thing I've told you? It's fun skating on thin ice but you never, ever, let yourself fall through the cracks."

In a tone of absolute horror, Madeleine said, "Auntie, they can't have... not *that*..."

"Sadly, I've been around too long not to recognise the signs. She's not denying it, is she? Oh, you little fool! Did you stop for one second to consider the possible consequences?"

Charlotte stared, one hand pressed to the red mark on her cheek.

"You've no right to speak to me like this. You know nothing about it."

Elizabeth raised her eyebrows. "I believe I know enough and I shall consider how much to tell your father – if we're to salvage what's left of your life."

Charlotte went sickly white at this threat.

"What have I ever done to you, Auntie? Why am I not allowed to fall in love?" She looked at her sister. "I wouldn't have hurt Maddy for the world, but –"

"I'll never forgive you for this," said Madeleine, her eyes glittering. "Never."

Charlotte's face was rigid as she walked out of the room.

"That's it, run away," Elizabeth called after her. "Your answer to everything." But she thought, *This time I've broken her. At last!* This gave her the means to crush Charlotte to the absolute depths of torment and shame. Once she was at her most wretched, that would be the time for Elizabeth to become the loving, forgiving aunt... and to re-form her niece in a more conventional shape.

Charlotte walked along the corridor into the upper hall, too stricken to weep. The gilded mirrors, paintings and gleaming furniture, all looked sharp and unreal. She had only ever wanted to love, and be loved by, her family; instead they apparently hated her. She'd hurt Madeleine and in any case, neither of them would be allowed to see Karl again. *All my fault.* Talons of fear and misery tore her heart.

"Charlotte?" Anne put out a hand and stopped her. Charlotte hadn't even noticed her. "Karl's back, did you know?"

"Yes, I've seen him," she responded tonelessly.

"Has he upset you? You look awful."

"No, but Elizabeth saw us together and she guessed... what I told you last night."

"Oh, lord," Anne breathed in dismay. "It might have been prudent to deny it."

"I'm no use at lying. The worst thing is that Maddy was there too – the things Elizabeth said in front of her... I can't bear this."

"What did Karl say?"

"Only that he'll explain later, and that he intends to stay in Cambridge."

Anne sighed. "It's not likely, after David's confronted him. He'll have to ask Karl to leave."

"He has no right!"

"But if Elizabeth tells David and your father what she knows, it will be ten times worse."

Charlotte appreciated Anne's bluntness, but their friendship was like driftwood in the ocean. She clung to it, but it wouldn't save her.

Anne went on, "You can't see Karl clearly. He's untrustworthy: he attacked his own friend. Either that, or they were kissing –

you decide which is worse. He seduced you, for heaven's sake! Whatever you say, it was very wrong of him. You must be realistic. What if you found you were pregnant?"

"Then Aunt Lizzie would take me on a quiet trip to Paris and Father would lock me up for the rest of my life," Charlotte said bitterly. "Please don't lecture me about being realistic. The things that have been going through my mind, you wouldn't believe."

"I'm on your side, you know," Anne said quietly. "Elizabeth's being downright cruel to you. It's unforgivable."

The front doorbell rang as she spoke. There were faint sounds from the lower hall: doors opening, voices.

Charlotte touched her arm. "I'm sorry, Anne. If you weren't here I don't know what I'd do. I've disgraced myself... and I'm losing Karl. I remember I once said I'd kill him if he broke Maddy's heart. Now I think I should kill myself."

"Don't you dare talk like that –" Anne began.

A voice interrupted.

"I wish you would!" Madeleine came marching towards them. "Oh yes, cry on Anne's shoulder, as if *you* were the one who's been wronged. If you're miserable you deserve it, you little – *whore*!"

Charlotte was beyond reacting, but Anne looked outraged.

"Maddy, for heaven's sake. There's no call for that sort of language. I think you should consider yourself lucky that Karl wasn't interested in you. Don't you?"

Maddy started as if Anne had thrown cold water in her face. There were footsteps on the stairs, an uneven thudding muffled by the carpet. Newland was bringing a guest to the upper hall. In a swift, mutual transformation, Madeleine dried her eyes and tucked her handkerchief into her sleeve, while Charlotte also swallowed her misery. By the time Newland reached them, the three women presented a tenuous front of normality.

The visitor was Edward Lees. His grey suit hung on him, emphasising his thin frame. Leaning on his walking stick, he stopped and smiled. The smile did not quite erase his anxious expression.

"Mr Edward Lees to see Mr Neville," Newland said solemnly. "I shall inform Lady Reynolds of your arrival, sir."

"It's all right, we'll look after him," said Anne. The butler

172

nodded and withdrew. "Edward! This is a surprise! Is David expecting you? He never said."

"Hello, Anne." Edward shook hands and greeted each of them in turn, his gaze lingering on Maddy. The distraction of his arrival was a relief. "No, David doesn't know, and I'm most awfully sorry for turning up without notice."

"Don't be silly, you know you're welcome here, day or night," said Anne. "Besides, you virtually work here."

"Well, that's just it," said Edward, smoothing his mousy hair. "I've been lazing at home quite long enough. This morning I woke up with an extraordinary feeling that David needed me and I thought right, that's it, no more of this convalescent nonsense. Time to pull myself together and start work."

"Oh, that's marvellous news, as long as you're well enough. David will be thrilled."

"Is he around?"

"Not at the moment," Anne replied. "He's gone up to the manor with Karl. I'm sure they won't be long."

At this his fragile smile wavered. "Is he alone with Karl?"

"Well, I presume so, but they'll be back soon. Do come and have some tea." She glanced at Charlotte and added, "We all need it."

Edward hesitated. He stared down at the front door.

"Actually, if it's all the same to you, I'd rather go and make sure David's all right."

"Why shouldn't he be?" said Charlotte.

Edward cleared his throat. His head twitched nervously.

"I know you're all being polite in not mentioning it, and I know everyone thinks I'm crackers – but I can't shake off this bad feeling about Karl. Maybe that's why I'm here." Edward moved towards the top of the stairs as he spoke. "I hope I'm wrong – but if anything happened to David, I'd never forgive myself. If you'll excuse me…"

His stick slipped on the top tread and he almost lost his balance. Anne caught his elbow.

"Edward, I'm sure everything's all right. But we'll go with you, if it will set your mind at rest."

Anne was clearly alarmed by Edward's state of mind. She gave Charlotte a meaningful look, implying, *"We'd better humour him."*

"I'm coming too," said Charlotte.

"So am I!" Madeleine, suddenly combative, ran down the stairs ahead of them.

Without pausing for coats, they hurried out to Edward's car, a small, boxy Austin Seven with a canvas roof. As he cranked the engine into life, Anne climbed into the front seat, Charlotte and her sister into the back. Maddy was visibly composing herself, squaring her shoulders and tidying her hair, a warlike gleam in her eye.

I wish I had her spirit, Charlotte thought as Edward swung the car onto the narrow farm track that led to the manor house. *Gods, what am I going to do?* Then, *Poor Edward... but what if he's right?* Memories of the awful things David and Anne had said last night... *No, don't be ridiculous. How could Karl be any danger to David? Whatever's happened, I know he's a gentle, good soul. I refuse to believe any of it!*

In the entrance hall of the manor house, a fire blazed in the grate and estate workmen could be heard talking over the sound of hammers and saws from the kitchen. It was good to have some life in the place, David thought, but the cheerful sounds didn't seem to reach the vaulted ceiling. The stairs and landing had a grey, brooding look.

"Mornin', Captain Neville, sir." The foreman, a tall good-natured man of about forty, leaned through a doorway and touched his cap. "If you need us for anything, just give us a shout." He disappeared into the kitchen again.

"They're doing well with the plumbing," said David. "We have a bathroom and running water – and not only down the walls." His gaze travelled up the stairs; no workmen up there, so they wouldn't be overheard. "Let's look upstairs first."

"As you wish," said the dark, elegant figure at his side. David was no stranger to difficult situations, yet for some reason the prospect of this conversation made him nervous. Best to get it over with.

As they climbed the long sweep of stairs, David said, "I'll come straight to the point, if you don't mind."

"Of course not." Karl smiled, inclining his head. "I appreciate directness."

"Well, it strikes me you've been taking rather more than a friendly interest in Charlotte. If you have sisters of your own you'll understand the responsibilities a brother feels. This is nothing personal, but you appreciate it's my duty to establish the truth."

"Naturally," said Karl, his eyebrows lifting slightly.

"Perhaps I've got the wrong impression, but I don't think so." Karl said nothing. "I must warn you, our father is very old fashioned about these things and I rather take after him. Casual affairs may be all the rage elsewhere – but not in this family."

"I assure you, my regard for Charlotte is anything but casual," said Karl.

Good God, thought David, *I was so sure he'd deny it.*

"She, ahm – claimed you were in love with each other. Are you admitting it?" he asked.

"I should not like to lie to you, David. I hold her in great affection and esteem. Sadly for both of us, there is no future for our love – so there would be no point in asking your father's permission to court her. She is aware of this."

David was taken aback by the candour of this reply.

"In that case, there is all the more reason to leave her alone," he said.

"I agree with you," said Karl, but his face was unreadable.

"I'm glad to hear it," David said with a touch of belligerence. "You know, the poor girl broke her engagement because of you. It's caused a great deal of disruption in my family. A man might almost read some kind of mischievous intent into it. I hope I'm wrong."

Karl moved along the landing and leaned on the balustrade.

Calmly he said, "I am very fond of all your family and it saddens me that you think I could wish them any harm. Perhaps you would explain why you have this idea."

David hesitated, battling an irrational feeling that it would be very dangerous to tell the truth. He was used to dealing with people in a straightforward way and this eggshell dance disconcerted him.

"Very well," he said at last. "I'll come clean. I overheard part of a conversation between you and your friend Pierre last night." He didn't intend to implicate Anne. "I didn't mean to, I just happened to be on the terrace while you were in the library…"

"Ah." A slight shadow touched Karl's face. "What do you think you heard?"

"Enough to convince me that your friend Pierre is not the most pleasant of fellows."

"To be honest with you, he is not. Yet he is my friend." Karl gazed up at the beamed vault. "As I said, Pierre is rather like your friend Edward: he appears normal enough, but he can be… unstable. Sometimes he has to be protected from himself."

David was offended at the comparison between Edward and the obnoxious stranger, but tried to repress it.

"Unstable in that he might actually become violent?" he asked.

"It has been known," Karl answered, giving David a long sideways glance. "That was why I took him away."

David said gravely, "There's no chance, is there, that Madeleine's 'illness' was due to her being attacked or frightened by Pierre?"

"That happened days before Pierre arrived."

"But didn't you imply that he was responsible?"

Karl looked straight at him with eyes like embers; dark and cold, yet glowing. It was the first time David had noticed how compelling his eyes were.

"You must have listened for quite some time."

"Long enough to see that you have a damned strange way of dealing with your friend. Apparently by trying to tear his throat out."

"I don't know how you may have misinterpreted what you saw and heard, but I can assure you there was nothing sinister in it. Pierre was distressed over a private matter, hence his erratic behaviour. Surely you realise that old friends develop a way of communicating that makes no sense to outsiders? It must be the same for army men." And still those eyes were on him, gleaming from the marble-pale face.

"Yes, of course, but –"

"You would not expect me to explain my private business with an old acquaintance – unless, of course, my word is not good enough for you."

This sounded perfectly reasonable to David. In fact, he was

beginning to doubt what he *had* seen. *Must've got my wires crossed somewhere...*

"Of course I accept your word, Karl, one gentleman to another. You have me at a disadvantage because I shouldn't have witnessed a private conversation. I apologise for that – on condition that you consider your relationship with Charlotte at an end."

"No need to apologise," Karl said politely. "And if you feel honour would be satisfied by knocking me downstairs, I shall understand."

David smiled uneasily. "I'm sure we can sort this out in a civilised way. You'll appreciate that it may be for the best if you don't go back to Cambridge."

"That rather depends on Dr Neville," said Karl, his voice razor-edged. And he gazed not so much at David as through him, as if he knew that David had no power over him. Not mocking, but something worse: not even caring. Preoccupied. And David knew he was lying, that *something* was going on, yet he felt powerless to unearth the truth.

There was a red glint in Karl's irises, a reflection of the hall fire, but it gave him a deathly malevolent look. *Surely he wasn't so pale when we came in...* Karl never had much colour, but now his face was less human flesh than alabaster. He gave off an eerie, hungry glow.

And suddenly he said very softly, "David, if I were you, I should leave here now."

Karl's hands tightened on the rail, his knuckles shone through the skin.

"Anything wrong?" David said, disconcerted.

"I am more tired than I realised, that's all." Karl turned, came towards him. David took an involuntary step backwards, and pressed himself against the balustrade. Since the War he had feared nothing, so why was he sweating?

The front door creaked open and watery daylight spilled across the hall below them. Karl halted, unnaturally still save for the slow smooth turn of his head as he looked down.

"David?" a voice called. "It's me. Thank God..."

David recognised the thin figure silhouetted in the doorway.

"Edward!" he called, surprised but strangely relieved. "This is unexpected. What brings you here?"

Edward answered hesitantly, "Just come to, er – make sure you're all right, old man…"

Anne, Charlotte and Madeleine came into the hall after him. Odd, despite the autumn chill, none of them were wearing coats.

"Don't come up, we're on our way down," said David.

As he spoke, he saw Edward's gaze shift sideways to Karl. Edward tensed visibly. He seemed to struggle between growing panic and the instinct to behave correctly. David recognised the onset of a nervous attack and he willed Edward to control himself, thinking, *Keep a grip, old friend. Don't let it happen again.*

Karl went straight past David, as if glad of this opportunity to leave.

"If you will excuse me," he murmured.

As he started down the stairs, Edward's eyes turned wild with horror.

Edward, no, David thought in alarm. *Control it, for God's sake!*

But the change was too swift to be prevented. Before David could move, Edward was shouting hoarsely.

"Keep away from him, David! He's evil, can't you *see*? Get out of here!"

Karl stopped, halfway down the stairs.

Rather than fleeing the house as David expected, Edward started forward across the hall. He came limping and stumbling up the stairs with his walking stick held like a fixed bayonet.

"Run, David! I'll hold him! For Christ's sake, *run*!"

"Edward, no!" David yelled. He started towards the stairs, but too late to intervene. Edward hurled himself upwards and thrust the stick hard into Karl's stomach.

David's own gut tightened in sympathy – yet Karl didn't flinch. Instead he clasped the stick in both hands, turned it aside, then used it to drag Edward towards him. Edward seemed unable to let go. David couldn't see Karl's face, he could only see his friend's expression collapsing from battle frenzy into abject terror as the Austrian's hands shot out and closed on his shoulders.

Karl's strength looked too swift, too effortless to be human.

It happened so fast. David could only stand and stare. Afterwards, the words went through his mind over and over again. *I should have stopped them but it happened so fast!*

With Edward in his grip Karl turned a little, so David could see him from the side. His face was bone pale, his expression blank, demonic. His iris was an arc of scarlet fire. Then, most horrible, his mouth opened and David stared in utter disbelief as the canines visibly *grew* into fangs. Less than a second, it took. Then Karl lunged and sank those vicious ivory wolf-teeth into Edward's neck.

Edward gave a strangled, bubbling cry. A line of blood spurted out. Karl's lips moved to stem the escaping flow, and he clutched Edward to him with ghastly intent. A feasting panther. *Monstrous.*

David glimpsed the girls down in the hall. Anne was clutching Charlotte. He knew from their expressions that they'd seen everything. Madeleine had her eyes tightly closed.

David's paralysis broke and he sprinted downstairs.

"What the hell? Let him go!" he shouted, striking Karl on the shoulder. It was like striking a marble column. Karl's arm shot out and sent him sprawling down the stairs on his stomach.

David scrabbled madly to save himself and ended up on the hall floor, bruised and winded. Something fell against him, warm and heavy. A body.

Edward.

A moment passed before David could clear his head, then he felt hands on his arms. He looked up into the shocked faces of Anne and Charlotte.

As they helped him to his feet the hall was suddenly full of people. The workmen had rushed out to see what the commotion was and they were crowding around him. Madeleine stood a couple of feet away, her eyes shut tight as if to squeeze the sight from her mind.

"Stay back! I'm all right," David barked, and they all jumped away from him.

Edward lay crumpled on the bottom stair. Blood stained his jacket lapels, and his throat was a purple-red mess, with two ragged wounds glistening in the gore. With a groan of disgust – not at the blood, but at what Karl had done – David bent down and tried to find his pulse. Nothing.

A fist of grief punched through him.

He stood up and cried, "Someone get him to a doctor! Quickly!"

He looked up. Karl von Wultendorf had vanished, but the workmen were rushing by on either side of him.

"He's nipped in one o' the bedrooms, sir," said the foreman as he dashed up towards the landing.

David started after him, shouting, "Be careful, he's dangerous."

He glanced back, saw Anne and Charlotte bending over Edward, Maddy staring at them unmoving.

He thanked God that the estate men had acted so quickly, at least. They'd trapped Karl in a room with a window too small for escape – if he'd chosen to throw himself from the upper storey. David found the foreman and three others just inside the door. The Austrian was at bay in the centre of the stone-walled room, facing them. The air was consumptive with dust and damp, the light cobweb grey.

As long as he lived, David would never forget the look on von Wultendorf's face. There was nothing demonic about it. He looked so damned *tranquil*. His skin was softly coloured now – with Edward's blood? Almost expressionless, just a minimal curve of the lips that was not quite a smile. But his eyes! One moment they seemed sad, the next full of sleepy contentment, then coldly ruthless. Yet they never changed. The varying impressions were in David's mind – Karl's true thoughts remained hidden.

"Give the word, sir, and we'll rush him," said the foreman. No one moved.

David shouldered through them, so angry he could hardly find his voice.

"Well, you've revealed yourself for what you are, von Wultendorf. If Edward's dead, I'll swing for you! Now you can give yourself up quietly, because there's nowhere you're going except straight to the police station."

Karl held up his palms, a gesture of supplication.

"I cannot express my regret for what has happened," he said in a low voice. "But I must warn you that it would be dangerous to try to detain me."

"You have the effrontery to threaten us, after what you've done?"

"I'm telling you that I don't wish to hurt anyone, but if you try to prevent me leaving, I will. I know you to be a man of high courage, David, which is why I rather doubt you will heed my warning. But I wish you would."

"Bloody nerve!" said David under his breath. "So, you refuse to give yourself up?"

"I have no intention of doing so."

"Right." He heard movement behind him, glanced round to see a short, heavily built worker come panting across the landing with several lengths of lead piping. "Oh, good man!"

As the man distributed the makeshift weapons, David whispered, "We'll spread out and surround him. Only go carefully, he's damned strong."

"It will do you no good," said Karl, as if he had heard. "I implore you not to. You cannot win."

"We'll see about that." Six men began to move across the uneven wood floor towards von Wultendorf, who, disconcertingly, resembled a statue.

"What's going on?" said a female voice from the landing. Madeleine. David ignored her, willing her to go away. Then, louder, "What on earth do you all think you're doing?"

The men halted in their tracks. David glanced round, cursing. Madeleine stood in the doorway, arms folded, cheeks red with anger. She must have seen Karl attack Edward, yet she was behaving as if it hadn't happened – or as if she couldn't accept it.

"Maddy, please keep out of the way," David said firmly.

"This is ridiculous!" she exclaimed. "Leave Karl alone, you've no right."

"Maddy!"

In advancing on Karl, the men had left the doorway clear. To everyone's astonishment, she simply walked straight between them and went to Karl's side. There she stood, facing them indignantly.

"This is barbaric!" she cried. "Put those pipes down and let's sort out this misunderstanding."

David froze. It was like watching someone touching a match to spilled petrol. Karl looked at Madeleine. Then, with that same awful intensity in his face, his hand flashed out and seized her wrist.

She gasped with pain. "Karl, you're hurting me," she exclaimed, trying to ease his grip. When she couldn't, she looked into his eyes and her indignation dissolved into confusion.

"Now," said Karl, with the same incongruous politeness, "perhaps you will listen to me. I have no wish to harm anyone. Nothing will happen to Madeleine, as long as you do as I say. Everyone must leave the house. I shall remain here, with her as my hostage to ensure against any further attack."

"What?" David said furiously.

"I can't tell you how much I regret this. But I must be left alone."

He held up Madeleine's bird-thin wrist in his hand, to emphasise the point. The grip seemed to immobilise her.

"Karl?" she said.

David saw the revelation strike her as the horror sank in at last, as she was finally forced to see Karl for what he was. Her face fell with terror, as had Edward's, and she began to struggle like a dying bird.

"Karl, let me go," she cried, breathless with fear. Then, when he did not respond, "David, help me!"

Charlotte helped Anne to carry Edward to his car, and somehow got him into the rear seat while Anne cranked the engine. He felt so heavy, lifeless. She sobbed unconsciously as she arranged his limbs, while images seared her mind: Karl on the stairs, his eyes like fire through rubies as Edward rushed him; Karl seizing Edward, ferociously tearing into his throat, sucking his blood then throwing him aside like a doll. Pushing David down stairs – *God, no, impossible, all of it* – but she had seen it, witnessed every detail.

Horror clotted in Charlotte's throat like blood. Her mind raced. *Edward kept on about vampires – no, it can't be. Karl was always so tender, so kind... but the way he looked sometimes, strange things he said.* She remembered his lips on her throat and shivered. *Those times when he... No, no, it's unthinkable... but could he, would he have done that to me?*

Maddy had lent a brief hand with Edward, then run straight back inside the house. She'd seemed furious, muttering that it was "a mistake, a misunderstanding." *She closed her eyes when it happened*, Charlotte thought. *She refused to see it!*

"Some blasted use Maddy was!" Anne grumbled. She struggled

with the starting handle, swore, finally brought the car to life and jumped into the driving seat. "Get in, Charli. We're going straight to the village doctor."

Charlotte felt her duty lay with Anne and Edward. *But if anything happens to Maddy or David – dear Lord, don't let them be hurt.* And Karl – whatever he had done, she was afraid for him too. No choice.

"Go without me!" she shouted.

Anne, thankfully, realised there was no time to waste in arguing.

"Right," she replied, already pulling away. Charlotte ran back into the house and upstairs, almost choked by the thrust of her heartbeat.

She reached the landing too late.

Charlotte stared through the doorway and saw Maddy in Karl's grasp, abject with disillusion and terror. And Karl, ignoring her fear, was speaking quiet, understated threats of death.

Like a serrated knife the truth drove through Charlotte. What was he, to have attacked Edward – yet to be standing here afterwards as if nothing had happened, unmoved and sublimely beautiful – just as he'd looked when he had kissed her, declared love with the same mouth that now uttered callous threats against her own brother and sister?

The Devil. Only the Devil himself could possess such twisted glamour, and look so calmly on his own crimes.

How else could he disregard Maddy's pitiful pleas for help? *He must listen, he can't be so cruel* – yet Karl remained untouched, glacial.

"Let her go, damn you!" David said fiercely. "Good God, Karl, to think we trusted you! If you've a human bone in your body –"

"But I have not. I am sorry, David, but I have stated my conditions and if your men carry them out, your sister will not be harmed." Karl's presence held a charismatic power impossible to resist. His very calmness and the eerie, commanding quietness of his voice were part of it.

Charlotte had never seen David so completely at a loss.

"For God's sake, man, she's just a girl. Be reasonable. You can't do this!"

"If you want to help her, I suggest you all leave. Now."

Charlotte stared at Karl, and felt that she had lost her mind. Reality had shifted, entered another dimension. Driven not by bravery but by a rash, internal compulsion, she found herself running into the room. One of the workmen tried to catch her round the waist but she pulled free, gasping, "For pity's sake, don't take Madeleine. Take me instead. Please, Karl, take me."

There was a moment of absolute silence. She couldn't see properly. Everything was spinning, blurred. The only clear figure was Karl, and danger flowed from him, as bright and sharp as lead crystal. Glass stained with blood.

Then Karl said, "Very well."

He let go of Madeleine, who flew to David's arms, and in the same instant he took hold of Charlotte, very gently, by the wrist.

Softly he said, "Now you will all depart. You may bring Charlotte food and clothes and leave them by the front door, but if there is any attempt to enter the manor, she will suffer."

"What – you can't keep her here, damn you!" David cried.

"You'll have her back when I'm ready to leave," Karl said evenly. "Now, if you value her life, go."

David's face turned bleak with defeat. He began to back out of the door, taking Maddy with him, followed by the disconsolate workmen. That was the worst shock of all, the moment when they gave up and abandoned her. Grey stars rolled across Charlotte's eyes, blotting out the last sight of them and the fading echo of their footsteps.

I love Maddy, I couldn't let her suffer, I had to save her... She drew the half-truth around her for warmth, but it dissolved like snow in rain. Hopeless to deceive herself. *Would I have been so noble if it hadn't been Karl? I don't know. I'm not selfless, not brave... just a wretched hypocrite.*

Her real motive was more complex, painfully selfish; despair had overridden her fear. She felt her disgrace was complete, making her an expendable member of the family... a scapegoat to take away their pain. And deepest of all ran the need to know the truth about Karl, however unbearable that truth might be.

Expensive, such selfishness.

Karl's grip felt as hard and delicate as bone. She had the horrible impression of a skeleton holding her. She looked up at him, desperate for a word, a glance, to ease her anguish. But as he turned his face towards her, all she saw was an exquisitely beautiful mask: eyes fashioned from jewels that mimicked human emotions to perfection. Love, sorrow, pain. How clever, how utterly hollow and cold.

Then a devastating wave of terror broke over her and she thought, *I don't know this creature, I don't know him at all! God help me, what have I done?*

She tried to cry out, "David, don't leave me!" but the blood was spinning out of her head and she could not speak. All life had bled out of the house and she was alone, sinking through a black and grey netherworld where nothing mattered.

PART TWO

Like an angel crying mercy to a storm
You call from shadows where you don't belong
And the candle that I carry in my dark
Was once a torch to love that I held back

When I tried to comfort you, I lied
Now I speak with effort, my tongue forever tied
When you walked across the meadows towards the moon
You made the midnight stranger welcome much too soon...

HORSLIPS, "RING-A-ROSEY"

CHAPTER TEN

ABOUT THE FIRE

When Charlotte awoke, she was convinced that she lay in her own bed. She felt she'd slept for days, and her only recent memory was of a vivid, recurring dream: Karl in a doorway, lighting candles on a candelabra. Slowly he turned to face her, his face glowing eerily white, the flames turning his hair to a blood-red halo, and he seemed utterly alien, supernatural, no longer the man she had loved. He was staring at her as he approached, his eyes as brilliant and compelling as fire scintillating through garnets.

She knew then that this was no mortal being. She was aware only of the white face, the burning, chilling eyes, and the roaring grey cataract of terror...

And then of waking in her bed...

But why was the canopy so old and faded, like a medieval tapestry? She took in a vaulted ceiling, stone and plaster walls. Everything looked wrong. This was a nightmare she'd sometimes had as a child, that she'd awoken in the wrong place, a prisoner...

Nightmare, or premonition.

"Father," she whispered. "Are you there? Father..."

This was no dream. The unfamiliar room was real. A fire glowed in a cavernous grate. On a rug in front of the fire stood two high-backed chairs with dusty, age-worn upholstery.

Someone spoke. "Don't be afraid, Charlotte. Do you remember where you are?"

Memories drenched her. She sat up, sweat branching coldly

down her back. Her whole body felt twisted with tension like barbed wire.

"Where's David? Where's Anne?"

"They've gone. You fainted, don't you remember?"

She looked round and saw Karl sitting in a chair next to the bed, in waistcoat and shirt sleeves, his collar undone.

"When?" she gasped.

"Ten minutes ago, no more." His face was sublime, impassive, his voice polite. Detached from her distress.

"I feel as if I've been asleep – unconscious – for days."

"You have not, I assure you," he said. "The mind can play tricks when you're in a state of shock. Here, drink this." He placed a cup in her hands. She stared at the brownish liquid as if it were poison.

"It's whisky and hot water," he said. "One of the workmen was good enough to leave a hipflask in the kitchen."

She sipped cautiously at the drink and felt fierce heat spreading through her, restoring her senses. She realised that they were in the solar, which in the Middle Ages had been the family's private apartment above the hall. Now her prison. She put the cup aside and stared at Karl, hardly believing he was the same person. She had seen him attack Edward, fling both him and David down the stairs, seize Madeleine...

She wanted to die.

She could see his unhuman quality now, so powerfully that she could not comprehend why she hadn't noticed before. As he spoke, she watched his sensual lips, the glint of light on his canine teeth. They appeared normal again, but a vision tormented her of his savage open mouth and thorn-cruel fangs... Impossible to grasp. *Vampire.*

"It's true, isn't it?" she said. "The things Edward said about you. We didn't believe him but he *knew*, didn't he? Is that why you killed him?"

Karl sat back in the chair, crossing his right knee over the left.

"Is he dead? I don't know," he said, with the detached, kindly interest of a doctor.

"You –" She clenched her hands, waited for the spasm of emotion to pass. "Just tell me the truth. You can't make things better by lying, and you certainly can't make them worse."

Karl paused, folding his hands.

"Very well. Yes, Charlotte, I am a vampire. Does it help you at all to know this?"

"I – I don't know."

"No, because it is only a word. I don't know what associations it has for you, but I doubt they are the same as mine."

She drew her knees up to her chin and hugged them, as if by holding herself very still she would be safe.

Not looking at him, she said, "When we were children, Fleur used to frighten Madeleine and me by reading us ghost stories. There was one about a vampire, called *Carmilla*, that haunted me for weeks. But it was a long time ago. I don't know how to answer. Everyone's heard folklore, but I've never given it any thought."

"That is strange, for someone with a scientific interest in ghosts."

"People do see ghosts, but I never thought vampires were real!" she said angrily.

Karl shook his head and said in a clinical tone, "So anything you think you know is based on fiction and hearsay."

"I know what I saw today! That was worse than any book!"

He did not react.

"Well, *Carmilla* and the other stories are the culmination of myths which have some basis in reality." He leaned towards her. "So, how do I look to you now? Like a fiend? Or the same as before, the same man to whom you declared such deep affection?"

She shrank away. "Don't! Don't torment me."

"I have no wish to torment you, Charlotte." He went over to the grate and cast fresh logs onto the fire. They hissed and popped, showering sparks up the chimney. As he turned round, she huddled back against the carved headboard. His lips thinned, very slightly. "However, it seems that I am unable to avoid doing so."

So cold, he seemed. The tenderness he'd shown her was all a sham; a brittle shell over a blood-black pit of ice.

"And you don't care," she whispered. "It wouldn't be so bad if you cared, but – God, I can't speak. How could you do this?"

"But this is what vampires are like, don't you see? Utterly selfish. Capable of any lie to get what they want. Capable of any pretence."

"Vampires don't exist! This is some awful delusion you're under," she said helplessly.

"As I said, it's just a word. I do not sleep in a coffin, nor turn to dust in sunlight. But the fact is I am not human, and I need human blood to sustain me. I want to explain what happened to Edward; not to excuse myself, because it is quite unforgivable, but so that you may understand what I am."

"'O wonderful, when devils tell the truth!'" Charlotte whispered bitterly.

Karl sat down on the corner of the bed, one pale hand curled around the post.

"'More wonderful, when angels are so angry'," he replied. She bowed her head onto her knees, unable to look at him. "And you have every right to be angry, of course. But if you will let me continue: I also have an extreme instinct for self-preservation. I came here with David simply to set his mind at rest about last night – not to harm him. Can you believe that?"

"Hardly, but I'll try."

"Regrettably, I made a mistake. In normal circumstances I can control the appetite for blood without conscious effort, but last night I had a fight that left me very weak." He paused, as if unsure whether to elaborate. "Another vampire had drawn all the blood out of me."

She was shocked. Suddenly there were hidden layers to his story she had not suspected.

"Another? Was it Pierre?"

"He is a vampire, but it wasn't him. It's irrelevant. The point is that when I met David, my thirst was growing unbearable… This is disturbing for you."

"You must tell me. I can bear it, as long as it's the *truth*."

"Impossible to understand the thirst unless you've experienced it, but it can become a delirium beyond which nothing else matters. I knew I had to send David away before hunger overrode my will. I told him to leave, and was about to go my separate way, when Edward came to the door. If he had not attacked me, if he'd stood aside – or if I had not been in that trance of extreme thirst – all would have been well. No vampire deliberately betrays himself by feeding in front of mortals. It was my own fault, for underestimating my state of starvation. So the moment he set upon me, my control vanished. Self-preservation, you see:

he attacked me, I needed his blood. He did not stand a chance."

A moan escaped her lips. *What reply can I make to this horror?*

Karl went on, "I would not have harmed him for anything – but I am a vampire, Charlotte. If human values and morals had a hold on us, we would not survive. I never, if I can help it, prey upon people I know. But don't mistake me. I am not sentimental, nor merciful. If your family persist against me, they may die."

"That's vile." She pressed her forehead so hard against her knees that the bones ached. "How can someone so callous have mimicked such tenderness? You must have hypnotised me. Is that what vampires do?"

He paused. "I can't deny that I have betrayed you."

"You only pretended to love me."

She wanted him to contradict her. With all her soul she wanted him to deny any pretence.

Eventually he said, "Now you see the full extent to which I have deceived you, all under the guise of honesty. You thought I was being honest, admitting I could not marry you?"

"Yes."

"But that was a less than white lie to hide a truth far more hideous; I could not marry you because I am not human. I must drink blood to live."

The image hit her like nausea: the passionless yet bestial intensity of his face as he'd lunged down and torn into Edward's throat...

"But you never drank mine."

He looked at her over his shoulder, his profile shimmering against the fire.

"No. But I wanted to." She stared at him. "I longed to. You never knew what danger you were in, alone with me. It is stronger than lust and far harder to control. I might have killed you."

"I don't believe you," she said, but she did. Now she knew why he always seemed to struggle against a deeper need than passion. The way he had sometimes kissed her throat, shuddered, turned his face away... *God in heaven.*

His gaze shifted away from hers. In the same impersonal voice he said, "Then I had better tell you the very worst of it, which will certainly make you hate me – if you don't already. Vampires do not reproduce, neither with humans nor with each other.

Therefore we rarely feel physical desire, but when we do, it is for a very specific purpose. Do you want me to go on?"

She gave a convulsive nod. "I don't follow."

"When a vampire is in constant proximity to a potential victim but resisting the instinct to prey upon them – as I was with you – then sexual desire can develop as a way to break down the intellectual resistance to feeding. The loss of control in love-making leads almost inevitably to the fulfilment of the *real* need, which is for blood. Do you see?"

She hunched over the sick ache in her stomach. She felt utterly betrayed, destroyed.

"Dear God. To think I was worried I might have a child!"

"I knew there was no danger of that."

"*You* knew –" Bitterness welled up. "Why did you go to all that trouble? It would have been easier just to – to seize me as you did Edward. Why didn't you?"

"I came to your father to gain knowledge, not his family's blood. I don't need to go to such elaborate lengths for nourishment." There was a touch of contempt in his tone. "I never wished you harm. In seducing you, my instinct was trying to override a conscious decision. I should have resisted, I should have left you alone – but I did not. I was playing with your life. You don't know how close I came to it, Charlotte. One more night, and I doubt that I could have resisted any longer."

"And I would have died?"

"Our bite is not invariably fatal – but it can cause madness, which perhaps is worse."

"And that's the only reason – not because you loved me?" She choked, unable to go on.

"I was drawn to you, I don't deny it. It was so easy to take advantage of your feelings for me."

"Devil," she whispered. "I loved you."

"How could it be love, when you did not know my real nature? It is a characteristic of vampires to appear enthralling to humans. What you felt for me is only what Madeleine and Elizabeth felt also: a kind of bewitchment."

He sat very still as he spoke, and more than ever she sensed him as an alien creature, beyond her comprehension. Misery and anger rushed up, with bitter resentment.

"It's not true. You're saying these things to torture me!"

Karl blinked impassively.

"If you think I wish to torture you, surely it proves that what I'm saying is true."

"I suppose you seduced my sister and aunt too, made them believe they meant something to you?"

"No. I have never touched either of them."

He did not elaborate, and somehow this statement made the pain worse. She was sinking in confusion.

"But you were going to abduct Maddy! Would you have fed on her as you did on Edward, and killed David if he'd tried to stop you?"

"I hope it would not have been necessary. But I am quite merciless, when I have to be."

She sat rigid. Everything, from their first meeting to this moment, was in her mind at once; every word and look, all the closeness they had shared; and now this smashed and red-stained mess, and the unbearable pain...

"Why did you bother to control the thirst?" she cried. "Why not just kill me? Why don't you do it now?"

She flung herself at him, pulled at his shirt sleeve – but when he turned to look at her, she froze. That glowing stillness, that beauty so heart-rending it could only be evil – suddenly she saw what he was so clearly that terror sheeted through her like flame.

A line between life and death.

The next she knew she was off the bed and running to the door, wild with the need to escape.

Down the stairs she rushed, only half aware of the treads slapping painfully against her stockinged soles. In the hall the fire had waned and the lofty desolation swallowed her. She struggled with the front door, found it locked, spun round in a panic and headed for the kitchen. Stumbling over piles of rubble that the workmen had made, she fought uselessly to open the outside door. Then, with no clear plan, she headed into the cellars.

Blindly she ran across the cryptlike space – where she'd seen the shadow-cat, a lifetime ago – bruising her feet, stumbling against the barrels, until she collided with a wall.

The stone was slick with damp and exhaled the mustiness of age. She felt it sucking the heat out of her body through the thin material of her skirt and sweater, yet she didn't move. She flattened herself against the harsh surface, letting the cold leach away her panic.

There were voices whispering in the darkness. Something brushed her legs, a cat – or a subterranean draught that breathed in and out like a living thing. Nothing could make her more terrified than she already was. The presence was simply an extension of the blackness inside her, and she surrendered to it, almost pleading.

"Help me," she mouthed silently. "God help me."

She wanted to weep but couldn't. Tears contained healing, and there was nothing to repair the ruin of her soul.

After a few moments, she heard the echo of footsteps.

"Edward Lees, yes... I see. Thank you." George Neville replaced the mouthpiece on its stalk and turned to the others. "The hospital tells me he's been given a blood transfusion and is resting."

"But will he live?" David said in agitation.

"It's too soon to say." Dr Neville sank down into an armchair, grey-faced. "They're doing their best."

Anne had joined Elizabeth, Madeleine and the two men in the main drawing room. Shock lay heavy on them all. They sat like waxworks, bound together by tension and dread. A tall, silver-haired police officer, Inspector Ash, stood quietly by the fireplace. Only David showed any animation, but his restless pacing was beginning to drive Anne mad.

"Charlotte was so brave," said Madeleine. She was curled up in a chair, her face streaked with tears. "It would have been me. And I was so hateful to her this morning. I shall never forgive myself."

"But, Madeleine, why the devil did you approach him?" her father said angrily. "Why put yourself and Charlotte in such danger?"

"I thought I was doing the right thing!" Madeleine twisted a handkerchief between her fingers. "I thought it was all a mistake, that Karl couldn't... Don't shout at me, Father. Don't you think I feel bad enough, realising what he's really like?"

"It's not your fault, Maddy," David said soothingly. "If it's anyone's, it's mine. God, if only I'd listened to Edward at the very beginning! I *knew* there was something wrong about Karl, I *knew* and I've entirely failed to protect my family." He gave Anne a heartfelt glance. "Lord, it could have been any one of you."

George Neville leaned forward and put his head in his hands.

"For heaven's sake don't blame yourself, David. I'm the one who took him on. He seemed so plausible – to think of the times I left Charlotte alone with him!" He sat back, pressing a hand to his shiny forehead. "If I'd only had the sense to turn him away… If any harm comes to her –" He broke off. Anne's heart ached. Dr Neville so rarely showed his emotions.

"This is all too incredible," Elizabeth said sharply. She stubbed out a half-smoked cigarette in an ashtray, then promptly lit another. "Has everyone in this family gone mad? There are no such things as –" She stopped, to Anne's relief. They'd all agreed not to use the term "vampire" in the hearing of the police. If they portrayed Karl as anything other than a criminal, they risked branding themselves as cranks, and Charlotte's plight being taken less seriously.

"It doesn't matter what we call him," said David. "What he's done is real enough."

"Unbelievable," Elizabeth said contemptuously. She sat forward over her knees, her long back taut and gaunt. The ashtray beside her was full of stubs.

"I suppose you'd prefer it if he *had* taken me," said Madeleine.

"How can you say that?" gasped Dr Neville.

"Father, it's no secret that you've always loved Charlotte the best."

"Do stop it, dear," said Elizabeth. "We're all upset and carrying on like that won't help anyone. *I* should have realised about Karl. Heaven knows, I was never easy on Charlotte – but I was firm for her own good. It's a hard world and she needed to learn how to live in it."

"Why?" barked Dr Neville. "She lived perfectly well in the academic world. I should have kept her safe at my side, away from the likes of Karl, and as for your precious 'high society', Elizabeth – all that did was make her miserable."

"I was trying to broaden her horizons! Any criticism I offered was never meant maliciously, she knows that." Elizabeth ground out the new cigarette as if trying to crush it to death.

"At least Edward's hanging on," David sighed. He sat down on the arm of Madeleine's chair and gripped her shoulder. "But if anything happens to him or to Charlotte, I shan't be answerable for what becomes of Karl von Wultendorf."

"It's in *our* hands now, sir," Inspector Ash said pointedly. "We have the house surrounded and there's no way out for him."

"Just be damned careful," said Dr Neville. "If he sees a bevy of policemen around the house, Lord knows what he might do."

The inspector replied in a level voice, "We shall do nothing to endanger your daughter's life, sir, believe me."

"We know that, Inspector," said David. He stood. "Right. Now I know how Edward is, I'm going back up to the manor. I won't rest until Charlotte's free. Shall we go?" He indicated for Inspector Ash to precede him to the door, nodding to Anne as he left.

Anne didn't follow. They'd argued earlier because David had insisted it was too dangerous for Anne to go with him.

So much for the modern man, she thought. *I'll wait a while and join him later, then he won't be able to stop me. I'm damned if I'll sit about chain-smoking, bickering and blaming myself when I could be doing something to help Charli. If only they knew how they sounded! Is this what it takes to make them realise how much they love her?*

Madeleine looked so wretched that Anne felt only sympathy. She knelt by her armchair and said, "How are you bearing up?"

Elizabeth and Dr Neville were in the doorway, talking to Newland. Maddy glanced at them and then at Anne, her eyes brimming.

"I saw such awful things when I was ill, Anne. I thought I was in a tomb, that I was actually dead."

Anne was taken aback. "A nightmare, that's all."

"But I was wide awake! I was seeing things. I know that now."

"You must have been feverish."

"Perhaps, but it was so real. I had this idea that only Karl could save me. He was all I could think about. I saw his eyes everywhere. The frightening, the really frightening thing is that I felt perfectly sane. In the manor, I thought that if I helped Karl, he would realise he loved me. But when he grabbed me –" she took Anne's wrist, unconsciously digging in her fingernails "– I suddenly saw what he was. He'd never loved me. He *couldn't*, because he was evil. It was as if someone had pulled a blindfold off me. Am I making any sense?"

"I think so."

"Now I don't know if I'm crazy or not. But I *do* understand how poor Edward must have felt when he made such a fuss at my party." Her mouth turned down at the corners and she wept. "I've been so stupidly cruel to Charlotte... because she's under Karl's spell too, and it's not her fault."

"Charlotte." Karl's voice struck echoes from the walls. "Please come out of here. It's cold. I am not going to harm you."

She hugged herself, shivering. "What will happen to me?"

"Nothing," he said. "As soon as I can, I shall let you go. You will return to your life in Cambridge and forget me."

She raised her head in amazement, straining her eyes to see him in the darkness.

"*Forget?*" she gasped. "What kind of life have I to go back to? You think you can make me fall in love with you – then reveal yourself as some kind of fiend, and expect me just to forget it all?"

"Our relationship had to end, Charlotte." His emotionless voice chilled her. "The truth is, I did not know how to end it. I never wanted this to happen. Given a choice, I would simply have gone away quietly."

"You would have left me, and I'd never have known why?"

"Exactly so. And you might have been unhappy for a time, but at least you would not have endured this misery. However, now it has happened, at least you will understand why we could not stay together. And, of course, you will not want to. Remember me with hatred if you must – and I am sure you will – but go on living. In time you will get over it."

The cold hit her then, and her teeth began to chatter.

"You want me to get over it? But why should you care, why the hell should you care? Don't tell me you feel guilty! Of all the unbelievable things you've told me, that is too much." Her bitterness felt loathsome. She added miserably, "I don't hate you, I haven't the spirit."

"You will, in time."

"No! How can I make you see? This is not something I *can* get over, Karl. It doesn't matter what you say or do, I shall never get over it! Don't you understand?"

When he fell silent in the darkness, she felt he wasn't there at all. The sudden emptiness wrenched her soul.

Then she heard him take a slow, soft breath, and he said, "Oh, Charlotte, I can't go on with this."

There was pain in his voice. For the first time, real pain.

She froze. What could the change in him mean, except danger? She felt him move towards her but she was pinned against the wall, unable to move. She closed her eyes, felt his hands on her shoulders and waited for the unimaginable stab of fangs in her neck. But he simply put his arms around her, drew her away from the wall and held her close.

She could not return the embrace. Her heart was breaking.

"Don't touch me," she whispered.

He let her go, it was like being dropped in mid-air. Then she felt his hand, very light and impersonal, on her elbow.

"Come back to the fire," he said. "We must talk."

She let him lead her across the cellar towards the hazy smear of light from the kitchen. It was all she could do to walk.

Once in the solar, she suffered him to wrap his coat around her and sit her by the fire, but all the time she stared at the flames and couldn't look at him. He sat on the floor, one knee drawn up and his arms resting loosely on it, the other lean leg stretched out.

"We won't be here for long," he said. "Until then I'll make sure you are warm and comfortable." He seemed different again: gentle and considerate, as he used to be. That, far more than his coldness, made her want to cry.

"Why are you being kind to me now?" she said thinly. "I don't know what you want."

"I don't want you to be in this pain." His voice was calm, but had lost its impersonal edge. "I thought the simplest path was to make you loathe me. I assumed that if I was cruel enough, any remaining love you had for me would die. With Madeleine, it worked, but…" He paused. "With you, Charlotte, I can't keep up the pretence. I cannot bear to put you through such misery… not after we have been so much to each other."

She gazed at the charred logs, black against scarlet embers.

"Are you saying that I meant something to you after all?"

"Yes."

"So, those awful things you said to me earlier were also lies, were they? How shall I know when you start telling the truth?"

"They were harsh things to say, I know, and I chose not to contradict certain assumptions you made. But I was not lying. The truth is horrible, Charlotte, but it is also much more complicated than you know."

She rubbed her forehead. The skin was ridged with tension. True love turned out to be demonic deceit. After this she could never love, never trust again.

"It's vile," she whispered.

"I know," he said. "I can't ask you to forgive me. I rarely feel any need to explain my actions, and I've never before spoken freely to a human. But I want to talk to you; not to excuse myself, only so that you may understand a little better – if you're willing to listen."

She allowed herself to meet his eyes. For an unnerving moment she was captivated by the amber irises, as she had been the first time they met, and every time since. She fought off the feeling.

"But the things you did! You terrified Maddy and you didn't care!"

"Charlotte, I took a hostage to keep them away from me, *because* I don't want to hurt them. It's as much to protect them as myself."

"I don't believe you."

"*Liebling*," he sighed, sounding weary, "do you really think I wish you harm?"

"I don't know."

"Well, I do not. But your family thinks otherwise, and it's what they believe that will preserve them – and me."

"You're happy to let them think I'm in danger of dying? That's cruel, too."

"I don't deny it."

"Why couldn't you have just run away?" she said savagely.

He half smiled. "Or turned into a bat?"

She stared at him. "You can't... Do you think this is funny?"

"No, I cannot turn into a bat, or a wolf or a cloud of mist," he said gravely. "Nothing so convenient. Yet vampires can vanish in a way that is perhaps even less believable. I could not, however, because I was still too weak from the fight. If I'd forced my way through David's men, I might have killed some of them, or they might have overpowered me; neither prospect was desirable."

"But when you recover your strength, you will be able to... vanish?"

"I hope so. But it may take days, or weeks if I am unlucky."

"And you need blood to recover your strength?"

"Yes."

"But there's only me..."

"You have no need to fear me, Charlotte," he sighed. "I am not going to touch you. The blood I took from your poor friend will sustain me for quite some time."

"What then?"

"I have to leave here, of course. And I shall have to take you with me, to prevent your valiant brother from following us. But once I know he cannot find me, I'll release you."

"And until then, I am your prisoner," she said, staring at her hands.

"Would you rather it had been your sister?"

The question flashed quick and sharp into the air and hung there, unanswered.

Eventually she said, "I remain your hostage while it suits you, then you discard me and I never see you again."

"Surely you would not want to see me again?"

"Don't twist my words! You're the most callous creature I've ever met."

"I'm sorry you feel that," he said, so gently that his voice melted right through her. "However cruel I seem, I feel anything but callous towards you. But you didn't answer my question."

For a brief, shocking moment, all the passion she felt for him rushed back, turning as swiftly to anguish.

"Don't, Karl. You're confusing me. First you torment me, then you apologise, then you go on uttering threats against my family in the same gentle tone. What am I supposed to think?"

"You have every right to be angry."

His composure made her more so.

"Angry is hardly the word for what I feel! After – after that first night we spent together, you said our love could only end in pain. Is this what you meant?"

"But you said, 'The feeling is worth the pain, whatever it is.'"

At that she tore herself out of the chair – away from his eyes – but there was nowhere to go. She sat on the bed, confused and trembling.

"That was unfair of me," said Karl. "To answer your question, no, this is not what I meant, because I didn't know this was going to happen. What I did mean is something worse, which perhaps you will come to understand. They're different facets of the same horror, which is as painful for me as it is for you."

"Oh, is it?" She glared at him. "Then why do you give the appearance of caring about nothing at all?"

"Vampires can detach ourselves from emotion; we have to. But that doesn't mean we don't feel. It would take time to explain."

"I don't want any more explanations! Why did you have to come here? You've disrupted our lives, stolen our hearts then revealed yourself to be –"

"What about you, Charlotte?" he said softly. "There must be reasons why you so selflessly took Madeleine's place. Am I the sole cause of your unhappiness?"

She couldn't answer. She felt torn to pieces, and now nothing fitted and the world made less sense than before. Her family seemed distant, like shadow puppets; she struggled to conjure their faces in her mind. In her wretchedness she longed for comfort, a few calm words, arms to hold her. Someone to say, *This is not so terrible after all. There is a reason. Look, this is what you have missed...* And she would find a scrap of logic that enabled her to understand.

But the awful, impossible thing was that she wanted this comfort from Karl. How could the one who had betrayed her heal the wounds? It was obscene: like asking her murderer to hold her hand as she died.

And yet, her body ached with longing to feel his arms around her. *I must be evil, to feel this,* she thought, curling up on her side, squeezing her eyes shut.

"You need to rest, Charlotte," he said impassively. "Try to sleep."

She sensed him standing over her. Her back tingled with the cold anticipation of his touch but he remained quiet, as if realising there was nothing else he could say to her in this state. At last she could bear it no longer. She pushed her hair out of her eyes, looked up, and received another shock.

Karl had departed soundlessly and she was alone in the room.

When darkness fell, Karl went down into the hall and opened the front door.

Charlotte was asleep. He was glad she'd succumbed to exhaustion, and found escape from the suffering he'd unwillingly inflicted on her. She had slept all afternoon, not even stirring when he returned to pull the coverlet over her.

Some time earlier, there had been a knock on the door. He'd waited until nightfall to chance looking outside.

They'd placed a bundle, presumably full of clothes and food for Charlotte, on the very edge of the doorstep, which meant he must step outside to reach it. Pausing, he sensed eyes on him; he heard the breathing of mortals in the darkness, caught their sweaty scent. Trees loomed against the sky. A number of policemen and estate staff crouched in the undergrowth, fondly imagining they were hidden.

Karl could see them all quite clearly.

They'd been watching the house all day. David was behind some brambles with a man in tweeds, whom Karl recognised as Elizabeth's head groom. He heard them murmuring to each other.

"There he is!" David's voice. Then the clean sharp *click* of a revolver's safety catch.

"You sure about this, sir?" The groom's voice was a gruff whisper. "You know what Inspector Ash said."

"Hang what Ash said," David replied crisply. "Is he alone? Damn, I can't see a deuced thing. Daren't risk it if my sister's there…"

Karl stood in the part-open doorway, staring at them. The night began to spin slowly around him. He felt weary. The blood he'd taken from Edward sustained him, but their heat in the darkness reminded him that he would need to drink again before long... and it would be so easy to entice one of them inside.

But he would not. Not with Charlotte there, even though he couldn't recover his energy without blood.

He should let her go, take his chances with David's makeshift army. He should never have taken her. The abduction achieved nothing, and was as cruel and wrong as falling in love with her in the first place. Yet he couldn't let her go; a perverse fascination held him, like the inability to let a wound heal on its own.

Kristian would kill me for revealing vampire secrets to humans, he thought. *But whether I escape or am destroyed, will he be so good as to protect them from Pierre? Ah, David, you think this situation is simple. Would you believe me if I told you otherwise?*

Karl stepped out and retrieved the bundle, moving unhurriedly. As he straightened up, he heard the groom saying, "Looks like he's on his own, sir. There's a bit of a glow from the doorway, no one else with him."

David's strong voice rang out. "Stay exactly where you are, von Wultendorf! There is a gun pointing at your heart and if you move, I'll fire."

Karl replied, "Don't be rash, David. The more difficult you make this for me, the more difficult you make it for Charlotte."

"You've been warned! Don't move!"

Karl ignored him. He'd barely begun to step back when a shot cracked the air. He saw the bullet winging towards him – a silver streak in a flower of fire – before it ripped into his shoulder. He staggered back against the door frame. He hadn't thought David would actually shoot. At least, not that fast.

Recovering his balance, he called out coldly, "This will do no good, David. You, too, have been warned."

There was a vehement curse in the darkness, then the sound of other voices whispering. Policemen were wading through the undergrowth, one of them hissing furiously, "Captain Neville, what the hell d'you think you're doing? If you want to put your sister's life in danger or end up on a murder charge, you're going the right way about it!"

Karl withdrew into the house and bolted the door.

* * *

There was a ghoul in Karl's form haunting the feverish twilight of sleep. Charlotte saw men seizing him, murdering him while he cried out her name. Then she saw him tearing out their throats, flinging their bodies aside like dummies. Now he was embracing her, kissing her hair and whispering endearments; now mocking her, his eyes shining like red glass and his mouth twisted in a cruel grin. She heard a crack of thunder. Images rained on her mind like hot coals, until at last she tore herself out of sleep like an arrow from a wound.

She was still in the same ancient room, and night had fallen. The window was a black oblong, but the fire burned brightly and Karl knelt in front of the grate with his back to her.

At the sight of him, her heart lurched and all her despair came streaming back. Her head ached, her mouth was dry and sticky. Her stomach churned with hunger. In the trauma of the past few days she'd barely eaten, and the previous day seemed a lifetime ago.

"How long have I been asleep?" she said, leaning on her elbows.

"All afternoon," he replied, looking round. "It's eight o'clock. You must have been exhausted."

She yawned deeply. "I still am. I feel terrible."

"You'll feel better after something to eat and drink. Your family brought food for you."

She followed his gaze and saw a plate of bread, ham and cheese on the black oak table beside the bed. Her stomach turned over.

"I don't think I can eat anything."

"Have some tea, at least." He came to the bed and placed a cup in her hands. She saw a kettle and teapot on the grate. "You must learn to look after yourself, Charlotte. Where is your instinct for self-preservation?"

As she sipped the tea, he sat on the edge of the bed and watched her. She sensed the radiance of his gaze and knew that if she looked up, she would see the tranquil warmth that always captivated her... so she wouldn't let it happen. *He won't deceive me again.* She kept her eyes lowered, feeling uneasy and closed away, as in those awful days when she had first known him. Yet those old feelings could never regain a hold on her. Too much had happened between them.

When she'd finished, he took the cup from her and placed the plate on her lap.

"I insist that you try to eat," he said gently, and went to pour her some more tea.

She nibbled at a piece of bread and butter, and instantly felt her appetite return.

"Aren't you having anything?" she said, then almost choked. "Oh God. I keep forgetting."

He did not reply, only sat down in a chair beside her with a wry twist to his lips.

Charlotte said, "I remember Sally complaining that you were always leaving cold cups of tea. Now I know why. It would almost be funny, if it wasn't…"

Still he did not speak. She saw the disturbing paleness and stillness of him – so beautiful, however eerie – and a splinter of dread went through her. She ate rapidly, letting the food distract her. After a minute or two he stood up.

"I'll heat some water for you, so you can bathe and change, if you wish."

"Yes… Thank you," she murmured.

While he was out of the room, she got up and began to shake out the assortment of clothes that Aunt Elizabeth – she presumed – had packed for her. *God, what must they be thinking?* She froze. *I wonder what's happening at the Hall? Poor Father…*

When Karl came back, she asked anxiously, "Karl, is – is anyone watching the house?"

He raised his right hand to his left shoulder and absently fingered a tear in his shirt.

"Yes," he said drily. "Your brother and half the local police force are keeping a vigil. Did you think everyone had deserted you?"

She bit her lip. The question was too close to answer.

"This is awful."

"It's worse than you think."

"What do you mean?"

He sighed. "I want to explain. There's much I would tell you… if we could speak freely, without this barrier between us. But I don't know whether it's possible."

He looked questioningly at her.

"Perhaps," she said. "If I felt I could trust you, or believe a word you said."

"You obviously think it unlikely. But we could try."

"I suppose it would pass the time," Charlotte said with a faint, arid laugh. She noticed the way he was pressing his hand to his shoulder. "Karl, are you hurt?"

"Your brother shot me."

Cold astonishment rippled through her. She reacted by instinct. "Oh, no. Let me see."

"If you wish. You didn't hear the gun?"

He sat down on the bed and she sat next to him, frowning.

"Actually, I did... but I thought it was part of my dream. How could he do this? He might have killed you!" As she unbuttoned his shirt, Karl began to laugh. She snatched her hands away and glared at him.

"Forgive me, beloved. I am not mocking you. It just seemed ironic that you should be concerned for me." He shook his head sadly. "But it is not funny at all, that someone of your sweet nature should have to endure this."

Then he pulled back the shirt to reveal the pale smooth flesh of his shoulder. There was no blood, only a white puckered mark – and on his back, a similar one over the shoulder blade.

"It looks as if the bullet went straight through," she said softly. "And it's already healed. Does it hurt?"

"A little. We are quite easy to injure, but very difficult to destroy. Bullets do not kill us, not even silver ones."

Tentatively she reached out and touched the scar. It was fading even as she looked. His skin felt so familiar under her fingers... recent memories went through her like hot wax, unbidden and overwhelming.

Karl caught her wrist and they stared at each other.

Then he said, "Go and bathe, before the water cools down."

She fled the room, burning with shame at the way her body was betraying her – as if it were a separate, animal entity, disconnected from her mental anguish.

The bathroom was only part finished, the new fittings shiny white and clinical, the walls and floor bare. She washed, changed and brushed her hair, shivering with nerves as she hurried through the tasks. When she finished, she felt better. Refreshed.

No amount of panic or hand-wringing is going to help, she thought. *I might as well try to be calm. "Be a scientist," that's what Father used to tell me when I was upset about something. "Don't react; think."*

She hoped he was following his own advice.

When she returned, Karl was seated in a high-backed chair by the fire, as elegantly relaxed as a cat. His eyes had a distracted look she'd seen before; a look that exposed the depthless chasm between his life and hers.

"I refuse to be frightened any more," she said, sitting in the other chair facing him. "I've decided that the worst you can do is kill me, and that you won't do it while I am useful to you."

"I don't blame you for sounding bitter," he said quietly.

"I'm not, I'm being realistic. Would you rather I was hysterical? I can't keep it up, it's such a waste of energy."

"I think in the circumstances you have shown a great deal of courage, Charlotte."

"Is that a compliment, coming from someone who's forced me to be brave? And you're so calm all the time. I don't think *anything* could upset you."

"There you are wrong. I'm not in the habit of showing my feelings, that's all. Some find it infuriating, I know."

"That only proves what I feared," she said. "What I see in your eyes and what you are actually thinking could be entirely different." He was looking at the fire, so she was able to study the exquisite lines of his face. "When I thought I saw love, you were thinking of blood."

"Not all the time. On the contrary, when I was with you, blood was often the last thing on my mind. Anyway, they are not so different." He glanced at her, a brief fiery gleam beneath the lowered lids. "But a vampire trying to explain himself to a human is like a wolf trying to apologise to a lamb. Unthinkable, really. I don't know why I thought I must act coldly to turn you against me; it is inevitable, whatever I do. All the same, Charlotte, if you do hate me it will cause me more distress than I can say."

"Why? You made it perfectly clear earlier that you were only using me! Don't start pretending to care about me again, unless you want to destroy me completely."

"No pretence now." He leaned forward a little. The intensity of his voice transfixed her. "Vampires do not disclose their secrets to humans. It simply is not done. You express doubt that you can trust me, but I also need to feel absolute trust in you. So, to prove that I do, I shall tell you that if you want to destroy me, you need not trouble yourself with stakes or fire. Just cut off my head."

"Oh." The starkness of the image shocked her.

A smile softened his lips. "I am going to be completely honest with you, Charlotte – but you must promise to do the same. Isn't that fair?"

"Of course."

"And I will answer your questions, if you answer mine. So, I ask you again why you offered yourself in Madeleine's place."

"Why –"

"No, Charlotte. Answer me."

She paused, one hand on her throat. Her instinct was to feel ashamed of her motives, to gloss over them so no one could see the wickedness inside her. But Karl made shame seem pointless and she thought, *Yes, why not the real reasons? What harm can it do to tell him?*

"It wasn't bravery," she said slowly. "It was despair. I was in disgrace with everyone. My aunt had guessed about us, and Maddy hated me for it. Perhaps you can't understand why these things matter, but they do. Yes, I put myself in Maddy's place without thinking, because I couldn't bear to see her so afraid... but the truth is, I resented you taking her. It sounds perverse; I don't know how to explain... *I* was the one who needed to know the truth about you, not Maddy! So I wasn't being heroic, only selfish."

She breathed out as she finished, feeling her tension fade a little.

"Well, no more selfish than me," he said drily. "Strange you should have resented what was hardly an act of love. Yet I understand. I have to confess that with Madeleine, this would have been easier."

"Easier?" Charlotte exclaimed. "In what way?"

"She is simpler than you. I don't mean less intelligent, but less complex, like David. I doubt that she would have sat questioning me. Her terror destroyed her infatuation, but she's also resilient enough to have recovered afterwards. However... it was self-delusion to tell myself that. I think I knew you would offer yourself in her place; I almost wanted to see if you would."

"Oh, God."

"And you did. And I'm sorry... because I knew we would both suffer for it. I thought it best to destroy your love with the harsh truth, but that was another delusion. I did not really need a hostage, Charlotte. I took you because it was my last chance to talk to you."

Charlotte laughed, stopped before it turned to tears.

"Dear God. You kill Edward, then you want to explain?"

"Yet you said you wished to listen, however bad it was."

"And I still do. I can bear this if I can *understand*."

"As I said, my attack on your friend was unplanned and I regret it." Karl folded his long, fine hands, looking down at them as he spoke. "There are some vampires who find it fun to make their victims fall in love with them, and you've seen how very easily we can do so. But it is a singularly cruel form of seduction and betrayal that I've never indulged in. As I said, only strangers need fear my footfall behind them in the dark. When I came to your father, I hadn't the remotest intention of touching any of you."

"Why *did* you come to us?"

"In search of enlightenment. We are thinking creatures, Charlotte, not mindless ones. Even your father admits there's more in nature than science can explain. I wanted to learn everything possible, in hope that I might discover an explanation of how such beings as vampires can exist, and how the Crystal Ring..." He broke off, then held out one hand in the firelight. "This is not human flesh. What is it? How is it that we remain changeless?"

Charlotte's eyes widened. "And have you found an answer?"

"Not yet. Now, perhaps, I never will."

"Were you – were you ever human?"

"Yes, long ago... at the beginning of the last century."

More than a hundred and twenty years... She couldn't grasp it.

"But you can't be more than thirty at the most."

"I was twenty-seven when I was taken. It's not a story I would relish telling. But before you ask, no, my victims do not become vampires. There is far more to the transformation than that."

"Thank goodness. I was thinking that Edward –"

"Well, don't," he said firmly. "It's quite impossible. But we were talking of your father. I'd heard of him before I came to England, of course. By chance I saw a photograph of your sister Fleur in a society paper and I…" He half smiled. "I invited myself to her party in the hope of meeting him. All so easy, really. I wanted to approach him only because of his reputation as a great scientist, I had no interest in his family. But humans can be very enchanting to vampires, and I was captivated by all of you – yet I was able to enjoy your company without sinister intentions. Other vampires might not have remained so disinterested, but as I said, I do not generally feed on people to whom I have been introduced."

He spoke with acid self-mockery. She didn't know how to respond.

"But you still needed to feed?"

"Yes, but I fed elsewhere," he said dismissively. "There was no *need* for me to harm you. I admit that the charm and compliance of one such as Madeleine can make it torture to resist my nature. Nevertheless, I am very well practised in doing so."

A vision hit Charlotte, of Karl moving through different places and times, with women – and men – sighing after him wherever he went, and he passing by with the friendly insouciance that he'd shown to Maddy and Elizabeth. The image shook her.

"You must have the most unbelievable degree of will power," Charlotte said sceptically.

He smiled. "No. Avoidance becomes an ingrained habit. Too easy to look at a beautiful woman and imagine what might have been. But there's no point in desiring her companionship, and if I desire her blood, I may destroy her… Do you see, it is the *pointlessness* that makes it no trouble at all to be detached?"

"It sounds lonely," she said.

"Yes. It can be. Very rarely am I emotionally drawn to a mortal. I don't allow it to happen. But when I met you, Charlotte, I saw qualities within you that cut straight through my defences like light. You are obviously unaware that you have this power."

"But why me?" She only half believed him. "Madeleine's prettier than me, she's confident and witty, she –"

"Charlotte, I've never known anyone with so little self-regard, and quite undeservedly. Do you think I can't see beneath the surface? Your sister and aunt are like sparkling streams without depth. They expect to be the centre of attention as their due, and why shouldn't they, if it pleases others to worship them? I've seen that bright, transient charm too often to care. Yet you held my attention without trying... You were all nervous, unselfconscious beauty, like a gazelle. Your demeanour said, 'I am nothing, kindly pass me by,' but your eyes were telling a deeper story. I saw such intelligence there, restlessness and a strange mixture of cynicism and passion. Most humans are transparent to me – but you were a mystery, and still are."

"It sounds as if you couldn't resist a challenge," she said.

Karl laughed softly. "I was right about the cynicism, at least. But you are unjust. Gods, if you could only see yourself with my eyes! You are as enthralling to me as a vampire to a mortal: glowing with golden life, filled with love, fear, hope – every precious human emotion. I saw you as... as a possible soulmate, if only circumstances were different."

Her throat closed up. She could hardly breathe.

He went on, "Yet I managed to control my feelings and be only a friend – until you sang '*Der Doppelgänger*'. A song of appalling loneliness, of searching endlessly for someone who's no longer there... and it made the gulf between us, mortal and immortal, unbearable." His voice became very quiet. "I wanted to pretend it did not exist. To close the gulf, just for a short time."

"I was aware of the distance between us," she said. "I couldn't work out its source."

"I still should have mastered my feelings, but I let passion and delusion take over – even knowing the effect it would have on you. I did not mean to be cruel. I simply discovered that it's possible to live for years thinking that you are in control and that nothing matters. And then something happens to make you realise that, for all that time, you were completely desperate... and the desperation will not be denied."

"But that's exactly what happened to me!"

"I know. Which makes this even more brutal. I am capable of love, Charlotte, though of unhuman and ungentle intensity."

"But you said you don't love me."

"No, I didn't say it. I tried to make you think it. There is a difference. Can you remember the nights we spent together, and still doubt what I feel for you?"

Tears stung her eyes. "I didn't doubt you at the time. Now I don't know what to think."

"What I told you so harshly about vampire instinct is true. It may be harder for you to understand that it can also be an expression of love, yet it is; and I had to resist, for your sake. Every desire I have felt or shown for you, Charlotte, was born of tenderness."

She raised a hand to touch her throat. Her emotions were in wild confusion.

"Every time I was alone with you I was in danger of being your... your..."

"Victim," he finished for her. "Yes, the danger was there. But if I'd taken advantage – what then? One moment of fulfilment that would destroy you... How could I have borne that? It was wrong of me to place you in such danger, but I averted it time and time again, because your life means everything to me."

She looked up, stunned by the strength of feeling in his voice. His eyes were fixed on her, glowing and predatory. She felt strangled. What sort of passion was it that would leave her not dishonoured or regretful, or with secret joyful memories – but dead? As she stared at him, another waking vision struck her: Karl, wandering in a great house like Parkland, desperately searching for her, finding all the rooms deserted. He was weeping as he searched and she was a ghost watching him, calling his name but unable to make him see or hear...

He spoke. The vision ended.

"I don't blame you for looking at me with horror. You see me now as my victims do in the split second before I strike. I can never hope for you to look on me with love again; nor have I any right to."

The despair in his voice wrenched her heart.

"If – if you had fed on me, would I have died – or gone mad?"

"A careful vampire does not kill, but I wish it were only blood that we take, Charlotte. Our victims suffer mental derangement:

irrational terrors, delusions or mania. The madness may last a few days, or it may be permanent. Outright killing might sometimes be preferable."

"Why does it happen?"

"There are theories. Perhaps, having glimpsed the pit of darkness beneath the skin of normal life, the victim never feels safe again. So, you realise now that Madeleine was ill because Pierre had attacked her?"

Although she had guessed, hearing the admission horrified her.

"You knew all the time? But who is Pierre, why did he come to you?"

"A long story. He delivered a message from another of our kind... the one I fought with last night. But Pierre is indiscreet and savage. He was a danger to your household, and that was why David saw me feeding upon him. I weakened him and took him away. As for Madeleine... I am so sorry."

"Will she get better?" Charlotte asked desperately.

"I believe so. She has a strong spirit. The sensitive ones suffer the most... Of course, there is no way to explain this that makes it anything other than what it is: evil."

Moments passed before she could speak, then when she tried, her voice almost failed.

"When you said that people fall in love with you for the wrong reasons, is this what you meant?"

He looked down, his long, dark lashes curved on his pale cheeks.

"Yes, this is precisely what I meant. They become infatuated with evil, and so meet destruction."

"And what I felt for you – was it only infatuation? Not real love at all?"

"Ask yourself that, Charlotte!" His voice was sharp with pain. "How do I know? I have no right to expect genuine love of anyone. If either of us had hopes, it is all the same hopeless... I thought myself long hardened against such feelings, but I was wrong. I would do anything to keep you with me, but it's impossible. I can offer you nothing – not marriage, not children, not a normal life. *Nothing*."

"Those things have never held any meaning for me," she responded. "I asked nothing of you except your company. The man I thought I loved – was he so different from this monster you claim to be? I can't separate them. You sound and look the same. You say you truly love me, after all…"

"I was always myself with you, *liebchen*. I was not acting, if that's what you think. There was just an unfortunate fact about me that you did not know."

She put her face in her hands. She'd been tempted by the Devil and had fallen. She felt ruined, her heart shattered. Was it worse to know that his devotion was real?

Yes. Yes, it is worse.

Karl's love for her made it impossible for her own feelings to die. As long as she felt the smallest degree of sympathy for him, that surely made her no less evil than him.

"I don't know what to do," she whispered.

Then she felt the light touch of his hand on her arm as he drew her out of the chair and gathered her onto his knee. Her limbs felt weightless. She put her arms around his neck and they held each other, auburn and russet hair mingling together.

"Dear God," he said. "I haven't the heart to keep you prisoner, beloved. Your brother is outside. I will come down with you and unlock the door, and deliver you safely to him."

She raised her head. "Then they'll try to arrest you, and you might kill some of them."

"I will not touch anyone."

"Then they might kill *you*."

"Perhaps. I rather thought you might wish me dead by now."

"Well, I don't!" she said fiercely. She knew her decision might be wrong, but she let the knowledge settle cold and dark within her. "Don't send me away, Karl. I won't go."

"I set you free, and you choose to stay?"

"Even if I left this minute I would still be a prisoner! How can anyone understand? This has taken over my life completely, there is nothing else! You can't put it right, Karl, by pretending it never happened."

He was silent for a moment.

Then he said, "Do you regret it?"

"No." She looked at the shiny blackness of the window, listened to the wind moaning around the house. She thought of David waiting grimly in the dark; she thought of Anne, Madeleine, her father, but they seemed to be on the far side of a night that would never end. "You can't show me a glimpse of another world and then shut the door," she said. "I want to know everything."

CHAPTER ELEVEN

WHISPERED SECRETS

"David, I cannot believe you did something so rash!" George Neville's voice trailed off into a cough and he leaned heavily on the marble mantelpiece, thumping his breastbone. They were in the main drawing room with Elizabeth and Inspector Ash. Midnight was approaching and they were all red-eyed with strain. David was concerned to see his father suffering. Only a few hours spent outside the manor, earlier in the day, had affected his weak chest.

"It wasn't rash," David replied, calm but grim. "Von Wultendorf was on his own, outside the house, standing on the steps as if deliberately making himself a target. Damn it, he had fair warning! And he was so infernally arrogant! I had to shoot. He was about to go back in the house and do God knows what to her. It was my only chance to stop him."

"But you didn't stop him."

"The bullet went clean into his chest, I swear. He fell back against the door, then straightened up as if nothing happened."

Dr Neville scratched his head, smoothed the thinning hair.

"I wish to God you had killed him, David."

The inspector said, "If you had succeeded, Mr Neville, you may have found yourself facing a criminal charge."

"I tell you, I'd happily hang if it meant getting Charlotte out of there!" David retorted.

"Unfortunately, as you only seemed to inflict a flesh wound, you may have made things worse for Miss Neville," said Ash.

My aim's not that bad, David thought angrily. *The fact that a bullet through the ribs didn't floor him only proves that he's not human.* He bit down on his frustration.

Ash went on, "Under the circumstances, sir, no action will be taken against you. But I warn you, unless you give your word not to take matters into your own hands, I'll have to insist that you stay away from the manor."

"The hell I will," David said under his breath. "Very well, Inspector, you have my word. But don't ask me to keep away. I'm going back there now."

"Oh, David, you really should get some sleep," said Elizabeth. "You'll be no use to your sister if you collapse with exhaustion."

"If you'd spent a few weeks in the trenches, you'd know the true meaning of exhaustion," David said quietly. "This is nothing."

"How disrupting all this is," Elizabeth sighed, turning away.

David resisted an angry response. Underneath her brittle surface, his aunt was as upset as anyone.

"Just keep the supplies of hot food and drink coming, Auntie."

"I'm coming up there with you," said his father.

"Oh, no, you're not!" said David. "Two hours in the autumn air, and you sound like a consumptive. Maddy needs you here."

His father shook his head, pushing his hands into his shapeless pockets.

"Damn my blasted lungs! Here, David." He produced a bulky envelope and held it out, speaking gruffly as was his habit when he felt awkward. "I've written Charlotte a letter. Will you take it for her? I put your mother's cross in there, Charlotte needs it more than I do." Brusquely he wiped moisture from his eyes. "If only I hadn't been so harsh on her the other day. I was so bothered about losing Henry, I never gave her happiness a thought. This might – this might be my only chance to tell her I'm sorry."

In response to a knock at the door, Karl went down and – more cautiously this time – retrieved a second parcel of food for Charlotte. When he returned to the solar he looked at her, sitting waiflike by the fire, her woollen sweater barely softening the tense angles of her shoulders. In candlelight, the chamber had the mellow quality of a Vermeer painting: a moment frozen in time, telling a story that ran far deeper than first appeared. Charlotte seemed stretched thin, like glass held up to the light. Her eyes were shimmering violet gems, thirsty for knowledge, for *understanding*. Their light burned him, making demands he could not satisfy.

Karl wanted to tell her everything, but how to begin? He hardly dared touch her. So much passed between them, unspoken, but the veil of danger kept them apart.

He was sharply aware of her mortality, her blood running like quicksilver beneath the delicate skin, her enticing warmth. Her beauty stole his detachment to a perilous degree. But he sublimated his hunger, and would do so for as long as he must.

"Charlotte," he said, walking to her, "here is a letter for you."

She looked at the envelope in his hand with astonishment.

"Where did that come from?"

"They brought more food. It was in the parcel, with a message from David imploring me to release you."

"Oh God," she breathed.

"Open it. Perhaps they expected me to tear it up without telling you."

She extended a wary hand and took the envelope. Her hands shook as she tore it open. A necklace slipped out and fell on the floor, but she ignored it. She scanned the letter once, then read out loud in a level voice:

My dearest Charlotte,

In hope that this reaches your hands, here is a token for your comfort and protection. Be assured that you are in our thoughts every moment of the day and night and we are praying and working constantly for your safe release. You have done no wrong, only been the victim of your old father's selfishness. For the words that passed between us recently I beg your forgiveness, you are the most precious thing in the world to me.

Do not despair, but join us in praying that we shall very soon be reunited. All our love is with you and this darkness will soon be behind us. Have faith!

Your very affectionate,
Father.

Karl bent down to pick up the necklace, and found it was a gold chain with a cross made of tightly woven hair. When he straightened up, Charlotte was weeping, her face in her hands.

"Your father sent this for you," he said softly. "Won't you wear it, for his sake?"

She raised her head, wiping tears away with the back of her hand. "Oh, dear God, it's my mother's cross."

"It is strange, isn't it," he said, "the way that Protestants suddenly embrace Catholicism at times of crisis?"

"People used to have crosses made from their loved ones' hair. It's my mother's hair. Father never parts with it." She broke off, staring at the cross dangling from Karl's fingers. "But you can touch it!"

"Of course, it is well known that vampires can't abide crucifixes. That's why he sent it for you," Karl said, amused. He fastened the chain around her neck and kissed her lips. "There, now you will be safe from me."

She blinked. "So it's not true that the sign of the cross terrifies you? I hadn't even thought about it." She rubbed her arms as if chilled.

"No, it's not true. But don't disillusion your father. He's trying his hardest. You had better write back and reassure him that you are well."

"Yes," she said vaguely, but he saw disturbing thoughts and questions in her face. He wondered if he would ever see her smile again.

"Are any of the superstitions about vampires true?" she asked.

"I've never discovered any symbol, herb or plant that holds any special terror for me. I cast a shadow and a reflection like a human being. Holy water does not burn me, nor do I find priests unduly repellent."

"But you never came to chapel with us."

"Because I don't believe in God," said Karl. "Actually I like churches. Didn't we agree that King's College Chapel is the most exquisite building we know? I love to go there."

Charlotte looked shocked. "Don't you – don't you worship anything?"

"Such as the Devil, you mean?"

Her eyes widened. "I must know."

"No, I do not worship the Devil. I told your father I'm an agnostic and that is true. There may be more to life than we can see, but I don't pretend to know what it is."

She was looking at him in obvious disbelief. He added, "What did you expect me to say?"

"How do I know?" she flared. "You tell me you are some supernatural creature, then you say you believe in nothing – it doesn't make sense."

Karl sat down on the rug beside her, resting one arm across her knees.

"Satan was not waiting in person to initiate me, nor God to vent his wrath. However, some vampires still believe in them with passion. There is no simple answer."

Weariness crept over him. He did not want to talk, only to sit quietly with Charlotte, to pretend there was nothing else; no distance between them, no blood thirst, no humans holding them to siege. Impossible. Charlotte's distress scorched him like flame.

"I must know how you became as you are. You said you'd tell me." Her voice was soft but insistent. Then her face changed and she touched his cheekbone. "Karl, you look so sad. This is hard for you to talk about, isn't it? I didn't realise."

"Yes, it is difficult," he said. "Still, they're only words, beloved. How can they have such power over us? I know you believe in God, which makes this doubly hard for you: the notion of sin." She bowed her head, her hand tightening on his. "Well, that is ingrained in all of us," Karl went on. "My family were Roman Catholics. Belief was unquestioned, instilled from babyhood. Repent, or burn in hellfire, the priests told us.

"Certain things I've told you are true. I lived in Vienna and I was a musician there. However, I couldn't specify the dates because I was born in 1793."

He heard Charlotte catch her breath.

"My parents weren't rich. My father was a schoolmaster, my mother worked hard to care for her children. I had two sisters and a brother; two others died in infancy. My mother's life was one of drudgery, yet it didn't seem so at the time. She never lost her beauty. My memory is of her always laughing and singing. We adored her, as did my father. She was so lovely, with dark red hair like rose leaves…"

"Do you look like her?" Charlotte asked.

"I suppose so. Ilona certainly does." Karl stopped. The memories were so vivid that he only had to speak of them to see their faces, hear their voices.

"Was Ilona one of your sisters?"

He paused. *Should I tell her? Everything, I said.*

"No, she's my daughter."

"*Daughter?*" Charlotte looked astonished, then dismayed. "You have a *daughter*? But you said you weren't married. I never thought…"

"I was once. Now you look more shocked than when you found out I was a vampire. But it was a long time ago, *liebchen,* and I want to explain it in order."

"I'm sorry." She swallowed, very pale. "Go on."

"It was not an easy time. We endured two French occupations of the city, then after the Congress of Vienna, the repressive regime of Metternich. But this was also the time of Schubert and Beethoven. I saw them, I played their music while they were alive and working. I still see the buildings of the Ringstrasse as new and gaudy, because when I grew up the Ringstrasse did not exist."

Charlotte looked incredulous. "So far in the past."

"Yes, but still vivid to me. In Vienna it was natural to grow up surrounded by music. I began as a chorister, then my parents made every sacrifice to educate me at a seminary where I learned the piano and the cello. Later, when I joined an orchestra and earned extra money by teaching, I was able to pay back all they'd given me. Treatment in the best clinic when my mother fell ill, a maid to keep house for her. But she had tuberculosis, fatal in those days. My father outlived her by only a year. They were both in their sixties, a fair age, for those times. I became a vampire ten years before they died, but I thank providence they never knew.

"I was twenty-seven. My orchestra played at the palaces of the Hapsburgs, at the Opera and the houses of aristocrats. My wife had just given birth to our first child. I was so perfectly happy it seemed nothing could go wrong."

Struggling to disguise the emotion in her voice, Charlotte said, "Your wife – what was she like?"

"Small, dark, very sweet, but she could terrify grown men with her temper. We met rehearsing a Mozart opera. Therese sang in the chorus." He smiled sadly. "Other faces I remember clearly, but hers is elusive. I don't know why."

"And you loved her very much. It's in your voice."

He clasped her hand and said gently, "I lost her a long time ago, dearest." The pain of recalling the past shocked him, far worse than he'd expected. He felt the touch of Charlotte's hand on his hair as he went on. "Therese was my life. We named our baby daughter Ilona after her mother, who was Hungarian. I was completely wrapped up in them. It never occurred to me that anything could intrude.

"I began to notice a man who came to every performance we gave. His appearance was very striking: tall and powerful, not exactly handsome, but with a strong, brooding face that fascinated me. His clothes were old fashioned and severe, giving him a puritanical look quite out of place in the flamboyance of Vienna. It's hard to describe his magnetic glow of strength and power. I often noticed others looking at him, too. But he always seemed to be watching me. Dark eyes, never blinking. He unnerved me a great deal.

"After he had stared at me through seven or eight performances, he approached me and introduced himself as Kristian Müller. He spoke Hochdeutsch – I mean high German, rather than the Wienerisch dialect – with an accent I could not place. He wanted me to give a private performance at his home, and offered a staggering sum of money. Therese and I were not in poverty, but a wealthy patron could make all the difference to our lives, make our families comfortable and ensure our daughter's future. I saw no harm in it. So I went alone to play my cello for Kristian, and he rewarded me generously and invited me again.

"He lived in lavish apartments but appeared out of place there, like an actor on a set. There was nothing of his personality in the rooms at all. To my relief, there were always others with him, graceful men and women with shining eyes, almost as intriguing as Kristian himself. I wasn't told who they were: guests, relatives?

I had no idea. He was always the centre. I can't emphasise enough the sheer presence he had, like a mountain – drawing people to him only to crush them.

"At first I was amused by the way his clique revolved around him, then it began to feel sinister. An evening in Kristian's company exhausted me. I couldn't wait to escape the smothering atmosphere and return home to Therese and Ilona.

"Soon I realised that Kristian resented me putting my family first. He would find reasons to make me stay longer. He was so hard to defy that I grew wary of him. Therese would say, 'Don't go again, Karl. It's more than music he wants from you.' Yet I ignored the warning signs and dismissed him as an eccentric. A great mistake.

"One evening, on my seventh visit, Kristian was alone. I played for him as usual and he plied me with wine and schnapps, trying to make me drunk. Wishing I'd listened to Therese, I planned my escape. But he never touched me. Instead Kristian began to talk of God.

"'Do you not realise how wretched your life is?' he said. 'Humans think they are alive but they walk around with closed eyes. They think they know God but they worship painted idols, wrapping themselves in delusions. They separate good from evil and pretend evil cannot touch them. Lucifer, they name the fallen one. But God and the Devil are the same being! One dreadful and avenging God who covers the world with his dark wings.'

"Kristian was like the most charismatic of preachers, you could imagine people falling at his feet, thinking they'd seen a terrible and awesome light. His words had a devastating effect on me. He said he was an instrument of this dark God. He was proof of God's existence, a dark angel walking the Earth to do God's work. And he said, 'I have chosen you, Karl, as one with the courage not to die in ignorance but to walk on the edge of life and death with me.'

"I had never questioned my faith, yet Kristian seemed to expose my beliefs for what they were: fragile, non-existent. I felt suddenly bereft and very afraid. And here was Kristian, promising to show me the true face of God. Offering salvation."

Karl paused, drew and released a breath.

"A very old trick. What made it so effective was that Kristian truly *believed*. He was like a prophet. In his presence, you could see nothing else. He filled the sky.

"'I can bestow life everlasting,' he said. 'I will make you one of God's dark agents on Earth. I can grant the power to fly inside the mind of God, which is heaven.'

"He overstated his case with these words, and the rational part of me began warning loudly this was not a prophet but a madman. I made excuses to leave and put my cello in its case, trying to seem unhurried although I was trembling.

"I'll never forget the way he stared at me. I should explain a little about Kristian. He hates humans, yet he searches among them – as if for diamonds in sand – for those who would make perfect vampires. And for some reason he fastened on me to join his brood. He thought I was under his spell. His ego is so great that he simply could not believe I was rejecting him.

"'Leave your family and come with me, Karl!' he said. He caught my arm and I felt his coldness bleeding through me, as if he were made of frozen granite. 'Once you see the wonders I can show you, the love of mortals will be as dust.'

"I was angry now. Who was this man, to think he could take over my life and dismiss my love for my family as *dust*? What did he want of me? I feared he wouldn't let me go, but he opened the door, saying, 'Come again tomorrow, my friend. By then you will appreciate what I offer.' I fled, with no intention of going near him again, however rich he might be.

"The next evening, when Kristian expected me, I stayed at home with Therese and the baby." Karl closed his eyes briefly, forced himself to continue. "I was completely happy that night. I felt released, as if Kristian had been a massive weight on my mind, from which I'd narrowly freed myself. *Liebe Gott*.

"We went to bed without a care in the world. When I woke I was alone, tangled up in the sheets, feeling desperately ill. I was confused; all I could think about was finding Therese, but when I tried to stand up I fainted. It took time to realise I was not at home, but in Kristian's apartments.

"That night seems blurred and endless in my mind, perhaps several nights run together. When I came round again, I found myself in the salon where I had played for Kristian. The room was all lit up with candles like a cathedral. Three people were with me, two holding me upright while Kristian faced me, looking fierce. He said, 'Why didn't you come back, Karl?'

"The other two were members of his clique, Andreas and Katerina. They looked very beautiful to me, but unreal, as if made of porcelain and diamonds… How can I explain how I felt? Perhaps you've had a dream where the most innocuous object fills you with terror. I was certainly in a dreamlike state, and these lovely life-size figurines terrified me. I felt their breath like frost on my neck. I knew what they were going to do, and that this wasn't the first time. They both struck at once, Andreas burying his fangs in the right side of my neck, Katerina the left. The pain was like being stretched on a rack, as if their sucking out my blood pulled every vein in my body.

"Then perhaps you've had the converse dream, where horrific sights leave you unmoved. Every reaction is irrational, and that's the true source of the nightmare. This was the state I entered now. I couldn't breathe. I was floating, a horrible sensation, as if all ties that anchored me to safety had been severed. The pain was a dark gold sphere in which I was weightless, detached from emotion as I waited for death. I wasn't even surprised that these were *vampires*, it all felt pre-ordained.

"When Katerina and Andreas finished, I stood half fainting between them, seeing the room through a thick golden light. A huge dark figure came towards me, rippling and distorted as if moving through water. Kristian was coming to finish me. Yet he didn't drink my blood, instead he touched my chest. I felt overwhelming coldness. I wanted to sleep, like a man buried in snow.

"Death is only oblivion, Charlotte. It doesn't hurt, any more than sleep hurts. And I was certainly dead. Yet they brought me back to life, or a form of it.

"I felt them carrying me. We seemed to be floating underwater, surrounded by strange colours. I became aware of crimson light throbbing through me, and I was struggling to take a breath, never quite succeeding… Yearning towards something. I had no idea what was happening, no conscious thoughts, but the hot ruby glow kept pulsing through me, drawing me towards some profound ecstasy."

Karl looked up and found Charlotte's grey-violet gaze fixed on him, rapt.

"Mingled with this were such dreams, feelings beyond my experience. The light throbbed brighter, until I experienced a revelation that I was part of a circle and therefore complete. I was now made of crystal. And when I opened my eyes, I found the three vampires around me, the four of us forming a circle and floating in a vast landscape – a sky, rather: a breathtaking sky of indescribable grandeur. Energy flowed between us. This was love, perfect happiness – heaven, as Kristian had promised.

"When Kristian saw that my transformation was complete, he broke the connection. It was like being dropped from the edge of a cliff. Being flung from bliss to terror in a heartbeat – I think no human would survive. However, eventually it dawned that I was not falling, but standing in the salon again.

"How can I explain? I was dizzy, as if full of opium, yet everything appeared wonderfully luminous and clear. A grey veil had been taken from my sight. Such colours... Even my own skin glowed like opal. And while these impressions held me captivated, I also understood that I was no longer human."

"What had they done to you?" Charlotte asked.

"Replaced my mortal life with their own energy. This new force transformed every cell of my body, changed me into a mineral replica of myself. Yet this new state was anything but inanimate. It's a deadly power with no real life of its own, yet it craves the life and energy of others... If that is the definition of a vampire, that is what I had become.

"I was in no state to comprehend this yet. Andreas and Katerina looked so lovely that I felt I'd never seen beauty before. They watched my reactions with the sort of pleasure people take in the first stumbling steps of a foal. Kristian was sombre, but his eyes burned me.

"My hearing was so acute that the silence itself echoed... and I remember thinking, *They only breathe when they are going to speak!* When I realised that I also no longer needed to breathe, a dreadful revelation struck me: these alien creatures had made me one of them. It was horrific, yet thrilling at the same time. I was standing on the threshold of a new universe.

"Outside the window the lights of Vienna shone like stars. I saw people moving through the dark streets as if it were day, all bathed in a beautiful soft light full of exquisite colours. I felt thirst pulling at my throat... a yearning I didn't understand. Andreas and Katerina came to me like loving friends, stroking my arms and hair, so beautiful I couldn't speak. Such pure beauty they had, like that of pearls.

"I looked at Kristian and asked, 'What have you done to me?'

"'Made you as myself,' he said.

"'But what are we?'

"He replied, 'Children of Lilith,' and began to laugh.

"His laughter was harsh to my oversensitive ears, malevolent. I felt the utmost revulsion towards him. Kristian exuded a dominating aura that made me feel trapped, and rebellious in a way that I don't think he had anticipated. I couldn't cope with all this beauty and horror mixed together. I was still far from my right mind, and I thought if I left him and went home, my life would return to normal.

"So I began hunting for my coat, but Kristian stopped me. He was like a great dark wall. He said, 'Don't you realise how I love you, Karl? I have given you this gift because I love you.'

"I was astonished, but his words only made me more determined to escape his lunacy. Like a drunk trying to sound sober I said, 'I must go home. My wife will wonder where I am.'

"At that his face turned livid. He assumed that once I changed, I would forget my family and worship him. He knew nothing of earning love through friendship. It's true that I was in awe of him – but emotionally, he meant nothing. He saw this, but was incapable of accepting it.

"'You cannot go home, Karl,' he said. 'You are part of my circle now.'

"I said something like, 'You can't keep me here. I'll call the authorities,' and at this, Andreas and Katerina went into peals of laughter. There was movement around me, doors opening and closing. I felt so strange, quite ill in fact. It was like a fever, a desire to tear off my own skin. There was a disturbing scent in the air... and I turned and saw Andreas bringing a human into the room.

"He was a boy of about fifteen, a beggar with huge brown

eyes in a grimy face. Just a boy. Yet I perceived him as if he were another species. Where vampires were like ice, he positively glittered with heat. Imagine your first glimpse of countryside after years in the desert. How your heart would ache for the first taste of rain on your tongue...

"He wasn't afraid. He thought some rich people had taken pity on him. Katerina was behind him and I'm sure he suspected nothing – she struck so quickly. Showing me what to do. And when I saw, when I caught the scent of blood, the urge pulled me in like gravity."

Karl stopped. "I should not tell you this, Charlotte."

"No, please go on," she said. "I want to understand."

"I was like two separate people. There was the monster I'd become, moving towards the boy as Katerina held him for me. It seemed natural to wrap my arms about him, to feel my newly sharp teeth slide down to reopen the wounds she had made, to feel the wondrous liquid flowing into me. There was no savagery, only the most luscious feeling of tenderness, relief. I was floating in a soft ruby light and I could feel tears flowing from my eyes and running down the boy's neck. Yet the other half of me witnessed what was happening as if I was outside my body. I stood aghast. *I am drinking blood. I am damned. God in heaven, how can I end this nightmare?*

"When the blood ceased to flow, I wanted more. The compulsion sickened me, yet still I wanted him... Andreas pulled us apart, and if the boy wasn't dead already, the others finished him. Then I came back to myself. With the stolen blood inside me, I was very clear-headed. I knew exactly what Kristian had done to me, and I was devastated.

"Andreas and Katerina caressed me with unspoken sympathy. Kristian spoke to me like a father confessor, kind and stern. 'This is what you are now, a vampire. You cannot go back to being human. You cannot return to your family.' He was right, there was no way back. My intellect could not overcome my new instincts. I knew he was telling the truth, but I still refused to believe him.

"So when he'd finished his lecture, I said, 'Now I am going home.'

"He was astounded. He said, 'You are not an imbecile, Karl, so why are you behaving like one? I have given you immortality, heightened perception, the power of life and death over mankind. A gift for which most men would sell their souls! Mundane responsibilities have no hold on you now. They are ash. Attend to me and I will show you the face of God.'

"His words were affecting, but desperate. He wanted me to say, 'Yes, I forsake my wife and daughter. Kristian, you are the centre of my universe.' He wanted me to say it and *believe* it. But I couldn't. I said, 'I don't care what you have done to me or why. It was without my consent.'

"'That is untrue!' he shouted. He grew furious because I was so calm. I believe he would have broken my back to force a reaction out of me. 'You told me that if you had no earthly ties you would accept the gift of enlightenment!'

"'But I have earthly ties. Why would I leave my wife just for the asking?' Although I spoke rationally, I felt a growing sense of dread.

"Kristian replied, 'You're wrong, Karl. You have no bonds with Earth. Come with me.' He took me along a corridor, where the air was so thick with the scent of blood that my head swam. By the time we reached a servant's room tucked away from the rest, the iron smell was overwhelming. Blood was splashed everywhere: dark wet stains all over the floorboards, walls, furniture. In my enhanced sight it glistened with a thousand shades of crimson and purple. In the middle, on a little white bed, was Therese. Dead."

"Oh my God," said Charlotte, muffled. "Had Kristian…?"

"He doesn't touch humans if he can help it, but he'd ordered one of his brood to murder her. Not Andreas or Katerina, one whose name I choose not to remember. But I don't blame that vampire, I blame only Kristian… and myself. In his twisted thinking, Therese was an obstacle to my freedom – so he removed the obstacle. He did so to demonstrate that if I actually lost her, I wouldn't care, that vampires do not suffer human grief.

"But he was wrong. I was blind with grief. All I could think was how she must have suffered, while I failed to protect her. I threw myself at Kristian, determined to kill him – not realising it was impossible. Instead he fastened his fangs in my throat. All the strength went out of me. He pushed me into the room and, as if she'd been waiting for a signal, Katerina came in with an infant in her arms. Ilona.

"They locked me in the room with Therese's body and my daughter, who was very much warm and alive. Kristian's way was to 'break' new vampires who were being difficult, as I was. And at the end, when the vampire was in the pit of despair, Kristian would become the fount of redemption, of love, sustenance, spiritual bliss.

"I was left there for hours while my hunger mounted – my only source of nourishment, my own daughter. The thirst was all-consuming, and I had no experience in controlling it. Outside I could hear Kristian talking to the vampire who had killed Therese. 'Tell me what you did. Tell me how you felt... and what did she do then?' Hours, it went on. That conversation taught me more about Kristian than I ever wished to know."

A sob escaped Charlotte. Karl folded his hand over her knee.

"But Kristian didn't understand that there are stronger instincts than a vampire's thirst. I would starve to death before I harmed Ilona. She was warm and full of blood and I was in torment – but I did not touch her. Such a hideous situation: her own father this white, dead thing, dying again for want of her blood; and the voices through the door... It was so monstrous that I went completely out of my mind. That's how I found the strength to do what I did.

"There was one tiny window, too small for a man to climb through. I smashed it, tore out the frame and ripped away part of the wall. With Ilona in my arms, I jumped down to the road, two storeys below – discovering in the process how resilient vampire bodies are. I ran to my older sister's house as if the Devil were after me – which he almost literally was.

"My sister was very shocked to see me in the middle of the night. I wonder if I looked like a vampire to her? I told her Therese was ill, could she please look after Ilona while I went for the doctor? All the time, I was aware of her human radiance, her heartbeat luring me towards her... My own sister. Gods. I left as fast as I could and, only a few yards from her door, I took my first real victim. He was a stranger, he could have been anyone. He could have been my own father, for all I knew when I dragged him into the shadows.

"As I fed on him I felt tenderness again, relief and ecstasy so intense it made me weep. But afterwards – and whether he lived or died, I didn't want to know – desolation overcame me. There was no escape from the thirst. I would be compelled to do this over and over again. How could I stay with my sisters or parents, how could I enter their houses with this evil within me? How could I look at them, when I saw them only as shimmering vessels of blood? How could I take them in my arms, when they might die there?

"Then I understood what Kristian meant. I could have no contact with humans, it would be betrayal even to try. There was a gulf between us forever. Charlotte, I cannot express how alone I felt at that moment.

"So I went back to Kristian. He found me halfway and we walked along the Kärntnerstrasse together, like two Viennese gentlemen after the opera. I told him my feelings. I told him I wanted to kill myself.

"He replied that if I was serious, there was a place where I could be frozen into oblivion forever, a place called the *Weisskalt*, so high and cold that even vampires could not survive there. The image frightened me, and I was so angered by his dispassion that I never seriously considered suicide again. To defeat him, I must live. I said I would go anywhere with him, do anything, if he would only leave my daughter alone.

"He agreed. I think he'd forgotten her already. But he said, 'It's not enough, Karl. You must come with me because you want to, not because I hold a threat over you.' I was incredulous, that he could do all this, murder my wife, try to make me kill my own child, then expect me to love him!

"Yet he did.

"No one could bring him to justice or hold him in prison. One thing I persuaded him to do was to help me cover up Therese's death, which he did by posing as a doctor who affirmed she'd died of a sudden illness. Yes, it sounds sickening, Charlotte, but understand: if they'd known she was murdered, there would be uproar, and I the obvious suspect. To disappear would prove my guilt, and I could never have seen my family again. But if her death appeared a quiet, ordinary tragedy, it was understandable if I left Ilona with my sister and went away to nurse my grief. And…

it would be acceptable for me to go back sometimes.

"So that is what we did, and then I went away with Kristian and his other vampires, in order to keep them away from my loved ones.

"In many ways Kristian was right, there are experiences more profound than human love. This strange new existence was wondrous, captivating me despite myself. Vampires can pass into another dimension, a world aslant from this, that we call the Crystal Ring. When we enter the Ring we seem to vanish. We can travel to any part of the world, feed in a different place every night, and thus pass unsuspected among mankind. It sounds unbelievable, of course."

Charlotte looked thoughtful.

"When Pierre came to Parkland, I recognised him. I'd seen him once in Cambridge, and I saw him disappear into thin air."

"He didn't speak to you or harm you?" She shook her head. Karl stroked her arm. "Oh, Charlotte. I didn't know he was looking for me even then. I should have been more vigilant."

"At least now I know I wasn't going mad," she said. "I saw a vampire disappear, so how can I not believe you? Tell me the rest, please."

"Ah, too much to tell, really. The Crystal Ring is beyond description." Karl smiled. "It's another existence... Kristian calls it the 'mind of God'. To give him his due, all the things he promised were real.

"I cannot truthfully say I regret what Kristian did to me. But was it worth Therese's death? No. I'd die a thousand times over in exchange for her life... and I can never forgive him, *never*. He elected himself king of vampires simply by being the strongest. I don't know his origins, but I believe he defeated immortals older than himself, and probably destroyed his own creators. He is the worst kind of egomaniac, one who believes he's doing God's work. An avenging God who visits disasters on mankind to teach them their folly. Sometimes he believes he *is* God. And his followers are his archangels.

"Everything about Kristian depressed me from the start: his fanaticism, his arrogance, his brutality. Yet I can't say I hated him, or if I did, the hatred was simply there like a sheet of snow, boundless, implacable. The same with love. Although the grief I felt for Therese was unbearable, I didn't fall under its weight. And with killing – however appalled I was by the idea of drinking blood, this inner tranquillity enabled me to do it. In order to stay sane, I embraced a state of deadly calm.

"I'm not saying all vampires feel like this. It was simply my nature, accentuated by the transformation. Perhaps it was my serenity that first drew Kristian to me, but later it began to drive him mad. However he provoked me, I would never react as he expected. I couldn't be what he wanted.

"Still, I wasn't the first. Time and again, he's destroyed vampires who fell short of his ideals. I've only escaped the same fate so far because he has a particular obsession with me. It has become his crusade, to see me on my knees declaring repentant adoration – *then* he can destroy me, and his pride will be satisfied."

"Might that happen?" Charlotte asked softly.

Karl laughed. "When hell freezes colder than the *Weisskalt*. Anyway, after we left Vienna, I went with Kristian to his Schloss on the Rhine. He lived like a monk there. Although he was rich, earthly wealth was just a convenience. His real craving was for devotion."

"Do you mean he kept you prisoner?"

"Not exactly. We were free to come and go, but if anyone stayed away too long, he would hunt them down. His punishments were horrible. The greatest fear he held over us was the *Weisskalt*, an effective death sentence. The irony is that the very qualities for which he chose his vampires – character, intelligence – made us intrinsically rebellious. Perhaps his greatest pleasure is the struggle of wills.

"I stayed away from the Schloss for longer each time, until I simply did not bother going back. He came after me, of course. The fights we had... so pointless. Yet he kept letting me go, giving me one more chance to return of my own accord.

"Instead, others began to leave him. Strange as it seems, Andreas and Katerina became my dearest friends and came to live with me. Pierre too, though he could never decide where his loyalties lay. Kristian couldn't tolerate our desertion. I believe that's why he began to hate me more than love me. He is a jealous lord who couldn't believe I had no desire to steal his flock.

"Meanwhile I often went back to Vienna. It was always a shock, to see my family ageing. Vampires do not change, you see; I saw their porcelain beauty around me every day. But in my loved ones I saw every line, every grey hair. I saw the blood rushing through Ilona like sap through flower petals. She grew so fast that I wanted to seize her and say, 'Stop! The faster you grow, the sooner you will die!'"

Charlotte said, "Did she – did she know you?"

Karl nodded. "She regarded my sister and brother-in-law as her parents, but she knew me as her real father. She'd been told her mother was dead, and that I played with an orchestra abroad. Ilona was the sweetest child. I adored her with human and vampire intensity. I couldn't bear her sadness, each time I left, yet she accepted it. My sister began to look at me with suspicion, though she never said anything.

"One day I returned to find Ilona married. I couldn't believe it. She was twenty-two already... and it's a terrible thing to admit, but I was jealous of her love for her husband. However, that's not why I made the decision.

"The next time I went, a year later, I did not make my presence known. Instead I followed Ilona and my sister as they visited our parents' grave. I was shocked to see how old my sister had become, now grey-haired, stooped and breathless as she walked. She wept, as she always did at the grave. God, I would have done anything to put my arms around her and say, 'It's all right, dear one, I am here...' But it struck me that I actually *could not* approach her. The disparity of our ages was too obvious. The risk that she might shrink from me in fear was agonising. So I stayed where I was, under branches that were all silver in the rain, watching.

"Here she was, weeping in a graveyard, she who'd once been young and so full of life... and I looked at Ilona and thought, *You too. I shall have to watch you grow old and die, my daughter, while I remain here like a stopped clock on a desolate landscape, watching your life shine and flicker and go out in the distance...*

"I couldn't bear it, Charlotte. I went to Ilona's house that night and took her away. She was so delighted to see me, it hadn't yet struck her that I showed no signs of age. She trusted me. And I believed I was saving her, as we travelled in a coach and pair to a distant hotel, but the truth is I was thinking only of myself.

"I didn't give Kristian a thought. It was Katerina who warned me he would be furious, but I persuaded her and Andreas to help me. And that night we made Ilona into a vampire.

"I didn't tell her my plan; I thought, rightly, that she'd be horrified. I took great pains not to alarm her, and she suspected nothing until the very last moment when I... when I drank her blood and killed her. I was terrified the process would fail, that she'd remain dead – because it can happen – but the three of us gave our vampiric energy back to her and her eyes opened again.

"And I shall never forget the anguish and loathing on her face when she realised what she had become. From that moment, she hated me.

"She had every right, of course. What I did to her was no better than what Kristian had done to me. I took her without consent, sundered her from her husband and everything human. I had what I wanted: Ilona, unchanging forever. But at such a price!"

"Karl..." He felt Charlotte's gentle hand on his shoulder.

"She changed completely. She lost all her sweetness, became cold and vicious. A perfect vampire, perhaps; but no longer my daughter.

"Kristian allows no one else to create new vampires, so he was outraged. With more subtlety than I knew he possessed, he found that the best way to punish me was to let me alone and to destroy those I loved instead. He took Andreas and Katerina from me and condemned them to the *Weisskalt* for their sins. I feared he'd do the same to Ilona. But no, he was entranced by her and she, perversely, adored him in return. She couldn't have taken better revenge on me than to become Kristian's perfect angel." Karl fell silent. Such pain in these memories.

Eventually Charlotte asked, "What did you do?"

"What could I do? Many times I tried talking to her. She was implacable. In the end I had to let her go. But I still love her. That will never end.

"Since then I have lived alone. Anyone who befriended me was in danger of Kristian's jealousy, I couldn't let anyone take the risk. Oh, I could tell you more, of travels I've made in search of some meaning behind all this, the wretched confrontations with Kristian... but it would add little to what I've said.

"There are only a few dozen vampires that I know of in the world, Charlotte, all of us subject to Kristian. He is always there, like a great dark storm. I always hoped he would give up and leave me in peace, after all this time... I should have known the hope was in vain. His patience is running out. He's so desperate to tame me that he even resorted to harming Ilona, his favourite. He sent Pierre to tell me that she was in the *Weisskalt*, and would remain there until I surrendered."

"But you didn't?" said Charlotte.

"No. The night I went missing, I rescued her myself. Kristian attacked me, and that's why I was too weak to spare poor Edward."

"Oh, Karl," Charlotte said softly. "Did you save her?"

"For the time being." Karl shut his eyes for a moment, weighed down by hopelessness, soothed by Charlotte's touch. "But while Kristian lives, no one is safe, no one free."

In a cautious tone, she said, "Could he be killed?"

"Try beheading a vampire, they'll slip away into the Crystal Ring laughing. And taking him to the *Weisskalt* would be impossible. He's too strong. That's why I came to your father, Charlotte. Not the only reason, but the main one was to discover something that would be fatal to Kristian. Perhaps a substance created in a laboratory that is never found in nature."

Charlotte looked startled but intrigued.

"Did you find anything?"

"No corrosives affected my flesh, radium did not burn me, no gas poisoned me... I reached the conclusion that only extreme cold has any effect on us at all."

"You were trying these things on yourself?"

"*Natürlich*. How else could I find out?"

"But you might have killed yourself!"

"Yes, there was that risk," said Karl. "But it was one worth taking, for a chance of destroying Kristian. Do I sound heartless, to speak so coldly of killing him?"

"I'd feel heartless too, if he'd done those things to me. I'm not very good at showing sympathy, I never know the right words... but I am so sorry, Karl... especially about Therese."

He stroked her arm. "Thank you. I cannot change what happened so I've learned to accept it. The sorrow is distant now."

"I wish you could have told me before," said Charlotte.

He looked into her eyes, trying to read the changing violet shadows. He saw no condemnation in her face. Rather, she looked contemplative.

"So do I," he said softly. "There it is. I don't know what I am, or why I exist. I have encountered no gods, angels or demons. I wish I had Kristian's faith, but what's the use of seeking an invisible God when you can see the very life essence pulsing through plants? What does it mean to be immortal, when the universe itself cannot last forever? I'm still searching for answers. I hoped to find them in science, but I think if there's any truth to be found, it is inside us."

Charlotte was silent for a time. The fire crackled, a slight wind curled around the house, bringing faint voices from outside.

Then she said, "I don't know what I expected, but what you've told me is like nothing I imagined. There's one thing I'm certain of, Karl: you are not evil."

"I doubt that your father and brother would look on my story so favourably. Don't lose sight of what I am. I was human once, but if I still had a conscience, I would not have survived this long."

"But who can claim to be perfect?" she said fervently. "The War, all those young men who never came back, or who came back like Edward —" She stopped, swallowing. "That was the doing of men, wasn't it? Or are you going to tell me that you and Kristian started the War between you?"

Karl laughed, despite himself.

"No. Men perpetrate evil to match that of vampires, it's true. Ours is on a small scale by comparison."

"You say you've always been your true self with me." Her expression was intense. "I don't doubt you at all. I still love you, Karl. I can't help it. I can't just make it stop."

"Nor can I," he said.

She was leaning towards him. He only had to slide his hand through her hair and draw her head down a little for their mouths to meet. And at her warmth, he felt the heavy pull of desire again, her compliance drawing him into the whirlpool… It would be so sweet to make love to her again, but at the last moment, in the exquisite loss of control that felt so poignantly human, would he still have the strength to turn his face away from her throat? He doubted it. Not this time. He forced himself to end the kiss, to hold her away from him. She stared at him, her lips parted, her eyes misty with longing and dismay.

"Charlotte, please..."

"What? What am I supposed to do? I can't accept that you're evil! You're like light streaming through a door from another world. I was afraid at first, but you, *you* told me not to be frightened. You can't just take the light away."

"Oh, God." He held both her hands firmly. "You know we can't stay here. It's not only my need for blood, Charlotte. I have to ensure that Pierre doesn't come back."

"Why should he come back?"

"He has a very dangerous sense of humour. He's already attacked Madeleine, and threatened to do worse once he recovers his strength. He knows the best way to hurt me is through you, and your loved ones. I can only control him as Kristian does, by physical force."

"To hurt *you*?" Charlotte turned pale with fury. "What about my *family*? He can't! How dare he even think it!"

"It's my fault," said Karl. He released her hands, stood up and returned to sit in the other chair. "I never meant to endanger your family, but by coming to them, I've drawn other vampires after me."

She stared at him, aghast.

"What are we going to do?"

"Initially, I shall write a note to your brother informing him that I'll release you in exchange for letting me go unhindered."

"Why?"

"Because that is what I intend to do."

"No."

"Charlotte, this situation is impossible! We cannot stay together, whatever happens."

Her lips were dark against the pallor of her face, her eyes circled with shadows of tiredness and strain, but this only accentuated her beauty. She was utterly different to Therese, yet now when he recalled his wife's death, he saw Charlotte in her place. Despair filled him. Karl wanted to forget his hopelessness in the warmth of her arms... but would only put her in danger, and he must protect her. Horrible, that he could still desire her blood, yet he did. He wanted her silken skin against his, her passion flowing into him... to pretend he was human again, and that all would be well.

Cruel delusion.

She spoke, breaking his trance. "No, Karl, let me finish. I think I know how we can leave without being seen."

He looked doubtfully at her, and saw that he'd misread her expression. The look was not fear, but determination.

With a tentative smile she added, "You are not the only one who has secrets."

CHAPTER TWELVE

WRITTEN IN BONES

Charlotte stoked the fire, then sat in the chair opposite, watching Karl in the firelight. His pale skin was burnished by a watery red glow, his hair a mass of black and deepest auburn, eyes shadowed pools of amber and jet. The more they talked, the closer she felt to him; yet, paradoxically, the more enticing and mystical he seemed.

"When I was a child," she began, "my sisters and I used to play in this house. It had been derelict for years and was such a gloomy, haunted place, but we felt drawn here."

Karl smiled. "Ah, the delicious torment of frightening oneself."

"But that was all Fleur and Maddy wanted to do, they were insensitive to the building's true aura. They had no regard for its age or secrets…"

Charlotte paused. She'd never expressed this, for fear of ridicule, nor realised how strongly she believed it.

"We came here once when I was nearly ten, and Fleur and Maddy were challenging each other to see who dared to go farthest into the cellar. I wished they wouldn't be so childish, they didn't even know what they were scared of, except the dark and spiders… but I felt there was a presence down there and I knew it was wrong to disturb it. Almost sacrilegious, like running and shouting in church. I was too timid to say so. They thought I was hanging back out of fear, and they teased me until I got upset and told them how disrespectful they were. I probably sounded like a ten-year-old prig as well as a coward, so they decided to teach me a lesson. Fleur insisted we all three go down into the cellar together – and once we were there, they fled and locked me in. Well, I was afraid, but –"

"Wait," said Karl. "Why would your sisters play such a cruel trick on you?"

The unexpected question deflected her thoughts and she felt wings of self-concealment closing around her. She didn't want to talk about it, but his gaze was insistent.

"It matters, Charlotte."

"Haven't you guessed, Karl? You're so perceptive. You've seen pictures of my mother, you know how my father is with us…"

"Your sisters resented him loving you the best," Karl said softly.

"But I didn't *want* to be favoured – not if it meant my sisters rejecting me. How can I explain? God knows, he can be stern and difficult, but he's the best, the dearest of fathers to me. The trouble was that I knew he missed my mother, and although I looked like her, I *wasn't* her. And that made him sad."

"And this made you feel responsible for your father's happiness?"

"Yes. I suppose it did."

"That is a dreadful burden to place on a child."

"Oh, but I don't blame him!" Charlotte said quickly. "He loved my mother dearly. It wasn't my sisters' fault either. They were lucky in other ways, growing up free and self-confident. Perhaps it was healthier for them, not to have him hovering over them with schoolbooks the whole time. I don't know if they were jealous of his attention, or pitied me. Both, perhaps. Whatever the case, they saw me as *different*, which I hated. Half my childhood was spent trying to win their approval… letting them have their own way in everything."

"And you found you cannot buy love in that way?"

She nodded ruefully. "Yes, I know that now. And the other half, I spent creating a shield of indifference to protect myself. Don't misunderstand, we do love each other, of course." She half smiled. "I became an object of affectionate exasperation to them. Poor Charlotte, stuck in the lab like a tortoise in its shell. That was me. But secretly… often I so longed to be like them, to be part of their world, and I never could. Oh well."

"But this has caused you real pain." She saw concern in Karl's eyes. "Have you ever told them how you feel?"

"I couldn't. The roles we assumed as children are too ingrained. I couldn't change now if I wanted to, and they could never see me differently."

"But you *have* changed, Charlotte, and you are changing still."

"Yes," she murmured, recalling the wild nights in which she'd found a new, deeper self that was nothing like her outer mask.

"And they fear the changes, more than you realise. They must accept that you can't stay the same forever, just to make them feel safe."

She swallowed. His words and the warm glow of his eyes brought her close to tears.

"I was telling you about the cellar."

"Yes. Go on."

"I was fearfully upset they'd shut me in, and the atmosphere… it was a heaviness, like layers and layers of age… with hundreds of voices murmuring, almost beyond earshot. So cold, so full of grief. I ran back up the steps and implored them to let me out. They wouldn't answer. I refused to humiliate myself further by pleading, so I went back down and across the cellar. It was pitch dark, and I kept tripping over things. Finally I stepped into a hole and really bruised myself. I didn't fall far, I'd landed on more steps. I sat and cried for a while, but when my aches eased, I went down the steps and found myself in another cellar, or a corridor. In the blackness I'd no idea where I was. There were twists and turns. I felt my way along a wall. I kept walking and walking."

"Don't ever again tell me you are not brave," said Karl.

"I was nervous, of course, but more than that I was… fascinated. Something guided me through that tunnel. It must sound strange – but whatever haunts this house is sad, not evil. I almost wanted to offer comfort.

"I don't remember how far I walked, but I've worked out since that it was just over a mile. The tunnel led from the manor house to an old ice house in the gardens of Parkland Hall."

Karl looked intrigued. "Does anyone else know the tunnel is there?"

"No one's ever mentioned it. It may have been an escape route in the Reformation or the Civil War, or even older. Meanwhile my sisters had opened the cellar door and found that I'd vanished. They were so alarmed, they fetched my aunt. They got into terrible trouble, of course. When I reappeared I was scolded too, because I refused to explain how I'd escaped. That's why I'm sure Aunt Elizabeth doesn't know about the passageway. I don't know why I was so stubborn about explaining, except that it was my secret, and keeping it was the only revenge I could take."

Karl was looking into the fire, thoughtful, his face half in shadow.

"So you never told anyone. Can you find this tunnel again?"

"I hope so. If we could slip away so no one knows we've gone…"

"Now I understand why you ran into the cellar when I had frightened you so badly. You were going to escape."

"Not consciously, but I suppose it was half in my mind."

"You are still free to go whenever you wish," he said.

Charlotte looked down.

"Don't, Karl. I've made up my mind."

His voice was grave, sad. "And by giving you the choice I have made things even harder for you. If I'd forcibly kept you prisoner, the blame would have been mine alone. Instead, I've made it partly yours. I'm sorry. As I warned you, my sense of morality is lamentably deficient."

A trickle of coldness went through her.

"That's true. But if I took no responsibility for this at all, I'd be deceiving myself."

"That's a brave admission." His voice and face were now deadly serious. "We should go soon, while we have the cover of darkness and most of the night to escape," he said.

Yet he didn't move, only went on gazing at the flames.

"What are you thinking?"

He gave a slight shake of his head and met her eyes.

"That I would rather brave your brother and the police than the cellar."

"Why?" she exclaimed. "Don't tell me you're afraid, I won't believe it!"

"Did I ever claim to be fearless?" He spoke with a touch of self-mockery. "The atmosphere you described in the cellar – I sensed it too, both times I was there. You say you felt nothing evil in it, Charlotte – but I did."

His words froze her. Suddenly she was very aware of the ancient house that contained them, its silence and shadows.

She said, "The first time I really spoke to you was in the cellar, do you remember?"

"Of course." His eyes warmed.

"We talked about ghosts, then you said we should go back upstairs because it was cold..."

"I was not being considerate. Something down there disturbed me. It still does. But I won't be stopped by what is only a remnant of human superstition."

"No, don't dismiss it." An old pain surfaced inside her. "I believe that events can imprint themselves on a place forever. My mother... died after giving birth to Madeleine. Sometimes at night I still hear the echoes – as if her screams never stopped."

Karl was silent for a moment, watching her.

Then he said, "Yet you don't fear your mother's spirit."

"They are two different things! Her pain is not her *self*. The pain is not a ghost."

"Still a terrible thing of which to be aware."

"Yes. And yet even that doesn't really frighten me."

"You are extraordinary, Charlotte," he said quietly. "Just when I think I understand you, there is another twist. To be sensitive to pain and death, yet unafraid..."

She felt defensive. "I know I'm strange, that I don't react as people think I ought to. To be in such pain and only released by death – the idea makes me feel awe. It stops me breathing. I want to touch it..."

"Not to turn away?"

"No. To understand. Perhaps it's all my imagination, I was less than two years old when she died, and I can't separate memory from dreams. But I feel very close to my mother. I talk to her and she listens. She is everything I'm not."

"You don't think," said Karl, leaning forward, "that the spirit you commune with is simply an idealised version of yourself?"

Charlotte stiffened with indignation.

"Don't say that! You don't know anything about us. You've no right to make such judgments."

He reached out and took her wrist, stroked his thumb over her pulse.

"Forgive me, that was uncalled for. But, dearest, it's not your fault she died, or that you aren't her. In trying to please your father and family you have lost sight of your *self*. When they attack you, you don't defend yourself, because you see no self to defend. People adore Madeleine because she believes she deserves it. But you are just as worthy, and have every right to consideration and respect – not only from others but from *yourself*. Do you believe me?"

He sounded so earnest, so purely human, that the knowledge of what he was – the incongruity of the two – slid through her like ice. Her friend, her lover; yet also a ruthless creature that fed on life... She knelt down on the rug, leaned across his knees, felt his hand stroking her hair.

"I dare not be my true self, Karl."

"You can't let the patterns of your childhood poison your whole life."

"It's not that. Father thinks I'm some kind of angel; my sisters and aunt think I'm a mouse. But inside I'm neither of those. That's why I seem shy, why I hide from everyone. I am scared of what I really am. I am a bad person, Karl. The fact that I'm here with you, doesn't that prove it?"

Pierre lay in the hedgerow where Karl had abandoned him, collapsed like a toppled mannequin, watching the half-globe of night slide towards morning. The loss of blood had turned his limbs stone-heavy and he was paralysed.

Not once did he lose consciousness. It would be a blessing, he thought, if vampires had that human weakness. Instead he remained aware of every second dripping into the lake of time, every tiny shift of the stars across an interminable night.

You bastard, Karl. You won't get away with this. Throw me as far and as hard as you like, and still I will come creeping back...

Now the grass was sheened grey with twilight and he watched tiny beetles on the blades, frantically busy, yet desperately slow. A robin began to chirp in the hedgerow, he was aware of its bright eyes through the stiff mesh of twigs. *Oh, shut up*, he thought. *You are no use to me.*

Pierre hallucinated. Revolutionaries were rushing towards him, arms raised, ragged clothes flying. All had bandaged necks. They dragged him towards the guillotine and he was fighting them, shouting, "I am no aristocrat, you fools, I am one of you..." But they knew what he was, and their only option was to decapitate him.

He shuddered from head to foot as the figures faded... all but two who kept coming towards him, their necks wrapped up. They must be real, he could feel their heat...

Fool, he told himself. *These are human beings, not figments of my imagination!*

Their heat flowed before them like a bow wave as they came along the lane. Relief swelled through him, and with it the lashing, ravenous snake of thirst. Yet still he could not move.

Two boys on their way to school: twelve-ish, muffled in caps and scarves. He forced a groan from his lips, and they saw him.

"Is it a scarecrow?" said one.

"Nah. It's a tramp. P'robly drunk."

Scarecrow? Tramp? Don't they realise how much this overcoat cost? They leaned over him, exhaling clouds of breath, sweet with milk. Bright hard eyes they had, like the robin. *Yes, that's it, come closer...*

Pierre pushed the words through his fossilised lips. "Help me..."

"Sounds foreign," said the second boy. As he reached down, starvation cracked through Pierre like a whip. His arm shot out as if controlled by a primitive brain of its own. Suddenly he was half sitting up, pulling both children towards him. Tearing a scarf away with his teeth and then, *oh then*, life was flowing hot into his collapsed veins.

While he fed on one boy he held the other to his chest, his grip tightening as his strength returned. It happened too fast for them to struggle, although one let out high-pitched moans of protest.

As he fed on the second child he found himself sobbing with gratitude, murmuring, "*Merci, merci...*" But as his head cleared he pushed them away, appalled at himself for being thankful. He propped them against each other on the grass verge and thought how sweet they looked, a pair of grubby sleeping cherubs.

"Gratitude is so undignified," he said, regarding them with affection. "But thank you anyway, children."

Pierre suspected they were not quite dead. Perhaps they'd

survive, if someone found them soon. He shrugged, he wasn't interested. Turning away, he tried to enter the Crystal Ring.

Nothing – like pushing against a closed door. No awareness of a dimension shimmering beyond the visible world. He felt he'd lost a sense as important as sight, become human again, or a mole pushing blindly through a tunnel...

It will come back. It always does. Yet there was an undercurrent of panic. *What if this time it doesn't?*

No choice but to walk. *I should have asked the boys where the hell I am before breakfasting.* He sighed, but as he strode along the lane his spirits began to improve. It was a cursed nuisance to travel like a human, but perhaps he could catch a train. To move among them, pretending to be one of them, was always pleasant. *And by tonight, my dear Karl, I shall return to Parkland.*

"Dress warmly," said Karl, "and bring some food. I think the workmen have left an oil lamp in the kitchen."

Now the moment had come, Charlotte did not want to leave. Talking to Karl, she'd become at ease with him, bathing in his radiance as she had that night in the study, when all she wanted was to sit with him and listen to the rain... But time, as always, stabbed cold claws of reality into their refuge.

She glanced out at a black sky streaked with smoky lavender. David was waiting out there, worried sick, his heart aching for Edward and for her. *Dear God, what am I doing?*

She wrapped herself in the warm brown coat that they had left for her, trying fiercely to suppress her guilt; trying to think of nothing except finding the way out.

Pulling on a hat and gloves, she followed Karl onto the landing and down the stairs. Lit only by faint fire-glow from the solar, the hall was as dark and fathomless as a cathedral. No longer did the house feel benign to Charlotte, the air was fogged with malevolence, as if the dreaming ghosts imprinted in its walls were stirring.

She kept her eyes fixed on Karl's back as they descended. He was calm as always, but the ring of their heels recalled other echoes. David shouting a warning; Edward rushing up the stairs, blindly heroic. The narrow gleaming fire of Karl's eyes as, silent and ruthless, he tore into Edward's neck then sent him sprawling down the stairs...

The house had absorbed these events and now screamed them back at Charlotte's heightened senses.

Strange and terrifying, that her perception of Karl could change so suddenly. In the fire glow he'd seemed gentle and protective, but this darkness, cold and pain-laden, stripped away his humanity and reclaimed him as its own.

In the kitchen, they found a well-fuelled hurricane lamp.

"We won't light it until we're in the cellar," said Karl, "in case someone sees the light moving across the window."

Someone outside. Oh God. She moved stiffly to the cellar door and opened it. The latch felt heavy and clammy, shedding rust onto her fingers. Karl went through and she pulled the door shut behind them.

Blackness enveloped them, as thick as cobwebs. Karl struck a match. Lamplight flared and spilled down the steps.

Where the beam fell, a four-legged shadow slipped across the steps. It no longer looked catlike but elongated, sinister. Karl placed a hand on her shoulder.

"You're trembling," he said. "I thought you weren't afraid of being here."

She couldn't answer. In the lamp glow, against the shadows, he appeared exactly what he was.

"Shall I go first?" she said. "I think I remember the way."

"If you feel safe with me following you." He spoke drily, but as she looked at him, something as black as night and thorn sharp passed between them. Knowledge that if he grew desperate enough for her blood, his promise not to harm her might prove meaningless, and she would not be able to stop him. He would not be able to stop *himself*. No, she did not feel safe. This danger had always hovered between them, but the eeriness of the cellar stripped it to its stark essence.

She took the lamp from him and began to walk down the steps. A miasma of damp, dirt and mould sucked her in, like stagnant water, chilling, repugnant. She found herself beginning to recite the Lord's Prayer, stopped herself. *How dare I ask God to help me?*

With pillars arching to form the ceiling, the space seemed

cavernous, labyrinthine. She led Karl through a maze of barrels, jars and ancient storage chests, all coated in centuries of grime and mildew. Shadows leapt and contorted in the lamp beam; rats and insects scuttled unseen over debris on the floor.

Ghosts, reverberations from a lost time, she sensed them all around her. Wordless whispers flowed from the walls, full of malice. Their mood had changed. Something was rousing them to anger... *Have we intruded once too often?*

"What are you looking for?" Karl's voice in the stillness made her jump. "Another door?"

"No, a trap in the floor," she said raising the lamp. "I thought it was here somewhere. It's hard to remember."

"Shall we try there?" Karl pointed into a far corner, where the beam didn't reach. Unnerving, to realise he could see in the dark. Charlotte pushed on through the murmuring shadows as if through a nest of spiders, holding her breath, her skin crawling.

The lamplight spilled over the edge of a hole, half hidden behind a pillar. The trap door had long rotted away.

The steps looked steep and forbidding, the walls slick, mottled, dropping into a pitch-black space as horrifying as an oubliette. How much simpler this had seemed when she was a child. A mile was a long way, underground. As she hesitated, she felt the touch of Karl's hand on her back.

"Go down a little way," he said. She obeyed, almost losing her footing on the slimy treads. She saved herself, only for the screech of metal on stone to set her heart pounding again.

Karl was hauling a chest across to conceal the opening above them. The easy strength of the action astonished her, but the sense of being sealed underground was disturbing. Lamplight danced on the wooden base of the chest and on the narrow walls.

Seeing her worried expression, Karl said, "I can move it again, if we have to come back this way."

You could... but I couldn't, she thought. She turned and began to descend as quickly as she dared. The wall felt furry and damp under her hand. A scent rose of sour mouldering earth. Thick cobwebs broke over her fingers. Karl was so quiet behind her that once she turned with a stab of panic, thinking he was no longer there.

"It's all right," he said. "I'm here." But in the lamplight he looked supernaturally pale, his eyes too intense.

The stairs led deep underground, curving at the base into a small, claustrophobic chamber. The stonework was crumbling and drifts of soil lay across the floor. Before them yawned the inky mouth of a passageway.

Charlotte stopped, her chest so tight she could hardly breathe. Whispers swirled around her like fog, turning her cold and giddy. So hard to think. Karl's gaze moved over the walls and ceiling, distracted. No need to ask if he could feel the presence of malice, if anything, he was more affected than Charlotte.

She recalled how she'd groped her way along this tunnel, following the left-hand side of the wall. They only had to do the same now. Simple.

Steadying herself, she walked into the tunnel with Karl at her side. The light sketched grainy, dancing shadows on the stone. There was tension poised in the air, like a held breath, presences flattened into the walls, watching, waiting. She wished Karl would speak; yet instinct told her that talking would make this worse, like invoking demons.

The passage dipped, rose and meandered, so they could see only a few yards ahead. The air hung thick and clammy. An oddly clotted shadow appeared... She halted as the beam illuminated a pile of barrels and planks that lay heaped in their path, blocking the tunnel.

With a twinge of dismay, she remembered, as a slightly built child, squeezing through a narrow gap in the barrier.

"There's a way through," she said. "Look."

Where the barrier met the wall, there was a thin space between the curve of a barrel and the stonework. The gap was hardly large enough to admit an adult, but she handed the lamp to Karl and edged sideways into the gap. The weight of wood and stone squeezed her ribs, pressing the breath out of her lungs. Then she was through. Karl passed the lamp along the floor and followed her with fluid ease.

Beyond the barrier, the temperature fell. Charlotte was perspiring and shivering at the same time. The left-hand wall was flat, but on the opposite side she noticed an archway leading to a small round chamber. Uneasy, she raised the lamp.

Iron-grey stones and shadows lay within. Also a chair and table, cracked with age, and on the table, a thick black book.

For some reason the sight of the book terrified her. Words came into her mind from nowhere, *Ledger of Death*. She looked at Karl but he was staring too, his face dead white, his eyes as red as rubies.

"Don't touch anything," he said. "We must go on."

She turned away and walked on through the tunnel. Bright flames of fear licked her throat. The moment they'd seen the book – that was the moment the phantom voices rose into the level of hearing. They were chattering, insistent, pressing on her. *Don't listen, don't think of anything, just walk.*

Suddenly Karl said, "It's cold. Don't you feel it?"

"A little," she said truthfully.

He reached out and touched her cheek. His fingers were so icy she started.

"Your skin is hot," he said, staring at her.

God, he's freezing! she thought, pulling away by reflex. *Why should he be concerned about the cold? I thought nothing could harm him. Only the cold of the Crystal Ring, he said...*

"Don't you know what is here?" he said intensely.

She wasn't sure whether he meant *Tell me*, or *Haven't you guessed?*

"Emptiness," she whispered. "As if someone died here and left... not their spirit, so much as their pain. Like my mother..."

She trailed off. Karl said nothing, and his silence unnerved her. The cold began to penetrate her clothes. Last time, she had experienced these lost spirits as sad and desolate, yet guileless. Letting a child pass by unharmed. There hadn't been this bitter rage, sharp as a knife at her throat. And such a sense of loss; grief that made her want to weep with fear, a void that sucked the heat out of everything that came close.

They rounded a bend in the tunnel, Karl now walking ahead, apparently so disturbed that he'd forgotten she was there. As she hurried to keep up, he stopped abruptly and she almost fell into him.

"*Mein Gott*," he breathed.

"What is it?"

She could see nothing, only the grim corridor diminishing into blackness. She moved forward, holding up the lamp. The light slid into an alcove on the right, through a low entrance and into a circular chamber that contained a tangle of strangely gleaming firewood. Then she recognised what she was seeing, and clung to Karl's arm in shock. Not firewood.

Human bones.

Shiny brown with age, skeletons lay crumbled and shored up in the chamber. There were half-buried skulls grinning at nothing, pelvises like bizarrely knotted driftwood, femurs worn down to sponge and coral. She lifted the lamp, saw ribcages jutting up like shipwrecks, vertebrae scattered as if from a broken necklace.

Near the entrance, a skull as brown as polished oak lay with its face pressed sideways into the dust, jaw hanging open in a scream that went on forever. And she could hear it. She could hear the skull screaming.

She backed away, trying to block her ears. The lamp swung against her arm and burned her. Hopeless anyway, she could do nothing to shut out the clamour.

"Dear Christ," she said. "To think I walked past this and never knew. What is it, a burial chamber?"

Karl turned to her. She wanted him to steady her, but his eyes were glazed in the half-light. Distant, almost ill.

"No. A vampire."

"What?"

"These were the victims of a vampire," he said.

The statement bewildered her. She took a moment to form a question.

"How do you know?"

"I can't explain, I simply know. A vampire lived here, underground. He lured his prey here, drank their lives, and hoarded their bodies. Their bones are those of his victims, and the pain we feel in the air – their pain."

The distant chill of his voice and eyes were terrifying.

"But he's not still here?"

"No," said Karl. "He is long gone, I think." As if in response to his words, the tunnel vibrated with a long, echoing groan of distress.

Charlotte had a sudden vision of a spidery creature in rags, sitting at the table, entering the details of his victims in a ledger of doom. Then she knew. It was Karl's presence that had disturbed the spirits.

They knew what he was. What did they want of him? Revenge?

"We have to go past them," she said. "I know it's horrible, but the quicker we go the sooner we'll be out of here."

Karl only stared at her with ice-glazed blankness.

"Did you hear me?" she said. "What's wrong?"

"It's so cold." He touched her arm and she felt his hand shaking. "We should go back. Too cold…"

Fear swept over her, fear of what was happening to him. She tried to speak, but the anguished murmurs of the dead swelled to a crescendo and swept her words away.

A wail of tormented rage poured from the walls, the floor, and from the remains of the victims who had been left to rot here, unburied, unblessed. Her brain was spinning in white webs of terror. Not ghosts but the opposite, an absence of energy, hundreds of souls sucked dry and gasping to be filled again, their agony swelling and contracting like a giant heart whose beats dragged at her mind as they rolled over her.

Thirsting not for her, but for Karl.

Charlotte dropped the lamp. Total blackness enveloped her, and the cold that bit into her was deeper than winter.

"Karl!" she cried.

Nothing. Then she moved, felt something against her foot and realised that Karl was lying stretched out on the tunnel floor. In panic she bent down and touched his face. He did not respond, and his lifeless skin leached the warmth from her hand like frozen metal.

The manor was a black bulk of shadow against the night sky, one upper window gleaming with fire and candlelight. David settled down for the remainder of a cold night, watching for shapes moving against the light. He saw nothing. There was only the tantalising fire glow to tell him that Charlotte was inside – a few yards away, but unreachable. He and Inspector Ash had gone round and round the house, hoping to find a way in, but the only way was to force a door or window.

"Which leaves us with the same problem, sir," Ash had said. "Whether we enter by stealth or force, it would put Miss Neville in immediate danger. All we can do at this stage is wait."

"I'm well trained in that, at least," said David.

He tried not to dwell on what suffering von Wultendorf might be inflicting on Charlotte. No use tormenting himself. *Edward always had too much imagination and it's no good for a soldier*, he thought. *No good in a situation like this. Watch the doors and windows, keep hoping for a break in the deadlock. That's all we can do.*

He had good men with him – estate men, including the head groom and the foreman, Ash and his force – yet he felt alone, solely responsible. It was hard not to keep asking himself, *How in hell did I let this happen? Why didn't I do this, or that, to prevent it?*

Anne was a little way behind him, distributing hot drinks. He was annoyed with her for coming here when he'd told her not to, for being so damned stubborn.

"You'd better go straight back to the Hall," he said. "They need you there."

Anne saw straight through his attempt at diplomacy.

"Don't be so bloody condescending! Elizabeth's holding the fort, she doesn't need me. I want to be with you."

"For goodness' sake, Anne, this is no place for you."

Anne looked at him, her dark eyes sombre with determination.

"It's no place for Charlotte, either. She's my friend, David, almost as much my sister as yours."

"Well, I'll let you stay a little while, at least," David said grudgingly. Then wondered why she turned away without showing any gratitude for this concession. Inside, he was glad she was there, glad of her support – but he thought, *It won't do, she'll have to go home.*

The impenetrable walls of Charlotte's prison loomed through the trees. *This feels like the bloody War again.* And it was too true to be a joke. The sense of futility, of waiting blindly for disaster, was the same.

"Karl," Charlotte whispered urgently. The darkness was in motion, as if thousands of people were jostling past her, all invisible, insubstantial, weeping and muttering with unearthly voices. "Please answer me. Karl!"

He was so still and cold that she was sure he was dead. *He's not breathing. He said vampires don't need to... should he be breathing or not?* She was almost out of her mind with terror.

But when he spoke, it was a worse shock still; heart-stopping, as if a corpse had sat up in its coffin.

"*Ich kann nicht... kalt, zu kalt...*"

"Can you hear me?" She pulled at his arm. "What's wrong, what's happened to you?"

"Charlotte," he said hoarsely. "So cold. I cannot move."

"You must! We've got to leave!"

The noise was turning her limbs to water, a multi-voiced sobbing and groaning, full of echoing discords. She discerned a ghastly looping repetition: one scream in particular swept up the register, again and again, to end in a strangled gasp. It set her nerves shrieking. She was certain that if they lingered, the void would drag them down into itself, beyond help, beyond light.

"Help me," he said, raising a stiff arm towards her. She seized his hand, drew his arm across her shoulders and braced her body, struggling to haul him to his feet. He tried to help himself, but he was like a dead weight. He had always been so strong, so composed, that his weakness horrified her.

At last he was on his feet, leaning almost his full weight on her. But he was slender, and she could bear him.

"The lamp," she said. "I can't see a thing without it."

"I can see," said Karl. "I will guide you."

It was all he could do to walk, even with Charlotte's aid. Wherever his body touched hers, cold radiated from him and her teeth chattered as the warmth left her. They moved with painful slowness, while all around them rolled the empty souls, yearning to steal back what had been stolen. She felt as if she were swimming against a tidal wave of darkness – sinking as if the earth itself were made of quicksand.

Then Karl stumbled and collapsed, pulling her down with him.

"I am sorry," he gasped. "I can go no further. Go on without me."

"No, I'm not leaving you. It can't be far now. Please try."

A short silence, in which the voices of the dead grew quieter, as if retreating across the gulf of time.

Then Karl said, "I can't move. I am frozen."

"What can I do to warm you?" she asked frantically.

A longer pause.

"Nothing."

She traced her hand along his face and neck. His eyes were closed, his cheeks smooth and lifeless as quartz, but she felt the movement of his throat as he swallowed. And she knew. Her hand rested on his collarbone, turning icy as her heat sank into his flesh.

Eventually she said, "Would it kill me?"

Although she couldn't see his eyes opening, she felt his gaze on her.

"What are you saying?"

"You know what I mean. You're starving. My blood would warm you, wouldn't it?"

"Yes." He breathed in and out, human-sounding. "It would help."

"So would it kill me?"

"Not if I took only a little."

"Take it, then."

"It will make you ill, Charlotte."

"It doesn't matter. I don't care if it does."

"God," he said very faintly, and groaned. "I can't ask this of you. If I take too much..."

"I'm not leaving you. Please, Karl. We can't stay here any longer."

For the space of a few heartbeats, he paused. Then he lifted his hand, too weak to do more than brush his fingers against the elbow of her coat. Shivering with something worse than cold, she leaned towards him, holding her breath.

"No, give me your wrist," he said. "Then it will be easier for me to stop."

Easier... A shock, to realise that from the neck it would be too intimate. As compelling as the physical act of love. Suddenly there were thorns between them, the tension between the desire and the danger... And she was afraid but she wanted it, wanted to give this to him with sensual eagerness.

She gave him her left hand. She felt his bone-cold grip around her palm, not gentle but hungry, startling. The speed with which he pulled her wrist to his mouth shocked her so much that she tried to struggle, to say, "Wait!" But it was too late. She felt two stabs of pain and the word came out as a cry.

She didn't know what she had expected. Nothing so painful,

a deep, paralysing ache that numbed her whole arm. Nothing so intense. It was horrible. She tried to pull away but he held her as if in a vice, his mouth tautening on her skin, locking her to him while her energy flowed away with her blood. And he shuddered as if with a wave of exquisite, overpowering relief.

Then she stopped trying to fight and gave in, gave herself completely to his need. One thing turned the horror back on itself and that was seeing, feeling, understanding, what the blood meant to Karl. She leaned down until her head rested on his – strange, the contrast between the softness of their hair and the hard pull of his teeth in her wrist – and curled her free arm round his shoulders. Cradling him. *Yes. Take this warmth from me.*

She felt the fragmenting sensation of faintness and knew this could be the beginning of death, that if he could not stop she would slide down into unconsciousness and never wake again.

God, such a sacrifice. She hadn't understood.

Was this what Madeleine had felt, when Pierre fed from her? This cold dark fall from a cliff, no comfort to be found. To be alone for ever. She saw clearly now how some could never gather in the threads of sanity and reweave the veil of beliefs that shielded them from death.

But if the blood is given out of love...

This was no violation. She knew the blood meant so much to Karl *because* he understood how great was the sacrifice. A dark jewel beyond price. To give him this was a pleasure as intense as the repletion he drew from her veins. She held him as he drank, her lips against his hair... falling slowly through a silver cloud of bliss...

She was walking between rows of beds and in each one was the deadly white face of a gassed soldier, tormented with the effort of drawing the next breath, and the next... "I would breathe for you if I could!" she cried, stretching her arms towards them – but she could move only her right hand, her left was pinioned. The pain brought her back to herself.

It seemed a century had passed but they were still in the darkness, Karl's mouth on her wrist, the faintest groan of relief or ecstasy issuing from his throat. The ghost voices mourned in the far distance. Charlotte lifted her hand from his shoulder to stroke his silky hair and, without knowing why, she began to weep.

CHAPTER THIRTEEN

IN THE STILL OF THE NIGHT

Charlotte felt the darkness tipping and dropping away beneath her. Through the tingling vertigo she realised that Karl was carrying her, while the voices of the empty souls blew away along an endless corridor... and, after a time, she felt him setting her down with utmost gentleness. There was a dim, luminous rectangle before her. The lukewarm sweetness of the night air felt warm after the unnatural cold of the tunnel.

Slowly she became aware that they were in a small stone chamber with a low doorway, open to the night. Beyond, the night sky gleamed like pewter through layers of leaves, and the whispering she heard now was only the soft rustle of leaves. She began to shiver.

"Charlotte," Karl said softly. "Can you hear me?"

"Yes. Where are we?"

"I think we are in the ice house that you spoke of. Is it down in the belt of trees that runs along from the hundred steps?"

"Yes. Hidden," she said, trying to orientate herself. It was hard to fight the faintness. Karl held her until the shivering ceased, keeping her wounded left wrist loosely against her chest. She felt only a dull ache in her forearm, worse was her overwhelming lassitude.

"I needed more than you could give," he said. "I almost did not stop in time."

She shifted a little to look up at him. His lids were half lowered, the long lashes shading the gleam of his eyes. And he was looking at her with such affection that she almost began to weep again.

"But you have your strength back?" she said.

"Yes. At the expense of yours, beloved. This is one thing I can never ask you to forgive." She tried to sit up and he helped, watching her closely. "How do you feel?"

"I saw strange things, but I wasn't afraid. I don't think I have gone mad, if that's what worries you. I am rather weak. It doesn't matter." She probed her left wrist, felt two tender scars. "My God, it's healed!"

"The bite does heal swiftly, as a rule," said Karl. "It helps us avoid suspicion. Ah, *liebe Gott*, I would not have done this for the world..."

"I'm glad," she said. She leaned in towards him. Their mouths met and she tasted her own blood on his tongue, and did not care. "There was nothing to be so very frightened of, after all."

He held her, his face against her hair. She felt his hand slide into her coat pocket and out again. She smelled the strong sweet fragrance of an orange.

He said, "You must eat to recover your strength."

He peeled it for her and she accepted the segments from him. The burst of liquid sweetness in her dry mouth seemed the most heavenly thing she had ever tasted. As she ate, memories of the cellar and tunnel sleeted across her mind, so vivid and distorted that she wondered if his bite had unhinged her after all.

She said, "Karl, did I imagine what happened down there?"

"No, unless we both did," he said. "Believe me, I was more afraid than you."

"But what happened? Why did you collapse?" She knew, but wanted her theory confirmed.

He shook his head. "We cannot talk about it now. You must rest for a while, but as soon as you feel well enough we must go."

"I feel better already. I'll be all right."

"I know," said Karl, "because you are going back to Parkland Hall."

Charlotte thought she must have misunderstood him.

"What are you talking about?"

"I am sending you back to your family. I have my chance to escape now, and I can ask no more of you."

His words cut her heart like a whip. The prospect of him

leaving her was devastating, to be denied with all her strength.

"But the moment I go back, they'll know you're free and they'll come after you! I know what David's like. He won't give up."

"He won't find me."

"What if he does? Suppose he actually caught you up, tried to stop you – you'd kill him, wouldn't you?"

"I would hope not."

"But there is that danger, so nothing's changed! I have to stay with you, to protect you *both*. Wherever you go, I'm coming with you."

"Charlotte –" he began, then stopped, gazing at the doorway. His sudden alertness was like that of a cat, distracted by an intangible call that no human could hear.

"What is it?" she whispered.

"There's another vampire in the garden," he said, "somewhere near the Hall. I think it's Pierre. Stay here."

Before she could protest, he stepped under the lintel and was gone. She stumbled to the doorway after him, but he'd already vanished, leaving no movement of foliage to betray his path. Another vampire… Pierre? *What if he's stronger than Karl this time?*

Charlotte felt herself turning faint again, while the birches and conifers seemed monstrously overdrawn against the night sky, grasping and threatening. If this was the beginning of madness, she couldn't fight back with reason, she was too tired, too afraid. She felt completely alone, while the garden – once her sanctuary – seemed drenched in malevolence.

Karl ran lightly up through the belt of trees, through paths twisting between great banks of rhododendron, and across the side lawns until he reached the stone balustrade that edged the upper lawn. As he ran he was thinking, *Pierre is going to sense me… how can I take him by surprise?*

Karl leapt the balustrade, paused in the darkness between shrubs and rose bushes. The plane tree under which they'd found Madeleine loomed over him. Although it was two or three hours before dawn, the Hall was lit up as if the entire household had stayed awake all night. He sensed them, suspended in cubes of light, illusions of safety, sensed their helplessness and anxiety. And on the terrace, silhouetted against the tall yellow windows of the drawing room, he saw the motionless figure of a vampire.

Pierre seemed to be watching, listening. He looked round, down into the garden; straight at Karl. There was a slight stiffening of his shoulders, controlled anger, then he began to move towards the windows.

Karl had no choice. Swift as sound he crossed the lawn, ran – all but flew, too fast for humans to see – up the steps and onto the terrace. And at the very windowsill he caught Pierre, seized his shoulders and thrust him down onto the flags.

Pierre fought, struggling and cursing so viciously that Karl feared the humans would hear him. A shadow moved into the light and he heard Elizabeth's voice say, "Did you see something on the terrace?"

Karl held Pierre close in against the wall.

From deeper in the room came Dr Neville's voice, thick with sleep. "What? What is it?"

"Get off me!" Pierre spat. "I'll give her something to see!"

"It's nothing," said Elizabeth. "Go back to sleep, George. God, my nerves are in rags. How long is this absurd situation going to last?"

The oblong of light narrowed to a pencil strip as Elizabeth closed the curtains.

Karl held Pierre in place, looking up to make sure no one could see them. *All I have to do is send Charlotte back to them and take Pierre away. Then it will all be over.*

Pierre twisted beneath him and bit Karl's arm. Karl broke free but the pain brought sudden anger, a tingling energy that moved softly into his limbs and his eyes.

"You can't keep me from them," Pierre said furiously. "You think you can treat me with such contempt, tell me what I can and can't do, half kill me –"

"Be quiet," said Karl. He spoke softly but the sheer commanding force of his voice reached Pierre. It was the same power that Kristian possessed, that all vampires had in one degree or another. And the hypnotic clarity of Karl's will was stronger than Pierre's, always had been, although Pierre was older. "How dare you come back, when I told you to stay away?"

Pierre would not be cowed. His eyes were half closed, steely with hatred.

"You are not my master. I said I'd come back for them and there's nothing you can do to stop me. You have to learn this lesson: you made this mess, my friend, and you cannot put it right by threatening *me*. Such interesting things I learned. Aren't you meant to be shut up in some derelict house with poor Charlotte as your hostage and the police outside? How did you get out? You could do this trick in the music hall. Now *let me up*!"

"But think of this first," said Karl. "Which would be the most rewarding – to sate yourself on this family, for whom I don't care so very much – or to present me to Kristian?"

Pierre was disarmed by this. The glitter of anger vanished and he said idiotically, "What?"

"Give me your word you will never go near the Nevilles again, and I will return to Kristian with you. Well?"

He pulled Pierre to his feet, drew him sideways into the ivy that veiled the wall.

"I don't understand you," Pierre said. "Nothing in the universe would force you to go back before, yet you'd do so to save these people? Don't tell me they mean nothing to you!"

"The truth is, I'm sick of this," said Karl. "These wretched games Kristian plays with you and me and Ilona. Why don't I just go back and confront him?"

"And you'd let me have the credit for persuading you?"

"Just so," said Karl, smiling. He smoothed Pierre's dishevelled curls and led him off the terrace, down into the garden. "Pierre, I wish you'd decide whose side you are on. You have no more love for Kristian than I do, so why treat me like an enemy?"

"I don't. This is how I treat my friends," Pierre replied sarcastically.

The trees and the tattered leaves of autumn folded over them. To Karl's eyes the darkness shone as if jewelled with deepest emerald, umber and bronze. He and Pierre walked slowly, a peculiar kind of razor-edged empathy between them.

"I wish I understood why you behave as you do," said Karl.

He expected a sharp-tongued response, but instead Pierre answered in a pensive tone.

"What do you expect of a vampire? I'm not an angel, nor a devil. Unlike you, I went with Kristian willingly. You know that, don't you? My mother and I, we lived in the utmost poverty in Paris but I had this dream of being an artist and she, poor fool, encouraged me. She worked her hands to the bone to support me. Then I met this glorious gentleman. Imagine, Satan and the Pope in a single figure, who looked like a hangman and scattered money about like holy water. 'Why not leave this struggle and come with me?' he says. He could give me anything. Riches, immortality. Oh, I was not like you, Karl, wanting to stay human for love. I was greedy for what he offered me. After he'd transformed me and I was desperate with the thirst, he took me to his coach – remember that magnificent black-and-gold coach and four he used to have? – and said, 'Inside you will find something to fulfil every hunger, every desire you've ever felt.' And there inside was my mother. My first victim, my mother."

Karl gazed up at the stars glittering icily through a web of branches.

"Didn't you hate him for that?"

"Hate him, for proving that I had made the right choice? I fed on her without a qualm. The silly witch had already made herself a martyr for me, so what better way to go than to give me her last drop of blood? I expect she got her reward in heaven. It was my goodbye to the old life. Not *au revoir*. Never."

"But you don't share Kristian's beliefs. You never have."

"Of course not. I think he's insane. But that's part of his charm, isn't it? I believe in *him*. He is the centre, isn't he? *Magnifique*."

"And you can't cross him, can you? You can't go back to him and tell him you've failed to bring me with you."

Pierre's gaze darkened, fixing on Karl.

"What are you getting at? You know, I am sick of being the one who has to pay and pay for *your* stupidity. It can put a strain on friendship, you know."

"Nothing, Pierre." Karl touched his shoulder. "Our agreement stands. As long as you remember it includes Charlotte."

"Oh, she is untouchable," Pierre said, lifting his hands in acquiescence. "A virgin in every sense, I'm sure."

* * *

Karl was such a long time. Charlotte couldn't get warm, she barely had the energy to shiver as she huddled in the doorway of the ice house. The suspicion crept on her slowly. *He's not coming back. He lied to me, he's abandoned me so I'll be forced to go home.*

And suddenly she saw the gleam of eyes in the darkness and almost leapt out of her skin. They seemed to materialise out of nowhere, these two pale creatures who were so clearly not human.

"Charlotte, don't be afraid," said Karl. He bent down, lifted her up and hugged her. "Pierre is coming with us – with me. We have had a talk and he will hurt no one now."

Over Karl's shoulder she looked at Pierre with suspicion. Her head throbbed with every heavy beat of her heart and she was shaking with weakness. Yet she could see so clearly. Too clearly, everything looked magnified, tremulous with meaning. She could even see the brilliant blue of Pierre's irises, as if they contained their own light. He stared right into her eyes and smiled.

"Looking a little pale, isn't she, Karl? So much for your impeccable self-control. Oh, how I love your wonderful sanctimony. 'Don't touch them, don't hurt them.' What can I do to them that's worse than what you have done already? Some friend of the family, was it, you finished off? And now your untouchable china doll on the path to damnation…"

His words stung Charlotte to anger.

"It's nothing to do with you!"

Pierre stared at her with exaggerated amazement.

"Bless me. Has he deceived you with his talk of love, Ophelia? You're defending the indefensible."

Karl held Charlotte protectively as he faced Pierre.

"Leave her alone. This is not a game, Pierre."

"No? To me, that's exactly what it is, and if I did not treat it as such I'd go mad. The rest of you *are* mad, which only goes to prove my point."

Charlotte disliked Pierre as much as she feared him. He had an intriguing aura in common with Karl, yet she felt no attraction to him. There was hardness in his sharp-boned features, a sly cynicism in his overlarge eyes that repulsed her. His character showed in his face. Yet Karl's did not… was that any better?

"We must decide how we are going to leave here," said Karl, disregarding Pierre's remarks. "I assume you still cannot enter the Crystal Ring?"

"Thanks to you," Pierre said resentfully.

"And neither can I. I will explain why later. So we shall have to travel to Dover and take the ferry."

"Tedious." Pierre scuffed up some leaves with his foot. "Are you bringing Ophelia?"

"Don't call me that!" said Charlotte.

"Why not? If you are not completely insane, *chérie*, you are obviously on the way."

Karl spoke to Charlotte, ignoring Pierre.

"It would be best if you went back to the Hall now." He turned in towards her, holding her hands against his chest.

She had hoped he would change his mind. Again came the terrible pain, like wire cutting her heart.

"Best for whom?" she exclaimed. "I suppose it's easy for you to walk away and leave me!"

His gaze moved over her face, disturbed.

"No, *liebchen*. I find it almost impossible. But you know we cannot stay together. You know what I am, and I know how much you care for your family…"

Every reminder tore her in two. *What am I doing, this is a vampire, he almost killed me to live!* And then there was an image of her family sleepless and wretched in the Hall while Pierre's face loomed like a death mask at the window; David outside the manor, waiting… She tried to close her mind, but it wouldn't go away. All that anguish she could put right… yet what she truly could not bear was being parted from Karl.

An idea came to her, a reprieve.

"Let me come to London, at least. I can go to my sister's. It will give you a chance to get away."

"Your sister…"

"Yes, Fleur, in Bloomsbury. You know where she lives. I can telephone the Hall from there and by the time they come for me you will have vanished before the police can do anything."

Karl hesitated, his eyes dark with fugitive emotions.

Then he released a soft breath and said, "Very well. But don't let us delude ourselves, we are doing this for all the wrong reasons. It is only delaying the moment."

"This is very touching," said Pierre, "and God knows, I am a romantic at heart, but if you have managed to make up your minds, can we go?"

"Do you have a car nearby?" said Karl. "Charlotte cannot walk to London, she needs to rest."

"I came back by train and taxi-cab," said Pierre. "Where's your beautiful Hispano?"

"Still at the manor, unless someone has driven it back to the Hall. I can't go back for it. We shall have to find a car on our way."

"Steal one, you mean," Pierre said with a soft laugh. "What a deliciously human crime."

Another long, icy wave of doubt went through Charlotte. *It's not too late to change my mind.* But in her heart, the choice was made.

They crossed the lower lawn – passing the fountain where Charlotte had first fallen under Karl's spell – and descended a flight of stone steps into the woodland below. They walked through the woods until she was stumbling along in a dream, too exhausted to keep her feet without Karl's help. Loss of blood had caused this weakness – while the energy with which Karl moved was hers.

The trees flowed down to the boundary of the Parkland Hall estate, edged by hawthorn with a narrow lane beyond. They climbed a gate and turned left into the lane, taking the way that led south. The surface was rough and flinty, churned up by centuries of horses' hooves, rutted by the motor vehicles for which it had never been intended.

After they had walked for twenty minutes or so, Pierre and Karl looked at each other and drew back into the shadows of the hedge. Charlotte could hear nothing at first, then a beam of light swung around the bend behind them, fanning over the hedgerow before swivelling onto the road. A car came bouncing slowly along the track, a black shape half seen behind the glare of its headlights.

The light blinded Charlotte, after so long in darkness. But Pierre calmly moved out into the middle of the road and waved his arms at the vehicle. It drew to a halt, braking with Pierre almost on the bonnet. A door opened and the driver got out, moving with ponderous self-assurance, curious rather than alarmed.

A policeman.

"Damn," Karl said under his breath. "And he has probably come down from the manor house. Stay here."

A chill gripped her stomach.

"What are you going to do?"

"It's all right, Charlotte," he said, his voice strange and distant. "Don't move. Don't watch." The words fell into the silence like stones into a dark pool as he left Charlotte and moved towards Pierre. And in spite of his warning she could not stop herself from watching with horrified fascination.

"Good evening, sirs," said the constable. "What seems to be the trouble?"

"There's been an accident," Pierre said vaguely. "My friend..."

"Nothing to worry about," said Karl, his voice so coldly hypnotic that it was like icy fingers being drawn along her limbs. "But if you could come here a moment..."

The policeman stared at the two vampires, then his expression changed. His eyes widened with bafflement and fear. With the light shining from beneath, reversing the shadows, his face looked horrible. And suddenly Charlotte shared his terror, like a great weight of ice on her chest, and she saw Pierre and Karl as he must see them.

White, luminous beings, spare and hard and pitiless. Not human. *Not human*. Impossible, turning belief upside down, tearing away the veil of normality to reveal the glittering evil beneath.

The constable muttered something.

"What's going on? Just a minute –" but he was moving forward, a fly caught in honey. And it was Karl who struck. One moment he was standing as still as marble, the next the policeman was in his grasp – yet Charlotte had not seen him move. And she saw the mutual convulsion of both their bodies as Karl's fangs drove into the man's neck.

"God, let me –" Pierre gasped. His blue eyes held pure burning hunger as he moved behind the man, bent his face to the other side of his throat.

Charlotte stared at the hideous scene. Then she found herself running along the darkened road, sobbing for breath, out of her mind. The strange, dark swimming sensation was inside her and could not be escaped. She felt she was flying and sinking, the illusion flooding her body like a drug, and at the same time she was alone in an infinite landscape, being drawn down into a warm darkness that she could not fight, almost did not wish to.

The feeling was unmistakably one of desire.

Only a few moments passed, then there was someone beside her, catching her, holding her up. But it was not Karl. It was Pierre. She recoiled from him, close to passing out with terror. His grip was inescapable and as he pulled her round she caught a glimpse of Karl still bonded to his victim.

"Don't be an idiot, I'm not going to hurt you, much as I'd love to," Pierre hissed. His lips shone dark with blood. With no strength left to resist, she let herself be guided back to the car.

She went with her eyes closed. *God, let me wake up out of this dream.*

Pierre stopped and she heard voices. At first they made no sense through the ringing of her ears, then she became aware that Karl and Pierre were arguing. "Of course we must take it with us!" said Pierre. "If we leave it here, they are going to realise you came this way."

"I am not taking it in the car," Karl replied adamantly. "Not with Charlotte. We'll have to leave it under the hedgerow and take the chance."

She realised that they were talking about the policeman.

Pierre helped her into the back of the car. She felt the smoothness of the upholstery sliding against her clothes, but the leather smell made her feel sick. She did not watch what they were doing. Pierre's voice, just outside the window, made her jump.

"Awful, this starvation, isn't it?" For the first time a softer quality replaced the sneering tone, a hint of sympathy, a link between the two vampires that reminded her all the more that they were foreign beings of whom she knew so little. "You take someone and you simply cannot stop. Now you know how I felt, when you did the same to me. Fortunately it does wear off. Eventually."

"I know," said Karl. His voice went through her like an electric shock. "It wasn't the first time Kristian had feasted on me. You drive, Pierre."

"Oh, must I? I want to sit in the back with Ophelia," the Frenchman said gleefully. But Karl gave him a hard look and he obeyed.

The car door opened and Karl slid onto the seat beside Charlotte. He remained in the opposite corner, as if he did not trust himself to touch her. Astonishing that he looked as composed and tranquil as ever. Although why she had expected otherwise, she didn't know.

"Are you all right?" he asked, as Pierre engaged the gear and set off at reckless speed.

"I don't know."

"You know that you have no cause to be frightened of me."

"I wasn't frightened," she said tightly. "Please don't ask me to explain. It's too dreadful."

He looked at her and she could not avoid his eyes, they were sad, brooding.

"I know what it was, Charlotte."

"You don't. How could you know?"

"You felt something unholy and alien to your nature. You were less frightened of what was happening than of your own feelings. That's what you were running away from."

She was horrified, because he was right.

"Karl, please don't speak of it!"

"It has to be faced. Don't be under any illusions about me."

"I don't think I am," she said. "Not now."

"Then you must look into your heart and examine what is there. You don't have to tell me, but you must do it." He went on looking gravely at her. He offered no apology that she had been so upset, but she understood and was glad. She wanted no comforting sophistry, only the truth.

"I don't know what I feel. It's all confusion, except for one thing…" She shook her head. Surely it was impossible to go on loving him after what she had seen, after what he'd told her about himself, yet she could not stop. The longer she stayed with him the worse it became: a complete infatuation with his every look or gesture. The idea of leaving him was unthinkable.

"And the one thing... is what?" he said.

"God, Karl, surely you don't need to ask!"

"No," he whispered. "Any more than you need to ask what the gift of your blood meant to me." The hypnotic swaying of the car suspended them in a bubble of time, opening a dark communication that hardly needed expression in words. "These bonds between us cannot easily be broken."

After a few minutes he reached out and clasped her hand, and now her fingers were icy, while his were warm.

Anne went back to Parkland Hall at David's insistence, but long before dawn she set out again for the manor. She went alone. Elizabeth and the Prof were dozing uneasily in the drawing room, Madeleine had gone to bed, and Newland – considering it his duty to stay awake throughout the crisis – was red-eyed and largely indifferent to anyone's welfare except Elizabeth's. There was no one to stop her as she put on a pair of wellington boots and David's old trench coat, picked up another bundle of food, and drove off in Edward's car.

It was five o'clock, the dreary time before dawn, when their hopes reached a nadir and the darkness massed between the trees seemed immovable. She parked some distance away and walked up the path until she found David. He was sitting on a folding stool under the scant cover of bushes.

"I've brought more food for Charlotte," she said. "Anything happening?"

"Not much. Ash sent a man to report back to the police station a while ago, that's all." David looked at her with disapproving concern. "You should have gone to bed, Anne."

"I couldn't sleep, any more than you can. Any sign of activity?"

"See for yourself," he replied grimly. The upper window, which throughout the afternoon and evening had glimmered golden red, was now dark. "He's let the fire go out."

"Charlotte's probably asleep."

"I doubt it, and she must be freezing."

"I expect they'll light it again in the morning."

"It *is* morning!" David said bitterly. "For heaven's sake, how long does he think he can keep her in there?"

A policeman went to place the fresh bundle on the doorstep. He knocked at the door, but there was no response. Heavy wet twilight striated the sky, but the fire was not rekindled. David and Anne remained at their post, staring grimly at the sullen walls of the manor. More than ever it seemed an unbreachable fortress, with no sign of life inside. The windows remained dead and cold.

Inspector Ash came wading towards them through wet leaves.

"If I'm not much mistaken, Captain Neville, there's no one in there."

Anne's heart turned cold.

"That's impossible," said David. "Your men have been watching every possible exit, haven't they?"

"Of course."

"Have they been asleep at their posts?"

"Certainly not, sir," Ash said in a hard tone.

"Then they can't possibly have left, can they?"

Anne said, "Could they have slipped away under cover of darkness?"

"No, Miss Saunders, we've been watching every inch of the place. If they'd come out of a door or even a window, we'd have heard as well as seen them."

Quietly, she said, "It does look awfully deserted, all the same."

"Well, I'm going to try the door again," said David. He marched up the path, took the four steps in one stride and pounded hard on the old arched door. Anne followed. The sound resonated and died as they stood side by side, looking up at the ancient stone walls. Minutes went by, but nothing happened.

David stood back and yelled at the top of his lungs. "Von Wultendorf! For God's sake, man, what are you playing at? Let me know my sister's alive, at least! Light a candle, let her come to the window!"

As he stopped shouting, silence billowed down like a stage curtain. The manor remained lifeless, impenetrable.

For the first time Anne saw real fear in David's face. She shared that moment of helpless terror, heavy as stone and impassive as the violet-streaked sky.

"Right," he said. He took Anne's arm and led her back to the bushes where Inspector Ash and two constables were waiting. "I think it's time we made a move, Inspector."

Ash looked dubious. "What did you have in mind, sir?"

"I'm going to force a window open and go in."

"You realise he could be setting a trap – maybe waiting for us to break in one way so he can escape by another?"

"Forewarned is forearmed, isn't it, Inspector? Your men will be ready for him."

"Well, you have a point, sir. We could wait until kingdom come, at this rate. It looks as if *something's* changed."

"I've got to know, one way or the other," David said grimly. "Have one of your men escort my fiancée back to the Hall."

"Will you please stop treating me like a child?" Anne said indignantly. "If you're going in there, I'm coming with you!"

"Anne, it's much too dangerous!"

She spoke with calm insistence. "If Karl is still there, I think he's more likely to negotiate with me than anyone. Besides, if anything *has* happened to Charlotte, I should be there to look after her. I can act as a mediator – but if there has to be a fight, I can at least keep her out of it."

"Anne, I can't possibly expose you to the sort of danger Charlotte's in. I absolutely forbid it."

"I thought you believed in equality for women!"

"I do – but this is different, old girl, you must see that."

"I'm not your old girl," she said thinly. "And it is not different. I've as much right as you to try to help Charlotte." Anne felt resolute, able to outface David because she had no choice. "When it comes to it, you don't practise what you preach, do you? You had better have your ring back."

She took off her left glove, slipped the ring off her finger, and held it out to him. He stared at the gold circle, flummoxed.

Finally he burst out, "Good God, is it a crime for a man to try to protect his fiancée these days?"

"We should protect each other! We agreed that we would be equal partners in marriage. If you didn't mean it, there's no point in us getting married, is there?" Her throat ached as she spoke. She'd sometimes imagined a real test of their relationship, never thought this moment would actually come. Now she had to see it through.

"You're being ridiculous!"

"If you think that of me, it only proves I'm doing the right thing. It's not because you want to protect me, David, it's because you don't even understand why I feel like this. I'm sorry, but I can't live with that."

"Anne." David went on staring at her, hurt and angry. Then his expression softened into resignation. "I do understand," he said in a low voice. "And you're quite right. Put the ring back on, please. All right, equal partners. But agree to one thing, will you? Let a couple of us go in through a window first, then, if the coast's clear, we'll let you and the police in through the front door."

Anne nodded. She accepted the ring, replaced it on her finger. David kissed her cheek. "I do love you, old girl," he whispered. "For God's sake, be careful."

"And you," she said. As he turned away, she drew a deep breath of relief, and found herself trembling.

David and the Inspector drew up a plan of action, decided to tackle a hall window near the front door. They broke a pane and opened it easily enough, but Anne watched with heart in mouth as the two of them, followed by a constable, scrambled through the embrasure. *However quiet they are, Karl's bound to know they're inside. Oh Lord, David, don't take any risks...*

Long moments of silence passed. Then the front door creaked open, and Ash beckoned the four men he'd assigned to go in with Anne.

David stood in the hall, white-faced.

"There seems to be no one here," he said faintly.

Darkness soared over them, barely touched by their torch beams, vast and full of menace, like the vaulted heights of a cathedral... or the dead grey sky over a battlefield.

"Have you searched the whole house?" Anne's voice echoed.

"Just a brief look upstairs. We'll do it more thoroughly now, but I can tell, Anne, the place is deserted."

"I feel it too," she said.

Side by side they went up the stairs, followed by the Inspector, while his men explored the lower rooms. The solar was empty and the ashes cold. There were signs of Charlotte's presence: the workmen's kettle on the grate, remains of food, clothes lying on the bed. While Ash moved slowly around the chamber – *Looking for signs of blood?* Anne wondered with a shudder – David went back onto the landing.

"Charlotte!" he shouted. "Von Wultendorf, if you're here, for God's sake show yourself!"

His plea fell into a well of silence.

They descended to the entrance hall again, where the other police reported that there was no sign of anyone, no clue as to how Karl and Charlotte might have escaped.

"How the hell could this happen?" David's eyes glinted with frustration and pain.

"I don't know, sir," Ash said gravely. "There's no way they could have slipped past us – unless there's another way out of the manor that we don't know about. My men kept the house under full observation at all times. It's impossible that they could emerge without being seen. We'll search again, see if there's anything we missed."

No one said it, but Anne knew what they suspected. *Karl's killed Charlotte, concealed her body, and now he's hiding somewhere...*

She said, "I didn't see Charlotte's hat and coat upstairs. That could mean they've left somehow."

"We haven't had a proper look in the cellars yet, Miss Saunders," Ash said grimly.

She and David waited on the cellar steps, watching faint beams of light criss-crossing the darkness, throwing shadows of barrels, boxes and pillars into grotesque motion. They heard the frantic scuffling of rats evading the light. Anne saw a horrible vision of Charlotte lying somewhere amid the dust and debris, rats clambering over her... *Stop it, you idiot!*

"Nothing, sir," Ash said eventually. "We can try again with more men and stronger lamps, but in all honesty I don't think there's anyone to find."

David visibly slumped with relief.

"What next?" he said.

"I'll initiate an extensive search of the grounds," said the Inspector, leading the disconsolate group up into the kitchen. "If von Wultendorf's escaped, he must be somewhere. No one can vanish into thin air."

"God," whispered David. "I am going to hunt down that fiend and I don't care if they hang, draw and quarter me, I swear I'm going to kill him."

Anne curled a steadying hand through his arm and he clasped it, plainly glad of her presence. Around them, the house remained brooding and insouciant, keeping its secrets.

CHAPTER FOURTEEN

DREAMS AND CHAINS

Charlotte slept for a time, woke feeling stale and exhausted, with the car's movement vibrating through her bones. Karl's arm was around her, and a deep blue glow brushed the sky.

"Where are we?" she asked, sitting up. There were trees, roofs black against the horizon, the deep rumble of a train. She could see nothing ahead. Pierre was driving without headlights, not needing them with vampire sight.

"Just on the outskirts of London," said Karl. "It's almost seven o'clock."

Charlotte yawned. "I feel worse for having slept," she said. "Karl, have you been awake all this time? Do you know, I have never seen you sleep, not once."

"We don't sleep," he said. "Not on Earth, at least. Vampires don't need the physical and mental oblivion that humans find in sleep, but we still need our own kind of rest – and we can only find that in the Crystal Ring."

"You have to go there to sleep?"

"Yes. I hope I didn't give the impression that the Crystal Ring is merely convenient. It's essential to our existence. We have to take care, though, a vampire who lingers there too long may become torpid and unable to escape."

"It sounds dangerous."

"As with all things," he said. "We find a balance."

"But will it – will it harm you, not being able to rest?"

"Not greatly. It is fatiguing... and it makes the thirst worse."
He saw her apprehension, and added, "It is nothing for you to
worry about."

"I wasn't worried about myself," she said quietly. She was
remembering the escape of the previous night, the hunger with
which Karl and Pierre had taken the policeman. *And I watched.
Does it mean I condoned it, that I'm an accomplice to murder?*

Karl seemed to know what was in her mind.

"I can say nothing to make this better than it is," he said. "And
it is horrifying."

But I don't feel as horrified as I believe I should, she thought.
That's what I can't face...

From the driving seat, Pierre said crisply, "My dear Karl, is
there *anything* you haven't told her?" He steered the car into a
narrow lane near a railway siding, slowed and stopped. "I'm not
a chauffeur, you can let yourselves out."

"What's happening?" said Charlotte.

Karl got out of the car, came to her door and helped her out.
Beautiful courtesy, even in this situation. Pierre turned the high-
roofed black vehicle round, glancing at Charlotte with a cold grin
as he drove away. All was grey and black: sheer brick walls furred
with soot, a distant line of terraced houses backing onto the railway
line, straggling verges where nothing but weeds could grow.

"There is a roadhouse around the corner. It's best the car is not
seen right outside," said Karl. "Can you walk that far?"

"Yes, of course. I'm quite all right, really. But where's Pierre
gone?"

"To dispose of the car. I shall wait for him, and order a taxi-cab
for you to complete your journey to your sister's."

"Do you trust him to come back?"

Karl put an arm around her as they walked.

"I made an agreement with him. He won't break it."

The redbrick eating house was not open, but the lights were
on and the owner, a cheerful stout man, let them in willingly
when Karl murmured some story about his "wife" being taken
ill. He took them to a corner table and Karl ordered breakfast
for her. She could do no more than nibble at toast, but her thirst
for strong, sweet tea seemed insatiable. She drank cup after cup,

letting the warmth and nourishment seep inside her, miraculously restoring her well-being.

Karl sat and watched her across the table. He was quiet. Perhaps there was nothing to say except goodbye.

She said, "When the taxi comes for me… will this be the last time I see you?"

He did not answer the question.

"We have some time to talk," he said. "Pierre will be a while."

"I hope he takes forever. I hope he doesn't come back."

Karl put his hand over hers. She wanted to make this small island of time into a wall against the world. Just to stay here, where she felt safe, talking to Karl forever.

She said, "I was thinking about what happened in the manor. It frightened me, the way you collapsed, I didn't think anything could hurt you."

"Apart from severing of the neck, only cold seems to affect us. I don't mean the extremes of weather on Earth, but an unnatural cold, like that of the *Weisskalt*."

"And the temperature of the tunnel was unnatural," said Charlotte. The memory chilled her, but still better than dwelling on the future. "Like complete emptiness. I always felt my mother left her pain in the house as well as her spirit, but those poor people who died under the manor left *only* their agony. You mentioned a vampire."

"Yes. I must be more attuned to such things than I thought." Karl spoke softly, as if this was a difficult subject. "I don't know how I knew. It was pure intuition, that a vampire had lived there once, hundreds of years ago, lured his victims in and kept their bones. A collector, an obsessive. Some vampires feed not only on blood but on the aura, the life force itself. So the victims' energy was taken and only their pain was left."

"That's what coldness *is* – an absence of energy," said Charlotte. "Yet it only affected you, not me. I've been through that tunnel twice now, and both times I was unharmed."

"Presumably the spectres recognised me for what I was," Karl said drily. "They wanted back what had been stolen. It didn't feel conscious, their revenge; more mechanical, like a vacuum sucking air into itself. It was a truly horrible feeling, Charlotte. I have felt the chill of the *Weisskalt*, and this was worse. I think I would have died if you had not been there to help me, beloved."

"Thank God I was."

"I don't think God would appreciate our gratitude." He was half smiling, his eyes so warm they dissolved her. "Obviously that vampire left its lair centuries ago. I can't think who it could have been. I wonder if Kristian would know."

"I wish we could go back to the manor and find out."

"You would go back there?"

"I'd do anything, if it meant we could stay together."

Karl did not reply. She caught his hands, her nails dug into his flesh but he did not flinch. "Take me to Europe with you."

His long-lashed eyelids swept down.

"I can't. I am going back to Kristian."

"After everything you said?" Charlotte exclaimed.

"How do you think I persuaded Pierre to leave your family alone? Being in favour with Kristian means more to him than taking revenge on me. Besides, I think perhaps I should have done this before. Tried to talk to Kristian instead of fighting and running all this time."

"Take me with you," she said desperately.

Karl shook his head. "Charlotte, I can't. There will be other vampires there. You can't have forgotten what Kristian did to my wife?"

"Oh, God." She sat back on the hard chair, so shaken by the image that she thought she might faint again. "After you've seen Kristian, can you – can you come back?"

The distress in his eyes burned her.

"He may not let me go again, but even if he does, what would be the point? You have your family, your work. Gods, I should never, ever have let this happen. It cannot go on. We both know it."

She tried to control her feelings, but couldn't.

"Are you telling me that this is the last time I'll see you?" she whispered harshly. "I can't bear it, Karl, I really can't. How do you expect me to live, after this?"

Karl remained as still and composed as marble, only the anguish in his eyes betrayed him.

"I'm trying to say goodbye to you and I can't. Go to Fleur's as you agreed. I am not leaving London immediately. There's someone I want to see, someone who knows Kristian. After that, if your family haven't taken you home by then, I will come and meet you."

She thought, *What's the use? It's only delaying the moment, as he said. If he doesn't say goodbye now, it will be later.* But it was all she had to cling to, a reprieve.

"Where?"

"In the garden in the centre of the square where Fleur lives. About twelve noon."

"It's too dangerous, Karl. What if David's there by then?"

"Don't worry. I will see him long before he sees me. If you are not there, I'll know they have taken you home."

"I won't let them. I'll run away."

"Don't, Charlotte," Karl said gently. "It will do no good." He leaned forward and kissed her. From the corner of her eye Charlotte saw the owner pause in the act of laying a table, slightly startled at this public display, but shaking his head indulgently. She was past caring what anyone thought.

They must have sat in the roadhouse for an hour, but it seemed only moments before the taxi-cab arrived for Charlotte. Pierre had not returned, and she was glad, she did not want to see him again. Numb, she walked outside with Karl and climbed into the back of the cab, lost for words, feeling dislocated and bereft.

"Twelve o'clock," he said, and kissed her again.

The cheery down-to-earth banter of the cab driver disorientated her, so incongruous after all that had happened. Misery enveloped her as she watched Karl's tall figure dwindling, until he seemed no more than an ordinary man. Already she was thinking, *What if he only said we'd meet to stop me arguing? What if he has no intention of coming? And Fleur must know what happened – how can I stop her ringing Father at once?*

She leaned back in the hard seat, flattened by exhaustion. London oppressed her, such a harsh contrast to the hours of solitude with Karl. Such heaviness… Chimneys, towers, gasometers… The endless rows of buildings were a huge, grey weight of brick and stone that seemed to be crushing her. An hallucinatory grandeur wreathed in smoke and mist, vibrating with noise and people, the rasp of motor horns, the cries of street traders rising and dying away like the voices under the manor... She felt a hot stab of panic in her chest. *Does everything look so strange because I'm tired – or was Karl right, his bite has twisted my sanity? No. While I can still think rationally, I won't give in to this, I won't!*

I know I'm losing Karl. He's trying to let me go gently, as if he thinks I can't see how impossible our love is. My heart can't accept that we're not free to love each other... but these physical and moral bonds hold us into the pattern of our lives like chains. Karl can't break them any more than I can.

In the cold morning light Charlotte stepped from the taxi and looked up at Fleur's house in its elegant row, the tall windows set in warm grey brick, the flight of steps up to the door and the neat black railings in front. *I can't face this, I can't go in... But what else can I do?*

"Are you sure you're all right, miss?" said the driver.

"Yes... yes, perfectly."

She put her hand in her coat pocket, only to realise she had no money. Before she had time to be embarrassed, the driver said, "The gentleman paid me, miss. Very generous, 'e was too."

"Oh, of course. Thank you." Charlotte turned away and hurried up the steps, her heart thumping. She heard the rough, throaty engine of the cab as it rattled away; she heard birds singing in the square, where Karl had said he would be... *How long? It's nearly nine. Three hours.* With an unsteady hand, she rang the doorbell.

She had expected Fleur's small plump maid Jenny to open the door; instead it was Clive who stood there, handsome and imposing, dressed for the City. The dismay she felt was a reflex, she'd never known what to say, how to behave with him. He stood with the morning post in his hand, surprised to see her.

"Hello, Charlotte, I didn't know we were expecting you. Come in, come in. How are you?"

Charlotte was lost for words. He spoke as if he knew nothing about events at Parkland, as if this was just a social call. She hadn't prepared a story. As she stepped into the hallway, Clive's mouth spread in a grin.

"Goodness, still too shy even to say good morning? We shall have to do something about this. I don't bite, y'know."

She found his manner threatening, not friendly. Clive was the sort of man who despised weakness, used it to torment those who could not defend themselves. He gave her an appraising look – taking her apart with his eyes, as Pierre had – because he knew it upset her.

After all she had endured, it seemed the last straw, but years of practice saved her dignity.

"Good morning, Clive," she said coldly. "Where's Fleur?"

"In the dining room, and I'm off to work. Perhaps see you later?" He tipped his hat to her and she watched him leave, only glad that he had gone.

Fleur sat at the dining table in a flowery silk dressing gown, her auburn hair falling into her eyes as she pored over a magazine. Jenny was clearing the table from breakfast. The atmosphere was of serene normality. As Charlotte entered, Fleur glanced up and stared at her sister with arched eyebrows.

"Charlotte? Good heavens, what are you doing here at this hour? I'm not even dressed yet. Was I supposed to know you were coming?" Fleur stood up and came to embrace her. "Darling."

Charlotte was stunned. *She doesn't know!*

Hesitantly she asked, "Hasn't Father or anyone telephoned you?"

"Not for a few days," Fleur said off-handedly. "Should they have done, to let me know you were coming? Oh well, it doesn't matter. It's rare and lovely to see you. Jenny, take Charlotte's coat and hat, bring some fresh tea."

The little maid obeyed. Alone with her sister, Charlotte felt like bursting into tears. She'd assumed Fleur would know the situation at Parkland, but it was possible that no one had thought to telephone her, or decided that, as there was nothing Fleur and Clive could do to help, there was no point in worrying them. *It only happened yesterday*, Charlotte thought. *It feels like a lifetime...* and suddenly, helplessly, she sat down at the table and began to cry.

"Oh, Charli," said Fleur, sitting by her. "Whatever's the matter? I thought you looked pale when you walked in. There, there..."

Charlotte longed to tell Fleur everything. Confess her sins, pour out the hopelessness of it all. The affection between them seemed a surface affectation to Charlotte, they'd never shared real openness. She and Fleur hardly knew each other, really. *You should talk to them*, Karl had said. The words twisted in her heart. Impossible, but she had to try.

"Are you sure you haven't spoken to Father or David? Not even Aunt Lizzie?"

"No, truly, darling."

"You don't know what's happened, then?"

Fleur draped her arm across Charlotte's back, shook her gently.

"You're making me worried, dear. Is it so terrible?"

"I – I caused a row at home. I broke my engagement with Henry. He resigned and stormed out and Father's absolutely furious with me. And I love someone else and it's such a mess…"

"Oh, Charli." A trace of astonishment in Fleur's voice gave way to complete sympathy. She gave Charlotte a handkerchief. "So you ran away? I would have done the same."

Charlotte blotted her eyes and nose.

"Fleur, can I stay here for a while?"

"Of course."

"And will you promise not to tell anyone I'm here?"

Fleur looked dubious. "Don't they know where you are? I should let them know, really, or they'll worry."

"Oh, just – just give me a few hours, at least. I need some time to think."

"All right, darling. You telephone them when you feel ready."

Charlotte was so grateful for her older sister's kindness that she almost started crying again. This sudden closeness between them was unexpected, yet so natural, as if it had been there all the time and neither had been able to reach out for it.

"Thank you."

"But who is this someone you're in love with?"

"I can't – it doesn't matter."

"It's not Karl, is it?" Charlotte didn't answer, and Fleur did not press her. "All this going on… I never guessed."

"What, that I have feelings?" Charlotte said with a touch of sourness.

"You do keep things to yourself, rather. You always have." Fleur hugged her. "It's awfully bad to bottle it up. If you're staying tonight, though, I think it's only fair to warn you that I'm having a little party this evening. Just a few friends, artists, poets – you know, all the sorts Father can't stand – nothing formal. I know you hate being sociable, Charli, but please don't stay in your room. It might help take your mind off things, to meet a few new people."

For Charlotte, *tonight* seemed to be on the far side of the Atlantic Ocean. She could see nothing beyond noon.

"That's all right," she said.

"I have to tell you a little secret," said Fleur, caressing Charlotte's hair. "I'm just as terrified of social dos as you are."

Charlotte was so startled by this revelation that she almost forgot her own problems.

"I don't believe you!"

"But I am. I've taught myself to hide it, that's all. Much as I would love to hunch up in a corner and speak to no one, I force myself to relax and smile. Looks jolly impressive, doesn't it? All a sham, my dear. Of course, there are substances that help… better than booze, even, and then one doesn't have to pretend. You shouldn't be afraid to try it, dear. Could make all the difference to you."

Charlotte didn't want to spoil the closeness between them by voicing her disapproval, so she only nodded. *Besides, who am I to disapprove of* anything *anyone does?*

She said, "I'm rather tired, Fleur. Could I lie down for a while?"

"Of course. But come and see the paintings I'm working on first. I'm awfully proud of them. I work all night, sometimes."

Charlotte let Fleur lead her into the conservatory, thinking, *It must be the cocaine, keeping her awake all night.*

"Doesn't Clive mind? He never seemed to like you painting in the first place."

"Oh, it's only his habit, to complain about everything. He's a sweetie, really, and he adores the work I'm doing now. There, look."

Breathing in the evocative scent of oil paint and turpentine, Charlotte wandered into the maze of plants and easels. She expected to see the light and colourful themes that Fleur loved: flowers, friends, country scenes. What she saw instead made her stop dead in disbelief.

The canvases were dark and macabre, painted in fierce strokes that vibrated in constant angry motion. They portrayed medieval nightmares of plague and death: narrow gabled streets, houses with crosses on the doors, piles of corpses on which ugly carrion crows were feeding. The hues were black and purplish browns, relieved only by stark highlights of deathly white and blood red.

Charlotte stared, incredulous. Then she turned to her sister. Fleur looked breezy, unconcerned, but for the first time Charlotte noticed something strange about her eyes. The pupils were different sizes, giving her an unfocused gaze.

"Well, what do you think?" Fleur asked.

Before she could stop herself, Charlotte said, "Why are you painting such awful things?"

"Are they awful?" said Fleur, as if Charlotte were criticising the style rather than the content.

"They're horrific." She swallowed, turning away to stop the angry brushstrokes hurting her eyes. "I'm sorry, Fleur, I don't mean to be rude, but you don't usually paint such ghastly subjects."

Fleur shrugged. "Ghastly, do you think? I just paint what comes into my head. It's so very cleansing. It's no good to turn away from reality, is it?"

Charlotte hardly knew what to say. *Can she really see nothing unpleasant in them?* The gentle normality of Fleur's house was turning sour and she felt a cruel sense of deception, as if she'd woken from a nightmare only to find she was still dreaming. *Is this the effect of cocaine, opium or something else? Oh, Fleur, what are you doing to yourself?*

"You don't think you're taking too much... medication, do you?"

Fleur only smiled. "Oh, Charli. Don't be narrow-minded. Besides, we've found something even better now; you'll see, tonight. But if you think my work's that terrible, you had better not look at it. Here's Jenny with the tea."

And then Charlotte thought, *What if it's me who's seeing things? Maybe the paintings are perfectly normal and I am losing my mind... How can I tell?*

Charlotte went to lie down in Fleur's guest room, but had her eye on the clock so often that the hands seemed to have frozen. Then sleep crept over her, and she didn't realise until she woke violently, her heart trying to leap out of her chest. It was ten past twelve.

"Oh my God!" In panic she leapt off the bed, ran downstairs and pulled a coat off the hall stand, not pausing to tell Fleur she was going out. Across the road she ran, through the gate in the iron railings, into the public gardens. The lawn was deserted, the benches empty, no figures moving between the autumnal trees.

Sobbing for breath, she made her way to a bench and sat down, pulling the beige coat – one of Fleur's – around her. She thought, *Karl came and I wasn't here and he's gone... Then, No, he would have waited longer than this... Unless he never meant to come anyway.*

The grass was very green, the trees black webs draped with mist and bronze leaves. Footsteps – she started, but it was only a lavishly dressed woman, walking a Pekinese on the other side of the railings. Nothing looked as it should. Charlotte sensed poverty seething beneath the thin varnish of wealth... ghostly queues of the unemployed, the destitute, jostling around her... *What a sheltered existence I've had. How could I have dared to envy Maddy and Fleur when I was so privileged?* And it was all about to cave in, the buildings were crumbling around her, the monuments to wealth reduced to rubble, the whole of civilisation vanishing like a stage set in flames. The woman walking past with clicking heels was dressed in rags, draped with cobwebs and dust, her little lapdog a skeleton trotting on the end of its lead.

Charlotte closed her eyes. *I won't go mad. I have always lived on this line between life and death. It can't hurt me, I belong here.* When she opened her eyes, the world had returned to normal, and she saw Karl.

He was outside the garden, a hundred yards from her on the far side of the square. But he was talking to someone – a small, slender woman, wrapped in a fur-trimmed red coat, her hair hidden under a scarlet cloche hat.

They knew each other, Charlotte observed with a sinking feeling. Several times Karl touched the woman on the elbow or shoulder, a familiar, affectionate gesture he had often shown to her, but never to a stranger. She could see his face over the woman's hat, but she was too far away to read his expression. He was shaking his head a little. Were they arguing? The woman in red stepped away from him. He went after her – asking her not to go?

Karl seemed to glance at Charlotte, though he gave no sign of acknowledgement. Then he took the strange woman's elbow and walked away with her.

Charlotte stared at his retreating back. The ache inside her became actual pain, as if he were holding the strings of her heart and stretching them thinner and tighter as he went away.

He lied to me. There is someone else…

No, it's not true. Be rational… But if he could keep his true nature hidden from me, he could keep anything secret.

He's not coming back.

And that last thought, she knew, was the truth. He was not going to come back. Yet she sat in the square for an hour before the cruel truth sank its barbed hooks into her.

Finally she went back into the house, not knowing what to do with herself. She ran back up to the guest room, went to the window and stared through the curtains of net and lace at the square.

Nothing is going to help me. Not panicking, not weeping, not telling Fleur nor telephoning Anne. Nothing. I am completely on my own and only I can decide what to do.

A strange sense of calmness came over her then. She seemed to feel her mother's presence: soft hands stroking her forehead, a golden glow of comfort and strength. She heard her father's voice too; *"Don't react; think."*

Karl was *coming to see me; that woman stopped him. (Who was she?) But he'll come again, surely. He knows where I am. I only have to watch and wait for him… and I can't telephone David yet. God, I pray they'll forgive me for this.*

She took a bath and changed, borrowing a dress of soft red marocain from Fleur, which was too long and came down to her ankles. Then they had lunch together, just the two of them. The calm feeling stayed with Charlotte, all emotion was suspended, while her mind healed. Waiting.

Diffuse sunlight slanted through the room, falling on the creamy walls, elegant modern furniture, the flowers gleaming fresh and bright in Chinese vases. The sunlight also rimmed the grotesque paintings in the conservatory. They were real after all, not a figment of Charlotte's imagination. But now she thought, *Perhaps Fleur is exploring death in her own way because she needs to. Who am I to condemn her, or to think it's strange? She may be more like me than I ever realised – and it's my fault I didn't know.*

"I wish you would try to eat more," said Fleur. "There'll be supper at the party but it's a long time until then. You're getting as thin as me. You've gone quiet again, do you know?"

Charlotte reached across the table and took Fleur's hand.

"I want to tell you about what happened. I can't yet – but I will one day. I'll tell you everything."

Fleur smiled, her brown eyes affectionate.

"You seem different, Charli, not a closed book any more. I think something very shocking must have happened to you. I'm sorry you're unhappy, but I'm glad you're here. I wish I could cancel the wretched party, so we could talk instead. But tomorrow, we'll sort all this out." She sighed. "Aren't we silly, not to have been real friends before?"

For the first time that day, Charlotte smiled. Perhaps one, just one good thing had come out of this. *The wounds don't have to stay open for ever, the past can be healed.*

Charlotte expected the day to drag unbearably, but when she went up to her room, fatigue overcame her and she slept dreamlessly all afternoon. When she awoke it was dark. She became aware of car headlights outside, voices lifting and fading, music drifting from downstairs.

Eight o'clock, she saw with dismay. The party had begun... but what about Karl? Surely he could not have come and gone away without making sure he saw her – yet if he hadn't, where was he? Despair kicked through her heart, but she forced it down.

She smoothed her dress, tidied her hair. She could go out into the square and look for him. Perhaps he would come, now it was dark...

The hallway was lit up, Jenny poised to answer the door, light and music spilling from the drawing room. In a lull between guests arriving, it would be easy to slip out, with no questions asked. As

Charlotte descended the stairs, Clive came out into the hallway, and stood looking insolently up at her.

"Ah, there you are," he said, blowing out wreaths of cigar smoke. "Joining us at last?"

He demanded her attention, blocking her path. He was slightly drunk, his handsome face flushed, his manner oppressively over-friendly. She tried to smile and slip past, murmuring, "Excuse me, I just have to…"

He caught hold of her arm.

"Don't run away, Charli. Not much of a chummer, are you? We'll have to see about this. Come along with me and we'll have a drink and a little talk."

She was taken off guard and didn't know how to refuse without being downright rude. She thought, *He's nothing compared to Karl, nothing. How can I still feel awed by him? What can he possibly do to harm me?*

So she let him lead the way, but Clive avoided the party and took her into the empty dining room. Hoping to deflect his bizarre attention, she said, "I was looking at Fleur's paintings earlier. What do you think of them?"

She expected a disparaging comment. Instead he replied, "I think they're very truthful, don't you?" He shut the door behind them. "Anyway, I don't want to talk about Fleur. I want to talk about you."

Charlotte heard the key turn in the lock.

The dining room was in near darkness, except for reflections of city lights scattering through the glass roof of the conservatory, fanning dimly into the room.

She felt nervous, threatened.

"I don't understand," she said, voice hardening. "You never took such a great interest in me before."

"That was before," Clive drawled, his gaze moving over her. "I thought it was about time I got to know you better. Fleur tells me you're in a spot of trouble. I assumed you must lead such a dull life, but you can't be so dull underneath, surely?"

"What do you mean?"

"Come on, a pretty girl like you? Can't tell me a fellow's never taken an interest in you. I don't believe this mouse act. I want to know what you're *really* like."

Charlotte felt trapped and so indignant that she could barely contain herself. Clive's attitude was designed to intimidate her. He was only a man, not a vampire. How could he, how *dare* he wield this power? Yet she knew that if she tried to leave, he could and would stop her physically.

"You don't know the first thing about me," she replied with the delicacy of frost. "What I am like is none of your damned business."

Clive looked startled, then he grinned.

"Aha. Never expected to hear such bad language from your prim mouth. That's promising."

She took a step towards the door. He blocked her way.

"Where's Fleur?"

"Entertaining her guests, as I am trying to entertain you. Oh, come along, Charli. There's no need to be afraid of me." He touched her shoulder and she wrenched away.

"I'm not afraid of you," she said contemptuously. "I don't wish to talk to you, that's all."

"Why don't you relax and trust me? I'm trying to do you a favour, old thing." She saw his teeth glinting in the semi-dark. "Do you know, there's something better than alcohol for releasing the inhibitions?"

"Oh, I see. You want me to try cocaine. Why make such a great mystery of it? I've no interest in it, it's sordid, not to mention illegal. Now would you kindly unlock the door?"

Clive was laughing, shaking his head.

"No, no, you've got it all wrong. This is something far better than any drug."

He came towards her. As she tried to dodge around him, he caught her arm and turned her to face the conservatory. The glass doors stood open and she saw leaves swaying, shadows stirring between Fleur's canvases. Anticipation rose, squeezing her breath into an unborn scream. It seemed incredible that anything still had the power to alarm her; yet there was always something to draw fresh fear from the well. With effort, she held back the scream as two figures stepped into the doorway.

There was a faint click as Clive switched on a lamp. A pool of rusty light pushed feebly through the darkness, but the newcomers seemed to gather every photon and radiate it back with splintered brilliance.

"Stefan, Niklas," said Clive. "I would like you to meet my sister-in-law, Charlotte."

The two young men were vampires. They were like delicate, identical porcelain figures, white and gold, their nature unmistakable. Two blond vampires, regarding Charlotte with a look of knowing serenity, and blinking in unison.

CHAPTER FIFTEEN

SOMEONE TO BLAME ME

As a second night fell over Parkland Hall, David looked back on a day of unrelieved misery. They had made no progress in finding Charlotte. When he returned to the Hall that morning, his father had been waiting, grey-faced, with information from the hospital: Edward's life was out of danger, but he had started raving, apparently believing he was back in the trenches. The doctors had had to sedate him.

A couple of hours after David received that disheartening news, Inspector Ash came up to the Hall and informed them that a police officer had been found dead under a hedge on the estate boundary.

"I'd sent him to report back to the station, then to go off duty," Ash said. "The cause of death isn't clear, the only marks on him were some odd small scars on his neck. I know what you said about von Wultendorf attacking Mr Lees with his teeth, but I can't believe a human bite would be fatal unless there was severe crushing of the windpipe. Anyway, the post-mortem will tell us." He showed no emotion, but the lines on his stern face sank deeper. He added, half to himself, "His wife's expecting their second any day."

That was their only clue that Karl *had* escaped the manor. Of the police car, no sightings were reported, no trace found. But Anne said, "Karl must have taken Charlotte with him. She must still be alive."

"It's a whole day and a night since she was taken," David said in a low voice. "And now we're farther from rescuing her than before."

"We're making every effort to trace the car, sir," said Ash.

"I know, Inspector. And I'm deeply sorry about your constable. If there's anything I can do to help his widow…" David smoothed his dishevelled hair. "If von Wultendorf wasn't a murderer before, he is now for certain."

David's aunt and father tried to insist that he sleep, but as long as Charlotte was in danger, he could not. He'd spent the day going back and forth with the police, but inside he knew he was doing nothing to help and the knowledge drove him mad with frustration. Now darkness fell again and another long night stretched ahead…

He stood in the upper hall, rubbing his aching neck, needing a breather from the anxiety that permeated the house. Anne came out to him and they hugged.

She said, "They're right, you really should get some sleep. I didn't want to but I went out like a light this afternoon and I feel much better for it. You would, too."

"I dare say," David sighed. "But I just can't. You know, I've been thinking it's time we let Fleur know what's happening here. There didn't seem any point in worrying her when we thought it would all be over quickly. Now it's obviously going to drag on, I think she should be told."

"Yes, you're right," said Anne.

David went to the hall telephone and was swiftly connected by the operator. His heart grew heavier as he listened to the ringing tone. *Hell of a thing, breaking bad news… almost as if someone's died… No, mustn't be so damned morbid.*

When the telephone was answered, all David could hear was a buzz of voices and gramophone music.

"Hello?" he said. "Jenny? This is David Neville, is anyone there?"

Then Fleur's voice replied, "Hello, dear. Jenny's busy and I was right by the phone in the drawing room. This is a nice surprise." Her voice was languid, the words slurred.

"Not a social call, I'm afraid. I've some rather serious news. It's about Charlotte."

A pause. He got the impression Fleur was being distracted by someone else.

Then she said, "Can you speak up? It's frightfully noisy in here."

Losing patience, he said brusquely, "Have you been drinking?"

"Of course I've been drinking. I'm in the middle of a party."

"Well, I'm sorry to interrupt your fun with bad news, but will you listen, for God's sake?"

"About Charlotte, you said? Heavens, hasn't she rung you yet? It's too bad of her."

"What? What are you talking about?"

"She's here, David. I did tell her you'd be worried."

David was speechless.

Anne said, "What is it?"

"Fleur's drunk. She's talking gibberish." He tried to speak slowly and clearly into the mouthpiece. "Fleur, it's Charlotte I'm talking about. She can't possibly be with you, she's –"

"But she is, dear. She's been here all day."

"Since when?"

"Oh, sometime quite early. About nine-ish. Turned up in a taxi."

"On her own?"

"Yes. David, don't be so irate. You can't count visiting her sister as running away. She's perfectly safe."

He was so shocked he could not work his tongue.

Finally he burst out, "Why the hell didn't you let us know?"

"Don't shout, dear. I didn't know I was supposed to. She said she'd had an argument with Father about Henry and wanted to stay here until the fuss died down, that's all. I didn't think it was so awful."

"She said *what*?" David paused for breath. "This really isn't making sense, Fleur. Is Charlotte there?"

"Yes, she's around somewhere… probably still in her room."

"Well, would you ask her to come to the phone? It's vital I speak to her."

"Of course, dear, as long as you promise not to be too hard on her. Hang on…"

David heard a *clunk* as Fleur put the earpiece down.

"What's happening?" said Anne.

"Fleur says Charlotte's there. Turned up in a cab this morning, alone… but I won't believe it until I speak to her. What the hell's going on?"

Anne's face was alight with astonishment.

"But don't you see, David? She must have escaped! Perhaps

Karl was on his way to London and Fleur's was the nearest place she could run to."

"Sensible girl, if it's so. But why didn't she let us know straight away? Oh, come on, come on…"

Two minutes became five, then ten. The murmur of the party went on, but no one came to the telephone. David shouted down the mouthpiece, hoping to attract someone's attention, but no one responded. He replaced the receiver, tried to call again, but the operator said the line was busy.

"Oh God," he said, despairing. "She's left the thing off the hook. I don't like this, Anne. Fleur didn't sound right, somehow… If she's been taking dope of some kind, she could be telling me any nonsense. What if Charli's there… and Karl's still with her?"

Anne looked at him, clearly sharing his thoughts.

"Well?"

"Hang the blasted phone, hang the police. I'm going straight down there now. Should do it in less than two hours."

"Not on your own, I hope?" Her head was on one side, a glint of excitement in her eyes.

"I should think not. Get your coat, old girl, and meet me on the drive."

David went into the gun room for his service revolver and ammunition. In the corner of the glass cupboard a dull sheen of leather and metal caught his eye. His sword bayonet. On an impulse he took it, strapping it on as he hurried out.

God knows, if bullets won't stop him, I'll try anything.

Charlotte stared at the two vampires, feeling as if someone had looped a cord around her throat and jerked it tight. How exquisite they looked, and how terrifying in their unhuman stillness, the way their stares burned deep into her. They were identical except for their eyes: one had irises of radium blue, with a look of glittering mischief, the other's were pale gold, expressionless.

Clive said softly, "Charlotte, this is Stefan…" The blue-eyed one inclined his head to her. "And Niklas…" The gold-eyed twin went on staring through her without any sign of acknowledgement.

Charlotte could not move or speak. Impossible to say either,

"I'm pleased to meet you," or, "They're vampires!" A dozen thoughts swirled through her mind. *Clive's presenting me to them as prey. No, he can't know what they are! But what are they doing here? How is it possible that they're in Fleur's house?* A few seconds passed, expanding with unspoken malevolence.

Then the door handle rattled. Fleur's voice, muffled, called, "Clive? Are you in there?"

For a moment the tension dissipated. Without a word Clive went and unlocked the door. Light spilled in, and Charlotte ran to her sister.

"Whatever are you doing in here?" said Fleur, moving into the room.

"Introducing Charlotte to our friends," said Clive.

Fleur began to say something else, but as she saw Stefan and Niklas her face changed. Softened. She went past Charlotte and straight to the twins, walking unsteadily, her eyes dreamy.

Charlotte's relief was short-lived.

"Fleur?"

"Ah, darlings," said Fleur, holding out her arms to the vampires. Charlotte watched helplessly as she embraced Stefan, while Clive looked on with apparent approval. Suddenly the whole safe world had creaked out of joint. Fleur turned, one arm around Stefan's waist, her head on his shoulder.

"We wanted you to meet our special friends, dear."

"But they –" Charlotte's words froze. *If they realise I recognise them, what will happen to me?*

One thing she could see: Clive and Fleur were too heavily under the influence of drink and drugs to be reasoned with. She gasped in horror as Stefan lifted Fleur's wrist to his mouth – not kissing her there, but biting, sucking. Charlotte's pulse thudded thin and rapid in sympathy. Even as he drank, Stefan went on looking straight at her, clear-eyed and as lovely as a golden-haired doll.

Charlotte looked at Clive, but his expression was rapt. His only reaction was to clear his throat and slide his hand inside his own collar as if it were too tight.

The door was open. Charlotte could have fled, but was paralysed.

Stefan held his victim only for a second or two before letting her go as dreamily as he had taken her. And still his sapphire eyes were fixed on Charlotte, cruelly amused. Charlotte was unconsciously holding her left wrist – which began aching again from Karl's bite – against her chest as if to ward him off.

She took a step back, shaking her head in denial. They must have seen simple fear in the gesture; they could not begin to know the complexity of her feelings.

As if nothing had happened, Fleur said, "Take our guests into the drawing room, Clive. We mustn't be selfish and keep them all to ourselves, must we?"

With a piercing glance at Charlotte, Stefan put his hand through Niklas's arm and followed Clive out of the room, leaving Fleur and Charlotte alone.

Fleur smiled, her eyelids heavy, half closed.

"I'm afraid Clive frightened you a little. It was very naughty of him." Her words ran together, the consonants indistinct.

Now the twins had gone, Charlotte found her voice.

"But don't you know what they are, what they just did to you?"

"Oh, don't say it. It's an ugly word for such beautiful creatures."

"You're in danger, they'll kill you!"

"Nonsense." Fleur lifted her hand, ran her thumb over the pale crescent marks. "They only take a little. Makes one feel so light-headed and wonderfully creative." She half turned towards the conservatory, swaying a little. "Such dreams I have... I can't wait to paint them."

Behind her, scenes of horror gleamed darkly on their easels, with stark patches of white standing out: a skull, a winding sheet. Beneath Fleur's blithe manner lurked a derangement that sent Charlotte dizzy with alarm.

"But who are they, how long have you known them?"

"Oh, I don't know... a month or two, I think."

Since Karl came to Cambridge? Charlotte wondered.

Fleur continued, "Does it matter who they are or where they come from? You needn't frown at me for enjoying cocaine, they are more delicious than any drug. Now, come along to the party, dear, and I'll make sure you relax and enjoy yourself too. Was there something I meant to tell you? Oh, I don't know. It can't have been important."

Charlotte let Fleur lead her into the hall, but once there she broke away and ran up to her room. Shutting the door she leaned against it, one hand pressed to her head. She felt like a scrap of paper in the wind, helpless.

Why would Stefan and Niklas be here, except because of Karl? Did Kristian send them, as he sent Pierre?

She imagined a huge dark figure moving through the house, scoring the polished table tops with his fingernails, crushing the glass lampshades to dust in his hands. Utter contempt for wealth and all it could buy. But her image of Kristian was vague and had no face.

It's as if Fleur and Clive are addicted to them in some way... A shiver went through her. *Addicted, yes, just as I can never have enough of Karl, his face, his eyes, the way the light burns on his hair... this dreadful craving I can't tell apart from love.*

She thought of Madeleine, her infatuation with Karl, and the way her gaze had hung on Pierre, that night he had forced his way into Parkland.

"They fall in love with evil and so meet their death," Karl had said. It was like a drug, this craving that had taken her heart, soul, her whole being by the roots and torn her to pieces. *Name the demon, they say*, she thought, hugging herself. *Name the demon and it loses its power.*

She looked at the black and gilt stalk of the telephone on the bedside table. Of course, she must ring David. *I should have done it hours ago. I must have been out of my mind!*

An eerie murmur came from the earpiece and she jumped as if it were a scorpion in her hand. Either it was out of order, or someone was on one of the extensions. She replaced the receiver and said aloud, "But what could David do anyway? What use would it be to invite him into more danger? I must help Fleur and I must do it alone."

Her terror subsided into calm. In control, she left her room and went downstairs to the party.

The drawing room was decorated on a fashionable Egyptian theme, in sandy gold and desert red, the lines geometric and stylised. Dimly lit, with shawls draped over the lamps so their light glowed through embroidery and lace, the room was a warm red den, enticing, threatening. Layers of smoke swirled and tipped below the ceiling. Women in lace and beads and feathers, men casually dressed with their collars undone, reclined on sofas, chairs, even on the floor. They all seemed either too languid or too animated; their laughter too wild, eyes unfocused, their slack faces moist and bronzed in the feverish light.

Charlotte moved into the room, looking for Fleur. For once, she felt not so much self-conscious as invisible; they were all so wrapped up in themselves. In one corner, a young man was reading a morbid poem to a small but attentive audience. As he finished, a self-styled literary critic, an overweight woman with a prim, pinched face, began demolishing his poetic efforts on technicalities. "Your similes didn't *quite* work for me, Teddy, because I think you'll find liver isn't *quite* the colour you describe…" On a sofa near Charlotte, two plump, bespectacled women were engaged in an earnest if drunken discussion of Irish politics – oblivious to anything else, even to the two young men tangled in an embrace in the armchair opposite.

Father would be horrified by this, Charlotte thought. *And vampires here, taking their rationality and their life in sips. They're only willing victims because they've been bewitched. They don't know the danger and they don't care.*

The men in the armchair disentangled themselves, and she saw that they were Stefan and Clive. Charlotte stared, too astonished to avert her eyes. She was almost as shocked as she would have been to see David there. Clive, of all people… always so conventional… now raising his fingers to wipe away a red streak on his throat, his eyes closed and his face flushed with fever or pleasure.

Charlotte turned away, swallowing hard. And at last she saw Fleur, languishing in an armchair between a man and a woman who were perched on the arms, talking and laughing with her. She stretched out a lazy hand to greet Charlotte, but made no move to go to her.

One of the blond vampires sat on the floor, leaning back against her chair. Niklas. His face was pale and cherubic, his golden hair almost white in a splash of lamplight. His irises glittered like sovereigns with an oddly vacant tranquillity.

Stefan moved to sit next to his twin; two lions, guarding Fleur's chair. The woman beside Fleur leaned down to Niklas, offering her wrist. Blank-eyed he bit into her until the woman flopped forward like an abandoned marionette. The others laughed. Fleur leaned down to stroke Stefan's hair, her smile serene, her eyes sleepy. The room was blurred, dim, shadowy, yet to Charlotte this tableau shone like an altarpiece in a spotlight. The twins sat upright and cross-legged with their admirers around them, like gods before their worshippers. Stefan was the one who smiled and talked, while his golden-eyed brother said not a word. Again, she noticed that they blinked in unison.

All my life I've felt powerless. Perhaps I am, but I must do something to stop this.

She caught Stefan's gaze and held it meaningfully. After a few seconds, as if intrigued by her attention, he rose to his feet and came to her.

"I would like to speak to you in private," she said.

He looked at her, quizzical and amused. A peculiar thrill went through her. Almost as seductive as Karl, his white-gold beauty, but he lacked the inner tranquillity that, in Karl, had swept away her better judgment. Nor did he look as unpredictable as Pierre. But there was a deeper edge to him that she couldn't read. Danger.

"Are you sure? Very well, Charlotte." His light accent sounded Scandinavian. "I am so pleased to meet you at last. Shall we go into the conservatory?"

She knew what a risk this was, but she let the mask of coldness come down over her face, as it had so often in the past when strangers tried to engage her in conversation. For once it was not her enemy but her friend. He held open the door for her, but as they went into the hallway, she shivered with the sense of being followed. Glancing back, she saw the golden-eyed vampire following them, moving like a ghost in blank silence.

"Don't mind my brother," Stefan said. "He likes to stay close to me, and I have to take care of him."

"Can't we talk alone?"

"He will not repeat anything he hears. He is mute."

She found Niklas even more unnerving than Stefan, but she said, "Very well, I'll speak to both of you."

In the darkened conservatory, Charlotte felt swamped by the brilliance of Stefan's aura. She was uncomfortably aware of

Niklas standing amid the forest of plants and dark paintings, as beautiful and mindless as a waxwork.

Suddenly Stefan put his hands on her arms and said, "Don't move; I want to know what he sees in you. You look haunted, which is more interesting than simple beauty. I think you would be perfect..."

"I don't know what you're talking about, but I know what you are," Charlotte said. "I want you to go away and leave my sister alone."

Stefan smiled. "Have you been tormenting yourself about this? Is this why you look so unhappy?" he said, quietly mocking. She tried to free herself of his touch and suddenly she felt his incredible strength. "If you really know what we are, you are very brave to confront us. This won't protect you," he added, touching the cross that still hung around her neck.

She could do nothing to evade him as his lips moved on her neck. A burst of pain, then with hallucinatory acuteness she felt him take a single swallow of blood, and withdraw.

"That is all we take from your sister and the others," he said into her ear. "They are in no danger from us. I should take no pleasure in killing them."

"But you're destroying them mentally!"

"That is a very subjective point of view. Unleashing their creativity, they tell us. It is a game to them, a novelty, something to try like a new drug. They seek eagerly the clouded nightmares and the daydreams that our bite can bring. We are supplying a need, if you like..."

"An addiction."

"Yes. They are addicted to us. Yes, I like that."

"It's sick, horrible."

"But not as bad as killing them, surely? There's no fun in that."

She doubted it would do any good to appeal to his mercy, but she had to try.

"Stefan, I can't make you leave. I'm *asking* you. There must be someone other than my sister you can prey on."

"But she would not want us to leave. She dotes on us, as you saw."

He had a gentle, implacable air of superiority that Charlotte could not penetrate. He was playing with her. If he and Niklas closed in, there was no one to save her. She could scream herself hoarse and no one would take any notice. Yet she would not let her fear win.

Her voice abrupt and icy, she said, "You can stay only as long as your presence here is useful to Kristian."

Stefan drew back, looking genuinely surprised. It was a tiny victory, revealing that she was not as ignorant as he had assumed.

"I beg your pardon?"

"I know you can do nothing without Kristian's permission. Didn't he send you here to look for Karl?"

The vampire blinked at her.

"Not to look for him as such. But to put pressure on him…"

"By hurting Fleur?"

"By showing him there's nowhere he can hide and no corner of his life he can keep secret from his master."

Unexpectedly she felt tears locking her mouth. She swallowed.

"Then you should know you are wasting your time. Karl has gone back to Kristian. So there's no reason for you to be here."

A smile touched Stefan's bone-china face.

"I can think of one very good reason. I understand you are Karl's friend. And it seems he has told you a great deal that Kristian would rather you did not know…"

"Don't touch me!" Charlotte took a step back, realised Niklas was directly behind her.

"Not afraid, Charlotte?" Stefan said sweetly. "I thought you liked vampires."

She turned, meaning to run – but they moved faster than thought to seize her, four arms binding her so tight all her breath was squeezed out. The certainty of death petrified her. Suffocating, she felt the steel touch of fangs on her neck and waited for the stab of pain…

A voice cut in sharply, "Let her go, Stefan."

Suddenly she could breathe again. She almost fell as they released her, but Stefan caught her – a gentle action at odds with the violence he had just shown. Then she saw Karl in the shadows, his silhouette blending with the leaves against indigo panes of glass. He came towards her, receiving her in his arms as she ran to meet him.

"Charlotte, Charlotte," he said. Then to Stefan, "If you ever touch her again, or allow Niklas to – I'll destroy you both."

Stefan did not look cowed or even resentful. His face seemed too sweet for an evil thought ever to have crossed his mind. He opened his hands to Karl.

"It's your responsibility, then, that you have told her too much. I shall say nothing to our master, but you know the dangers of caring for humans. Don't blame us for the knots in which you have tied yourself." As Stefan spoke, Niklas's serenely empty expression did not change, he showed no awareness of what was happening.

"It's Kristian I blame for everything," said Karl, "as you should, my friend." He kissed Charlotte's forehead and said, "Wait here a few moments."

She watched him take Stefan and Niklas to the edge of the conservatory. She heard them whispering, but couldn't hear what they were saying. Then there was a draught, the click of an outer door opening and closing.

Karl came back alone.

"It's all right, I've persuaded them to go," he said. "I had no idea Fleur was in danger, that Kristian would go to such lengths... What were you thinking, trying to confront them? There are worse creatures than Stefan and Niklas, and I have no quarrel with them – but all vampires are potentially lethal to humans. You took a terrible risk."

"What else could I do? You weren't here!" she exclaimed. Tremors of shock and relief went through her as she explained what had happened that day. "They've been feeding on Fleur and Clive for at least a month." She waved a hand at the canvases, her anxiety twisting into rage. "Look, look at these dreadful things that are in Fleur's mind. I had to try to make them leave. I waited for you this morning, I saw you walk away with someone else! I thought you weren't coming back! Who was that woman, who is she?"

As if sensing his touch would not calm her, Karl stood apart, watching her with shadowed eyes that still dissolved her. Even through her anger she felt the ache of wanting his arms round her, wanting to hurt him and hold him at the same time. Love, obsession, whatever this feeling was, she could not conquer it. One touch of his hand was all it took to start the fire again.

Softly, Karl answered, "It was Ilona."

"Your daughter?" She was stunned. "But she looked the same age as you – from a distance, at least."

"Did you expect her to be a little girl? I told you she was in her twenties when…"

"I know, but actually seeing her was different," said Charlotte, subdued. "Ilona… it sounds strange, but I could never quite believe she was real."

Karl's eyes were sad and he looked away from her.

"You are very angry with me, dearest, and with good reason. Let me explain. It was Stefan I wanted to see this morning. He is often in London, though I had no idea he was here. I couldn't find him. When I came to meet you, Ilona appeared and stopped me. I could hardly bring another vampire to you, so I took her away instead. The rest of the day I have been talking to her and Pierre…" His shoulders rose and fell minimally, as if the talks had been fruitless. "And the truth is, I almost did not come back. I thought you would have gone home by now. However, I couldn't resist the temptation to pass Fleur's house and make sure. When I sensed vampires inside, I had no choice but to come in. Is there some reason why your family haven't yet taken you home?"

"You should know better than to ask that," she said thinly.

"You haven't contacted them? Well, if I condemn you for that, I condemn myself. I should have said goodbye, and meant it."

"But what did Ilona want?" Even knowing their relationship was one of father and child, Charlotte felt a spasm of jealousy. "I thought she wouldn't speak to you."

"It is quite a rare event," said Karl. "But Pierre had seen her, and told her I intended to go back to Kristian. She's angry, even after the way he's mistreated her, his castle is still her home and she does not want me there. So she came to tell me that if I went back, she would leave Kristian and neither of us would ever see her again."

"Would that be a bad thing?" Charlotte spoke sharply, before she could stop herself.

Karl gave her a dark look.

"Don't be jealous of her. The hatred she feels for me must be bitterly painful – as is the love I feel for her. But the fact that I love her does not mean I love you any less."

She felt a little ashamed. "So – has she made you change your mind?"

"Nothing has changed," he said, pinching out the faint glimmer of hope. "I have to go away, Charlotte. You know that. As long as I stay, you and your family will be in danger from Stefan and Pierre and Ilona… but when I leave, they'll all go with me."

"Even Ilona?" said Charlotte.

"Yes. I'll make sure of it. I know her. Whatever she says, she will not miss a chance to cause trouble between Kristian and me."

She was quiet, biting her lip until she tasted the metal sting of blood.

"And I will never see you again. Can you just leave me and forget?"

"There is no other solution." He avoided her gaze, but there was such misery in his face that she almost cried out.

"There must be! Karl, I can't bear it! You asked me to be sure of what was in my heart – but the only thing of which I am absolutely certain is that I want to stay with you." She made to embrace him, stopped herself. "I know we can't always have what we want," she added bitterly.

He took her hands and held on when she tried to pull away.

"Charlotte, you don't belong with me. You belong with your family and friends. I would not wish it on you to stay with me, to deprive you of the normal life that is yours by right."

She stared at him. "Deprive? What is there left for me when I go back? You can't really think I could marry someone else and be happy, can you? How could I even contemplate looking at another man, after you? No one, no one could ever compare! All that remains for me is to stay at home and be a continual source of disappointment to Father, because I'm not the person he really needs. Karl, can't you see that you are the only thing that matters to me now? You've made everything else seem meaningless!"

She did not mean her words as an accusation, but they were. The anguish in his eyes cut through her.

"Yes, I have been cruel to you. Perhaps this pain was inevitable from the moment we first met. I've already made it worse by being unable to let you go. But now I must. I won't promise that you will get over it, *liebchen*. Nor will I. But this is the least painful way."

"I don't see how it could possibly be worse," she whispered. Tears clawed her eyes. "Tell me."

"Yes! I want you to understand!" he said with sudden intensity. "Ask yourself what would happen if we stayed together! Putting aside the guilt you've suffered since I gave you the choice of leaving the manor – it would be far worse for both of us. I described the anguish of watching my family growing older, suffering every wound that mortality can inflict. It was one of the main reasons I have distanced myself from mortals, deluded myself that I could not fall victim to love. I could not bear to go through that pain again, watching you grow old and die. Don't think I would cease to care for you. Unlike humans my nature is not fickle, my emotions not dulled by time. To lose you, however slowly, would be the pain...

"But it's nothing, Charlotte, to what you would suffer. How do you feel, knowing that I must prey upon humans to live, that my bite will bring them illness, madness, even death? I wonder how long the love of a sensitive and Christian soul can survive that knowledge. Have you any idea? No. But you would come to hate me eventually – or yourself, which would be worse. Our love has no future. None!"

She was utterly stunned by his words. Their truth was a dazzling, vitriolic light that she could not bear.

He added bitterly, "Well, have I not treated you in just the way you would expect of a vampire? You may be physically unharmed – just – but I seem to have drained your life of any prospect of happiness."

"God, don't say any more." She was devastated beyond weeping.

"But I don't want to spare you anything," he said. "There's a question you have never asked me, but I can't believe it's never been in your mind. Do you want to know whether I could make you like myself? A vampire."

"Yes – I thought of it – I daren't ask."

"The answer is no."

"Why not?" she whispered.

"Many reasons. It carries too much risk, Charlotte. You would have to die before the transformation takes place. Do you understand? Actually *die*. And sometimes it does not work. I could not even contemplate it. And my energy alone would not be enough to re-animate you, it takes the power of three. There is no one I can ask to help me. And even if there were, even if we succeeded, when Kristian found out he would punish us and destroy you."

She swallowed against the thickness of her throat.

"But he let Ilona live…"

"And I should never have changed her," Karl said abruptly. "Whatever motive anyone might have for seeking to become a vampire – the prospect of immortality, or power over others, or a fascination with evil – no reason can be anything but wrong."

"What about love?"

"Love is the worst of all! It would destroy you, Charlotte! I don't have the right to inflict this existence on anyone. It can be beautiful, yes, but also excruciatingly lonely. It's comfortless, the only true relief is in killing. And there are no answers. The passion and the life we have is stolen, paid for by the suffering of our victims."

"Would you rather be dead?" she said sharply.

"Your questions always go straight to the heart, like a needle, don't they?" he said with a faint smile. "I told you I have a strong instinct to live. I have come to terms with what I am. And I am frightened of dying, just like anyone else."

"So you don't want to bear the responsibility of changing someone. I understand that, but if the other person was to consent –"

"You can't consent, because however much I tell you, however much you think you understand, you would never truly comprehend until you actually became a vampire – and then it would be too late. And you don't want the responsibility of making such a decision either, do you? You would like me to take you as I did my daughter. But I will never do that again."

"That's the real reason, isn't it?" she exclaimed. "You're afraid that I'll change, as Ilona did!"

She saw then that she'd touched the thorn-sensitive root of his reluctance. Darkness collected in his eyes, frightening her, but when he replied his voice was level.

"Yes, if I am completely honest. I cannot tell you how much distress it caused me, the complete change in her character. If it happened to you, if you hated me afterwards, it would be more than I could bear."

"But it won't happen to me. I could never stop loving you."

"You can't be sure. It would alter your feelings. It always does."

She stared wildly at him. "You mean you might not love *me* any more. I'd be someone different."

"I would still love you, even if you were. But that is not the point. Think what it means, Charlotte! Can you really make a choice that will result in you going out each day to prey upon people by drinking their blood?"

She shuddered violently, lowering her eyes.

He went on, "Knowing, even should you choose to prey only upon strangers, that each one you strike down has sisters, or parents, or children who will grieve for them and ask why, why it had to happen?"

Now she was weeping, shaking with sobs.

"You know I couldn't."

"No," he said more gently. He drew her into his arms and held her, stroking her hair. "So now do you believe me when I say we must part, and the sooner the better? I cannot go on loving you because the longer I am with you the harder it is to resist my instinct."

"But it was not so terrible," she said, unconsciously touching her neck where Stefan's brief bite had left two small, sore crescents. "It was a bond between us."

"Yes. And that has made the desire a torment... and if it happened again, it would probably kill you."

She looked up at him, her eyes burning. Her fingers dug into his arms.

"I don't care! I would rather be dead than have to live without you!"

He seemed taken aback by the fierceness of her reaction.

"Why don't you do it?" she said, closing her eyes. "Put an end to this misery."

She felt his hands tightening on her back, his tension transmitted itself to her body, electrifying. She meant what she'd said, yet she was petrified to realise that this time he was not going to turn away. That he *could not*. He kissed her mouth, gently but with fervid intensity. His tongue touched the blood where she had bitten her lip and he caught his breath. Panic chilled her. His lips moved over her cheek, down her neck. Silvery waves of anticipation sheeted over her skin, while his arms tightened until she could barely breathe.

This was so different to the time she had given him her blood in the manor, he had been vulnerable then, dependent on her for his life. Not now. He held her in bonds of dark stone. And although he held her with love, that love had become a ravenous need that scythed away all her defences. The liquid ache of desire pinned her body to his. Every instinct warned her to stop him, but she could not. His dark thirst mesmerised her and she arched towards him, wanting him, *willing* him to sate it. Treacherous, this seductive yearning for self-destruction.

His lips were a whisper of warm silk on her throat. His tongue brushed over Stefan's marks as if to obliterate them. And then – two burning thrusts of pain. His mouth was a circle of heat, pulling, bruising her. She cried out softly, *Ahh*, and clasped his neck as a heavy ache spread through her chest, stomach, limbs, dragging her down until the rhythmic contractions of her heart and loins turned into the wing beats of a flock of carrion birds that swooped towards her as she slid under the surface of a black ocean... Down until the agony twisted on itself into perverse, excruciating delight.

She wanted this to never end. It answered her despair completely. This was more than predator and prey. Yes, it was unholy, dangerous, dark, yet she felt centred within the vortex, poised on the mouth of something rich and incomprehensible. *All your conventions, beliefs, values*, whispered the birds as they soared along the night. *Leave them all behind and come away...*

For every drop of life that Karl drank, she drew something out of him in return. The threads of his being. An insoluble bond.

But it lasted only a few moments. There was a wrench as his fangs slid out of her flesh, a tingling that centred in the wounds and dissipated down through her body. Her eyelids fluttered open. The world swung back into focus and she was sharply aware of every sensation: the moist air sweetly cool on her face, the texture of Karl's clothes and the touch of his hands.

He was holding her, one arm enfolding her shoulders, the other hand cupping her head. They were pressed together down the length of their bodies, an unspeakably sweet feeling. He breathed in, held the breath, let it go in a long, shivering sigh. Then, with gentleness that rent her heart, he helped her to sit down on a bench and kissed her, leaving drops of her own blood on her lips.

A sacrament.

"Beloved, I could not…" he whispered. Tears gleamed in his eyes. "Never. Not for the world."

"I know," she answered. "I know."

He wrapped his arms round her, buried his face in her hair.

"Everything we have said might just as well have gone unspoken. I don't know what we are going to do."

She held onto him, every last trace of fear gone, all the tension between them shattered and discarded like egg shell. They seemed to be inside each other's minds. Her blood was in him. Despair locked them seamlessly together.

"I don't care about any of it," she said. "Just stay with me."

"Charlotte…" He kissed her with purely human passion and at once she was adrift on a blood-dark ocean, sinking. Sweeter than any drug was this feeling, and a thousand times more addictive. They would have pulled each other to the floor amid the foliage and easels, the scents of greenery and linseed, not caring if they were discovered… But Karl suddenly drew back, his hands on her arms holding her away.

"What is it?" she said. It was a wrench to separate herself. How could he detach from her so abruptly? He was gazing past her into the darkness of the dining room.

"There's someone here." His sudden complete stillness and the concern in his eyes alarmed her. She turned starkly sober, her mind ice clear.

"Who? Not David?"

Not answering, he folded his hand round hers and drew her to her feet. As they went into the house she began to sense something wrong…

Then, in the hall, she realised. The house was silent: she heard no music, no voices, no sounds of the party at all. Terror washed over her.

"Karl, wait," she whispered, but he ignored her. His gaze was fixed on the closed door of the drawing room as he walked steadily towards it. Silence hung in cold heavy sheets and she wanted to pull him back, to warn him... but it was too late. He was turning the handle.

The door opened onto a cave of horrors.

The light dazzled Charlotte's dark-accustomed eyes, but through the glare she saw a scene of bizarre chaos. *A charade?* she thought, trying to force rationality into the sight. No. Death lay ravelled in the gold and rose-red shadows.

The room appeared to have been ransacked. All the guests sat motionless in their chairs. Only one figure was on her feet, a woman in glittering red with scarlet hair to her waist. She was moving slowly around the room with a deliberation that made her every gesture shine with malevolence. She pulled a shawl off a lamp, tipping it over; she picked up a photograph, slammed it down so the glass cracked. She stopped and glared down at each man or woman in turn, appraising and despising them.

Some of the guests were slumped in their seats, unconscious; others were staring at the woman, blank-eyed. She was in complete, hypnotic control. Charlotte didn't know why this slender creature inspired such terror, but watching her was like waiting for a scorpion to strike.

The woman stopped by a young man with shiny black hair. She pierced him with her malign gaze; he stared back, lips working as if he were trying to articulate a protest. Then she seized his collar and pulled him up bodily – he was tall and heavy, yet she held him one-handed – so that he hung from her grasp at an undignified angle, his eyes bulging.

She bit into his throat. Her shoulders rose, the muscles of her bare back tightening with pleasure. But after a second or two she threw him aside like a carcass. A groan trickled from his throat. His eyes were marbled red with burst vessels.

Even then, no one moved, no one reacted. Even Karl seemed transfixed.

At last he said, "Ilona."

The woman stopped in the centre of the room and faced him, hands on hips. She was smaller than Charlotte, with large brown eyes in a delicate, cloud-pale face. Her hair was brilliant poppy scarlet, circled by a bandeau and flowing to her waist over the fiery dress. Anger and venom flowed from her in a silent winter gale. She was the hub of the nightmare that was coiling around Charlotte's heart.

"I was wondering how long it would take you to notice me, *Father*." Her voice was accented, clipped.

"What are you doing here?"

"If you hadn't been so preoccupied with *her* –" she gave Charlotte a look of searing contempt "– you might have guessed by now. Games, Father. I will show you games."

As she turned away, Karl stepped into the room and pulled the two bespectacled women off their sofa.

"Get out," he said, pushing them towards the door. "All of you, get out of here!" Charlotte had so rarely heard him raise his voice, his commanding power was electrifying.

That broke the spell. Suddenly people were crying out, falling over each other to escape, and Ilona was snatching at anyone who came near her, her eyes demented, her hair as wild as snakes. The front door banged open and voices floated out into the square. Cold air swirled in, but the room was not quite empty. Seven people remained slumped in their seats.

Were they drunk or drugged, Charlotte wondered, or was it the bite of a vampire that had left them insensible? The delicate sips that Stefan and Niklas had stolen… or Ilona's murderous thirst?

Charlotte stood pressed against the door frame, horrified, powerless. To her alarm she saw that Fleur was one of those who hadn't moved. She remained in her chair, eyes closed. Clive, sitting upright on a sofa opposite the door, was the only one who appeared to be conscious, but he was staring into space as if too shocked to react.

His voice betraying no emotion, Karl said, "Ilona, stop this."

Ilona ignored him, went into the corner and picked up the fat poetry critic from a chaise longue. The woman came out of her stupor and squawked in pain as Ilona took a brief drink and hefted her aside.

Charlotte gazed at Fleur, willing her to wake up, to move, but her sister's eyes remained closed and her chest rose and fell unevenly.

"Fleur..." Charlotte went towards her, then stopped in her tracks. Karl was crossing the room almost faster than she could register, hands outstretched to seize his daughter – but as he reached her, there was a cold shifting of the air and Ilona vanished.

A moment later she reappeared next to Fleur's chair.

"No, leave her alone!" Charlotte cried. As she rushed forward, Ilona's hand lashed out across an impossible distance and caught her across the cheek like a whip. The blow flung Charlotte backwards into a wall and she slid to the floor with bloody points of light stabbing her eyes. Half stunned, she watched the scene unwind as a flickering slow-motion film.

Ilona gathered up the oblivious Fleur like a rag doll and stood facing Karl. She was a thin ruby-red flame, exquisite and lethal.

"What are you staring at, Karl? Isn't this how a true vampire should behave? You only play at it, just as you only play at defying Kristian. But I am not a ball to be thrown idly between you."

"No one has ever thought you were that," Karl said, his voice low and measured. "Let her go, Ilona. Come with me and we'll talk."

"About what? We talk all day and all I learn is that Kristian has wormed his way into your heart by threatening this human family. Harming *me* was not enough to bring you back – yet you'd come back to protect *these*?" She shook Fleur in violent emphasis. Charlotte tried to cry out, could not make a sound. "But what if they were dead, Karl? What could he threaten you with then?"

At these words, Karl launched himself towards Ilona.

Too late. Mouth open, Ilona lifted Fleur and tore out her throat as easily as a dog wolfing a mouthful of butter. When Karl reached Ilona, with a crystalline *snap* she vanished again to reappear on the far side of the room like a glinting red knife.

They were speaking German now, a thin cold stream of anger – but Charlotte could only stare at Fleur lying over the arm of the chair as if her back was broken. Her head hanging back, eyes open, the wound in her throat stretched wide like a mouth, dark and bright blood pouring from the torn vessels. She went on breathing for a few seconds, breath bleeding out of her in faint grunts until there was none left.

Charlotte turned sick and faint yet she found herself crawling across the carpet, out of her mind, half blinded by anguish. Sobs of shock came out of her like coughs. She hauled herself onto her knees on the arm of the chair and took her sister in her arms… but the body was a soft weightless husk, all the sparkling life force gone.

"No…" The strength of denial seemed to shake her apart, but when the wail burst from her mouth it was soundless. Her throat was full of rust. *You can't be – You must wake up. We were going to talk to each other, Fleur. Tomorrow. All the things we haven't said yet…*

A cold draught blew on her from the doorway, and she heard voices outside, the gruff crescendo of a car. She looked up, and that was when she realised Clive was not merely staring into space, but dead. That Ilona must have killed him too, before Charlotte and Karl had come into the room.

Charlotte only half registered the sounds outside: people shouting, footsteps, a man's voice. The sounds were in the hallway now but they were so far away, not her concern…

Then she felt another crisp shiver of air, like ice crystals sifting over snow, a brief wrenching emptiness. Ilona was gone, and this time she did not reappear.

A second later, Anne and David appeared in the doorway. Only Karl remained, Karl who no longer had the power to escape into the Crystal Ring.

Charlotte held onto Fleur's cold hands and despair rolled through her. This was what it came to, her love for Karl. This horror.

David had driven at reckless speed from Hertfordshire, arriving in London before ten o'clock. Turning into Fleur's square, he and Anne saw a number of figures on the pavement, shadowy in the streetlights.

"Lot of drunks about," he commented.

"No, not drunks," said Anne. "Something's going on."

Light was streaming from his sister's front door. People were running away from the house, some shouting for help, others wandering as if dazed. A terrified girl came straight at David. Startled, he took a moment to realise she was Fleur's maid, Jenny.

"Oh, Captain Neville, thank God it's you!" Jenny cried,

breathless. "I don't know what's goin' on: I was in the kitchen and I heard screamin' and carryin' on – I'm goin' to call the police!" She hurried onwards across the square.

"What the devil – ?" In a few strides David was inside the house, Anne close behind. In the doorway to the drawing room he froze, confronted by a scene worse than anything he had anticipated.

Charlotte was huddled on the floor, hair dishevelled, head bowed on Fleur's knee – and Fleur's face was turned to the ceiling, grape-mauve and sunken, her throat a lake of blood.

A wave of revulsion, grief. Such horrors he'd seen in the trenches but nothing, nothing to compare with this. His own sister, safe at home, *safe*, in her own drawing room... Behind him, he heard Anne gasp. He was too late to shield her from the sight. He caught the door frame for support, held down sickness. The War had trained him in this, at least. No quarter for emotion until the task in hand was finished.

Trembling, David looked around the room. Clive was slumped on the sofa, eyes glassy and staring – *Christ, him too* – and there were four or five others, whom David did not know, lying motionless about the room.

And in the centre of the room stood Karl von Wultendorf, gazing at David, a lamp behind him turning his hair to a blood-red halo.

David realised he'd turned Karl into an unrecognisable monster in his mind. It was a shock to see that he looked no different: slender and self-contained, with the same aristocratic face and intense honey-brown eyes. A gentleman... with the evidence of his monstrosity strewn all around him.

All at once, the rage within David was very controlled, smooth and hard as a missile. He knew with absolute clarity that he must kill von Wultendorf.

He raised his service revolver, although he knew bullets had had no effect on the vampire before. But the reassuring weight helped him focus his thoughts.

As he did so, Anne went past him into the room and hauled Charlotte up from the floor. David didn't try to stop her, he was glad of her cool head and swift action. His heart was in his mouth as he waited for some lightning counter-move on the vampire's part. Karl did not move. Anne half carried Charlotte the few steps to the door and took her into the hall: knowing what David planned and doing just the right thing.

"All right, von Wultendorf," he said, level and grim. "It's over."

He fired the gun, three times.

The bullets went through the vampire's chest. He reeled back from the impact, righted himself, stood gazing at David as if nothing had happened.

He heard Charlotte crying out, "Make them stop! Make them stop!" while Anne tried desperately to calm her.

Then von Wultendorf spoke. "Charlotte was to have been safely returned to you, and you would never have seen or heard of me again. There is no need for this."

"No need?" David could barely speak. "By God, you are a coward! You protect yourself by abducting an innocent young woman, commit the vilest of murders, and now you're trying –"

"I have harmed no one in this room," said von Wultendorf, emotionless.

David was suddenly blinded by tears.

"My sister!" he shouted hoarsely, pointing at Fleur. He blinked the tears away, hardened his voice. "A coward and a liar. I'll give you just one chance to answer for your crimes before I do justice – if you've the nerve to say anything in your own defence."

Karl looked at David in a strange, abstracted way, staring straight through him, his thoughts elsewhere. David began to feel disorientated and to lose his resolve. He guessed he was being hypnotised but there was nothing he could do to fight it. He was about to drop the gun… then the vampire lowered his gaze, shaking his head wearily.

"No, I have nothing to say. If a shepherd knew that a wolf had preyed upon his flock, what choice would he have but to pursue and destroy the beast? There is no doubt that you are a good shepherd, Captain Neville."

Shaken by this glimpse of his unhuman powers, David steadied himself. Could he really kill this creature in cold blood? Fleur, in the corner of his eye, Edward, Charlotte, Maddy… *There's not one of us this devil hasn't harmed – by Christ, yes I can.* Beneath his coat hung his bayonet: the type with a long sharp blade and a hilt like a sword. His only hope if bullets could not prevail.

"However," the vampire went on, "I would advise you to let me go unhindered. If you do not... I can kill you with considerably more ease than you can kill me."

From the doorway, Anne said, "Perhaps he's right, David." Her voice shook. "What use is it for anyone else to get hurt? Let him just go away and leave us alone."

"Anne, please don't interfere. Look after Charlotte."

"Charlotte said he can't be killed! If he murders you, where will that leave us?"

Karl said softly, "Miss Saunders has a point." There was nothing fiendlike about him, nothing mocking or ambiguous, not even simple defensiveness or anger. *Is it possible that Anne's right?* he thought. *No, even he can't be indestructible. If I don't act now I never will.*

"Anne, get back."

"David –"

"Get back!" he shouted, so sharp that she obeyed. And then he fired again, aiming for the vampire's head this time.

Two shots went wide. The third went straight through Karl's forehead. Surely, however fast the brain could heal – *if* it could heal – it would disorientate him for long enough...

But Karl was coming for him, impossibly fast, like flame. David never knew how his own hand moved swiftly enough, but wondrously the bayonet's hilt was in his palm in place of the revolver. He swung the blade to connect with the flesh of the vampire's neck, just before the white hands could seize him.

Von Wultendorf fell back, hands out to defend himself like skeletal supplicants. For a moment he gripped the bayonet with terrible strength. Then David wrenched it free and was hacking furiously, again and again, his own harsh breath and blood thundering through his ears, as the neck slowly split away from the body. The spinal column cracked, the stump gave up an ooze of semi-liquid blood... and the vampire lay dead, decapitated.

David lurched away, his sight turning black with dizziness, retching for breath.

There were shouts, dark uniforms moving around him... policemen. Drained and resigned, he dropped the sword bayonet.

Then Charlotte came rushing towards him – *Why didn't they keep her out of here? Idiots!* – and he caught her arms, tried to soothe her although there was hysteria in his own voice.

"It's all right, old girl. It's over. He's dead."

She wrenched away from him.

"No, he can't be dead, he can't be!"

To David's dismay she flung herself on Karl's body, choking out sobs of absolute, soul-racking grief. David gaped at her, almost more horrified by this than by anything that had gone before. *She's acting as if she still loves him, but she can't, it's impossible...*

And yet Charlotte was crying out his name with a desperation that turned David cold and sick with misery, went on crying even as they dragged her off his body and pulled her, struggling, out of that place of death.

"Karl. Karl. *Karl!*"

PART THREE

He's sure to come a-calling
When the shades of night are drawn
A twisted blackthorn in his hand
He'll linger until dawn
You wish to stay forever young
But only he knows how;
It's his blessing, it's his curse
And it's your decision now...

HORSLIPS, "RIDE TO HELL"

CHAPTER SIXTEEN

SILENT ALL DAY

Anne spent much of the stark, sleepless night sitting beside a hospital bed, watching over Charlotte. Dr Neville and Elizabeth were on their way to London, but until they arrived Anne was keeping the vigil on her own. Charlotte had been sedated but she fought to stay awake, her eyelids flickering in her colourless face.

"Where's David?"

"He's all right. He's safe," said Anne, and Charlotte drifted into sleep. Anne did not want to shield her from the truth, but now was not the time to tell her that David had been arrested for Karl's murder.

Anne was haunted endlessly by the dreadful scenes of that evening: Fleur, lying over the arm of her chair with her throat torn; the brief, bloody horror of David's fight with Karl; and Charlotte pouring out her misery over Karl's headless corpse.

What could have happened in the minutes before we arrived, poor Fleur and Clive? If only we'd arrived earlier... but, God, if we'd arrived later, surely Karl would have killed Charlotte too... Or if things had gone just a little differently, it would have been me weeping over David's body...

But how can it be, that Charli wept when Karl died? Anne brushed damp strands of hair off Charlotte's forehead. *Will we ever know?*

* * *

Kristian stood in the silent mortuary, looking down at Karl's long, lean body, as pale as the slab on which it lay. And the head, serene and cold as marble; and the two plum-red stumps of the neck.

Pierre stood beside him, blood-tinted tears rimming his eyes.

"God above, how could Karl let this happen?"

Kristian glanced at him with contempt.

"Only humans weep," he said. "Grief is their sickness, not ours."

"Don't you feel a damned thing for him?" said Pierre. "Are you glad? I suppose you are only angry that you did not do this yourself!"

"If you can say nothing sensible, hold your peace," said Kristian. "You cannot begin to comprehend what I feel. But that is not your fault."

Pierre turned away.

He thinks I patronise him, but he cannot argue, because he knows it's true, Kristian thought.

Although Kristian showed no superficial emotion, the vast thoughts and designs of God moved deep inside him, like whales beneath the surface of the sea. He had sensed Karl's death the instant it had happened. It had been a physical jolt, an ice burn circling his throat. *The dark strands that bond all immortals to God... how should they not vibrate, when one of His children is cut down?*

Kristian had raced along the dark canyons of the Crystal Ring, pulled by the shockwaves of Karl's destruction... and in London he had found Pierre, Ilona, Stefan and Niklas, all drawn together by the same wave. Deep in the shadows, they had watched the lighted doorway, the street busy with onlookers and ambulances, the police going to and fro. And after a long time, Kristian had seen them carry out three shrouded figures and drive them away in a police van.

"Who killed those two humans?" he had asked.

"Not us," Stefan replied.

Kristian had looked at Ilona, but she remained silent, not meeting his eyes.

"Who destroyed Karl?"

"I don't know, I swear I don't know!" she said fiercely.

"I will find out the truth of this, eventually," Kristian had said. His voice was low but he was glad to see them quail at his contained fury. "Now go home, all of you. It is finished with these humans, there is no cause for you ever to go near them again."

And at his command they had vanished. All except Pierre, who claimed he'd lost the strength to go through the Crystal Ring.

"Come with me, then," said Kristian, and together they trailed the van through the streets to the police mortuary.

They'd waited until the early hours of the morning, when activity within the building died down and Kristian sensed that there were no living presences within the morgue. Then he lent Pierre enough energy for them to enter the Crystal Ring for long enough to pass through the walls to the interior.

Sickening scents of organic chemicals, alien glint of tiles and metal... Kristian wanted to be away from this web of mortal evil.

"I don't see the point of coming here," Pierre whispered, as if he imagined someone might overhear them. "You say grief is human, but if you don't want to mourn, why bother?"

"Because I am going to take him home," said Kristian.

"For God's sake, he's dead!" Pierre laughed, but his voice was raw. "What's the use? Do you want to give him a decent burial – in the *Weisskalt*?"

Of course he is bitter. Was Karl not the most beloved and lovable of my flock? Who would not grieve for him?

Aloud, Kristian said, "I am not leaving him here for humans to probe and defile, to practise their *sciences* on him." He bent forward and lifted Karl's stiff, pale body, holding it easily against him with one arm. With the other hand he picked up the head by the hair... like a warrior carrying a trophy.

Pierre looked on in disbelief.

"Beloved Father, how will you take him home? It's impossible to take another being into the Crystal Ring alone and I can't help you."

"I hope you are not questioning my power." Kristian glared at him. "Don't judge me by your own petty standards. I have the strength. For Karl's sake, God will provide! You will have to find your own way home, Pierre. Feed well, and return as fast as you can."

Then Kristian let the room of death dissolve into the crystalline silence of the Ring. Karl's body had been no burden at all on Earth, but here it became so impossibly heavy that he almost let it fall back into the physical world. But God aided him. Clasping Karl tight to him, Kristian skimmed through the convolutions of the mind of God towards Schloss Holdenstein.

Charlotte felt as though she were drifting on a glassy grey river that had no beginning and no end and no meaning. Under the surface she could see shapes that made no sense. But at last, as she began to come out of the delirium of shock and hypnotic drugs, she realised what the shapes were. She was staring at windows and furniture and the brown oak-panelled walls of her room. She was at home, in Cambridge.

Memories came back like a picture torn in pieces. Lying in a hospital bed, Anne stroking her head... only a fragment, like a brief dream. Then in a motor car... *On my way up to London with Karl? No! Coming home with Father, Maple driving, Elizabeth holding me wrapped in a blanket. Why? We were all at Parkland... why am I here?*

Then pain gripped her, memories came back with the swish of a blade, cruel as justice. She wanted to scream but she couldn't breathe in or out, and his name was pounding through her mind, *Karl Karl Karl...*

Why am I still alive?

A voice said, "I think she's waking up. Charlotte? Darling, it's all right, we're here."

Charlotte woke properly then. All the shrieking turmoil had been deep inside her; her body, heavy with unnatural languor, remained motionless. Too numb to weep, almost too heavy even to speak, she looked up and saw Madeleine sitting beside her, her face puffy from crying. Aunt Elizabeth was on the other side of the bed, her bony face dry but taut, showing her age.

"We're here," Madeleine said again, taking Charlotte's hand as she had not done since they were tiny children. With her head bent and her copper-red hair falling forward, she looked so like Fleur. *Fleur. God help me, it was no dream. That's why she's been crying.*

"Maddy," Charlotte said with an effort. "What's wrong with me? I feel so tired."

"That's the sedative, dear," said Elizabeth. "It will wear off, don't worry. You were in an awful state when they took you to the hospital."

"How long have I been asleep?"

"You spent last night in the hospital, then we brought you home this morning. It's afternoon now. Dr Saunders said it was best you slept for as long as possible."

"I don't remember any of that."

"It's just as well."

"But I remember what happened before," Charlotte said dully. The tide of horror flowed in again: vampire eyes gleaming, Ilona biting through Fleur's neck and throwing her aside, Karl hurling himself at David and the deafening concussion of gunfire. The stark unbearable certainty that Fleur was dead – *We were going to talk... what is there to tell her now? It's over, Karl is gone... I'll never touch the light again, never* – but just as the wave threatened to overwhelm her, it receded along the dreary, endless shore. The pain was there, but she couldn't grasp it.

There was a moment of silence. Madeleine started to cry again, and Elizabeth said, "Don't think about it, dear. It won't change anything to get upset, will it?"

"But what about David? Where is he?"

"Downstairs," Maddy said quickly, as if glad to impart some good news. "They didn't charge him after all."

"Charge him – what with?" said Charlotte, confused.

"It's nothing to worry about," said Elizabeth. She shook her head at Maddy, frowning. "It was just a muddle. We'll explain when you're feeling better."

He killed Karl, Charlotte thought. Yet the words didn't really mean anything. It was too unreal, she could not blame David. She was only glad he was safe, yet her relief seemed distant. Each emotion drowned blindly in the edge of the savage implacable ocean: the knowledge that Karl... was... dead.

Through her tears, Madeleine said, "We've been so worried about you. I was longing for the chance to tell you I'm sorry for the wretched way I treated you. It was unforgivable, but I am truly sorry. Can you forgive me?"

It was all Charlotte could do to remember the quarrel they'd had over Karl. Although it was only a few days ago, it seemed to belong in another lifetime.

Before she could reply, Elizabeth said, "Can't this wait, Maddy? You know Dr Saunders said we mustn't excite or upset her."

"But what if she had – and I'd never had the chance to say it?" said Madeleine. "I don't see how it can hurt to tell Charli we love her." She hugged and kissed Charlotte, for the first time in years, with real affection.

Charlotte was taken aback, moved. Her sister's love was not only unexpected, it was – she felt – undeserved.

Madeleine went on, "The way you put yourself in my place and made – made him let me go." Her voice shook. "David says that's true courage, to act bravely even when you are terrified."

"I wasn't brave," Charlotte said quickly. She lacked the strength to explain her true, muddled motives – and how would it help if she did? *It's all past now... And he's gone, gone... Is it the sedative that won't let me scream or cry?*

Maddy's grief was uncomplicated; she could not begin to imagine the fogged complexities that lay in Charlotte's soul. And that made Charlotte feel helpless with guilt. She so wanted to return Maddy's love, but could not. *I'm too wicked... but I'm paying.* All she could do was to stroke her sister's bowed head and murmur, "It's all right."

But that was a lie.

"What on earth were you thinking, David?" George Neville's voice was hoarse with strain, anger, relief – all the anguish of the last few days. "Dashing down to London like a lunatic without telling a soul! And taking Anne with you! And to cap it all – for God's sake – nearly ending up on a murder charge!"

"We got Charlotte out, didn't we?" David said angrily. "And von Wultendorf is dead. If we'd told you and waited for everyone else to prevaricate, we'd still be at Parkland now and she might be dead as well as..." He stopped short of saying Fleur's name. He and his father were facing each other across the stuffy drawing room, both white with exhaustion, grief, rage. Anne's father, Dr Saunders, stood quietly, not intervening, but Anne had had more than she could stand.

"Oh, stop it, please!" she exclaimed. "Arguing won't solve anything."

"I suppose it did not occur to you," said Dr Neville, "that you were breaking your word to me not to do anything to endanger Charlotte's life? Bravado – idiocy – I don't know what to call it. And yet –" Suddenly he moved towards David. "Thank God you did. Thank God." The two men embraced. "I know – I know it was not your fault – what happened to Fleur and Clive. God in heaven, I can't believe it. I thought all the danger was to Charlotte, how could anyone have dreamed that *Fleur* –"

"I wish I could make some sense of what happened," David said, his voice rough. "Yes, we were in time to save Charlotte, but if only we'd got there sooner…"

Anne sat down heavily on the leather couch, shaking, the ticking of Dr Neville's numerous clocks echoing through her head. Someone tapped her on the shoulder. She looked up and found her father offering her a glass of whisky.

"Medicinal," he said brusquely. Anne knew he was angry about the escapade, and that he was also proud of her. His feelings were clear in his eyes, and there was no need to say anything. They both knew.

"Thanks, Father," she said. "And – sorry and all that."

Dr Saunders straightened up. "By the way, David, why exactly did the police decide not to bring charges against you?"

David and his father exchanged a concerned look.

Dr Neville began, "Well, I doubt the charge would have stuck anyway, with David's good character and excellent war record. Anne was the only reliable witness to the actual – erhm – event, and she testified that David acted in self-defence during extreme provocation. The Hertfordshire police would have confirmed that that – I hesitate to call him a *man* – was a maniac who'd put one man in hospital, killed a police constable and kidnapped my daughter." His voice rose. "And that's without mentioning Fleur and Clive! Charged? My son should be given the blasted Victoria Cross!"

David cleared his throat. "Thank you, Father, but of course it helped that the police somehow lost von Wultendorf's body."

"They what?" said Dr Saunders.

"Ash told us that it vanished from the police mortuary sometime during the night. There were no signs of a break-in, no one heard anything, not a single clue. How the devil can the police manage to mislay a corpse? Anyway, altogether the case against me wasn't looking very good."

"What on earth happened to the body?" said Dr Saunders.

"God knows. If I can believe in vampires, I can believe they turn to dust or vanish into thin air when they die."

Dr Neville sat down next to Anne, cradling a glass of whisky. Anne touched his arm; he patted her hand. The effort of suppressing his pain must be agony for him.

"As for the rest of it, I don't know what will happen," David went on. "There were five other people in the room, unconscious or injured, but they're all recovering. Only Fleur and Clive died. It's all confusion as to what actually happened. Some of the party guests mentioned a red-haired woman, but no two of them came out with the same story. Some had seen a blond man, or blond twins, some nothing at all. The trouble is they were all too drunk or doped to know what they'd seen."

His father made a faint noise of denial, distress.

"What do you think?" asked Anne's father.

David said, "I think it was Karl who killed them. I think Charli escaped, ran to Fleur and he followed. Perhaps Fleur and Clive were trying to protect her. As for this woman in red, well, Fleur has – had – red hair and Charli was wearing a red dress... or it could be some hallucination he planted in their minds. The police may never solve it, but as far as I'm concerned it's a closed episode, ended with the death of Karl."

David took a sip of whisky and stared out of the window, rocking slightly on his heels.

In a more introspective tone he added, "I lost so many friends in the War. One found ways to accept it. But to lose members of one's own family in such circumstances... there's no way to make sense of it."

"You have my utmost sympathy," Anne's father said gravely. Anne was glad of his impartial, kind presence. "And anything we can do – it goes without saying."

Dr Neville went to the sideboard to refill his glass, and turned to him.

"Tell me honestly, is Charlotte going to be all right?"

"I'm sure she is," the doctor replied. "I would not have brought her out of hospital if I'd thought otherwise. She's mainly suffering from emotional shock, in which case she's better off at home."

"So she hasn't been physically harmed in any way?"

Dr Saunders hesitated. "There are some marks on her neck and her wrist. They're barely visible, but I was concerned because they're similar to the marks on Edward's neck and that of the dead policeman. Also Madeleine, that time she collapsed. As I said, this is no proof that a vampire was responsible, but I keep an open mind."

Dr Neville's hand shook, and he spilled whisky on the polished sideboard.

"The damned fiend! To think I believed he'd keep his word not to harm Charlotte!"

"She is slightly anaemic," Dr Saunders said calmly. "I couldn't swear that the blood was lost through those wounds. But it's nothing rest and a good diet won't put right. What really concerns me is her state of mind. She's been through some appalling shocks and it will take her a considerable time to get over this."

"I think the best thing is to help her forget," said Neville. "We should keep her quiet and say as little about it as possible. Least said, soonest mended. I'm certainly not having the police asking her questions."

"I'll tell them she's not well enough to be interviewed. It's nothing less than the truth."

"I don't agree," said Anne. The three men looked at her. "I think she should be encouraged to talk. Oh, not to the police, but to us. It could do her terrible harm to bottle it up and feel she can't say anything to anyone."

She was thinking of how Charlotte had looked when they carried her from the hospital to the motor car: her eyes clouded glass, dead to this world, staring into another. That was not just the sedative. Anne was desperately worried.

"My daughter has a point," said Dr Saunders. "We need to know her state of mind. She may be in need of spiritual help."

David breathed out grimly. "I don't want to upset her – but I would like to know exactly how that swine mistreated her. One thing, though: we must all agree never to mention the fact that Karl's body disappeared. God knows what it would do to her, to hear that."

Dr Neville sat down on the edge of the couch. His shoulders were hunched, his head bowed and hands dangling helplessly between his knees.

"Very well, we'll talk to her – but not until she feels better. Perhaps it's this old fool who wants to be treated with kid gloves, not my daughter. I would like to pretend it never happened."

Charlotte was sitting up in bed the next day, staring at her lunch tray without seeing it. She'd eaten without hunger or revulsion, without even tasting the food. She felt nothing.

The door opened. She expected to see Sally, come to take the tray; instead it was her father, Elizabeth, David and Dr Saunders, filing in as if on an official visit. Because they were being so kind to her, she forced herself to smile.

"Hello, m'dear, how are you feeling?" her father asked.

"Very much better, thank you," she replied.

"We just want to talk for a short while, about – events. The last thing we want is to upset you, but it's very important. You don't mind, do you?"

"Not at all," she said tonelessly. They seated themselves around the bed, making nervous little jokes as they sorted out the chairs. Charlotte waited impassively.

She loved them; she shared their grief for Fleur, and knew they had her best interests at heart. She wanted to give them what they needed, reassurances that, yes, Karl was a monster, and she'd had a terrible ordeal but was getting over it now. She even understood why David had killed Karl, and she forgave him... and yet she felt so far away, as if seeing her visitors through the walls of a glacier. *If only I could make them understand.*

Dr Saunders, as a neutral party, conducted the interview. He spoke gently and firmly, as if to a patient.

"Charlotte, do you remember anything about the night you were rescued?"

"Rescued?" She blinked at him, then said, "Oh, I see. Yes, I remember."

"You know, then, that the man who kidnapped you was killed."
She looked down at her hands.

"You can say his name. Karl. Yes, I know."

"I appreciate this is hard for you, but we must know. How did he treat you? Was he unkind or cruel to you in any way?"

She raised her head and stared at a spot on the wall between Dr Saunders and David, her eyes burning. Shock cut through her apathy as she realised there was no one to speak in Karl's defence except her, and that she was facing a jury who had already found him guilty.

She knew what Karl would have said: *"What they believe of me means nothing. It is what they think of you that matters. Tell them I was the blackest villain imaginable, that I used you cruelly; tell them anything but the truth, because you will only lose by it."*

But to that she could only have replied, *"How can you think I could be so disloyal? What have I to lose?"*

She answered, "No, he was in no way unkind to me. He was as you knew him, a gentle and courteous man."

"That's nonsensical!" David exclaimed. Their father gave him a sharp glance.

"Are you saying that he behaved towards you with courtesy and propriety at all times?" asked the doctor.

Propriety… Are they asking if he raped me? God, this is sickening.

"He was a perfect gentleman," she said, her voice gaining strength. It was true – for the time she had been his hostage, at least. She glanced briefly at Elizabeth, silently asking, *Would you betray us?* – but her aunt remained inscrutable.

"Charlotte," Dr Saunders said gently, "you appreciate how strange it must seem, that you were so upset by his death. It isn't quite what one would expect of a kidnapper and his unfortunate victim. I know this is hard for you, but it's only in your interests that we need to know what happened."

"I know," she said. She wanted to cry out, *It's simple. I loved him. I don't care what you think or say!* The words stuck in her throat. At last she said thinly, "He – he knew I was frightened and did all he could to put me at ease. We came to understand one another. We were friends." She could feel their disbelief scorching her. This was not what they wanted to hear.

"Friends?" repeated her father, looking more confused than ever.

"Yes. You were expecting me to say I suffered terribly at his hands, but it isn't true. On the contrary, he was more than kind to me; he was honest. He taught me that the harshest truth in the world is not so cruel as deceit, however kindly that deceit is meant."

"You are telling us the truth, then," Dr Saunders said gravely. "Not trying to protect him?"

She had to make them understand. The need was as forceful as a gale blowing though her.

"The truth is that he was not the monster you seem to think. He had released me, and he would never have been seen or heard of again. He only came back because Fleur was in danger. *He did not harm anyone in that room.* He was trying to protect them from – from another vampire, but he failed."

David said, "Can you prove it?"

"Ask the other people who were at the party."

"The police already have. None of them has a clear story. There's no evidence that there was any other 'vampire' there except Karl. How could anyone else have been responsible, unless they vanished into thin air the moment we arrived?"

But that's exactly what did happen! How ridiculous it sounds. Whatever I say, they'll simply assume I've lost my mind. The other people don't remember, not because they were drinking, but because Stefan and Niklas or Ilona fed from them and clouded their memories.

Bitterly, she said, "I can't prove anything. But there was no need for him to be slaughtered in cold blood!"

David shifted, uncomfortable and indignant. "Charlotte, don't you understand why it had to be done? How can you claim he was not evil? He was a murderer!"

"David, he could have killed you easily, if you hadn't been too busy being heroic to see the danger. But for some reason he chose not to. He let you win."

David looked shocked, and said nothing. Perhaps he knew she was right. *I didn't mean to make them so uneasy. What am I doing?* Obviously they had expected to hear a tale of woe from a tearful and wilting young woman. Instead, her fierceness was proving a shock to them. She shocked herself, too.

"Very well, discounting the fact that he almost killed Edward and didn't much care whether it was you or Madeleine he took hostage," Dr Saunders went on, "you maintain that he was a kind, honest gentleman who was, perhaps, so fond of you that he would never have harmed you?"

"Yes."

"Then, my dear, how do you explain the puncture marks on your neck and wrist? Do you deny that Karl made them?"

Charlotte said nothing.

"We have reason to believe he killed your sister and brother-in-law. Don't you realise he might have killed you too, had David and Anne not arrived at that moment?"

Charlotte bowed her head, remembering how she had thought death preferable to being separated from Karl. That despair was still in her. *But if I faced death and found nothing to fear in it, why do I fear my own family? Why fear their opinion?*

Then she thought, *So, tell them the truth! Tell them you stayed with Karl of your own accord, that you're as bad as him! Why can't I say it?*

There was nothing she could say to explain the wounds. What lay behind them was too private. In any rational view, they were proof positive that Karl had been evil, and nothing could redeem him. *And how can I tell them about Ilona, argue and argue with David when he would never believe it? He can't afford to. It would make everything impossibly complicated. I can't do that to him.*

I can't tell them, because I'm incapable of making them believe me. It's as simple as that.

She glanced at her father. To her surprise he was looking at her not with condemnation but with loving concern.

"We won't go on if it distresses you."

"It doesn't distress me," she said faintly. "But if I spent all day explaining I still couldn't make you understand. I think it's better if I don't say any more."

"Would you – would you prefer to talk to a clergyman?"

The thought startled her. "Why, to confess my sins?"

Her father looked steadily at her. "My dear, you don't think you have sinned, do you? You might feel more able to talk to a chaplain than to us. If you feel you have done wrong in trying to defend Karl, a chaplain might help you to give thanks for your deliverance, and to pray for forgiveness. God's mercy is infinite."

The words went into her like hot knives. How could her father seem so imperceptive, then strike at the very root of her pain?

"Forgiveness?" she said. "But I'm not repentant. I can't renounce my love for Karl, I can't believe he was completely evil. If that's wrong I don't want – I don't deserve to be forgiven! Let God forgive Karl! I'll pray for him – not for myself. No chaplain, please."

Her outburst seemed to leave them all at a loss for words. Dr Saunders stood up, easing the tension.

"We've talked enough, you're obviously tired, my dear. We'll leave you to get some rest."

Subdued, they left, but she could hear their voices on the landing and moving away down the stairs, agitated. *I've hurt them.*

A few minutes later, Elizabeth came back on her own, sat beside Charlotte and studied her intently.

"Well, you have caused quite a stir," said her aunt.

"What did they say about me?"

"The consensus seems to be that you were almost literally tempted by the Devil." Her tone was tongue in cheek.

"I was what?"

"Karl mesmerised you and made you believe he was good and worthy of your love. Naturally he was not cruel to you. Satan is more subtle than that. He deluded you so consummately that you cannot believe he would ever have harmed you, even when the proof was right in front of you. So it was all his fault, not yours."

Elizabeth's candour astonished Charlotte, but she was glad of it. It was as clear and sharp as wine, after the cotton-wool kindness of the others. She lay back on her pillows, reflecting on the fear that had governed her life. Fear of people, not only of strangers, but of her own family. *I seemed to spend my life in hiding, wishing I could melt into the scenery. Now the anxiety's gone. Some of Karl's detachment has rubbed off on me, now that it no longer matters. I'm not even afraid of Aunt Lizzie any more.*

"What do you think, Auntie? You sound as if you don't agree."

"I'm not so sure that I do. They want to believe you are still a sweet, helpless girl, and it would take more than you are capable of to disillusion them."

"Of course," Charlotte said flatly. "I am not capable of forming a view which so wildly contradicts theirs, so I must be the victim of a delusion."

"Created by the Devil, no less! You should be glad that they are so determined to think highly of you... whatever the evidence to the contrary."

"Should I?" Charlotte exhaled wearily. "I feel I've returned to a world of deceit, where they're all kind and comforting to my face, then exchange looks they think I don't notice and talk in whispers behind my back. But I can guess everything they are thinking and saying. They are the ones who don't understand!"

"Naturally." Elizabeth raised her eyebrows. "And I am sitting here now because you are the only person in this household whom I do not find utterly predictable. You know, I've been wrong about you. You have spirit after all; true, independent, amoral spirit, which runs far deeper than an ability to shine at parties. After all, no one is without faults, for all their high words. And we can't help with whom we fall in love."

"You don't condemn me, nor think I've fallen under a spell?" said Charlotte.

"I could see he wasn't completely the fiend your father and brother thought him. Whatever you think of me, I never wished you ill and I am sorry that you had to lose him. But now you had better decide whether you are going to continue shocking your family until they send for an exorcist – or make life easier, for yourself and them, by letting them believe what they need to."

"I can't go on hurting them. It will just be my secret, won't it?"

Elizabeth smiled, in her thin cool way. "Even though my lessons were lost upon you, you have somehow learned the rules of the masquerade in another way."

"What do you call a masquerade, Auntie?"

"Society, people, life; what you will. You went straight to the heart of something while everyone else was tiptoeing around the edge, not daring to look. I almost feel proud of you."

Charlotte felt a silent, hollow amusement.

"That's ironic. Once, your approval would have meant everything to me, but all I had from you were cruel words and criticism. Now, suddenly, I've won your favour – just when, for the first time, your opinion of me doesn't mean a thing."

Elizabeth sat back in her chair, her lips narrowing.

"*Touché*," she said drily.

Charlotte was out of bed the next day and resting on the small sofa in her room, turning a visiting card round and round in her fingers. She had found it in the pocket of the dress Fleur had lent her, a white card with a Mayfair telephone number and the message, "we are here sometimes", scrawled in unfamiliar copperplate handwriting. Nothing else. She thought, *Someone put this in my pocket on the night of the party.*

She was still puzzling over the card when she received an unexpected visitor.

Henry.

He sat down nervously at her side, his familiarity oddly soothing. His large face was shiny behind his glasses, his hair as untidy as ever. The laboratory smell that clung to his clothes brought a cluster of memories and emotions into her throat.

"I – I hope you don't mind me coming to see you, but I heard you'd been ill, and…"

"There's no need to pretend," she said, unable to be either polite or hostile to him. "You know I haven't been ill."

He paused, embarrassed.

"I – I know. But how are you, anyway?" And after some laboured small talk, he said, "Thing is, I was rather hasty, storming out as I did…"

"Hardly that. I've never known you to 'storm' anywhere."

She wasn't making things easy for him, but he persisted.

"No, I was too precipitous, and in fact I have apologised to the Prof and he's asked me to come back, but the thing is…"

He seemed to be waiting for her to respond.

"I hope there are no hard feelings between us," she said. "I can go on as we were before, if you can."

"Well, that's just it. I don't think I can, actually. But – well, I – it occurred to me that, that when we had our, um, disagreement, you weren't feeling quite the ticket and, er…"

She stared down at the enigmatic card and said without feeling,

"Are you trying to say that when I broke off our engagement, I didn't know what I was doing?"

He took off his glasses and rubbed at the red marks they left on his nose. Without them, his face had a raw, schoolboyish look.

"Perhaps I'm wrong. The truth is I haven't enough pride to stay in a huff, Charlotte, and I do still think such a lot of you. I just wondered, you know, now it's all over, if you wouldn't, er, reconsider your decision?"

Charlotte felt nothing, not even surprise. All she saw, in a strangely distant, calculated way, was an opportunity to make her father happy.

"Do you mean that if I marry you, you will come back?"

"Just so," he said. "Exactly."

Charlotte regained her health swiftly, because she was young and strong and the mechanisms of nature healed themselves independent of her will. Her family showered her with love and she returned it, seeming content in a tranquil, removed way, all her painful shyness gone. Madeleine and David were delighted; only Anne suspected that her recovery was not what it seemed.

"You're not going to get away with this, you know," said Anne. She had found Charlotte in the garden shed that Dr Neville used for storing and making equipment. She was already working again, although only two weeks had passed since events in London, and six days since Fleur's funeral.

"With what?"

"Silence. You used to confide in me – don't you still feel you can?"

"Don't, Anne. I can put on a brave face for David, Father – anyone but you."

"You don't have to for me. Are you angry with me? Perhaps you feel I was partly to blame for Karl's death."

Charlotte was leaning over a bench, making some kind of wooden strut. She stopped, and her shoulders went rigid.

"Perhaps I do, however unfair it seems."

Anne moved closer to her. "I know you loved him, and it must have been terribly painful to be disillusioned. I tried to prevent the worst, but even if I'd pleaded with David on my bended knees

I couldn't have stopped what happened. However awful it was, I can't see what other solution there could have been."

"Don't worry, Anne." There was a distant, arctic edge to Charlotte's voice. "I know that you and David only acted in my own best interests."

"Don't be so cold!" Anne exclaimed. "I'd rather you shouted at me – said you hated me and couldn't forgive me – than treated me like a stranger!"

Charlotte flinched. "Oh, God, Anne, I'm sorry. Of course I don't blame you. Sometimes I think, what difference does it make whether Karl is dead or not? He was going to leave me – in my best interests, naturally – and so he has. He's left me. Gone." And then she suddenly turned and put her arms around Anne's neck. Anne held her, but Charlotte remained dry-eyed.

"You might feel better if you had a good cry," Anne suggested.

"No. If I started crying I should never stop. Oh, what kind of friend am I to you, Anne? I can see how terrible this has been for you, and for my family. Poor Father, especially… but it's as much my fault as Karl's."

"Charli, that's nonsense."

"But it was, because I was under no illusion about him, no enchantment. I understand why David thought he couldn't have acted otherwise. But I loved Karl and I always will. That makes me as evil as him, doesn't it? You don't know the half of it."

"I can see that," Anne said softly, thinking, *Obviously I don't know even the merest fragment.* "And you did try to explain it to your family, didn't you? You gave them a hard time."

"I didn't mean to. All I wanted… was for them to say, 'Yes, it's your fault!' I wanted someone to blame me, to acknowledge that I have a will of my own, that I'm capable of doing wrong as well as right. But they can't. Inside, I am not who they think I am. I never have been, really. I had one attempt to make them see, and that taught me that it's best to keep my mouth shut, to pretend everything's going to be all right – for their sake, not for mine. Do you understand?"

"I think so," said Anne. Charlotte's eyes were a grey-violet glaze sealing in a void of misery, but still she didn't cry. "It's too private, isn't it? I can understand that things may not be the way your father and David would like to imagine… and I've no right to judge you. Who has?"

"I don't deserve a friend like you." Charlotte kissed Anne's cheek, stroked her hair. "Actually I think it would break Father's heart to know the truth. That's why I have to hide it – because nothing can make it better. Because it's *mine*. And because Maddy and Father need me to be strong, to help them get over Fleur."

The door creaked. Anne ignored it, thinking it was a draught.

"We all have to get over it together," she said. "We'll help each other."

Charlotte nodded. "I'm going to marry Henry after all," she said.

Anne was dumbfounded. "But why?"

"He said he'd come back to work here if I did."

"Is that all? You have to have a better reason than that. If you don't love him you won't be happy."

"But I won't be happy anyway!" Charlotte burst out. "Don't you understand, that's exactly the point. Without Karl, nothing matters! I don't care whether I'm married or single, alive or dead. So I might as well marry Henry as not, because it just doesn't matter!"

Some instinct made Anne turn her head, and she saw Henry standing in the doorway. He looked stricken, bewildered; yet strangely, not surprised. And it struck Anne that he would still marry Charlotte, even after what he had overheard, because he loved her and was quite without pride.

They had dug the trenches by connecting each grave to the next, a line gouged across the limitless mud of the cemetery. The corpses stood on their coffins to keep watch over the battlefield, their sunken ribcages pressed to the clay, their uniforms pale and tattered shrouds.

And now the enemy was advancing, wave on wave, with animal heads under the grey helmets – but animals such as Edward had never seen before, deformed and primeval with huge prominent jaws and curved yellow incisors. And their hands… those were not hands on the ends of their arms but perfect little vampire faces with slanting green eyes and red mouths agape.

They screamed as they came. It was the screaming Edward could not stand…

He covered his head with his arms, but the sound receded and David was suddenly there in front of him. David, with his kind face and endless courage, always a source of strength in this hell. Of course David was here: he was their captain, but that meant…

"I didn't know you were dead, too," Edward said.

David looked at him with solemn, sad eyes.

"What do you mean, dead?"

"Well, you wouldn't be here if you weren't."

"Neither of us are dead, old man. You're in hospital. I've come to see how you are."

Edward looked up and down the trenches. The coffins were white, like beds… the trench walls were green, roofed in. Strange how the battlefield looked different sometimes, but the screaming never stopped. He saw two of the corpses struggling with a third, trying to force him down while he cried out with agony. Injured… his heart pounded with the reasonless fear that never left him now.

"We're all dead here," Edward said. "But I'm so glad you're with me, David. You'll help us to repel the attack."

"What attack?" David said gently.

"Oh, they attack all the time. First the bombardment to soften us up, then they come over the top through the barbed wire… the vampires, you know."

David nodded, but his face was grave.

"The War's over, old man." His voice was hoarse. "That's what I've come to tell you. I killed the vampire. He's dead."

Then Edward realised that David didn't understand. He reached out and clutched his sleeve, willing him to hear.

"But there are others. They're gone now but they'll come back… They always come back when it's dark…"

CHAPTER SEVENTEEN

GHOST IN THE LOOKING GLASS

The spring sky above the Rhine was capricious. One moment rain clouded the river as if the Lorelei had breathed on the mirror surface; the next, the clouds were torn apart and the green sides of the gorge were awash with glittering diamonds. At the top of the gorge, the castle turned from earth brown to golden russet in the ever-changing light.

Within the windowless lower rooms of Schloss Holdenstein, where daylight never came, Kristian was aware of the breeze dancing across the sky outside. He was aware of everything. The corridors that linked the twisted maze of cells and chapels also angled away into the Crystal Ring, into infinity. Kristian could see both realms at once, the solid world and the mind of God, overlaid. He and the castle were the symbiotic heart from which veins of wisdom branched in every direction.

And here was his inner sanctum, where world and Ring were perfectly interlinked, permeated by the power of God. Here was absolute purity; bare walls, one chair and one desk on which lay his Bible – the Bible he was writing – and in the centre, two coffins lying side by side on catafalques.

They were ancient stone coffins, lidless, the inner cavity shaped to fit a human form. Both were full to the brim with blood.

Kristian sent his flock far and wide each day to bring victims to replenish the supply. He would not let them hunt too near Holdenstein lest suspicion fall on the castle. He took care to avoid discovery, not because he was afraid of what humans could do to him – they could do nothing – but because he would resent the intrusion. For the same reason, he hated having live humans brought here at all. But it must be endured – as must the cloying scent of their blood, distasteful to one who only drank from vampire throats.

He recruited Stefan and Niklas to do the worst of it for him; they were the only ones he could trust to keep the secret. The others would be told in time. Each day, Stefan and his twin skimmed off the coagulated blood so that Kristian could inspect the progress. Then they replenished the fluid by bleeding new victims into the coffin, and took the bodies away. When it was done, they all prayed together.

The process was going well. Kristian felt expansive, optimistic. He relished the sense of his vampires moving through the corridors, beloved children of Lilith in dark robes like monks, ever returning to the fount of life to renew their faith in Kristian before they went out into the world again to feed. Here they were completely his; they called him Beloved Master and Father; they bowed to him and received from his wrist the single swallow of communion wine. The blood of their messiah, quite literally.

Kristian sat at his desk, staring at the gore-filled coffins by the light of a smoking torch. Shadows swelled and shrank on the stone walls and on the blood-blackened flagstones, making him think of other shadows. Three black figures who had ambushed him on a cold hillside as he went home from preaching at church. Hellfire and the wrath of God he had preached. Perhaps it was their revenge, an immortal joke to show the man of God what true evil was. Make the priest into a vampire. But the trick had recoiled upon them, because in the transformation Kristian had found deeper truth, had seen the face of God at first hand and become His ambassador on Earth.

The three vampires who had transformed him, he had tracked down and destroyed. And many, many others after them; those who set themselves against him, those who disappointed him.

But the ones who were most disobedient were the ones he loved best. Ilona, Pierre, Karl (of course, Karl) – so he would tolerate them, stretch out his arms to absorb their doubts, their bitterness and heresy. *Yes, sharpen your teeth on me, my children, the better to deliver my message to mankind.*

He had punished Ilona only lightly for her wilfulness. Slaying humans for personal reasons was a crime – not against humans but against Kristian's law. Humans were an anonymous mass, except the few Kristian singled out for attention. The mortals he'd used to put pressure on Karl were no use dead, and Ilona had killed them out of spite, to defy Kristian and hurt Karl. All Kristian had done in return was to starve her for a few weeks until she repented. He felt generous. Would it not be punishment enough when she discovered the miracle he was weaving?

It wasn't yet time for the blood to be replenished, but Kristian, impatient, went to look down into the coffins. In one, only the body and limbs were firmly defined, sheened by crimson, while the head-shaped cavity contained a semi-solid red mass that merely hinted at a face. In the second coffin, the reverse was true. The body was indistinct under a wetly gleaming blanket of clotted blood – taking shape so very slowly – but the face gleamed strong and clear. Beautiful, even though it was waxen and spattered with gore.

"Come back," Kristian said quietly. "In God's name you *will* come back." His fingers rested on the cold stone rim. He willed strength, healing and energy into the lifeless head.

Karl's spirit, those entrancing eyes so full of life and acid humour, were absent; yet there was a presence in this chamber. Something brooding, slow breathing, stirring in its sleep under layers of darkness. Clawing its way up towards life on strands of human blood.

Kristian's mouth thinned with satisfaction. The process could not be rushed, after all, but time and the Almighty were on his side.

Life went on, but Charlotte merely existed. She drifted easily through the duties that were expected of her, said and did appropriate things, but inside she felt like a bird that had died in the air, somehow still coasting along on fixed wings. Waiting for the inevitable crash.

The grief of Fleur's and Clive's funerals was followed by the subdued joy of Anne and David's wedding in the new year, then Charlotte's marriage to Henry in spring. There was a sense of shaking off a nightmare, a new beginning. Charlotte's father, being what he was, clammed up about "those unfortunate events". Anne and David took the healthier approach that there was no point in dwelling on the past. With distance, entrenched scepticism about the existence of vampires regained its power. How could they speak of it without taking those walls down again?

Charlotte now found it paradoxically easy to express the affection she had never been able to show her family. They were all closer than before. Silence had fallen, but memories imbued every word or kiss exchanged with unspoken affirmations: *"It's over, we're alive, we're together. It can't touch us again."*

Yet Charlotte was uneasy when Anne and David moved to Parkland Hall to take up the duties of running the estate. They were living in a wing of the Hall that Elizabeth refurbished for them, while the manor house remained unfinished, deserted. Although they issued endless invitations for Charlotte to go and stay with them, she could never quite face it.

Life was hard enough in Cambridge, where everything she touched released a silvery cascade of memories, like wind chimes in the lightest breeze. *Here in this study we truly talked for the first time and I realised I'd no choice but to love him. Here, at this laboratory bench we worked, and when Henry was pompous Karl would catch my eye and make me laugh. Here we walked, here we sat...*

The memories at Parkland would have been unbearable.

She had never been allowed to mourn Karl – by others or by herself. Who could mourn for a murderer, a demon in human shape?

Instead she tried to go on as before, locked into the magic circle of herself, Father and Henry, immersed in probing the secrets of matter. Fascinating still, but the laboratory walls seemed more confining than safe, and nothing was the same. She could have left, now she was twenty-one – but there was nowhere she wanted to go, nothing to fill the emptiness. This was home, all she had to cling to.

Marrying Henry had been a great mistake.

Was it that he had changed, or that she had never seen him

clearly before? Both, perhaps. Henry was not unkind but he was weak, and he possessed the immense stubbornness of weak men. She had assumed he'd be too obtuse to mind her apathy, but under his bumbling surface there was an unformed mass of resentment and frustration. It was partly her fault: for his sake, she shouldn't have married him without love. His reaction to her indifference was to become overbearing. Henry could not win her heart, so all that was left was to control her.

He would pick arguments, trying to change her life without reason. She was incredulous, shortly after their dismal honeymoon, when he actually suggested that she give up work.

"Whatever for?" she said.

"It is generally not the done thing for married women to work," he replied stuffily.

"What do you want me to do, arrange flowers all day while Father has to employ a postgraduate in my place and spend months teaching him how he likes things done?"

"Mother thought you could become more involved with her Methodist circle. They do awfully worthwhile work."

Charlotte regarded this suggestion with such contempt that she struggled to reply.

"That is your mother's life, not mine," she said tightly. "I should like to hear what Marie Curie would have said if her husband ever told her to stop working."

Henry gave a grunt of disapproval, sounding exactly like her father.

"You will have to stop anyway, when we have children."

The thought froze her.

"Very well, I'll stop then," she said with thin anger. "Not before."

It was easy to defeat Henry in any argument, but the war went on. She hated it. She almost hated him... but not quite, because sometimes she saw the world so clearly from his fixed point of view that she detested herself.

When Henry made love to her she never thought of Karl. She tried to think of nothing at all. But if her body responded independent of her will – desperation, perhaps, for what she had lost – her passion seemed to alarm him. He thought only wanton women enjoyed themselves. And he was inhibited, easy to put off when he knocked timidly at the door of her bedroom. She had insisted on keeping separate rooms.

And each month she dreaded finding she was pregnant, breathed a sigh of relief when she knew she was not. *Why don't I want a child? Because I don't want anything of his. I don't want anything to bind me to life – just in case I should want to leave it.*

Once she dreamed she had a grown-up daughter. Her name was Violette and she had black rippling hair and bore a striking resemblance to Karl.

There were pleasanter aspects to life. Madeleine, as Karl had said, was resilient, and soon returned to her vivacious self, treating Charlotte with an affection and respect that she had never shown before. Maddy went to London with Elizabeth for a second Season, but came home early in the summer, quiet and restless. Then she suggested to Charlotte that they go and visit Edward in the nursing home.

"I don't know," said Charlotte. "David says he hardly recognises anyone now. It might be terribly upsetting."

"But he was our friend, still is," said Maddy. "It must be awful to be deserted, as if mental illness is somehow worse than any other sort. Sometimes you have to face up to upsetting things, don't you? Please come with me, Charli."

The truth is, I still feel too guilty. Rationally I know I am not responsible for Edward's illness... but in loving Karl, it became partly my fault. Yet she agreed to go, for Maddy's sake.

Madeleine drove them to Hertfordshire in her sleek new open tourer. David had ensured that Edward received the best of care in a private nursing home. To leave him in an asylum would have been unthinkable.

At the home, a nurse led them into a pleasant sunny garden, where Edward was sitting on a bench beneath a chestnut tree.

"He's well enough to be outside," said the nurse. "We don't have to restrain him very often at all now. But he is rather in a world of his own, and I'm afraid there's little hope of improvement."

Little hope of improvement, echoed Charlotte's thoughts. Edward watched as they approached, but she was not sure he remembered who they were. His face was thin, looking nearer fifty than thirty, and his eyes had the hunted look of paranoia. *What does he see?* she thought. David had told her that for Edward, the War was still going on, looping endlessly through his mind – and his enemies were not Germans, but vampires.

This was the nearest Charlotte had come to weeping since Karl died.

"Edward, dear, it's Madeleine, don't you remember?" Maddy said, sitting beside him. "And Charlotte."

Edward looked up at Charlotte, squinting a little in the sunlight. Then he said, "There's a shadow behind you."

Charlotte glanced round by reflex, saw nothing.

"How are you?" she said.

He shook his head. "The shadow's still there. He's still with you. Following you. Can't you see him, behind your left shoulder?" There were strings of foam in the corners of his mouth. His words, his expression, rooted Charlotte to the spot.

"It's all right, Edward," said Maddy, giving her a concerned look. "There's nothing there, only us."

"No, you don't see! They don't go away, they come back! Can't you see it, the red tongue in the cage of teeth? The dead ones come back. There's a black aura all around you..."

"I'd better fetch the nurse," said Charlotte.

"No, sit down, Charli, quickly," said Madeleine. "I think it's because you're standing against the sun. Edward, I'm David's sister. We've met before, don't you remember?" Madeleine linked her arm through his, went on talking softly to him until his trembling subsided and his eyes clouded to relative calm. Charlotte sat next to them in silence.

Somehow Madeleine seemed to reach him. After a while, Edward turned to her as if he'd only just realised she was there and said, "Maddy? What are you doing here? Am I on leave?"

In the car on the way home, Charlotte hugged her stomach against the heaviness she felt there. *What was it he saw in me? Am I tainted? Poor, poor Edward... I wonder if he's really mad or just seeing the truth. The veil of safety gone and his nerves stripped raw, burning and shrivelling in the slightest breeze. We should listen to him instead of locking him away. Was it the War, or Karl's bite, or would this have happened to him anyway?*

She said, "You were so good with him, Maddy. All I seemed to do was upset him."

"Don't feel bad about it," said Maddy. She sounded thoughtful. "The slightest thing can set him off, David said. He knew who I was, that's a good sign, isn't it?"

"I hope so," said Charlotte. "Oh, I do hope so."

For a few moments there was only the sound of the engine, the wind streaming past.

Then Madeleine said, "Charli, can I ask you something? About... well, you know. Last year. I'll understand if you don't want to talk about it."

"No, I don't mind."

"Did you really love him? Karl, I mean."

It was the first time Maddy had mentioned his name since it had all happened. They had never discussed the matter.

Charlotte answered, "Yes, I did. I thought I did. I don't know what love is, really."

"Neither do I. It's nothing like, say, the love I feel for you and Father. How can love cut you to pieces like that?" Maddy sighed. "I used to think I was such a hero, you know? I was never afraid of anyone, I thought nothing could hurt me. It was no fun at all to find that I'm not brave but an idiot."

"You were never that, Maddy," Charlotte said, smiling.

"But I was so blind. With Karl... I was trying to think of something to compare. I was like a child, enthralled by a big beautiful dog, who assumes that all she has to do to possess the creature is to say, 'I want him.' It never occurs to her that she can be denied. Then she's told she can't have her way. While she's still clinging onto the dog and crying, she sees that it's not a lovely sweet pet at all but a wolf, with red eyes and fangs, and it's too late, she wants to run away but she's trapped and the whole world has turned dark..." She trailed off. "That's how I felt about Karl."

"I understand you, Maddy," Charlotte said softly.

"Do you? I can look back and see that I was quite insane for a few days. I can't stand to think of Karl now. It's his fault I don't feel safe any more. We've both been through the same thing, haven't we? Only it was much worse for you. There we were fighting over him, while he was betraying us both."

Charlotte felt tears pushing at her throat, and she thought, *No, don't let me start crying, not now.*

"I don't think he meant to. It was just the way things were –"

"I'm scared to fall in love now," Madeleine interrupted, as if she didn't want to hear qualifications.

If she's made sense of things, Charlotte thought, *I'll let her be.*

"D'you know why I came back from London early? I got sick of the Season. It all seemed so shallow, one party after another, Aunt Lizzie dangling me like bait for some stinking rich titled fish to catch. I've been doing an awful lot of thinking."

"What about?"

Maddy didn't answer at once. Then she said, "I like Edward so much. Did you see how he was with me? He quieted down until he was almost himself again. You heard the nurse say no one else has ever got through to him like that since he's been there, not even David."

"He was always sweet on you, Maddy."

A long, pensive silence.

"D'you remember how we used to help the nurses during the War? I was rather good at it. This may be an awful shock, Charli, but I want to do something worthwhile. I don't quite know what, but don't laugh, I'm deadly serious. And I'm going to stick by Edward."

As they drove back into Cambridge, the beauty of the town struck Charlotte as if she had never appreciated it before. A privileged life, cupped in shimmering gold and green grandeur, the dour buildings in which the secrets of the universe were being pried from their minute Pandora's boxes. It came to her that life might be bearable after all.

Karl felt that he had been *aware* for a very long time – years condensed into a single moment, or a moment stretched out for years – but dreaming, unable to reason. Like being suspended under the surface of rippling red water... only seeing, not thinking or feeling.

At some point memory began to return. First the vague fleeting sense that there was something he should know, some profound revelation just beyond the grasp of his intellect. His whole body ached, every bone of his spine alight with pain, while through him and all around him a velvety ribbon of melody flowed from a cello. A seamless run of notes turned endlessly around on itself like a Bach fugue. The ache in his spine and the music were the same thing... yet the music made the discomfort tolerable.

He was cold. The air itself cracked and froze around him, shattered into powder and fell away into an abyss under a blazing ice-cold sun.

And he was hot, turning slowly in an inferno while his flesh dripped from him like sweat. But the gliding notes of the cello carried him through the fever into self-awareness.

He began to remember who he was. No specific memories, only an untroubled consciousness of *self*.

Yes, the music... surely he must be drawing out the melody with his own hands... A glimpse of a dark-haired woman, playing with a baby, laughing. *Therese... why can't I move, have I been ill?*

Still no anxiety, only a persistent feeling that there was something he should know. Everything fell away except a dragging emptiness that, it presently occurred to him, was hunger...

And then, out of nowhere, a hideous, blazing image came rushing towards him. From a single point of light it came, expanding until it seared through the centre of his forehead in a flower of white-hot iron. A blade sliced into his palms as he tried and failed to seize it, hacking into his neck as he fell. His head was being cut from his body and he was aware of it happening. Searing panic. Consciousness dragged on after his head was severed, but emotion was suddenly gone as if cut off with his body. He only *saw*. Garish shades of red in carpets and curtains all tilted at wrong angles, someone sobbing, and thoughts circling his horrified mind, *I still live, I cannot die. Nothing can free me from consciousness.*

The horror brought him awake.

One second ago it had happened... But how could that one second be so deep and full of detail, an interminable nightmare that a vampire had murdered his wife and made Karl like himself and pursued him down the years until he had taken the only escape possible: death. Only to find even that escape route closed.

Am I sick or in hell? Therese, such a dream...

No dream. He opened his eyes and knew that it was all real. He wasn't human but a fiend, a luminous supernatural being who could not afford pity.

He recognised the walls that enclosed him. A stone chamber lit by candles and the fluid dancing of fire. Kristian's castle. He was lying on a straw mattress, naked, his skin prickling with cold and heat. His body felt strange. He stared at his limbs; he was physically unchanged, unhurt. When he stretched, his body obeyed and feeling returned, an almost drowsy sensation that warmed him back to normality.

But a shadow oppressed the room. Karl turned his head and saw Kristian standing a few feet away, looking down at him, arms folded. There was an intense expression of satisfaction on his strong pallid face, and his shadow on the wall behind him was the flowing black cloak of his soul.

"Karl," he said. "Can you speak? I have waited so long for you to look at me. Did you dream? Do you know what has happened to you?"

Karl sat up slowly, swinging his feet over the edge of the mattress. His hunger made everything shimmer with painful clarity. Apart from that he felt, physically at least, as if nothing had happened. Strong, perfect, as vampires were.

"You ask a lot of questions," Karl said. He felt completely calm; not angry, not afraid that Kristian had captured him at last. Not even resigned, simply calm. "You will have to help me answer them, Kristian. It may have been a dream… but I could have sworn that my head was severed."

Kristian's eyes widened and firelight gleamed in the orbs; eerie, horrible they looked. He leaned forward, his voice an eager whisper.

"Yes, your head was severed. Tell me about it, Karl. How did it feel?"

Karl sat back, felt the wall cold against his spine. He gazed candidly at Kristian, astonished yet in a bizarre way amused.

"Extremely painful," he replied.

"But when it happened – after it happened – were you still *aware*?"

"For a time, yes."

"I want to know about it!"

Karl paused, gazing coolly at him. He took a breath; the air felt raw, and thirst went through him like streams of sand.

"Then I shall tell you – in exchange for you explaining how in God's name you managed to put me back together. I understood beheading to be fatal."

Kristian paced slowly around the chamber.

"So it is, if no attempt is made to heal the immortal. But in God's name it was done. I brought you back here and tended you. I bathed the injury, I bathed the whole body with fresh blood every day, filled you with the power of the Crystal Ring, that is the breath of God. And by His grace your immortal flesh was regenerated."

Karl tried not to dwell on the words, *fresh blood*. He put a hand to his throat, felt smooth skin.

"Would you like a looking glass?" Kristian took a small mirror from a table and handed it to him. "I allowed this symbol of man's vanity into the castle just for this. Look."

Karl looked. His reflection in the silver was pale with starvation, his hair tousled, his amber eyes shadowed; otherwise, the same. No scar on his throat.

"How long did it take?"

Kristian sat beside him and ran his broad hand down Karl's arm. Karl resisted the instinct to pull away.

"Eight, nearly nine months."

Karl gave nothing away, but he was shocked. And the image that came into his head was Charlotte. *God, what did she feel when it happened? She was there, she saw. I heard her weeping. All this time, all this time, what has become of her?*

"Months…"

"No time at all, to us," said Kristian. "Karl, I've brought you back to life. Does it mean nothing to you? Are you not grateful?"

"It is difficult to take in what happened. I don't know."

A black passion moved behind Kristian's eyes. *He wants something from me*, Karl thought despairingly. *He's looking for signs that I've changed, relented.*

"How can you not be grateful that I've delivered you from death – not once now, but twice? I have given you this gift!"

"And both times, I did not ask for it," Karl said without feeling.

"You cannot mean that you wish I'd left you for dead. You

can't tell me you would prefer death!"

"You are the one who believes in God, Kristian. Perhaps I would have been in heaven now... or more likely in hell. It felt like hell. You have only saved me because you have unfinished business with me, isn't that so? I am not allowed to die before you bring me to heel. Afterwards, perhaps."

Kristian stood up, a swathe of ink-black that seemed to swallow light and energy from the room.

"In heaven's name, Karl. Do you feel nothing? You died, you rose again! *I* did this –"

"All we are missing is the Holy Ghost."

"Yet still you blaspheme! Do you feel no awe, no repentance?"

"What I feel," Karl said slowly, "is mine, not yours to plunder because you have no genuine feelings of your own. I am not sure it is a pleasant thing to discover that I can't die, even if I want to. I could go up to the *Weisskalt*, starve myself and go to sleep there, but you'd rescue me, wouldn't you? I cannot escape from you, whatever I do."

For the first time, he saw an actual flash of panic in the older vampire's eyes.

"Always you speak of escape, as if I am your gaoler! I gave you life, and the instinct of immortals is to live!"

"But your condition is too hard," Karl replied. "You want me to live for *you* and I cannot."

"I am the centre of your life! I choose who lives and who dies. I am the heart, I am God's right hand. You cannot turn away from me!"

"You expected me to come to you out of love, when you'd destroyed everything I loved. You wanted me to come of a free will that you would not let me exercise. And then by threats to Ilona, by scything down anyone who came near me; and now, gratitude."

Sheer desperation blazed in Kristian's eyes now.

"But it was all for your sake, Karl. I must have you back."

"So imprison me, starve me."

"It's your spirit I want!"

"You will have to break it first, and what use will it be to you, broken?"

For a moment he thought Kristian was going to attack him. But the carved-stone face cleared, and his dark aura seemed to shrink a little. His huge fists unclenched.

"I am unfair to you, Karl. You have barely recovered. You need time to think and reflect."

Karl relaxed a little. *Have I forgotten I meant to come back and talk to him? Hostility will never help us to understand.*

"Yes, you are right."

Kristian smiled, as if he took this as capitulation.

"You must be in need of nourishment. Why don't you go and dress," he indicated a door to another chamber, "while I attend to it?"

In the side room, Karl selected and put on clothes from a cupboard. Not the drab robes that Kristian favoured, but an everyday suit in charcoal grey, and a dark overcoat and hat. When he returned to the main chamber – the coat over his arm a statement of intention – the door to the corridor stood open and skeins of human heat drifted in.

The thirst throbbed through him so fiercely that he almost cried out. A female vampire came in, dressed in a black robe like a monk, a hood over her straight gold hair. Her expression was intense and solemn. In life Maria had been a nun, but now Kristian was her Lord. She brought with her a squarely built grey-haired man who exuded the aura of luscious vermeil life. Although he looked strong enough to break Maria like a piece of straw, her thin hands and vampire glamour held him.

Chains of fire and dust pulled Karl towards the prey. It was all he could do not to fall on the man, yet somehow he held back and said coldly, "Thank you, Kristian, but I prefer to hunt for myself."

He walked to the door.

"Where are you going?" said Kristian.

"To think, as you suggested. Am I a prisoner?"

"No. You are free to go... and to return." Although Kristian made no move to stop him, he gave Karl a strange look as he ducked under the lintel and walked away, fighting to control the fever of thirst at every step.

As he was on his way through the warren of corridors, Karl met Ilona and Pierre. They stopped and stared: their usually cynical faces were for one second slack with unguarded wonder.

356

Karl thought Pierre would have embraced him, had Ilona not been there. Hostility gathered swiftly in her eyes, where for a moment there had been the astonished pleasure with which, as a child, she used to greet his rare visits. That brief yearning look would once have torn his heart open, but now, for the first time, he felt almost nothing. No love, no anguish, only a weariness too stale to become anger.

"I heard," she said, "but I couldn't quite believe it."

"Well, we are immortal, it seems," Karl said off-handedly. He was going to walk straight past, but Ilona put out her hand to stop him.

"Is that all you have to say? I suppose you don't want to hear how I've suffered. Kristian tortured me! He sucked my blood so I hadn't the strength to go into the Crystal Ring, and then he locked me up and left me to starve. That I could almost bear. But he wouldn't leave me alone. Every day for hours, asking me over and again the same questions." She gave a vicious imitation of Kristian's tone. "'But what was it like when you killed the woman, when you felt her life going into you?' Hours and hours of it... I gave a different answer every time, to save myself from going mad. 'Cold,' I said, 'like a crystal waterfall to a man who has crawled out of the desert.'"

"Don't, Ilona," said Pierre.

"And I said, 'Warm. Like swallowing whole someone who loved me, so that their love was inside me and could never betray me again...'"

"Stop it!" Pierre said savagely. "There's nothing he's done to you that he hasn't done to the rest of us!"

"What do you want me to say?" Karl said without feeling. "Am I meant to be outraged? I could forgive you almost anything, but not for murdering Fleur."

Ilona seemed genuinely shocked by the lead-coldness in his eyes and voice. She drew back into herself.

"Do you know how false her name sounds on your lips? She was just a human. How many have *you* killed?"

"You did it to hurt me," Karl said, "but it was not me you hurt. That is what I can never forgive. Don't tell me how cruelly Kristian uses you. He put you in the *Weisskalt*; when I saved you, you came straight back to him. He starves and humiliates you, and you crawl back every time. You too, Pierre! You must have rejoiced when I died. Isn't this his ultimate crime, restoring me?"

How dreadful to see the twisted loathing in her heart-shaped face.

"I said I'd leave if you stay here, and I meant it. You will never see me again, and you couldn't bear that, could you, *Father*?"

"I don't care what you do," Karl said, and meant it.

Tears made pinpricks of light in his daughter's eyes.

"But this is your doing, don't you see? You ask why I come back. Without Kristian to love, without you to hate, I'd have nothing at all!"

There was real anguish in her voice, yet Karl remained detached, floating in ice.

Emotionlessly he said, "I wish I had left you in the *Weisskalt*, or better still, to live and die as a mortal. The Ilona I knew in life would not have let her existence become so hollow that her only reason for living was hatred. You are not my daughter."

He walked on past her, ignoring Pierre.

"Karl!" she said furiously. Then when he did not stop, "Father. *Father*!" Her voice followed him, more and more plaintive, decades of pain echoing along the bare stone corridors.

He did not look back.

After Karl had gone, Kristian went back to his inner sanctum. Here was the beautiful figure, dressed in a drab black suit, standing by the far wall and regarding Kristian with a serene golden gaze. Karl, to the life.

Kristian walked to the figure, touched his shoulders, ran his hands over the high cheekbones, the mass of hair that was like burgundy touched with fire.

"You are gone, yet you are still here. My blood is yours; you shall drink only my blood." Kristian bit his wrist and put it to Karl's mouth. He did not respond at once, then he seemed to realise what was required. Eyes widening, he began to suck by reflex, like a baby, conscious of nothing but pleasure. Then he bit down more savagely, and Kristian had to wrench himself free.

"Come here," said Kristian. He took Karl by the hand, led him to the chair and sat him down. He did what he was shown, stayed where he was placed; no memory, no real mind guided him, only vestigial instinct. Kristian went into the outer chamber, opened a tall cupboard and took a cello and bow from a case.

"Karl used to play the cello for me," he said as he returned and closed the sanctum door. He pushed the creature's knees apart, clamped them on either side of the cello. He folded one of the pliable hands round the neck, placed the bow in the other. Karl did not move. Patiently, Kristian pressed his fingers onto the strings and guided his arm back and forth to show him how the bow was drawn over the strings. Toneless sawing notes vibrated from the body of the instrument.

"You will play for me again, Karl. You must remember how. You will be everything he was not. You will never leave me, never look at me with cold eyes and deny God, never throw back the gift of life. Play for me, Karl."

He stepped away and watched from the other side of the room. The vampire went on sawing at the strings just as Kristian had shown him – like a clockwork doll set in motion.

"You must remember how to play!" Kristian shouted suddenly. "You must be able to learn!" Frustration and anguish flamed through him. "You must. You will!" Kristian rushed forward, hand out to strike the vampire. The creature was apparently unable to comprehend why this anger was directed at him, but like a dog he seemed to know he had done wrong. He drew back.

Kristian's hand passed through thin air and he fell, sprawling over the cello and the chair. He leapt up, cursing, but the chamber was empty. His exquisite replica of Karl had vanished into the Crystal Ring.

"Damn you!" he shouted. "I won't pursue you, you will not make a fool of me like that! *You* are the one who needs *me*. You will return, and you will be what I want!"

And Kristian was not even sure which one he was addressing, the double or the true Karl.

Elizabeth was sitting on the sofa in the main drawing room, reading a letter from her husband Lord Reynolds that outlined, in pedantic detail, the reasons for some journey he must make from India to Singapore. *Accompanied by his favourite young male "assistant", I don't doubt,* she thought wryly. She put the letter aside without finishing it. These days she seemed unable to concentrate on anything. She had done her best to forget the events of last autumn, and the busy social round went on, yet she often had these pensive bouts when she would sit for hours gazing out of the window.

It was night, but the curtains were open. Elizabeth preferred to have a view outside, to be absolutely sure there was no one lurking on the terrace. *The state of my nerves,* she thought in irritation. *No good to spend time on one's own, imagining things. That was the root of Charlotte's trouble. It's so nice to have David and Anne in the house. I'll go up and see Anne in a little while, yes.*

Her attempts to reassure herself could not douse a surge of fear. Suddenly her skin was crawling with the conviction that there was someone outside... Elizabeth shut her eyes, all at once terrified that if she looked, she might see something she did not want to see.

What's wrong with me tonight? Don't look at the terrace! No, stop being a fool. Look! Prove to yourself there's nothing there!

With her breath lodged in her throat, she looked. And there was the vampire, staring in at her through the French window. Suddenly there, like an actor appearing at the flick of a stage light.

The shock was like lightning, white hot, paralysing. Elizabeth shot to her feet but couldn't make a sound.

I'm seeing things. Inner strength or death wish; something compelled her to move towards the windows. *Confront it and it will go away,* she told herself frantically – but the man remained, three-dimensional, real.

She was shaking so hard it was almost a convulsion. His form was indistinct, his drab clothes blending with the darkness, but his face shone with its own light. Sculpted features, haunting eyes, his glossy hair catching red lights. His expression was blank but for a slight unconscious smile... and the golden clarity of his gaze, fixed straight on her.

Karl's face. *Karl.*

Once Elizabeth managed to start screaming, she could not stop.

CHAPTER EIGHTEEN

COME IN OUT OF THE DARKNESS

The apparition was still there when Newland and two footmen responded to Elizabeth's screams. Then, at last, she experienced a strange relief in thinking, *It's real. I'm not imagining things. He's real, real!*

David and Anne ran in a few seconds later. David took one glance and held onto his aunt as if to shield her.

"God Almighty," he said.

Anne simply stared. Then slowly she moved close to Elizabeth and the three of them clung together, like infants, for comfort.

Newland – like all good butlers, a master at controlling his reactions – said calmly, "Shall I send some men outside to apprehend the intruder, ma'am?"

"No," David answered promptly. "No one is to go outside. Make sure all the doors and windows are locked. Go on, Newland, it's all right. I'll look after things in here."

The butler left, followed by the other two men. The creature that looked exactly like Karl remained there, staring in at them, radiant in the light of the chandeliers. Suddenly the room seemed too bright. Elizabeth forced herself to look at him and he gazed back with no recognition, no emotion whatever on his exquisite face. Worms of horror pushed through her as her mind tried to unmake the evidence of her eyes. *People don't come back from the dead, they don't!*

"Oh, God," said David. He broke away and sat down in an

armchair, head in his hands. "Oh, God. I killed him. *Killed* him. For heaven's sake, you saw, didn't you, Annie? His head was clean off."

"David, for heaven's sake," said Elizabeth, her stomach turning.

"But I didn't dream it, did I?"

"No," said Anne. Her face was white, her mouth turned down at the corners with sour denial. "No, you killed him."

Elizabeth said sharply, "So what the hell is he doing standing on my terrace? I'm frightened. I've never admitted that in my life before, but now I don't care who hears. I don't like it and I want him to go away!"

"Christ," David muttered. He stood up, paced across the room and back again. He watched Karl; Karl watched him with that dreadful, mindless regard. "Do vampires have ghosts?"

"He looks solid enough," said Anne. "His body vanished, don't you remember?"

David turned to her, wild-eyed.

"Are you trying to tell me that after they put him in the morgue, his head stuck itself back to his neck and he walked out?"

"God knows, but he's standing there now, large as life!" said Anne. "How else could it have happened? This is horrible." Neither she nor Elizabeth were the type to need physical reassurance, but now they clung unselfconsciously to each other.

"If that's the case, why did he wait so long to come back? Why's he just staring at us?" said David. "What's he planning to do, break in, what?"

Elizabeth swallowed hard and took several deep breaths. *Now I've got myself under control again. Good.*

She said, "Perhaps we had better ask him, dear."

"What?"

"There was a time when he seemed a perfectly intelligent and rational young man. If he's trying to frighten us, don't let's show it. Let's try to reason with him."

"Reason?" said David. "Are you mad? Forgive my disrespect, Auntie, but…"

"I don't mean let him in," she snapped. "Just call through the glass. It's worth a try, surely?"

"I doubt it, but if you insist…" David made a move towards the window but Anne stopped him.

"Let me," she said. "I wasn't the one who cut off his head, was I?" With David hovering nervously behind her, Anne went to the glass panes and called out, "Karl? You've succeeded in giving us all a fright. Now won't you tell us why you're here?"

Karl showed no sign of having heard. His eyes were as beguiling and soulless as a portrait. Anne suddenly lost her nerve and backed away.

"Oh God, the way he stares through you. Is he doing it on purpose or..."

David took her place.

"Karl!" he shouted. "Now listen –"

Glass shattered and burst into the room. The vampire seized David's hand and began trying to drag his arm through the pane, towards the jagged edges. David cried out and Elizabeth's throat contracted as she saw his forearm turn deadly bluish-white in Karl's grip.

Anne reacted instantly. She grabbed a letter-opener from a side table and stabbed it into the vampire's hand.

Karl vanished.

There was nothing outside but darkness, tangles of wisteria stirring softly along the terrace balustrade. One broken pane in the window, glass on the carpet, and David – his face as white as plaster – rubbing at his bruised wrist.

"Are you hurt?" Anne said anxiously.

"Nothing broken. Thank God you acted so fast... but where the hell's he gone?"

"Disappearing was a talent Karl kept to himself before," Anne said drily.

"At least he *has* gone," said Elizabeth. She rubbed her forehead, tension pains were shooting through her skull.

"But what if he comes back? I suppose it's revenge he wants." David shook his head and heaved a huge sigh. "If beheading him didn't work, what else can I do?"

"Don't let's imagine the worst," Elizabeth said briskly. "I'm wondering what to tell Newland. I don't want to upset the servants, but I should never forgive myself if anyone was hurt."

"If he does come back, I think it's me he's after," said David.

Elizabeth's fear returned in a sick wave. Annoyed at herself, she said, "The three of us are all sensible and not easily unnerved. I can see no reason for us to start behaving like the three little piggies in the house of sticks."

But that was exactly how she felt. She loathed nothing more than feeling out of control, either of her emotions or her situation. Although the apparition didn't appear again that night, none of them got any sleep.

Karl left Kristian without a clear aim in mind. Kristian's revelation was swelling into a mass of hideous implications. Karl's disbelief at the manner of his resurrection became horror. He wanted to escape but the amorphous cloud of evil flowed with him.

Karl stretched out to touch the Crystal Ring. Ah yes, he could reach the subtle dimension again, despite his hunger. But he chose not to enter. It was enough to know that the dark wings of flight were no longer broken. *I want only to walk*, he thought bleakly, *as if connection with the physical world can somehow shield me from this despair.*

Nothing could shield him, of course. Haunted, he walked through darkness and light, unconscious of time, following the course of the Rhine through lush vineyards, steep tangles of rocks and trees, pine forests where sightseers admired the view from hilltop restaurants. He let his thirst gather and gather until he was almost delirious, drifting slightly outside his body, but still he did not sate it. When he saw humans they looked to him like children: defenceless, wide open to life and to danger.

I can't touch them, he thought, amazed at himself. *I have no right to be alive... Some immutable law has been broken, the law of God or of the universe. Abomination. My existence is an abomination against nature herself...*

The thought was as clear and vast as the evening sky. Karl had rarely before experienced such hopeless depression. Charlotte's pain. Ilona's pain.

Everyone I touch is damned... I drag them into damnation with me... One clean blow, and I should have died! I cannot feed, because to feed would be to accept it all. Immortality. Damnation. Kristian's law... and I can't accept it! All that had happened rolled over and through him like a gravid, purple-black thundercloud.

He climbed slowly along the peat-brown paths of a forest, letting his sight dim until he saw no more colour than a human could see. Pines soaring black against a clear deep violet sky: this simplicity was all he could bear.

The slow, obscene healing, bought with the blood of God knows how many mortals... Kristian's obsession, to put such a thing in motion without a qualm.

Such a sin, such a violation of nature, must be repaid... an equal and opposite reaction... or will it recoil with three-fold violence, like a curse? No one would speak so longingly of immortality if they knew what it meant!

A log lay across his path, near the summit of the hill. He stopped, lacking even the will to step over it, turned and sat down. Even through his pain, he was arrested by the vista that spread below him. The soft soot-blackness of the trees and hills, the river reflecting in long loops the violet and silver sheen of the sky.

In this beauty I can live... but what if it were gone?

Then Karl, who had been alone for decades, experienced the most devastating sense of loneliness. It attacked him with a fierceness that hurt like slashing knives, and it cut through him like wind-driven rain, as if he had no substance left at all, only desolation and thirst. If Charlotte were here... she would make this bearable. Sitting beside him, absorbing his words, her own thoughts moving behind her dark-rimmed eyes that were the colour of the sky. He imagined the soft weight of her hair on his hands, gold frost glinting on brown... Simply not to be alone with this despair.

I don't know if she's alive or dead... but if alive, surely she will have found a way to forget me. She had the strength to do that. How could I go back to her? Nothing has changed. I could only say again, "I cannot take you with me but neither can I leave you in peace." Why? To destroy her life a second time?

"Don't torment yourself with that," Kristian's voice seemed to tell him. "Come back to me." No, even this loneliness was preferable to that!

Yet do I really want to be free of Kristian? Perhaps I'm like Ilona. Without him to fight, I'd have no purpose. He is always there – like a father to a child who hasn't yet learned about death. He is to be rebelled against, but he is safe. He holds the promise of answers even if he can't give any except God, God, God. Then should I give in to him? Try to make myself believe what he believes, that God is on our side? That He takes revenge on mankind through us… We are His flood, plague, famine. We are part of Him – therefore no need to fear or to be alone.

But Karl looked at the sky and felt no God there. Power, certainly – but a blank, disinterested power. The majesty of nature, beautiful, pitiless, impersonal. Not requiring the services of dark messengers.

Of course Kristian needs God, to keep him from the abyss. And I haven't the imagination – or lack of it – to believe in deities. But Kristian is real so I need him instead…

Immortality had always been an abstract idea – still was – but Karl had always assumed he had the choice of death. Now visions crept over him of what it meant actually to be unable to die. The visions were stark. Hellish. His power to detach himself, to accept, was gone. And the hideous images marched past relentlessly.

Everything noble, the music and art and science that made life precious, familiar, were lost forever. Earth became a desert of ashes and cracked mud, caused by some inconceivable holocaust or the slow death of the sun. Then the Earth itself was gone, nothing left but the black void between stars… To go on and on through that nothingness, without escape…

The fear was simply that. *To be unable to sleep.* Never any respite from this curving line of consciousness that stretched on and on through time. A flame of clear white horror blazed inside him.

I am dead and this is the afterlife. This is hell. This is the evil and *the punishment: they are one and the same!*

The revelation hit him, dazzling white like the *Weisskalt*, heartless, inimical. A sword of glass stuck through him so that he could not move, or breathe, or think. And as he sat aghast at the knowledge, he saw a silhouette climbing up towards him; a headless hulking shape that dipped from side to side as it came. Karl was unable to make sense of the figure through his delirium, but his thirst leapt like a tongue of flame.

Soon he saw that it was a hiker with a knapsack bulging above his shoulders. A middle-aged man with grey hair, a strong bearded face, legs thin and tough in shorts and hiking boots. Karl's need was so intense that it could hardly worsen, but now his sharp thirst focused on the moving vessel...

Speak to me, Karl thought. *Then you will become a person, not just prey, and you will be safe. You* are *safe, because I cannot move, I am simply incapable of being a vampire any more...*

The hiker saw Karl and almost jumped out of his skin. He recovered himself quickly and said, slightly breathless, "*Guten Abend, mein Herr.*"

"*Guten Abend. Schönes Wetter,*" Karl replied without intonation. He willed the man to go by, but he stopped.

"*Sprechen Sie Englisch?*"

"*Ein wenig,*" said Karl. "Yes."

"Oh, splendid. My German is only *ein wenig* too, I'm afraid." The man's voice was deep, rather soothing. Karl liked him instantly, even through the despair and hunger. "That's quite a hill. Mind if I sit down?"

"Of course not." Karl moved along to make room. "Admire the view."

"I'm on a walking holiday. Nothing like it." The man took a huge breath and blew out a satisfied *Ahhhh.* "As Browning put it, 'God's in his heaven, all's right with the world.'"

"Browning is always misinterpreted!" Karl said. Amazing he could speak at all, with the horror still inside him; with human heat so close, the heartbeat pulsing like moist kisses through the arteries... "Pippa's words are overheard by an adulterous couple who have murdered the wife's husband. The irony is lost."

Taken aback, the Englishman gave him a curious look.

"I only teach geography, not English literature, I'm afraid. However naive the sentiment, I still agree with it."

"I did not mean to offend you. Then, of course, Pippa's innocence forces the couple to face their crimes..." Karl was beyond caring what he said, saw no point in pretence any more. The intensity of feeling came through in his voice. "I only wish I felt as you do, but I can see no God and nothing in the world but evil."

The hiker leaned forward, elbows resting on his knees.

"Tell me to mind my own business if you like, but you sound troubled, to put it mildly. It might help you to talk to a stranger.

I know what it's like to feel as you do, believe me, it was a long struggle to be at peace with myself."

"Had you killed someone?" Karl said sharply.

"Yes, in the War."

"In the War, as a soldier, under orders? You cannot truly blame yourself for that. But how can a murderer be at peace with himself? Worse than a murderer, a fiend who brings madness and misery even to those he most loves, whether he wants to or not, because his soul is damned?"

The Englishman was quiet, as if long practised in not reacting to shocking statements.

He must be a good teacher, Karl thought. *One who commands not just respect but love from his pupils.*

Then the man said, "Whatever you've done can't be so bad."

"No?" Karl was incredulous. "Why do you say that?"

"In my experience, people who've most cause to feel guilt don't feel it. They find ways to justify their actions. The ones who torment themselves have often done nothing to deserve it. But if they have, at least they recognise it and know their need to make their peace with God. It's a step in the right direction. Walking helped me, being alone with nature."

"I don't believe in God or the Devil," Karl said. "There is no way to justify what I am!"

The man breathed out softly. "No one's perfect. Whatever it is you've done – and you needn't tell me, because it's not my position to pass judgment – you will only find peace if you accept who you are."

The man had done nothing to hurt Karl, nothing even to offend him; yet suddenly he wanted to thrust through his unshakeable calmness. Part of his mind was saying, *He's made sense of life, let him alone* – but a deeper instinct was looming cold and white and pitiless through him. *Nature gives no quarter. Nor shall I.*

"You think I should accept *this*?" He gripped the man's shoulder, making him stare into Karl's face until he *saw*. All the order and logic of his life was turning upside down, his wise grey eyes whitening with horror. Then Karl let his fangs slide out to their full length, cruelly sharp. "Now do you understand? You speak of Nature, but it's Nature herself who has damned me and abandoned me! What should I do except pay her back?"

"No! Let me go!" The Englishman struggled to pull away.

"Yes, go," said Karl. "Run."

He released the man, watched him stumbling away through the trees, wasting half his energy in panic. He dwindled until he would have been lost to human sight and hearing, but Karl could still see his flailing form, hear his stressed breathing and the faint tap of his heart. He watched in absolute stillness, like a cat watching a tiny spider on a lengthening filament of silk. His thoughts were more shapes than words inside him.

Why not accept what I am? The pain, all the pain comes from denying it. This moral code I tried to keep is self-deception. If nature allows me to exist, forces *me to exist, let her bear the consequences.*

He stood up. Unhurriedly and without sound he loped through the trees until he caught up with the hiker, seized the strap of his pack and swung him round and off his feet. Karl cast no glamour on the man to soothe his fear. He saw the face haggard with shock and terror and he felt no pity.

"I accept it," said Karl, and drove his fangs through the salty damp skin of the neck.

And then came the blood. It gushed to fill the elastic cloud of emptiness within him, and transformed pain into scalding red ecstasy.

God, how could I have forgotten this? And he was clutching the man like a lover and weeping as he drank, with an overwhelming sense of returning home. The answer had been there all the time. And it was so simple.

Charlotte believed she had got over Karl. When he came into her thoughts she could drive him out again without pain. She felt calm, brisk, in control. Yes, life was bearable. She looked back on the months of desolation and felt a kind of grim pride that she had survived.

I don't love Henry but it doesn't matter, she told herself. *I don't want to be in love. No one is ever going to do that to me again!*

Only when it rained did she find it hard not to think of Karl, and it was such a wet summer. Rain had lashed the windows while they sat together in the study, warm in each other's radiance; always rain when he visited her at night – or when she waited for him in vain. Usually she found some way of occupying her mind to force out these thoughts, so why, on this particular evening, did her mind stray so persistently into the past?

Madeleine was staying with friends in London, and Charlotte hadn't seen Anne or David for weeks. She thought, *Of course they're too busy to come here often and it's my own fault I won't go there. But being alone with Father and Henry all this time is so wearing. Perhaps that's part of it.* She felt restless, sensitive to atmospheric pressure as if a summer storm were brewing. To sit with Henry irritated her unbearably, so she'd come to her bedroom, hoping to still her thoughts by reading. One electric lamp threw a red-brown sheen on the panelled walls, caught bronze highlights on mirrors and picture frames, on raindrops trickling down the window.

She found herself reading the vampire story *Carmilla* without conscious intention. The tale had always intrigued her: Carmilla was a vampire who seemed more vulnerable than her prey, taking victims by befriending them, falling in love with them. Yes, it was like a love affair between Carmilla and the female narrator, one that would end in death. The story still frightened Charlotte. How thrilling, that fear... but why?

Why is there a thrill in any kind of danger? To climb a mountain, to set sail for an unknown continent, to court Gentleman Death and not die, somehow to outwit him... but still, always that edge, that blood-red glint in the shadows... Oh God, without that danger, that feeling, what is there?

She slammed the book shut. *And why am I doing this to myself?*

She sat quiet for a moment, felt the atmosphere change with physical intensity. The house seemed to expand around her, while breezes sighed along distant corridors that did not exist. She could feel screams vibrating in the air. By reflex she put her hands over her ears. When she took them away, the screams had faded but she saw a face looking over her shoulder in the mirror.

Her mother. Translucent, bronze-golden. Suddenly there were tears in Charlotte's eyes.

"How could you bear it?" she said aloud.

Her mother seemed to answer, "Pain goes away and is forgotten. If it were not so, no woman would bear more than one child. But it passes, Charlotte. It is a valley of shadow you must walk through."

"Not just the pain, but to die after... to have no consolation."

"My consolation is you, dear. All my children. And knowing that your consolation will be something different, a passion completely your own."

Charlotte's throat felt tight, bitter. She closed her eyes.

"I had something and it's gone. I know I had no right, because it was evil; I know we lost Fleur and it almost destroyed the rest of us... but I can't stop thinking..."

"Walk gently through my shadow," said the ghost. Charlotte opened her eyes but her mother's face was gone.

Violent emotion knotted inside her.

"I hate Karl," she said. "I hate him for leaving, for doing this to me." Why this sudden rage? It was all entangled with a sense of dread that turned the inside of her skull cold. Frost ran all through her limbs. Terrible fear, and no one to tell, no one to help her – because the fearful chill lay within her own mind. "Damn you, Karl. When will you let me go?"

Why am I so morbid tonight? She decided to go downstairs and sit with Father and Henry. They were still up. It wasn't so late. Perhaps they would listen to some music on the wireless, or play cards. Yes.

Charlotte left her room, but as she went downstairs she heard voices from the morning room, at the rear of the house. Her father's voice, gruff and angry; then Henry's, rising in pitch as it did when he was agitated. And then Maple, subdued but puzzled. She leaned over the banister and listened.

"I went in the pantry for a bit o' supper, sir," Maple was saying, "and I saw the window wasn't closed properly, it sticks unless you bang it shut. So I opened it to do that and this hand comes through and grabs my wrist. Nearly gave me a heart attack. The hand was pulling at me, like it meant to take me clean through the window. I slammed the window on my own arm so it couldn't pull me any further, and it let go."

"Get Maple a brandy, Henry," said her father. Their voices

became indistinct. She went down to the half-open door of the morning room and heard him say, "We mustn't tell Charlotte."

"No. Absolutely not, Professor," said Henry.

Charlotte pushed open the door. "What mustn't you tell me?"

The three men froze and stared at her – the white-whiskered chauffeur on the couch, Henry handing him a glass, her father with his hands in his pockets – all looking distraught, and dismayed that she'd overheard.

Eventually her father said, "We, ah, we think there was a burglar in the garden. Didn't see any point in worrying you."

A potential intruder would have made her father more angry than nervous. She knew he was lying. Trepidation crawled up and down inside her but she went to him, slipped her hand through his arm and stroked his forehead.

"Are you all right, Father?" she said gently.

"Yes, yes, perfectly."

"You don't look it. If it was a burglar you would have called the police, wouldn't you?"

An uneasy silence. All the lights were on but the room still seemed dark, oppressive.

Henry said, "Look, Charlotte dear, why don't you just go to bed? It's all under control. Nothing for you to worry over."

"I am not five years old," she said, infuriated but keeping her voice steady. "I know when you're trying to hide something from me."

And she walked towards the windows.

"Don't touch the curtains!" Henry exclaimed. He moved in front of her and dramatically spreadeagled himself in her way. Charlotte simply moved to the next window and pulled open the drapes.

There was no one there. She looked out at the dark lawn, the trees against the sky, rain glittering in the light from the house. It was a tiny garden compared to the one at Parkland, but there were still borders, arbours and hedges where an intruder might conceal himself. Nothing moved in the shadows.

She heard distinct sighs of relief.

"What was it?" she said, turning round. "What did you see?"

"It was just some rogue," said her father, irritable now. "Probably a student playing a prank."

"Most of them have gone down for the summer," said Charlotte. She looked steadily at her father but he turned away, changed the subject, busily started organising Henry and Maple. She stood there, held in a trance. Sensing clear conspiracy, she thought, *It can't be what I think... but why else would they be so afraid – and why have I had these premonitions all evening?*

She went out into the hall and telephoned Anne at Parkland.

"I need to speak to someone normal," Charlotte said, trying to be light-hearted. "We've had such a peculiar evening. There was a would-be burglar in the garden and everyone's jumping out of their skins."

Anne went quiet. Then she asked, "Did you see the intruder?"

"No, and Father's being very evasive. It's driving me mad."

"I expect he... didn't want to worry you," Anne said in a strange tone. Then she, too, changed the subject. She sounded distracted, not her usual self, and she ended the call abruptly, leaving Charlotte more distressed than before. Anne knew something. She was hiding it. *Gods, Anne, even you?*

Whispered secrets, telephone calls behind closed doors, and a dark web of conspiracy netting the house... Charlotte went to bed and dreamed, for the first time in a year, of a desolate beach where hideous black crows flapped endlessly towards her across the ocean.

"David," said Anne, putting down the telephone and turning to him. "I think you had better call your father. There was someone outside their house too... and they wouldn't tell Charlotte who it was."

"Oh, no," David groaned. "Since he hasn't appeared here again, I was hoping that was the end of it."

"Perhaps it's Charlotte he's looking for – not you," she said.

Anne waited anxiously while David made the call. When it ended, he met her eyes grimly.

"Yes, it was Karl they saw. Poor Father, it could have given him a heart attack – not to mention Maple. They did the right thing, not telling Charlotte, though."

"She'll guess," Anne said bluntly. "What shall we do?"

"Well, you heard me tell him to call us immediately if the deuced thing appears again. If it does, we'll go straight to Cambridge. Aunt Lizzie too, I think it would be safest if we all stay together."

The next morning, Charlotte, Dr Neville and Henry worked as usual, not mentioning the previous night. Nothing was said at dinner, but as darkness fell, after nine o'clock, her father produced a stack of notes that needed typing and virtually bundled Charlotte into the study to work.

She knew precisely why he was doing it. If the mysterious intruder appeared again, he was determined that she should not see it. But she played the game. She typed mechanically for an hour, two hours, her mind not on the task. She felt the atmosphere tightening again, fear squeezing her ribs like whalebone.

Is there someone outside? In a strange way she didn't want to know, she wanted to ignore the feeling until it went away. *Perhaps I'm imagining all this. Perhaps Father really does need these notes by tomorrow...*

Headlights flashing through the curtains startled her. A few minutes later the front door opened and she heard voices in the hall: David, Anne, Elizabeth. They spoke rapidly, quietly, but she pressed her ear to the door and could hear them.

"He's still there," her father was saying. "I've sent the Maples and Sally to stay with Mrs Maple's sister. No point in putting them in danger too."

"Does Charlotte know?" said David. No answer. Charlotte imagined him shushing David, pointing at the study door. Then their footsteps were moving away and she heard David saying, "Best she doesn't..."

When Charlotte was sure they had left the hall, she slipped out and ran upstairs. Her room was at the rear of the house, the window overlooking the back garden. Now she had made the decision to face her dread, fear fountained inside her. Her legs weak and her pulse beating thinly through her head, she forced herself to look through the glass.

The moon was behind clouds, swelling the darkness with faint silver luminosity. She saw the stiff crowns of apple trees, the roofs of the shed and summer house gleaming; the untamed shrubs and sycamores, the dark box hedge that hid the vegetable garden. The garden looked poised, frozen. And there in the centre of the lawn she saw a dark figure. Too far away to be certain, but the shape of the upturned pale face was so familiar...

"No," she gasped. "No. Why are you doing this to me? Go away, go away!"

The dread kept rushing up until she wrenched away, arms wrapped around her stomach, holding herself against agonising stabs of fear. The coldness in her head became a snowstorm and she almost passed out. So sick, she felt. She lay on the bed, hearing nothing but her own heart roaring in her ears, thinking, *I'm dying, I'm actually dying of fear...*

The faintness passed and she sat up. Thank God for this numb control that always came to her rescue. The initial shock was over. Now there was a kernel of ice inside her, scepticism, even anger – both at her family and at Karl – and disbelief. A soul-deep instinct was telling her, *It is not him.*

Charlotte looked out again. The figure had moved closer to the house. Composed, she went downstairs again and found her family gathered in the morning room.

Silence dropped like a blanket as she walked in. They looked at her with guilt in their eyes, even Anne. They seemed lost, impotent. Although Charlotte was furious at them for trying to deceive her, at the same time she felt desperately for them. After a suspended pause, they all seemed to remember the need to act normally.

"Charlotte, dear, how are you?" said Elizabeth, coming to kiss her on the cheek.

"Finished that work already?" her father said with forced jollity. Their kindness was too intense and fragile, as if they were about to break bad news.

"I know what's happening," she said. "It's no good you trying to protect me."

Now they all looked sideways at each other.

"I doubt that you do," David began. "Look, Charli, this is very difficult. You must understand –"

"Even you, Anne!" Charlotte exclaimed. "The one person I thought I could trust not to treat me like an idiot!"

She walked towards the curtains – almost ran, as David and Henry came after her – and flung them open.

Six feet from her, on the other side of the glass, she saw Karl staring in at her.

She'd thought she was ready for the shock this time. She was wrong. She couldn't breathe. Sound and light came at her from a vast distance and all she could see clearly were those irises of palest gold – and the jet-black pupils boring through her with no humanity, no recognition, no emotion at all. Bleached, they looked. Beautiful, yes – *but not Karl's eyes.*

David was helping her into a chair and Henry was fanning her face with a scientific journal. The curtains were closed again but he was still there, she *knew.*

"We did try to warn you," Henry said feebly. They all gathered around her. Her father knelt down by her and stroked her hand, but she pulled away.

"It's not Karl," she said.

"Oh, Charli," said Anne. "I know this must be awfully hard for you. He was outside Parkland two nights ago, just the same. He tried to hurt David. I know it's unbelievable, but it obviously is Karl."

"It isn't." Charlotte spoke with unshakeable conviction. "It isn't him. You only have to look at his eyes!"

They looked on her with pity now: *Poor child, appalling shock, she can't accept it.* That's what they were thinking, but she knew she was right. But the horror...

Her father said, "We saw him last night. He tried to grab Maple through the pantry window – poor fellow was in an awful state."

"We're so sorry, old girl," said David. "We were only trying to save you from being upset."

"I know," said Charlotte, "but you can't. What are you going to do, cut off his head and see if he comes back *again*?"

Her brother flinched, so distressed that she felt ashamed of herself.

"Charli... I don't know. I just don't know."

She stood up, her back rigidly straight.

"I don't know who it is, but it isn't Karl. Now, I think I would like to go and lie down."

"Would you go with her, Anne?" said David. "I don't know

whether he means to get inside the house – but as long as I keep him in sight, we'll be as safe as we can be."

Charlotte had no intention of going to bed – but if Anne was with her, she couldn't do what she had planned. Then she thought, *Why be secretive? She can't stop me.*

Upstairs, Charlotte went to her dressing table, picked up the little white card and turned it round in her fingers. *"We are here sometimes,"* said the old-fashioned writing. She thought, *It may only be something Fleur left in the dress pocket. No, I know it wasn't there when I put the dress on. If it's not him, what does it matter? But if it is…*

She left her bedroom and went to her father's, the only upstairs room with a telephone extension.

Anne followed, saying, "What are you doing?"

"Telephoning someone who might help."

"Who?"

"One of Karl's friends."

"A vampire?" Anne almost choked on the word. "Oh, Charli, do you think that's wise?"

"It's my only hope! All my life, things have happened to me because I let them. I would like to be in control for a change. You can listen, if you like." Anne sat on the end of the bed as Charlotte asked the operator for the number and waited while it rang.

And someone answered. "Hello?"

"Is this Stefan?" Her voice was weak with nerves.

A long pause. Then something like a laugh, and the light, Scandinavian-accented voice said, "It would not be Niklas, would it? Charlotte? I never expected to hear your sweet voice again, especially after all this time."

God, it's really him. The sound of his voice sent shivers through her.

"You left a card in my pocket," she said. "You try to kill me then you give me your telephone number!"

"We were only trying to frighten you," he said, a smile in his voice. "I told you, killing is no fun. You were impertinent but I admired you for it. Why else do you think I gave you the card? I am so glad you have used it at last, but may I ask why?"

"I need your help. It's desperately important and I don't have time to play games. It's about Karl. You know that he was killed."

Another silence. When Stefan spoke again his tone was so guarded she was immediately suspicious.

"I heard, yes."

"He said he had no quarrel with you and Niklas, he made it sound as if you were more friends than enemies."

"Such human terms, Charlotte. We loved Karl. Everyone did."

"Good, because Karl is here now." Her voice was running away with her. "He's standing outside the window, watching the house. He's appeared three nights in a row and he just stands there. The point is, it's not Karl. It's something that looks exactly like him, but it isn't him! I want to know what's going on."

Again a long pause, and she thought, *Stefan knows what it means but he's not going to tell me!*

Then he said, "Don't upset yourself. What you have said is a shock to me."

"Is it him or not? I don't believe you don't know!"

"I – I have to think about this, Charlotte."

"There's no time to think," she said desperately, now convinced he was hiding the truth. "I need to know what to do."

"Well, I cannot give you an instant answer – except to warn you not to go near him. I shall try to find out, and one way or another I shall let you know. But I can't work miracles, it will take a little time."

He sounded helpful, even kind. There was no mockery in his tone. She felt a trace of relief, only a trace.

"We live in Cambridge, let me tell you the address," she began, but he interrupted.

"I know where you live." His words sent a feather chill down her neck. "And I'll be as quick as I can."

All she could manage to say in return was, "Thank you."

"I am glad you called me. I gave you our number for a reason, Charlotte. There is something special in you. Karl saw it and so did I. So if you ever wonder how it feels to live forever..." There was a click and Stefan was gone.

"Well?" said Anne.

Charlotte put her head in her hands. She was knotted with tension, her mouth dry, her head aching.

"I think he knows something and he can't or won't tell me. He said he'd try to help, I'll just have to hope he keeps his word. God, I hope I've done the right thing."

Anne made no comment, only sat beside her and gave her shoulder a reassuring touch.

"Oh, Anne," Charlotte whispered. The tension broke: she turned and they clung to each other. "Why is this happening to us?"

The long tree-covered slopes met the surface of the Rhine and fell onwards through the water in obsidian-green shadow. The pure blue of the sky dappled the surface, brightened by swift-moving, sun-edged clouds. Karl sat at a table between the trees outside a *Kaffeehaus*, lost in the view and the soothing flow of life around him; people at other tables, birds and squirrels feeding fearlessly among them.

When the young waitress brought the coffee and cake he had ordered, he saw the way her lips parted as her gaze moved over him. She lingered to wipe the table, looking back over her shoulder as she walked away, hips swaying. Karl felt a strange sense of melancholy mixed with pleasure. *What do you think you see, Fräulein?* He threw the cake to the squirrels, watched the steam curling in ribbons of tiny particles from the coffee as it cooled.

A breath of coldness made him look up and he saw two vampires approaching: Stefan and Niklas, white and gold angels, turning heads as they threaded their way towards him.

"We've been looking for you all night!" said Stefan. He sat opposite Karl, Niklas mirroring the action. Karl felt oddly pleased to see them. Stefan was a secretive, chameleon character whose relationship with his mute twin was unfathomable. Despite their apparent devotion to Kristian, their true loyalty was only to each other – but Kristian, of course, could never see that.

"Well, you have found me," said Karl. "How nice it would be to feel you sought me for the pleasure of my company and not because Kristian sent you."

"But he didn't." Stefan was uncharacteristically serious. "We've been in London and he doesn't know we're with you. There's something you should know. It's about your human friend, Charlotte."

To hear her name spoken aloud stunned Karl. Its resonance was ethereal, painful. He stared at Stefan with such intensity that the blond vampire drew back.

"What about her?"

"When I met her on that unfortunate evening, I gave her the telephone number of our London flat. Last night she called me. She said that she keeps seeing you at night, outside the window, watching her. She wanted to know if it was really you, and we were the only ones she could ask." He put his head on one side, sapphire eyes piercing. "She sounded... terribly upset."

Karl had deliberately distanced himself from his memories of Charlotte. She had become like a rose in his mind, perfect and transient; or an image on film, shining and alive, yet only a silent flicker of light. To think of her as real again brought the most extraordinary pain.

Finally Stefan said, "Aren't you going to say anything? You have not been watching her, have you?"

"No, I've been nowhere near her."

"No, we... did not think you had."

"She must have imagined it..." Karl trailed off, thinking, *God, has she still not put me from her mind?*

"I don't think she imagined it, my friend," Stefan said quietly. He seemed almost embarrassed. "You don't know, do you? I had a feeling he wouldn't tell you, although how long he thought he could keep it secret..."

"What are you talking about?"

"Your regeneration... what did Kristian tell you?"

"That he kept me bathed in blood until the injury healed." His eyes were fixed on Stefan as if to drink the truth from him.

"Think, if you lose a limb," Stefan said, "it cannot be grafted back, but you will grow a new one. The principle is the same. Two coffins. In one your head, and in the other your body. Filled with fresh blood every day. I know, because I was the one who had to do it. And in time the head grows a new body, and the body grows a new head."

Karl listened in complete abhorrence. He stared at his hands. Same hands he had always known...

"You mean that in healing me, Kristian also made a double of me? I don't believe you," he whispered. "I am no different..."

"Your brain, of course, contains your memories, your personality. But the replica's head, regrown from the body, has no mind... only some remnant of instinct."

"And this thing... looks like me?"

"Just like you, but rather as a statue of you, a moving photograph, a ghost. It is less beautiful than you because *you* are not inside it. Charlotte seemed to sense that."

"But what was Kristian's intention, nurturing this thing, letting it live?" He'd thought he had no capacity for horror or outrage left, but Kristian had surpassed himself.

There was a strange look on Stefan's face, almost resentment.

"If he cannot have you, a living double is the next best thing. Perhaps he hopes it can become everything you are not. Of course, he will be disappointed, because it lacks your character and intelligence..."

"Yet you say this thing is watching Charlotte! Why?"

"I am not certain that it is Kristian's doing. These doubles do not think, but they have some kind of awareness; like a cat, perhaps."

"Some kind of vestigial memory," said Karl.

"I believe so." As he spoke, Stefan was stroking Niklas's arm, staring at his profile in which the transparent dome of one pale gold eye caught the light. "I believe they know where they belong."

"*Liebe Gott*," Karl breathed. "I never guessed. I always assumed that you and Niklas were brothers."

"More than that. He's part of me. Long before Kristian met you, Karl, when I had been one of his flock only a year or two, some soldier found me dining on his comrade and struck off my head. Kristian saved me. I don't know whether he knew it would work, or if I was the first experiment, but when I woke from the healing, I found that I had this companion."

"Weren't you horrified?"

"Never." Stefan looked dreamily at Niklas as he spoke. "I loved him from the first moment."

"Isn't this taking narcissism to the extreme?"

Stefan laughed. "Perhaps. It was like finding my missing half, quite literally. We do not need anyone but each other... and Niklas will never leave me. He has the needs of a vampire, though he would starve if I did not take him to his prey. I cannot speak for other *doppelgängers* being so docile, and of course they cannot be reasoned with."

"Charlotte is in danger."

"Particularly if Kristian ever follows the double to see where it goes."

Karl gazed at Niklas, brooding.

"Is there any way in which these replicas are more vulnerable than the rest of us?"

"I don't know." Stefan put a protective hand on Niklas's arm. "I would not tell you if I did. But I have told you this for Charlotte's sake, not for Kristian's."

"I appreciate it – but why?"

Stefan gave a dazzling smile to make the most stony-hearted mortal fall in love with him.

"I like Charlotte," he said. "She reminds me a little of myself. What will you do?"

"I had made a decision not to go back to her," Karl said quietly, staring across the river. "Of course, I could disregard what you have told me, walk away and leave Charlotte to her fate... I have no choice at all, actually, have I?"

Standing under a dark arch cut through a hedge, with rain pattering around him, Karl stared up at the rear of Dr Neville's house. Creamy stone greying with age, ivy around the lighted windows. It seemed only days since he had last been here, the intervening months lost. He had travelled through the Crystal Ring from Germany to England, fed discreetly, and spent the remainder of the day watching the house. In daylight the double had not appeared.

Charlotte is alive, only yards from me. And some creature in my shape is haunting her! God knows what she must feel. And if I actually see her again... I could be noble: destroy the creature, drive it away – whatever it takes to make her safe – and vanish again without her ever knowing I was here. Or I could be true to my nature and simply take her...

Then, as the darkness came down, Karl saw the figure. It appeared to solidify out of nowhere with a black-ice crackling of the air. Tall, lean... the face in profile as dead white as the moon...

Dear God, it's the song! Karl felt a weird sensation like *déjà vu*, the world caught in a loop of time in which the same scene of horror played over and over again on a vast desolate stage. The echo of Charlotte's voice: "Oh! horror! For when I mark his features, the moon revealeth mine own visage there!"

Exactly that. Karl outside the house of his lost love... and the *doppelgänger* there before him, precisely mirroring his anguish.

The creature that masqueraded as Karl did not appear in daylight – but when darkness fell it manifested again outside the windows of the morning room. Watching. Charlotte couldn't bear to see it; nor could she bear to ignore it. David declared he would not try to destroy the monster unless it attacked them first, and the others agreed. All shared unspoken horror at the idea of a creature that could not be killed... They tried to play cards, listen to the gramophone or read – but it would have been easier to relax with a cobra loose in the room.

And Stefan hadn't kept his promise to help. Charlotte had tried to telephone him earlier but there was no answer, and at last her patience gave way. She stood up and made to leave the room.

"Where are you going?" David said sharply.

She raised her eyebrows. "Where do you think? And I don't need an escort."

"Oh, I see," he said, embarrassed.

They would have locked her up if she'd stated her true intention. Floating above a sense of danger, Charlotte began with careful deliberation to defy Stefan's warning. Her instincts cried, *Don't be such a fool!* but a stronger voice countered, *I can't bear this. I must know!*

She went down to the laboratory, taking a pair of scissors from a bench as she passed, and through a second cellar room to a door that led directly to the garden. Outside, a flight of moss-slippery steps led up to ground level.

The garden was full of movement: trees shivering against the sky, shrubs netted with moving shadows, ivy fluttering on the walls of the house. A thread of terror looped around her throat, drawing her away from safety and out into the darkness.

She moved halfway up the steps, barely noticing the patter of rain on her hair. She could see the figure a few yards along, staring in through the window, the face a pale smudge – *So like him but not him!* – but she knew that if she approached, David or someone else would see her from inside and panic. Could she make the being come to her instead?

She slipped a little way along the side wall, and from the cover of shrubs she looked across the grey lawn, the apple and plum trees all in silvery monochrome.

Very softly, she called, "Karl?"

He did not react at first. Then, as if sensing rather than hearing her, he turned with agonising slowness and began to walk towards her. The way he moved was not like Karl, too smooth, no grace or sinuosity about him. Even the clothes were wrong: he would never have chosen such a shabby old suit. Then with a wave of horror she thought, *What if he has come back to life – but without a mind?*

She began to shudder with suspended revulsion as he came closer. If she breathed she would scream.

Stop, don't come so close – but he kept walking until he was only inches from her. Completely rigid, she stared up at the face and thought, *God, it's him – except for the eyes, the eyes – like Niklas's, blank!*

He simply stood there, making no move to touch her; not even looking at her but straight past her at the wall. Long moments dripped by. She was transfixed, all emotion gathered up and suspended. At last, unable to stop herself, she reached a trembling hand upwards to his cheek. So pale, the high cheekbone, the beautiful face she had so loved...

"What are you?" she said. No response. A ghost clothed in flesh. Sudden raging anger twisted inside her. "How could you do this to me?" she cried. "Who made you, who sent you? Kristian, Ilona? Why are you tormenting me like this?"

There were tears streaming down her cheeks with the rain. She thought she heard a voice say, "*Charlotte*," but the being's lips had not moved. It was mocking her.

"What do you want? I hate you, Karl. Go to hell and leave me alone!"

And she struck out at him. Again a faint call, "Charlotte, don't!" but it was lost as the vampire seized her right wrist in a grip that deadened her whole body. The scissors were clutched in her left hand. She stabbed wildly at his shoulders, neck, face. Then she felt the sickening sensation of metal puncturing flesh and the whole garden swung around her like a carousel. A soft tearing of the air almost sucked her with it – and the creature was gone. She was lying on the earth, exhausted, weeping.

And a clear, soft voice right above her said, "Charlotte, don't be afraid."

Karl's voice. A black figure standing over her. Her heart gave a huge jolt that thrust out all her remaining breath and the night roared and spun around her. The shape was completely dark but for a long white hand stretched out...

"Let me help you up." The voice was soothing, the gentle Austrian accent burningly familiar after all these months. "There's no need to be frightened of me. Give me your hand." And he waited for her to do so, as if he would not touch her until she gave permission.

In a state of shock, Charlotte climbed to her feet without his help and looked into his face. Another spasm of terror – but this was not the gold-eyed demon. These eyes were glowing honey, scintillating with fire, not disturbingly vacant but full of life and fixed intently upon her. Karl's true beauty lay not merely in his form but in the intelligence that shone from within.

The first apparition hadn't given her such a flood of shock as this. Just as she'd known the other being was an impostor, she knew with absolute conviction that *this* Karl was real.

"I didn't mean to give you a fright," he said. "I was trying to warn you not to touch him, but I couldn't make you hear." He shook his head, seeming lost for words. Raindrops fell from the brim of his hat. "Won't you say anything to me, not one word?"

She went on looking at him, devouring every detail. Shock and terror bloomed into excruciating anger and she cried out, "Why have you come back? I saw you die!"

Such anguish in his eyes.

"*Liebling*... I would not have had this happen for the world. I don't know what use it is to explain, but I can't just leave you. I heard you say that you hate me. I deserve worse."

"I don't hate you," she said helplessly.

"I thought... What can I say to you?" He sighed. "I've missed you so much. Don't weep."

But she was weeping. Delicately, as if she might shy away, Karl touched her shoulder, and the next thing she knew she was in his arms, unable to stop herself. They clung to each other. There was nothing to say. When he kissed her she almost pulled away, then the deep familiar passion flared and her mouth met his like a butterfly seeking nectar.

All her self-possession was gone in an instant. Months spent healing herself, coping, forgetting – blown away like burned paper from a bonfire. There had only ever been this... everything else was a bereavement. And all it took was a single touch of his hand.

Ten minutes passed before either of them spoke.

Then all Charlotte could say was, "Oh, God. Karl." Then rage again. "If you weren't dead, why didn't you come back before? You can't, you won't do this to me!"

So Karl explained, while she leaned against him, listening in numb disbelief as his words streamed away softly into the rain. How Kristian had stolen his body, healed him, made the *doppelgänger*, how Stefan had delivered her message.

"I meant to rid you of the thing without you seeing me. But when you came out to it, when I saw you..."

"You can't leave me again!" she said fiercely. "Not now!"

There was a change in his eyes, an alarming surrender of will as if he was about to attack her. But he only pulled her to him again, so hard she could barely breathe.

"What can I bring you but pain? It would be better if I had died."

"No, no, it wouldn't. You don't mean it."

"I can't say it with any conviction at all at this moment." He brushed her damp hair out of her eyes. "We can't stay here in the rain. I assume the double has gone back to Kristian through the

Crystal Ring, but it may keep returning. You and your family are in danger. I have to stay to protect them until we find a way to destroy it."

They were both silent for a few moments, looking at each other. Then Charlotte said, "Stay... in the house with us, you mean?"

Karl smiled. "I can help them best in that way, yes."

She went cold with apprehension, tinged with excitement.

"You mean you would face my father and everyone, after everything that happened?"

"If I can speak a single word of explanation before your brother dismembers me." He spoke drily, but there was a hard spark in his eyes that made her think, *Has he changed? Did I ever know him, really?* "That my reappearance will shock and frighten them is certain – but I cannot say that I care. Understand this, Charlotte; you mean everything to me, but what they think of me means nothing at all."

The eerie being outside the window had vanished. Anne sensed a cautious relaxing of tension in the room, but she was thinking, *What if it's come inside?*

David looked at her as if he'd had the same thought.

He said, "Charlotte's a long time..."

The next moment they were all searching the house for Charlotte, calmly at first, then with increasing panic as it became clear she was nowhere to be found.

"She can't have gone outside!" said Dr Neville.

"Even she wouldn't be that reckless," said Elizabeth.

"Well, she's not inside," David retorted. "Come on, Henry, we'll check the garden."

He unlocked the door that led from the morning room into the garden, while Henry hung back, nervous. Anne saw Charlotte crossing the edge of the lawn, her light-coloured dress clinging to her, rain-soaked. No sign of the vampire.

"Charli!" David shouted. "What in heaven's name are you playing at? Come back inside now!"

Charlotte walked unhurriedly to the door and paused in the doorway, her hair sparkling with rain, her expression radiant. Her skin shone, her eyes were wide and full of light, she was luminous against the darkness outside. Anne felt a rush of relief. David, Henry and Dr Neville all began scolding her at once.

"There you are, thank God! We were worried sick!"

"It's gone," said Charlotte. "I told you it wasn't Karl." She moved into the room. Two heartbeats and someone slid out of the shadows after her. A tall slender man, dark hair strewn with ruby points of rain, eyes not blank but full of life and intelligence under the dark brows. Charlotte took his arm and drew him fully into the light.

"*This* is Karl," she said.

CHAPTER NINETEEN

WHO IS THE BEAUTY, WHO THE BEAST?

Karl.

Anne had seen him die – yet now he stood in the doorway as if the night at Fleur's had been a crazed dream.

Karl moved into the room as Charlotte closed the door behind them. David, Henry, Elizabeth and Dr Neville all backed away. Anne found herself retreating with them, unable to help herself. The power of Karl's presence was tangible, radiating fearful darkness into the room. Yet Charlotte remained by his side, her eyes alight with terrible joy.

Has he hypnotised her in some way? Anne thought, not doubting he had the power to do so. She was desperately trying to make sense of the confusion. *Was it him staring through the window at us? His eyes do look different now. What on earth is going on?*

David broke the silence.

"Charlotte," he said tightly. "You'd better come over here now. Come to us."

Charlotte did not move. She was very composed, almost defiant.

Then Karl spoke. "I realise what a great shock it is for you to see me alive." His voice was so gentle, yet sinister. Shivers ran over Anne's skin. "But don't be afraid. I've no wish to alarm you more than is necessary."

"How the hell have you come back?" David demanded. He was outraged, powerless.

"We are very hard to kill, David," said Karl. "Rather like trying to cut heads from the Hydra: strike us down and more of us come back."

"What do you want? Aren't you satisfied with the harm you've done us already?"

"Your anger is justified," Karl said dispassionately.

Dr Neville found his voice at last, hoarse with rage.

"You've got the cheek of the Devil, coming back here!"

"Hardly that." Karl's dark gaze moved over them each in turn, coming to rest on Dr Neville. "I did not kill your older daughter, sir, nor her husband. On the contrary, I regret their deaths more deeply than I can say, and would have stopped them if I could. However, I can't be absolved from responsibility. And I know it is equally useless to protest that I never intended you any harm; the harm is done. I have not come to ask forgiveness or even understanding. However, I have something to say and I must insist that you listen."

Karl spoke with the charming courtesy Anne remembered, but his tone had an ominous edge. *He simply doesn't care what we think or how we feel*, she thought, *yet he* does *seem to care about Charlotte...*

Without choice they all listened, transfixed. He went on, "Another vampire with my face and form has been watching you. You may be in great danger. I mean to protect you and to destroy the double – but if I am to do so, I must have your co-operation. Do you understand?"

Elizabeth exclaimed, "I don't understand any of this!" She moved to one side of the room, looking in the glass-fronted cupboards. "George, where d'you keep the brandy?"

Karl said, "Please, why don't you all sit down and have a drink? This has been a shock for you, but there is no reason for you not to be comfortable."

"You're damned right it's a shock!" said David, not moving. "You're trying to tell us that that thing we saw outside wasn't you?"

"Exactly. You have heard the expression *doppelgänger*? It will take some time to explain, but I shall do so – if you will be calm and listen."

"You're lying!"

Anne said, "I don't think he is, David. The creature wouldn't respond when we spoke to it and its eyes were the wrong colour. It seemed mindless." The memory made her shudder. "Elizabeth and I both said so. And you knew, didn't you, Charli?"

As Anne spoke, she was watching Charlotte for signs that she was under Karl's control in some way. There were none. Charlotte sounded normal, even matter-of-fact.

"I tried to tell you," she said. "I know I was reckless to go outside, but I had to be sure. The double nearly attacked me. Karl came to save me, and it disappeared."

"But it will come back," said Karl. "You have a choice: you can tolerate me until the creature has been destroyed, or I can leave you to its whims, whatever they may be."

"Are you telling us that we're powerless against this demon?" David said angrily. "That only *you* have the strength to defeat it, or secret knowledge of how to destroy vampires *permanently*?" He infused the last word with contempt.

"It could be suicidally foolish of you to refuse my help, yes," Karl answered quietly.

Anne saw the situation with sudden clarity. Karl's bewitching glamour had never affected her because she was down to earth and too much in love with David to notice. Now Anne saw the enthralling quality that Karl unfurled without effort, like threads of light. Yet still she wasn't drawn in, because at the same time he scared her to death. The veil had gone: the protective veneer created partly by Karl's deceptive charm, partly by their assumption that he was human. Only Edward had seen through his deceit. Now they all saw and the stark truth was terrifying.

And Karl was using their fear to dominate them. She remembered the first time she'd seen that menace in his eyes – the night she had spied on him and Pierre through the library window – and how she'd feared for Charlotte. Now she thought, *He could have used this power on us at any time and yet he didn't. We never saw it – but it was always there!*

Although Dr Neville was shaking visibly, he kept control.

"You're asking us to trust you?" he said.

Karl looked at him with a touch of sadness.

"You used to trust me, Dr Neville. I appreciate that it is difficult for you to do so again – but it would be in your best interests to try."

"Talk about the Devil and the deep blue sea." George Neville sighed heavily. "David, what in God's name are we going to do?"

"Von Wultendorf could start by giving us a sign that we *can* trust him," David said grimly, "by letting Charlotte come over to us."

Karl opened his hands. "I am not stopping her."

Charlotte still did not move.

"Charli!" David exclaimed.

She looked at Karl. His voice low and tender, he said, "You had better do as your brother suggests. For now."

What does he mean by that? Anne wondered. Expressionless, Charlotte walked over to her brother. And it was he who put a protective arm around her – not Henry, who hovered in nervous silence behind Dr Neville.

"Charli, you're soaked through," said David. "You'd better go and change. Anne, will you go with her?"

"Of course," said Anne. She went to Charlotte, never taking her eyes off Karl, as if he were a snake liable to strike at any second. She thought Charlotte would object, but she went with Anne quietly, only exchanging a single long glance with Karl as they left the room.

Upstairs, Anne fetched a large fluffy towel and sat on the edge of the bed while Charlotte dried herself and put on a dressing gown, moving as if in a daydream. Anne waited for her to speak.

Eventually she gave up. "Aren't you going to say something?"

Charlotte turned to her, towelling skeins of rain-darkened hair. "I wouldn't know where to start."

"Try starting with what possessed you to go outside!"

Violet flames of anger lit her eyes.

"Possessed, you said possessed! I *decided* to go out. As I explained downstairs, I had to know the truth!"

"And you just happened to bump into Karl in the garden?"

"Haven't you worked it out? The friend of Karl's I telephoned, Stefan, knew Karl was alive. Stefan went and told him that this *doppelgänger* was watching us. So Karl came to find out what was happening. Because he – he cares about us, don't you see?"

Anne breathed in and out slowly, trying to be objective. Failing.

"But how can Karl still be alive? I'm sorry, Charlotte. You will have to help me with this. Anything else I can cope with – but dark cellars, and people coming back from the dead…"

Charlotte sat down beside her and hugged her.

"Isn't this strange? Here I am comforting you for a change."

"Aren't you scared? Aren't you terrified?"

"I don't know," Charlotte said distantly. "I suppose I should be, but… Karl's come back. I can't think about anything else."

"The same goes for the rest of us! The difference is, we are not all starry-eyed about it like children on Christmas Eve!"

Charlotte clutched Anne's arms.

"But how do you think I felt when I realised that I was looking – not at some animated waxwork of him – but actually at *him*? I thought I should die. But when I got over the shock – Anne, what do you expect me to feel, but ecstatic?"

Anne held herself still, trying not to judge.

"Do you still love him?"

"I never stopped."

"Have you thought that you might just be in love with an image? Can't you see anything in him that's… pitiless? Evil?"

To her surprise, Charlotte did not leap to defend him.

"He can be, I know," she said thoughtfully. "But it's not all he is. In David, it's called heroic."

"Don't you dare compare – No, I won't get angry. I simply want to understand."

"Degrees, Anne! You don't know Karl. I do!"

"You think you do – but how do you know it's not some spell he's cast on you?"

"Why would he *bother* to cast a spell on me unless I meant something to him?" Charlotte retorted. "I'm too saintly to have a mind of my own, is that it? You know what contempt I feel for that idea. And you know it's not true! I am not under any illusions about him. Tell me, Anne, do I look hypnotised?"

"No. You certainly don't sound it."

"And does Karl look as if he's deceiving me, trying to play some game?"

Anne recalled the depth of feeling in every glance Karl had given Charlotte, the secret communication between them, even when they weren't touching. She tried to fault her own observation, but couldn't. Now she felt strangely defenceless, backed into a corner.

"No," Anne acquiesced. "As far as I can tell, he appears more fond of you than ever. I know that I'd still love David whatever he did. If he'd had to stand trial for killing Karl, I would have stuck by him. I understand that you can't just stop loving someone. But Charli – what do you think is going to come of it?"

Charlotte drew away, eyelids sweeping down to veil her thoughts. She could not or would not answer.

Anne asked herself, *Now, do I force the issue or leave it? Because she doesn't know, she can't know, any more than I do. And I think she's going to be very badly hurt again. Dear God, what has she done to deserve this?*

A brisk knock at the door interrupted Anne's thoughts.

Charlotte called, "Come in," and David put his head round the door.

"Everything all right?" he said.

"Yes," said Anne. "What's happening?"

David crossed the room and sat on a small couch that stood between the bed and the dressing table. He looked grave but businesslike.

"Von Wultendorf –" he spoke the name with distaste "– doesn't think the 'apparition' will come back until tomorrow night. He's going to keep watch in case it does. He suggested – rather, we decided that we might as well all go to bed and talk properly in the morning when we're fresh. He also said that anyone who wishes to leave is free to do so."

He looked at Anne with eyebrows slightly raised, lips compressed.

"Very magnanimous," she remarked.

"I thought it would be best if you, Charli and Aunt Lizzie go to your parents – wait, before you start arguing! I knew you'd refuse, and Karl says the damned thing will probably follow Charlotte wherever she goes... Sorry, I don't mean to frighten you, Charli. We're all here to look after you."

"I'm not afraid," said Charlotte.

"That's the spirit," David said without conviction. "Aunt Lizzie has decided to go up to London to make sure Madeleine's all right." Anne looked questioningly at him and he added, "Well, we thought Fleur was safe, didn't we? Anyway, Maple's going to drive her, so that's settled. I think Henry was pretty keen on the idea of saving his own skin…"

"Has he left?" Charlotte asked quickly.

David gave her a quizzical look.

"No. Didn't want to look a coward, I suppose. I shall have to have words with him. He's been worse than useless, giving Charli no support at all."

"Don't blame him," said Charlotte. "No one ever really explained to him what happened."

"I don't think any of us quite got the full story, did we?" David said pointedly. Charlotte didn't react, and Anne gave him a warning look. "Anyway," he said, "Henry's gone to bed."

Anne said, "If you'd join him, Charli, David and I could have this bed."

"I'd rather stay in my own room, if you don't mind," Charlotte said sharply.

"You and Anne have the bed," said David. "I'll rest on the couch. I doubt that I'll sleep anyway."

"There are other rooms," said Charlotte. "I don't need a bodyguard."

"Don't you? Don't even think of leaving this room until morning, Charli. I don't trust von Wultendorf one inch."

Is it only Karl he doesn't trust? Anne thought. She could sense Charlotte's resentment and frustration burning beneath her quiet surface. *We're right to keep them apart – but how long is she going to tolerate it?*

When morning came, Charlotte woke with a flame of anticipation inside her. There was a moment free of thought, only the lingering sensations of a dream – Karl alive, Karl's mouth on hers – then memory flooded back. Pure joy. *I didn't dream it, Karl's alive, he's here!*

When she and Anne dressed and went downstairs, there was no sign of Karl. Charlotte's disappointment was so extreme that she felt giddy, almost drunk with dismay.

David said, "I expect he'll be back. We couldn't get rid of him that easily."

Her distress flared into anticipation. She knew he would come back. *He will have gone out... to feed*, she thought with a shiver. *But he will come back!*

"Well, no use wasting the day worrying," said her father. "We'll just try to carry on as normal."

So Charlotte spent the day in the laboratory, but nothing was normal. None of them could concentrate. She could hardly bear to look at Henry. He was unusually irritable, and when they kept getting different measurements for an isotope of lead they almost came to blows.

Finally her father interjected, "For pity's sake, will you both stop this deuced bickering! I don't know what's happening to this family. I'm the only one allowed to lose my temper in this laboratory!" He leaned on the bench and breathed out heavily. "I suggest we call it a day. It's nearly four o'clock, anyway. Let's have some tea. Damn, I keep forgetting the Maples and Sally aren't here. I'm useless without 'em."

"I'll do it, Father," said Charlotte. She slid her hand through his arm and he clasped her hand. Henry was tidying up, keeping his back to them.

"I'm so sorry that you're having to go through this again, my dear," he said.

"It's you I'm worried about," she said. Awful, being torn apart like this: wanting Karl, but seeing her father suffering. Unbearable. For a moment she leaned against him, comforted by his familiar scent of tobacco and tweed.

"Oh, no need. I'm not in my dotage, and I've withstood worse than this." He shook his head. "It's this wretched feeling that we're never going to be rid of it."

David was calling down the stairs, "Father! Charli! Von Wultendorf's reappeared."

Charlotte's heart gave a bound that seemed to pull her up the stairs in a gliding arc. But as she reached the hall, David put a protective arm around her, and she found Henry guarding her other side, her father deliberately placing himself in front of her. In a rush of indignation, she saw that there was a conspiracy to keep her away from Karl, actually to shield her physically from him. She almost laughed in disbelief – then came alarm. *How am*

I going to speak to him, touch him? They simply won't let me!

"He wants to talk to us," said David. "I've a few things to say to him, as well."

"Oh, Lord," said Henry. "There's not going to be any – violence, is there?"

"Of course not," said Dr Neville. "We're all going to be perfectly civilised. Like a war conference, eh, David?"

"There's no need to be afraid of Karl," said Charlotte. "He wants to help us."

David turned on her. "Like he helped Edward?"

"He wouldn't have touched him, if Edward hadn't – Oh, it's hopeless to explain! But if you are so worried, let me speak to Karl."

"So you aren't frightened of him?" David said, exasperated. "It doesn't mean a thing! He's deluded you into trusting him."

"Why should he do that to me, and not to you?"

"Charli, will you stop for one moment and ask yourself *what* you are defending? We can't possibly let you anywhere near him! Not even to talk. If he says anything to you, ignore him." His tone became gentler. "Please don't fight us about this. It's for the best."

Charlotte, seeing it was hopeless to argue, fell silent. She felt oppressed by her father's concern, Henry's incomprehension, David's over-protectiveness. *Nothing has changed*, she thought. *They still assume I'm too innocent to be anything but a victim of an evil influence. But I've colluded, I have spent all these months letting them believe it.*

They went into the dining room, where dusty sunlight sheened the dark panelling and made the long mahogany table glow. And there was Karl, waiting for them, self-possessed and elegant in a dark suit.

His presence electrified the air. His beautiful eyes were on her at once, absorbing her, speaking without words. She wanted the others to vanish; she wanted to go to him, to feel his arms around her and... But her family walled her away from him, and the impossibility of touching him was the most exquisite ache.

* * *

How sombre, how mistrustful they look, Karl thought as the Nevilles came in. Karl sat down at one side of the table and David sat facing him with Anne on his right, Dr Neville, Charlotte and Henry on his left. It was an unconscious arrangement, as if the table were a battle line between them. Karl found it hard to take notice of any of them except Charlotte. Her eyes were fixed on his, the deep grey irises jewelled with amethyst.

"How are you?" he asked gently.

"Very well," Charlotte replied. He saw the pearly tips of her teeth as she smiled. "Very well indeed." David turned and frowned at her. Her family's protectiveness would have amused Karl, had it not made him feel so sad.

"I shall have to insist," David told Karl, "that you address yourself only to my father and myself."

"I would rather leave it to Charlotte, Anne and Henry to decide whether they wish to speak to me or not," said Karl. He respected David for his strong spirit, but at this moment David's wishes were irrelevant. He could easily have dominated them all with vampiric will power; only for Charlotte's sake was he using diplomacy instead. "I hope we can call a truce, at least until the *doppelgänger* is destroyed. I should explain, David, that after you severed my head, another vampire healed me. His method and reasons are not important, but he created a new body from my head and a new head from the body... thus a replica of myself, with vampire instincts but no power to reason. Do you see?"

"The whole bloody thing's unbelievable," said David.

"So it seems," said Dr Neville, "but in the absence of a rational explanation we have to trust the evidence of our eyes."

Henry, pressing a handkerchief to his forehead, looked incapable of saying anything. Of them all, he was suffering the most. Karl felt sorry for him.

"I will not go into detail," Karl went on. "But perhaps this knowledge helps you to understand the difficulty of destroying my kind. Only beheading is effective, and even that can be reversed. Disastrously so. I experimented on myself in your laboratory, Dr Neville, and found no substance that harmed me."

Neville looked astonished, fascinated.

"No? Not radium, or acid? Not even an electric current? Good God, the first time you came here – you picked up a beaker of boiling water and weren't scalded. D'you remember, Henry?"

Henry turned a shade whiter.

"In fact, the only thing that seems to afflict us is extreme cold."

Dr Neville smoothed his moustache, looking thoughtful. This had become a scientific problem to him.

"The coldest thing we can make in the lab is liquid nitrogen. Minus one hundred and ninety-six degrees centigrade. How cold does it have to be?"

"I am not sure." Karl spread his fingers on the glossy mahogany surface of the table. "I found that it paralysed my hand temporarily, nothing more."

"You poured that stuff on your hand?" Neville looked stunned. "So much for my lectures about safety in the lab. Are you claiming that you are indestructible... immortal?"

"So it seems," said Karl. "We can be wounded but we heal swiftly, even our brains... as if we were animated by something outside ourselves. We defy the laws of nature, do we not?"

"You're also defying the second law of thermodynamics," Dr Neville said gruffly. "Entropy always increases. You cannot live without changing. Deteriorating. But then, the behaviour of matter itself seems to come down to the study of probability. Nature resists precise measurement. We don't know yet what her laws *are*. If you were right, Karl, if creatures existed that were immortal, it could turn all of science, biology and philosophy on its head. Then again, if you exist outside nature – what we know of it, at least – perhaps you can only be destroyed by something outside nature. It's a fascinating puzzle."

"I wish we could talk in greater depth," Karl said with genuine regret. Dr Neville looked away, as if he remembered why he'd once liked Karl so much, and felt ashamed.

"I'd like to see you survive a mortar attack," David said under his breath.

"An explosion may fling a vampire into the air but it will not dismember him; shrapnel passes through his flesh as bullets do. Or mustard gas, or chlorine, David? No."

"How the hell do you know?"

Karl did not answer.

Charlotte said questioningly, "But the *Weisskalt*...?"

"No," said Karl. Again they spoke with an intensity that excluded everyone else, making them uncomfortable. "Our friend has the power to save him. It would not be final enough."

"He won't be happy if you do kill the double, will he?"

"He is not God," Karl said, thinking, *But Charlotte is right, of course. More fuel to Kristian's furnace.*

"Charlotte, please," David said in a severe tone, as if he couldn't bear this incomprehensible, private communication between Karl and Charlotte. "A stake through the heart, then. There must be something!"

"We do not sleep in graves, and the other superstitions are also false. Beheading is effective – as long as the vampire is not deliberately healed. I want the replica destroyed so completely that it *cannot* come back."

"Why?" said David. "Why d'you want it dead so desperately? It's one of your own kind. Won't it be rather like... killing your own twin brother?"

Karl felt a pang of obscure but wrenching pain. He hoped the feeling did not reach his face.

"Ask yourself, how would you feel if a perfect copy of yourself were haunting you? Haunting *Anne*? Would you tolerate it?"

Dr Neville said, "It's a presage of your own death, isn't it, to see your *doppelgänger*? In German myth."

"Perhaps that's what it is," Karl said, twisting his white fingers together. "We both live or we both die. I don't know."

"Doesn't it worry you," said David, "that if we find an effective way to kill it, we might use the same method on you?"

"There is that possibility," Karl said flatly. "I could be taking a very great risk."

"Why would you put yourself in such danger for our sake?"

"Because I know how much it would hurt Charlotte if anything happened to any of you."

David's strong face coloured.

"I don't know how you even dare speak her name, after what you did to her!"

Karl glared at David, dark contempt in his eyes.

"Has she ever said that I mistreated her?"

"She did nothing but defend you, but for God's sake – you took her hostage, we saw the wounds on her wrist and neck afterwards. She's never been the same since. Don't you dare claim you didn't harm her!"

"You assume I have no capacity for anything but evil. Perhaps you are right, but it doesn't mean I am incapable of love. However much it pains you to hear it, the truth is that I love Charlotte."

Henry glowered, flushing red. Karl saw Dr Neville grip his daughter's arm, a talismanic gesture of denial.

"You've got an infernal nerve," he growled.

"And supposing we destroy this creature," said David. "What then? Will you leave us in peace?"

"Of course."

"Damn it, I want to know what your intentions are towards Charlotte! You seem incapable of leaving her alone, but I am warning you –"

Karl raised his voice, just enough to cut across David's anger.

"I should not ask Charlotte to do anything against her will. Neither shall I embarrass her by asking her to make any comment on her own intentions." Charlotte, gazing at him, gave an almost imperceptible nod, as if to say, *"Thank you."*

"This is intolerable!" Henry broke in. "She's my wife, damn you!"

Mildly shocked, Karl looked at Charlotte.

"You didn't tell me," he said.

She lifted her shoulders apologetically. "I forgot."

"Forgot?" Henry spluttered. He looked as if he were about to have a seizure, but he seemed a distant figure, nothing to do with them.

"It doesn't make any difference… does it?" said Charlotte.

"No," said Karl. " Human conventions have no hold on us. I told you, don't you remember?"

"I remember," said Charlotte. "I have never forgotten a single word you said to me."

"Charli, will you stop this?" said David.

"Absolutely preposterous," Dr Neville exclaimed. "If you're suggesting that my daughter would even for one second consider –"

At the same time Henry was pushing his chair back, saying,

"I've had quite enough of this! Charlotte, I'm taking you out of here. Come on."

Ah, the rabbit has teeth after all, Karl thought, staring at Henry. *What possessed her to marry him? Grief? If so… gods, the harm we do has no limit.*

Charlotte remained in her seat, her expression set.

"I am not going to be ordered about," she said. "None of you has any right to tell me I can't speak to Karl!"

This confrontation was bound to break out eventually – *But not now, it is too soon*, thought Karl. He had to calm them. The air was so thick with tension that it seemed to contract and shimmer, as if their conflict were drawing an outside force. Karl began to interrupt the argument but the words died on his lips.

The shivering of the atmosphere was more than emotion, it was physical. He felt the air turn wintry and sensed a crisp concussion, like glass shattering in a vacuum.

And the *doppelgänger* appeared. It was inside the room, standing at Karl's shoulder.

Everyone leapt to their feet, Karl included. Sunlight fell across the figure but its dusty-black old-fashioned clothing drank the light, swathing the demon in darkness. It was so still that it hardly seemed alive. Even to Karl, the double was unspeakably menacing.

"Your bayonet, David," Karl said levelly. "A meat cleaver, anything. But move slowly."

"Bayonet's in the hall," David whispered. He began to back towards the door, but Henry turned in a panic, knocked over his chair and almost fell headlong across it.

The *doppelgänger*'s eyes widened and it came to life, starting towards Henry with a fixed, vacant smile. The movement seemed a reflex action, like a fox pouncing on a flapping hen.

Karl seized the creature's arms and held it back, the effort was like resisting the inertia of a toppling boulder. Shocked by its strength, he held grimly on and said, "Slowly, Henry!"

But Henry fled the room, and a door banged in the hall. David went out more cautiously. Anne, Charlotte and Dr Neville drew together and stared at Karl and his false twin.

Karl held the *doppelgänger* and turned it to face him. Close at hand, he found the being infinitely more disturbing than he'd anticipated. It was like a reflection in a mirror: perfect in every detail, but lacking its own inner life.

What does it actually feel behind those bleached-gold eyes? I don't think I can kill it... but I must! For if I don't... will it haunt me forever, as Niklas haunts Stefan? I could never love something that is no more than Kristian's hideous parody of me. I would despise it. I would have to kill it sooner or later, whatever happened...

As these thoughts circled his mind, he was leaning towards its throat. *Take its blood and weaken it...* But the instant Karl's lips touched the skin, the creature dissipated in his grasp and he was left clutching empty air.

The sensation was like being thrust over a cliff: blood thirst rising only for the victim to be snatched away. Karl knew his eyes must be filmy with hunger as he turned: he saw the others draw away from him, even Charlotte. Anne's gaze was fixed on Karl, serious, dark, accusing.

"God Almighty!" said Dr Neville, closing his eyes.

David was in the doorway, his sword bayonet in hand. Karl felt a trace of fear; memories of the last time he'd seen David in that posture, ghosts of sickening pain and nightmares. He pushed the fear away.

"Where is it?" said David, wide-eyed.

Karl could sense the creature in the house, he perceived a distant beat of human warmth, too.

"In the laboratory," he said. "I think Henry ran down there and shut himself in. His heat must have drawn the double after him – and locked doors are no barrier to us, unfortunately."

While the others ran into the hallway, and David began struggling with the cellar door, Karl stepped into the Crystal Ring. He pressed through walls as if through curtains of water. When the door at the top of the stairs finally burst open and David came rushing down, followed by the others, Karl was already in the laboratory. Henry was cringing back against a wall, the false Karl clamping one hand on his shoulder, almost with the guileless curiosity of a baby grasping a toy.

And still that slight curve to its mouth, like a demon in a nightmare feigning kindness. Evil, mocking. Henry had lost his glasses, and his face was contorted in a fight for breath.

Karl seized the creature, hauled it away. As if recognising Karl as a threat, it sidestepped into the Crystal Ring again – but Karl was ready, and went with it, binding the vampire in his arms. It tried to loop away but he drew it back into the space that contained the laboratory: a grey lozenge where all the angles were wrong and the humans invisible but for their auras.

He held the creature tight and nipped the skin of its neck between his teeth, then let his fangs slide out to puncture the vein. The blood, thick at first, thinned suddenly and ran scorching into his mouth like ice-cold brandy. So delicate, too strong to drink fast – both repellent and addictive. *Is this the taste of my own blood?* he wondered, aghast. He drank with steady intensity, eyes wide open to keep his head clear as he fought the tide of pleasure. And as he drank he watched the auras glittering against the strange shadow-shapes of the Crystal Ring.

David's aura was bright blue and gold; his father's indigo, complex and intense. Anne was a slender shape of green, red and brown. Earth colours. And Charlotte, unmistakable: needles of violet and golden-bronze, rose and black radiating from her, the corona of her soul. Henry's aura was barely visible, colourless.

Like Kristian, Karl could drink auras instead of blood if he chose. He did not, because stealing the life force seemed a worse betrayal than taking blood. It made death almost inevitable. It was like crushing an exquisite flower. And most of all, it left him feeling empty: the difference between standing by a fire and making love. Both were warming, yes... but it was the physical closeness and the lusciousness of blood he craved, as did all vampires. All except Kristian...

Gradually, as the creature weakened, he drew it back with him into the corporeal world. The laboratory solidified around them, strange perspectives resolving into solid walls, wisps of colour becoming hard shiny objects. Clamp stands, glass tubes, a row of Dewar flasks on a side bench. Slightly intoxicated from feeding, Karl let the *doppelgänger* go. He took a moment to let his canine teeth retract, to recover his composure.

The double stood impassively, as if nothing had happened, although the skin around its eyes was now waxy and drawn. The glassy, serene look belied what it was: a walking corpse animated only by blood thirst and some distant instinct to pursue what Karl loved. Horror dumbfounded him, yet at the same time he pitied the creature. *It did not ask to exist like this, understanding nothing...*

"I've weakened it," Karl said. "It can't escape now. We shall have to cut off its head, David, then cut the head into pieces. There is no other way."

David came forward, holding the bayonet's hilt two-handed. He hesitated, his mouth turned down with revulsion.

"I can't do it," he said. "Not in cold blood like this."

Karl saw the distress in his eyes, and understood.

"Then give me the blade!" He stretched out his hand, but as he did so the *doppelgänger* turned its head and pinned David with its blank gaze. Karl caught the vampire's arms. It pulled free and began to walk slowly and inexorably towards its prey. David backed away, holding the sword bayonet defensively, but the double – indifferent to the threat – persisted. The two of them began to make a gradual, bizarre circuit of the laboratory. *Does it have some memory of what David did to me?* Karl thought. Again he tried to impede the false twin, again it pulled away. Too weak to enter the Crystal Ring, in compensation it had the desperate strength that only a starving vampire could possess.

The mechanical quality of its movements seemed far more chilling than conscious evil. Although David wielded a weapon, Karl could see he was incapable of using it.

"David, throw me the bayonet!" Karl ordered. David, though, was not going to relinquish his only defence. He went on retreating, shaking his head in horror.

Karl looked around for another weapon. *Something to sever the head; wounding will only inflame it.* Charlotte was moving away from her father, sidling towards the bench that held the Dewar flasks.

"Charlotte, what are you doing?" said Karl.

Her eyes crystalline with terror and determination, she ignored him. She picked up a flask and began to edge towards David, removing the stopper as she went.

"Don't," said Karl. He spoke softly, watching in helpless fascination as Charlotte placed herself between David and the *doppelgänger.* Acting with swift precision she lifted the flask and tipped the contents over the double's head.

White smoke cascaded over its clothes, turning the material frost-grey. Liquid nitrogen. The vampire halted in its tracks, its auburn hair turning as white as its skin.

David backed up against a glass-fronted cabinet. Dr Neville was holding onto Anne's shoulder, while Henry had fled. Charlotte was pale and trembling, but moving deftly she seized a second flask and tipped the steaming bitter-cold fluid down the double's neck. The third flask, she flung into its face.

Colder than the *Weisskalt*...

The creature stood rigid, vapour flowing over its shoulders in a silent white-blue waterfall. Its clothes crackled with rime. Its face looked as white and friable as chalk.

Charlotte dropped the last flask on the floor and stared.

"Is it dead?" she whispered.

Karl took her arm. "I think you have paralysed it. Come away, before it recovers. You acted very bravely."

She obeyed and went to her father and Anne, who clung to her wordlessly.

Karl would have to pass the double to take the bayonet from David. If he could just do so before it revived... It stood as lifeless as a statue, hair and eyebrows crusted white. Something compelled him to pause and look into its face. To touch its cheek... irrational grief welled inside him.

As Karl touched the being's face, the skin crackled and shattered under his fingers.

God, its eyes! The orbs had shrivelled like raisins in the sockets.

He withdrew his hand in shock, then probed the face again. His own fingers stiffened with the vicious cold, but the face was brittle. The *doppelgänger* appeared frozen solid, and like a frosted rose its flesh yielded to dust under the pressure of his hands. David and the others looked on in revulsion. He heard them gasp and protest, but with horrible fascination Karl went on crushing the head between his hands until the skull creaked and popped and showered onto the floor in shards of glass.

Then the body crumpled to the floor. He heard the limbs snap like icicles.

Karl pressed his foot onto its chest. The ribs caved in. Frost granules spilled from the sleeves where the hands had been.

Ash. All that remained was collapsed fabric in human shape, spilling a grey and red-stained slush. And that was curling away into vapour as the liquid gas itself had evaporated. Even Kristian could not regenerate what was left.

A long, shocked silence.

"God," David breathed at last. "What happened?"

Karl picked up one of the flasks, tipped the last drops of nitrogen over his own fingers.

"Don't even think of it, David." He held out his hand to show that his flesh was unharmed. "It won't have the same effect on me. But you still have the bayonet. Cut off my head again, and this time cut my skull and my body into a thousand pieces. Perhaps a thousand vampires would return to haunt you – but I doubt it."

Glaring at Karl, David placed the bayonet on a bench.

"You've won," he said flatly. "You know I can't do it." Then he put his hands to his head. "God, you killed the bloody thing. You and Charlotte."

Karl stared down at the grisly remains. Horror and pity settled in his chest, clawing at him as if he were human.

"I don't think there is much chance of this returning back to life," he said, "but we shall have to dispose of what's left. Little more than a tattered old suit, really. Would you help me burn it in the garden, David, Dr Neville? If you have the stomach."

"Yes, all right." David pushed back his hair and swallowed hard. "Not Father, he's been through enough. I'll damned well make Henry help, though."

Later, the Nevilles sat in subdued silence in the drawing room, gradually recovering from the shock. Charlotte on the couch between Henry and her father, Anne perched on the arm of David's chair. They'd burned the double's remains – a bundle of dusty fabric and bone fragments – on a small bonfire in the vegetable garden, then buried the ashes, cleaned the laboratory, washed and changed. Now they sat drinking cups of tea – *The English answer to everything*, thought Karl with a trace of affection.

Henry looked rather green; the others were more resilient. Karl sat apart, aware that his presence made them uncomfortable. But he could not leave yet.

Eventually Anne broke the silence.

"I don't understand," she said, addressing Karl. "Why should liquid air be fatal to the double, but not to you?"

Karl answered conversationally, "Apparently the *doppelgänger* is more fragile than the vampire from which it was created. I don't know why, except that it had no intellect. Perhaps only I, as its progenitor, could destroy it; and also, I had taken its blood, of course. Another question of philosophy for Dr Neville. Does the true source of our energy lie in the mind?"

He smiled at Anne, but she looked away. No one answered him. Their hostility made him sad, but he would not be distracted from his purpose.

He said quietly, "Charlotte, are you feeling better now?"

Her gaze flashed to him, bright and intense.

"Yes, I'm quite well."

"Then would you come and speak to me – in private?"

Before she could answer, Dr Neville sat forward, one hand on Charlotte's arm.

"Out of the question!" he growled.

Charlotte pulled free of her father's grip and stood up. He, David and Henry rose too, trying to protect her again. Karl sympathised, but the human barriers between them were an annoying irrelevance.

"Please don't make a fuss," Charlotte said determinedly. "I'm going to speak to Karl and there's no point in you trying to stop me."

"The hell you are!" said David.

She said calmly, "I'm not a child, David."

"No, you're a married woman!" Henry put in, but she ignored him.

"Won't you believe I want to go with him of my own free will? He won't hurt me! Let us have a few minutes, at least."

"Charli..." Anne began.

"You can come and chaperon us if you want! I'm sure you don't mind listening to a private conversation!"

The three men looked desperate, realising they might as well try to persuade the sun not to set. Charlotte walked over to Karl. When Henry made a last attempt to stop her, Karl gave him a cold glance and he backed away, fear in his eyes.

Karl thought they would go into the study, but Charlotte took his hand and led him upstairs.

"Henry and I have separate rooms," she said. "They won't disturb us. They wouldn't dare."

Her room was dark, glowing with rich browns and reds in the afternoon light. Charlotte closed the door behind them and they clutched each other as if they were drowning.

"I did mean to talk to you," Karl whispered. "Only to talk…"

"So did I." Her breath was warm against his neck, her skin flushed with nervous excitement. "Weren't we being unrealistic?"

"I just couldn't stop them." David paced about the room. "It's as if I can't do a thing to resist von Wultendorf's will!"

Trying to calm him, Anne said, "Do you think it's likely Karl is actually going to harm Charlotte?"

He stood still, leaning on the back of the couch.

"Strangely enough, I don't think he is. But how do I know that's not an idea he's planted in my head?"

"I don't think so, David. Whatever Karl is, I think his feelings for Charlotte are genuine and I'm sure he won't –"

"But that's the danger, isn't it? He may not hurt her physically, but if the poor girl thinks she's still in love with him – God, it's worse, much worse!"

"This is outrageous!" Henry exclaimed. "I'd like to remind everyone that I happen to be her husband!"

Dr Neville turned on him testily. "Why don't you sort this out, then?"

Henry subsided, wiping sweat from his forehead with a crumpled handkerchief. Dr Neville patted his shoulder.

"I'm sorry, Henry," he said. "Why are we all paralysed? How the deuce can we let him take her away right under our noses?"

"Give them an hour," said Anne. "Just one hour. It won't change anything to panic, and if they've something to tell each other we can't deny them that. They probably want to say goodbye, that's all. I'll make more tea and sandwiches and then we'll just sit down and be calm, shall we?"

"Good idea," said David. "I'll give you a hand. God, I hope you're right."

"One hour," said Henry, looking at his pocket watch as if willing the hands to speed up. "Not one minute more."

In the luminous circle of Karl's embrace, Charlotte didn't stop to think that she was in her family's home, that her father and her husband were downstairs. Inhibition, guilt, self-control, all vaporised. From the first glance, the first touch they exchanged in the garden, this had been inevitable. All that went before was forgotten and there was only this ring of crystal, sword-sharp and achingly sweet.

How have I lived without this? Charlotte cried to herself as they entwined on her bed, limbs glowing like fire in the blush of sunset. His new, regrown body was achingly familiar, exactly as she remembered the old one: muscular, slim, flawless. A miracle. *How could I ever have thought I was alive?*

This should never end, she knew; this wild dance, by turns warm and smooth, hungry and blazing. *This is where we both belong.* Always with Karl there was a fresh revelation and now, as if his hands shaped her into a goddess, she saw that her own flesh – the body she'd ignored and hidden for most of her life – was his equal in beauty, creamy pale like a summer moon.

As their final crest of ecstasy faded, Karl groaned and turned his face away from her neck. He pulled away from her, actually left the bed and went blindly towards the window as if to throw himself through. She sat up in alarm but he stopped, leaning against the glass. After a moment he came back to the bed and sank down onto the carpet, clutching her hand and bowing his head against her forearm. They remained there, tangled up in love and despair.

"Is it always going to be like this?" she said faintly.

"You are still human, and I am still what I am," he replied. "All the reasons why we could not stay together are the same."

"But you took my blood twice, and I'm still here."

"The fact that I did so only makes the desire worse."

She leaned towards him.

"So drink from me! I don't care!"

He looked at the floor.

"But I do. However little I tried to take each time, it would have no end except your death. I could not bear that. I want you, Charlotte, but I cannot have you without destroying you. It's a brutal thing to say, but it is the truth."

She began to get up, unable to face what he was telling her.

"There's no hope, then," she said, wrapping a dressing gown around herself, tying the cord.

"There never was."

She sat down on the small couch, watching Karl as he dressed, still dumbstruck by his beauty, aching from head to toe with everything that had happened. Most of all, with the helpless anguish of thinking, *He's going to leave me again. I can't, I can't bear it, not again...*

Eventually, her heart breaking, she said, "What are we going to do?"

He sighed, sat down beside her and took her hand.

"I wish I knew, beloved. I have no answer."

"Unless you make me into a vampire."

He looked at her, long lashes fringing his eyes with darkness.

"Charlotte, have you forgotten the conversation we had in London?"

"I remember every word."

"Then you know it's impossible."

"But it isn't, not if you really want it! You say my conscience couldn't bear it, but I don't have one, or I wouldn't be with you in my own home –"

"Vampires take away conscience, too."

"Don't blame yourself for this, Karl," she said fiercely. "Don't be like my family, assuming I'm incapable of having a thought of my own."

"You don't know what you're asking!" Karl shook his head, exhaled softly. "I should have stayed away. I tried, but the *doppelgänger* seemed to know it belonged near you. It must have known my heart better than I did. When I saw you standing there in the rain I had to speak to you..."

"I'm glad you did."

"Don't be. It was unspeakably cruel. I have never caused you anything but pain, and now I've returned to cause more. This is selfishness. Vampires are like this, don't you see?"

"It was when you were being unselfish that I hated you! Trying to leave me because it was 'for the best'. I've thought of all the arguments: that I might change, or die, or Kristian might kill me. Even simply what it would do to my family if they knew. It's all hopeless. All I know is that I want you. Won't you take a single risk so we can stay together?"

Her words seemed to touch him.

"You've told me with your heart why you should become like me," he said, his voice low. "We love each other. Simple, yes? But now let your head speak."

"Do you want one reason, or all of them? It's not that I'm unhappy, I love my family, but I've always felt empty. Even before you came, I was looking for something else, and it's what you showed me, a wild and strange world beyond this one. I can't go through life wondering what it would have been like – to be immortal, to see the future unfold…"

"Charlotte –"

"Please, let me finish. Aunt Elizabeth once said I was amoral and it's true. Everyone refuses to believe any ill of me, which says a lot for them but nothing for me. I am not good. I can accept that without wanting forgiveness for it – not even from God. You've shown me the path I want to take. Shouldn't we be responsible for our own destinies? I want to take responsibility for mine."

"Ah, *liebchen*," said Karl. His hand curled around her knee, so tight it hurt. "But to take such a risk with your life…"

"But if I lose you again, I shall die anyway! I don't believe you're afraid. What will you think in a few years' time, when I am gone? 'If only I had taken the chance, she would still be here?'"

His pain was so palpable that it shook her.

Softly, he replied, "I have often dreamed of what it would be like to have you at my side, a companion who is more than a wife, far more than a beloved friend… but dreams are like us. They bite."

"Let them."

Then he looked at her, and his expression was no longer troubled but dark, intent. Her heart threw itself in circles of anxiety. She realised that arguing was the easy part; winning the argument, terrifying.

"I can't promise you happiness," he said. "I can't tell you what to expect. Don't turn to me and say, 'You didn't warn me!' because there are no words to prepare you for what will happen…"

"You've changed your mind?" she gasped.

"No," said Karl. "The moment I saw you again I knew that I would take you with me, whatever the dangers, but not without your consent. I had to be sure it was what you wanted. But now I'm certain of it I must warn you that I shall be completely ruthless. I won't let your family stand in our way. Nor must you."

Cold rivulets of foreboding went through her, but she said, "I won't."

"And I shall find two vampires to help me with the transformation…"

"Stefan," said Charlotte. "He and Niklas will help."

Karl looked astonished. "How do you know?"

"He virtually offered!"

Karl fell quiet, but he was smiling.

"I see. You have this all worked out." He moved to sit on the arm of the couch, leaned down and kissed her. "Well, now we have decided, there is no point in fearing it. Take this off."

He lifted her left hand. She realised with a chill that she was still wearing her wedding ring. She removed it.

"I only married Henry because I thought it would make Father happy. It was the most dreadful mistake."

"And I told you it doesn't matter." He took a signet ring from his right hand and slid it onto her finger in place of the wedding band. Red gold with a crimson stone. "For eternity."

Charlotte caught his wrists.

"Karl – something you never told me – do vampires make love to each other?"

He had no chance to reply. There was a light, hesitant knock on the door. Charlotte tried to ignore it but the tapping was repeated, louder and more insistent.

"I ought to answer," she said.

"Yes, do," said Karl. "There's nothing they can do to keep us apart. Don't be afraid."

"I'm not," she said, and meant it. They kissed, parted with lingering touches of hair, arms, hands. "I'm truly not afraid."

"Charlotte!" came a voice from outside. "Are you all right?"

She opened the door a few inches. Henry was there alone, overstrung with nervous anger.

"What are you doing?" he demanded. "You've had an hour to talk. I must – must insist that you, you come downstairs at once. Why won't you open the door properly?"

Charlotte found she didn't care what he thought. Her indifference to him was so complete that it felt like euphoria. Freedom. She opened the door fully and stood back, as if inviting him in.

Henry remained on the threshold, his bewildered gaze moving over them. Charlotte in her dressing gown, hair loose over her shoulders; Karl, sitting casually on the arm of the couch in shirt sleeves, his collar unfastened. The bed in disarray. Perfectly obvious there was nothing innocent in their meeting. And both of them looking back at him with a searing lack of shame.

"I see," said Henry, oddly dignified. "Well, you've succeeded in making a complete fool of me, Charlotte. Only you made a fool of me from the beginning, didn't you?" His voice rose. "Perhaps it's my own fault – I know you think I've no pride and no feelings, but you're wrong! I won't stand for this!"

His fury startled her. He marched into the room as if he meant to hit Karl. Karl outstared him until he shrank back from the unhuman gleam of his face.

"You'd better go," said Charlotte. "I've wronged you and I'm sorry."

"But you're still my wife!" Henry cried. "*My* wife."

His distress only infuriated Charlotte.

She said savagely, "Karl is my husband in the eyes of God!"

Henry stared at her through misted glasses, as if she had turned into a different person.

"You mean – before we married – you –"

He seized her shoulders and shook her. She was so astonished that she couldn't defend herself. Then his palm slammed across her face, so hard that she sprawled headlong onto the carpet, almost blacking out.

Her head ringing and her cheek on fire, Charlotte sat up, sobbing more with shock than pain. Karl was in the doorway, pinning Henry against the frame. Beyond, Anne and David appeared at the top of the stairs, followed by her father.

Karl, with his hands like claws on Henry's shoulders, said thinly, "I should kill you for that."

Henry's face bleached with terror. For a few moments, Karl looked certain to carry out the threat.

David shouted, "Get your hands off him!" Karl stepped back and released Henry, thrusting him away contemptuously.

"Whatever else I am," said Karl, "I do not hit women."

Henry hurried away to her father, still halfway between rage and fear.

"Shameless – in our own home," she could hear him exclaiming as Karl helped her to her feet.

"Beloved," said Karl, touching his finger to her inflamed cheek. "The truth is going to be a rather brutal shock to them, thanks to Henry, but we would have had to tell them eventually. Remember what we said. Nothing to fear."

But he was wrong. Charlotte was afraid, suddenly. She and Karl moved to the doorway and stood there defiantly, arms around each other. It had been easier to confront Henry's fury than the helpless silence of her father and David.

They can't still be thinking I'm Karl's victim, not after this...

No. She had finally torn their belief in her innocence to shreds, and how terrible it was to see the disillusionment in her father's eyes. It flayed her raw. She had once told Anne, *"It would break Father's heart to know the truth."* Now she saw how true her instinct had been, she felt she would have done anything to turn back time, to mend the illusion... but it was too late.

Even Anne looked shocked. Perhaps more sad than disapproving, as if to say, *"Oh, Charli, what have you done?"*

As evenly as she could, Charlotte said, "I'm going away with Karl."

"Over my dead body," said David.

Karl said icily, "If it comes to that."

"There's no point in trying to stop us," said Charlotte. "Please don't be angry. I'm an adult, you can't make my decisions for me, even if you think I'm wrong!"

Her father said, "Don't worry, we won't try to stop you." He spoke in the tone of granite disapproval that she dreaded. He walked up to her, and the look in his eyes shrivelled her. Utter hostility, as if she were a total stranger.

She started to say, "I'm sorry..."

"Damn your apologies!" he cried. "You can just pack your bags and leave! I don't want you under my roof a moment longer. I don't even know who you are."

CHAPTER TWENTY

THE DARK BIRDS AND THE WALKING DEAD

Years of habit made it possible for Charlotte to leave the house – her home – with no trace of emotion on her face. Utterly callous, she must have seemed. But if she had said one word to anyone, she would have broken.

Now, in a taxi-cab that was taking her and Karl from Cambridge to London, she wept as if she would never stop.

"What will this do to Father? I can't be this cruel... After he lost Mother, and Fleur..."

Karl held her without trying to soothe her. Simply understanding.

"Ah, it is difficult, *liebling*," he said very gently. "And this is only the beginning."

"Nothing could be worse than this."

"I warned you there would be pain. But it is too late to turn back now."

Emotion subsided and she lay against him, drained, watching trees and houses sweep past in a blur.

"Tell me what will happen," she said at last, speaking too softly for the driver to hear. "Why must there be three of you to change me?"

"To move into the Crystal Ring takes a certain amount of energy," said Karl. "There's a limit to the external objects we can take there. Our clothes go with us – indeed, it would be awkward if they did not – and in some way they become part of our substance in the other realm. And small items, without great difficulty: money or a watch, for example. But the heavier the object, the more difficult it becomes. If I tried to take a human into the Ring with me, I simply could not do it. But part of the transformation involves taking the mortal, on the very point of death, into the Ring. One vampire, even two vampires don't have sufficient strength. There must be three of us, to feed sufficient energy into the mortal to take them over the threshold. I was told this, and I found it to be true when we transfigured Ilona."

"So I – I die, then you take me into the Crystal Ring – and I come back to life?"

"Yes. We feed the Ring's life energy into you to replace your own."

"It doesn't sound so dreadful," she said, but she thought, *He said it doesn't always work...* and to die, actually to be facing death when there was no need, when if she chose she could simply walk away and live, go back to her father...

Karl was asking the driver to stop. They were somewhere in Mayfair, but Charlotte was lost, the graceful houses all unfamiliar to her.

"We have a little way to walk," said Karl, as they stepped out onto the pavement. "If your brother should have some idea of finding us, I don't want the driver to know the precise address."

The cab pulled away, and they walked along tree-lined streets between tall Georgian villas. The evening sky was creamy grey and a cool breeze tugged at the leaves. Washes of gold bloomed and faded as the sun tried to break through. A cart went past, the metallic echo of the horse's hooves startling in the quietness. They walked for five minutes before Karl turned and ascended a flight of steps to a house.

"This is where Stefan and Niklas live, when they are in London," he said.

The house showed a hint of dilapidation, white paint turning grey, plaster flaking off the columns. The front door stood open, revealing an inner door inset with stained glass. There was a row of doorbells on the wall, each with a nameplate. The bottom nameplate, Flat 5, was blank.

Charlotte stopped in the porch, overwhelmed by dread that rushed up from her childhood.

"Don't be afraid," said Karl.

"I can't help it. When – when I was very small, Father took me to hospital to have my tonsils out. It sounds trivial but it was the most terrifying thing that ever happened to me." Impressions came back with hideous sharpness: a small child's uncomprehending terror at naked walls and alien chemical smells, the sense of being abandoned to some horrific doom. The smell of ether, pain and the taste of blood, and worst of all, the knowledge that even her father could not protect her. When she tried to imagine what David and Edward had gone through during the War, that was the sensation that came to mind. Everything that had been safe – ripped away. "I've got that feeling again."

"I know," said Karl. His hands were gentle on her shoulders. "But a little child has no choice. You have. No one will force you into this, you can have as much time to think as you need."

She took a breath so deep that her chest ached.

"No. I've made up my mind. I'm all right."

They entered a black-and-white-tiled hall with a wide staircase curving around the walls. With his arm around her, Karl took her up the stairs to the top floor. He'd obviously been here before. She had a brief impression of him as a faceless official, taking her to the gallows for some unnamed crime. Apprehension set solid in her bones as Karl knocked on the door of Flat 5.

"It's so eerie, to think of vampires living here among ordinary people," she said softly.

"Well, we are not such ethereal beings," said Karl. "We need somewhere to leave our belongings, to be alone. And Stefan always liked to entertain."

Parties for his victims? she thought.

The door opened and Stefan stood on the threshold; a gold and ivory angel dressed in eighteenth-century clothes, a frock coat and breeches of blue satin, white stockings, buckled shoes. He was smiling, not at all surprised to see them.

He said, "I was wondering how long it would take you to come to us. I expected you yesterday!"

And Karl's first words were: "Why is Pierre here?"

Another lurch in her stomach. *How does he know? But of course, Karl always senses other vampires...*

"Don't worry, my friend," said Stefan. "It's for a reason.

Come in and I'll explain. Miss Neville, you are very welcome. This is a delight."

Stefan took her hand and kissed it. He seemed so charming, so genuinely pleased to see her, that she forgot her fear for a moment and smiled back. As he led her into the hallway, she saw Niklas standing to one side of the door. She almost jumped out of her skin. Dressed identically, he mirrored Stefan's stance. The only physical difference between them was the colour of their eyes: Stefan's were cornflower blue, Niklas's watered gold, unnervingly blank.

Shivers went through her at the memory of the *doppelgänger.*

"Come into our parlour," Stefan said with a theatrical flourish. "I don't blame you for being nervous, Charlotte, I would be too, in your place."

"Is it so obvious?" she said uneasily.

The flat was lavishly decorated with Persian carpets, chandeliers, shining Italian furniture. On a striped-silk chaise longue sat Pierre, dressed in everyday clothes, just as Charlotte remembered him. He exuded insolence and mockery, even in the casual way he sat. For some reason the sight of him almost jarred her into changing her mind. He paused just a second or two, looking her over, before bounding to his feet and taking her hand.

"*Ma chère* Ophelia, I am so very sorry to see you are still insane enough to run away with this fiend..." He turned to Karl, embraced him and bestowed kisses on his cheeks. Karl received the embrace solemnly, with a kind of sad affection.

Charlotte looked questioningly at Karl, dismayed that Pierre was here and deeply suspicious. Karl shook his head as if to quiet her.

He said, "We have come to ask your help, Stefan."

"So I guessed. You want to bring Charlotte into the Crystal Ring. Of course. I only marvel that it has taken you so long to decide."

Karl smiled. "You seem to know my mind better than I do. I am impressed."

"You shouldn't be," said Stefan, shrugging. "It has been blazingly obvious since the first moment I saw Charlotte that she is perfect."

"It will be a complete disaster," said Pierre, flopping back onto the chaise longue. His words sharpened her sense of dread.

"You understand," said Karl, "that I am doing this without Kristian's permission or knowledge?"

"Naturally." The blond vampire grinned. "If he *approved*, you'd change your mind."

Karl did not respond to Stefan's gibe.

"I ask your help on the understanding that you don't tell him. The fewer people who know, the better. I'd rather you had not let Pierre in on the secret."

"I appreciate your good faith!" said Pierre.

"He is here to help," said Stefan. "You know there must be three of us."

Charlotte said, "But I thought Niklas…"

"Niklas… he cannot take part in the process," Stefan said with a trace of sorrow. "He would not understand what was required of him, you see."

"Ah." Karl nodded. "I suspected as much. So you've agreed, Pierre?"

"Yes, I drew the short straw," said Pierre.

"Why?"

"Your trust in me is positively touching. You and Stefan can always twist me around your fingers – and so can Ophelia, for that matter. I just couldn't say no."

"The trouble is, you can't say no to Kristian, either," Karl said grimly. "I trust you not to tell him, but we know he will find out eventually. When he does, we may all be in danger. Knowing this, why do you want to help me?"

Neither Pierre nor Stefan replied. Stefan touched Karl's arm and they simply looked at each other. Charlotte sensed an unspoken current passing between them, unfathomable but strong.

Then it struck Charlotte hard that she was alone with four vampires. She felt encircled by their pale, deadly beauty. She looked out of the window at roofs and treetops, trying to anchor herself to the real world, but it was no good. The mythical otherworld was crystallising around her, entombing her in a sphere of glass.

Frightening, yes, but also perfectly wonderful and astonishing.

Then Karl said, "Is there a room where Charlotte can rest for a while?"

"Of course," said Stefan, indicating a door. "Through there."

As Karl went to the door with her she whispered, "I still don't trust Pierre."

She forgot the acuteness of vampire hearing.

"Should I be offended?" Pierre's voice was as brittle as the light glittering on the chandeliers. "In fact you are very sensible. Never trust a vampire, Ophelia."

"Stop it, Pierre," Karl said quietly. "Don't make it worse for her."

Pierre stood up, came to her and fixed her with his large, cold blue eyes.

"It is not so terrible. It is like jumping out of an aeroplane: once you are over the biggest step it is all terribly easy."

"The biggest step?"

"Dying."

Karl left Charlotte alone in the bedroom. It was decorated in the same rich, delicate style as the drawing room. She was grateful for his perceptiveness in guessing that she needed time to prepare herself. She couldn't hear their voices. The atmosphere was so still that she almost panicked for a moment, thinking they had all left.

Calming herself, she sat at a dressing table and looked at her reflection in the mirror. Her brown cloche pulled low over her forehead, wisps of crinkled wheat-gold hair escaping from under the brim. Eyes large with anxiety, the heavy lids darkened with tiredness. Mouth solemn, deep red because she had been unconsciously biting her lip. *How different will I look after…?*

She opened the one small suitcase she'd brought and took out the photograph of her mother. For a long time she looked at the tinted sepia.

"Tell me what to do," Charlotte breathed. Was it wrong to invoke a ghost? Nowhere near as bad as the destiny she planned. "Oh, Mother, is this really so evil? A word from you, and I'll go home… Just a word of guidance. Help me…"

She felt soft hands on her hair, so vividly that she jerked her head up and stared into the looking glass. It was her own reflection she saw there, yet there seemed to be another face looking over her shoulder, identical to hers.

"You are no angel, Charlotte," said the soft voice in her head.

"You are like me; selfish, wild, beyond human convention."

"You weren't like that, Mother," she whispered. "They all spoke of you as if you were a saint."

"All pretence. Nobody knew what was inside me, least of all your father. And the hiding of my true self killed me."

"No, I don't believe you!" Charlotte exclaimed out loud.

"Don't make the same mistake. Don't let their love destroy you with guilt. Listen to your own voice..."

The ghost – if she was ever truly there – was gone. And Charlotte thought, *Will I still see you if I change? Mother, you didn't let me say goodbye!*

"Charlotte, is anything wrong?" said a voice in the doorway. Karl came in and leaned on the edge of the dressing table, looking at her in concern. "I heard you cry out."

"I thought I saw my mother," she said, embarrassed. "She said the most extraordinary thing."

"What was it?" said Karl, his eyes intent under the dark curves of his eyebrows. He was all flame and shadow, mesmerising. And never, ever, did he make her feel she was being foolish.

"My mother said, 'The hiding of my true self killed me. Don't make the same mistake.' What did she mean? It's as if she was someone my father never knew!"

"He probably did not, any more than he knows you," said Karl, taking her hand.

"But I need to be sure... Is it only my mind recreating her, or does her ghost exist independent of me, which would make her... immortal?"

"I wish I could answer you."

Yearning for reassurance, she whispered, "I cannot imagine how it feels to know you will live forever."

"Completely terrifying," Karl said frankly. "Because I don't know what it means any more than you do. The Church taught me that if I sinned a little I'd be sent to purgatory; a lot, and I would go to hell. Whether or not I deny God, such ideas are too ingrained to be discarded altogether. When I recovered after Kristian healed me, and discovered what he'd done, I was not glad. I was in despair. All I could think was, 'If I cannot die, then there's no respite, no mercy!' It seemed to me that the punishment for evil is hell, and that in becoming vampires we enter hell forever, with no escape. Do you see? The sin and the punishment are concurrent."

Charlotte could not speak for a few moments. She found it hard to get her breath.

"I have to tell you, Karl," she said, "you are not helping."

"It would be dishonest to try. You're not someone who can accept comfort readily; you are always pressing for the truth, not platitudes." He lowered his head, his mahogany hair shading his forehead. "All the same, there's no need for me to make this harder. Forgive me."

"Anything," she said, pressing his hand to her face. How cold his fingers were.

"This is far worse for you than it was for me, because I was given no chance to anticipate or doubt. I didn't know what was happening until it was too late. And I told Ilona nothing, you see. Now I overcompensate."

"No," said Charlotte. "I'm glad. The worse you make it sound, the better I am able to face it. I doubt any vampire could describe how it feels to live forever, could they? The sun itself will die, not for millions of years, but who can visualise living that long?"

"Perhaps we are dying, very much more slowly than humans. That was something I hoped to learn when I came to your father, but maybe it's better not to know."

"Science predicts that the universe itself can have only one end," she said. "Disorder will increase until all matter is at the same temperature and all energy is evenly distributed as radiation."

"The dissolution of the universe... that's a prospect infinitely more bleak and hard to imagine even than our own deaths," said Karl.

"I've often felt I wouldn't mind so much," Charlotte said thoughtfully. "Loss of self, I mean. When it seems too much of a burden to be this feeling, walking thing, expected to act and react all the time... how wonderful, just to dissolve."

"To die?" said Karl.

"Not exactly... No, to be somehow part of the wind, still aware, but without emotion. Just to observe without feeling pain."

"Or pleasure."

"Pleasure brings pain too, doesn't it?" she said sharply. "Then there are theories that radiation might turn back into matter and create a new universe... but I don't accept that. It's against the second law of thermodynamics, as my father said. So what does 'immortality' mean?"

"But your father also said that there's more in nature than science can define. Can the Crystal Ring exist after the known universe is gone, some transcendent dimension like heaven? No one can answer that. But then, philosophers can't even explain the world around us. When I asked your father where he thought the universe came from in the first place, he said that we can't know, any more than figures in a painting can see the painter outside the canvas."

"And the painter is God, of course." Charlotte smiled. "I think he believes it."

"Don't you, any more?"

"I don't know. I think God's forsaken me, hasn't He?"

"You're trembling," said Karl.

"When will it be?"

"Now, if you like. We are ready."

Although Charlotte had thought she was prepared, his words sent renewed spasms of dread through her. She fought the fear so hard that the battle was almost exhilarating.

"Yes, why not?" she said, standing up. She took off her coat. Karl tenderly removed her hat, unpinned her hair and shook it loose. "But give me a moment," she said. "Hold me."

"*Liebchen*," he whispered. His arms were around her, his head resting on hers. She pressed herself to him, closing her eyes. So warm, so human he felt. *Hold this moment forever.* It was the last moment they would embrace each other like this, while she was still mortal; perhaps the last time ever.

She felt his breath in her hair as he spoke.

"I shall take your blood and your life force, but everything I take I shall give back. But if you would rather one of the others..."

"God, no!" she exclaimed. "It must be you. But if I don't come back to life –"

"You will. You must."

"But if I don't, don't blame yourself, Karl. It's what you most wanted and could never have until now, isn't it? My blood and my life. I want you to understand that I give it to you completely, with all my love."

She felt his tears on her face. He so rarely wept.

"Yes," he said. "There's nothing for you to fear." His voice was soft, distracted, torn between his dread of hurting her and his desire for her. And so imperative, that desire. She barely understood it yet the heat of his excitement carried her along, melting all instinct for self-preservation. All she craved was the fulfilment of giving such pleasure to him...

She felt him sigh, shudder slightly. Then her throat turned hot under the pressure of his lips and she felt the stab of his fangs, a paralysing wire of pain from her shoulder to her head.

She hadn't expected this so suddenly. It hurt. It was terrible. Yet she gave herself up willingly, thinking, *Yes, why not now, why prolong the pain of waiting? There's nothing else to think or say... I've nothing to fear, Karl's the one who's afraid...* and she held onto him hard, conveying that she understood, forgave him... that she shared this wanton bliss. His hands – one on her waist, the other cradling her head – felt like trails of fire.

Wing beats again. Slow and heavy, shaking her apart.

Leave everything behind and come out into the darkness...

Her sight and hearing were dissolving into a hissing cloud of silver. She was fainting, losing the power of speech. Yet she was still aware... Karl was no longer drinking from her throat but only kissing her there, his lips pressed to the wound... Now he was lifting her in his arms and carrying her into the drawing room. Fleeting impressions... Niklas sitting at a table with his elbow bent and his chin resting on one finger, as if he had been posed there like a doll. A thin figure crossed the room in the background, someone who wasn't there before... no, hallucinating now.

Her head cleared a little and she found herself swaying in the centre of the room. Bleached pink it looked, expansive. The three vampires surrounded her, stroking her arms and her body, larger than life, unearthly. Karl's eyes were full of anxiety. Pierre looked gruesomely amused. Only Stefan had any power to soothe her, his eyes sparkling like azure lakes. She focused on him and somehow she was in his arms and his mouth on her throat...

I can't spare any more, if you take any more I'll die...

She had no will to resist and it hurt less this time. Stefan drank from her with such tenderness, like Karl, but without Karl's passion and anguish... and after a few moments he relinquished her to Pierre.

She felt numb, outside herself, wanting this to end but lacking any power to halt the process. Pierre's touch she hated... too eager, the way his teeth fastened in her, sucking her strength... His was the only false note, the only trace of revulsion she experienced. Dimly she was aware that Karl had to drag him off her. Then there was the heavenly relief of being in Karl's embrace again, his mouth on her throat drawing her along the sweet tunnel of drowsiness. No pain this time. His ecstasy as he swallowed the last drop transmitted itself to her all down the length of their bodies and she gasped, clung to him...

She was falling, all thought and feeling fading into granular darkness. They caught her, let her down gently onto the carpet, but still she did not quite lose consciousness. Part of her was clinging to life and would not let go. This was what Pierre had meant about jumping from the aeroplane... She could not find the courage to leap. She was a child again in the hands of doctors – witch doctors, these – and she was fighting the anaesthetic with all her strength.

Karl, kneeling behind her head, leaned down and kissed her. She parted her lips to the kiss, felt sudden bitterness flood her mouth. Her eyes widened. He had bitten his own tongue and let the blood run into her mouth. It jolted her system like poison. He took her left hand, Stefan her right, then both linked hands with Pierre so they formed a circle. That was the last thing she saw. All the warmth was being sucked out of her; more than heat, they were taking the intangible energy that animated her. *Life.* All that remained was frigid emptiness. Impossible to resist because all her spirit to fight was gone. No feelings now, neither pain nor relief, nothing at all...

As Pierre had said, it was not so terrible. Just a single thrust off the cliff edge and a short drop into darkness.

* * *

Charlotte stood on a beach, the barren extension of her soul. The sand was sooty brown, all torn up by mines and barbed wire, the sea as turbid as oil, the sky black. There were distant specks winging towards her from the horizon, and she knew that when they reached her, something unspeakably evil would happen. She must run. She turned but the air hampered her like water, and a figure barred her way.

Fleur.

Fleur was dead, yet here she was alive again, staring at Charlotte with watered-gold eyes, her throat torn open and something inside the wound pulsing and glistening like a heart. Charlotte tried to scream, her breath emerging as a soundless rasp. She heard the steady thump of wings behind her. She was trapped between the dark birds and the walking dead.

And all her family were there with Fleur: Anne, Madeleine, David, Father, Elizabeth, their faces deathly white with terror. This was her fault. She must save them but she could not move, could not warn them. Edward came rushing out of nowhere towards the flying creatures, brandishing his stick, shouting, *"Run! I'll hold them off!"* But he was only a small frail sentry against a legion of beasts...

Now Charlotte was lying on the edge of the tide, thin waves washing over her, her life leaching away into the sand. As her soul dissipated, a new energy flared in with the sea. It entered in a thousand different ways: pierced her with needles of ruby light, and with coiling white-gold tendrils of fire. It stampeded through her like a vast crowd of people running. It came in like a whisper that grew louder and louder, a single bird singing far away on a mountain. It blew through her with all the relentless illogic and colour and power of dreams. *Dreams...* subconscious thought patterns that symbolised every fear and desire and memory. Fragments of a broken mirror rained down, each holding an entire image. She saw a brightly lit room full of people who for no reason made her dizzy with terror... Her aunt and sisters in supreme control, looking down on Charlotte, flaunting their smug knowledge of secrets she was not allowed to share... Edward, face distorted, hoarse cries tearing from his mouth, *"Can't you see what he is! Death! Get him out of here!"* A closed door behind which her mother screamed, cellar walls shielding her from the weight of her father's disapproval, from the demands of the world. *Alone I can be myself but when I look into that self I see darkness, horror...*

Charlotte dared to open the door, and saw another world. The strange world was dark yet she wanted to enter... wanted the dissolution into night that was both escape from her fear and into the forbidden paradise of love. She yearned towards the amber, ruby and violet fires she saw moving far away in the forest of darkness, burning in Karl's eyes.

"What are you doing?" said her father.

"I'm turning into radium," Charlotte replied. She felt it to be literally true. She was lead turning back into radium.

"But it's completely against the laws!" he said angrily. "Spontaneous decay does not reverse itself!"

Yet atomic particles kept flowing into her and as each one struck she glowed brighter. She became a single electron that filled the universe, its energy spreading in every direction – the curves of space-time bringing the waves back to where they began and so round again, interference patterns rippling across each other without end... *And so it is with everyone... We are particles, yet we are waves. Every thought we have is electricity, releasing waves that flow through space forever...*

She could see into the structure of matter itself. Not only protons and electrons but other particles of which her father had not dreamed, splitting and joining in an unfathomable dance that in her dream-state made perfect sense. She wanted to share the revelation with him.

"Look, Father! You were right, the neutron exists, but there are tinier particles inside. Can't you see? We must find out what they are!"

"Damn your theories!" he said. "I don't even know you!" And he stared at her with harsh condemnation until she backed away and went running out into the darkness, heart broken.

And found herself once more on the war-racked beach.

The dark birds were very close now and she was fleeing beside David, filled with terror, knowing that however fast they ran they would never escape. She heard their hissing breath and felt their claws in her hair...

Her fear was like metal hooks through her lungs. Her mouth gaped, her breath was paralysed. She could not escape. She sprawled forward, but the claws closed on her shoulders and she was being lifted into the air. The whole landscape slanted and her head whirled with vertigo.

I knew they would come for me. They could never be avoided...

The crows took her swooping along the wind with them. Mixed with her horror came euphoria. Below, tiny and defenceless and in despair, her family stumbled through the craters and the cruel wire. Charlotte stared down at them and wept.

How can I feel guilt and sorrow at the same time as this elation and freedom? But I can. I embrace everything. Every feeling and every perspective. I see myself from the ground as you must see me, Father, Anne, David, and I see you from above. You are afraid but I want to surround you with love, to absorb your fear and take you completely into myself...

The beach heaved and flowed, licked by waves of bronze and red and deep blue. The tilt of the landscape took her breath away. Not desolate now but full of mysterious fire. And the flying creatures no longer seemed hideous but graceful in their unearthly way. Fierce, mystical, laughing. She was just like them. Their long wings were really arms, and they were joined by their hands in a circle through which energy poured like ripples along a rope of light.

They broke the circle and she fell.

The jolt of falling that dropped her into darkness was the same jolt that brought her back. Like waking from an operation, thinking, *But it can't be over, I haven't even slept, I didn't let them put me to sleep!* Yet sensing in her bones that the entire world had changed.

Charlotte had thought she was lying down, but now she found herself on her feet. The room was phosphorescent, brushed with light, softly coloured by the prismatic sparkle of the chandeliers. She could see so clearly and in such detail, it was as if she'd spent her life looking through frosted glass.

Only Karl was in the room, watching from a few feet away, but something else seized her attention. A spider was walking across the carpet. She could see the way its joints articulated, the marvellous subtle hues of its body. She could even hear the scraping of its tiny feet on the fibres. The smallest sounds were extraordinarily clear. She could filter them from the louder noise of her own clothes rustling, the wind gusting along the street outside.

Everything was so brilliantly clear and sharp that she dared not move for fear that it would all shatter around her.

Awe held her motionless. There was discomfort under her ribs, a pulling like the need to draw a huge breath. She filled her lungs convulsively – the strangest sensation, because it came to her that she did not *need* to breathe, and the breath did nothing to ease her strange longing.

Panic. She tried to turn round, only for the whole room to tip sideways around her. Everything went dark and she was aware of another room rushing at her like a train. Narrow dark walls streaked with light, all the angles askew – she cried out, half fell and grasped the edge of a table.

The room turned bright and solid again. Even as she hung desperately onto reality, she was aware of the surface of the table under her fingers; the individual grains of wood beneath the varnish, the last faint energies of sap: the blood of trees. Awareness of that life-giving fluid struck a harmonic within her, and made the pulling sensation worse.

Surely the world had changed, not her. Reality revealed all its secrets, all the dancing particles of light and matter that human eyes could not see. And the world itself was no longer stable but likely to fragment around her at any second.

It was as if she'd awoken to find herself poised on a wire hundreds of feet above the ground. Horrifying insecurity.

A year seemed to pass before Karl came to her. Even with his hands on her arms, holding her, she felt no safer. Now they were both trying to balance on the wire. But she was distracted from the danger by her first sight of him in this strange new world.

Such unutterable beauty. The face of a saint, luminous and serene, like an altar piece illuminated by a single candle. His eyes were exquisite jewels, ruby and amber. If Karl had seemed beautiful before, now he was incandescent.

All she could do was stare at him in a mixture of wonder and panic, like a kite cut loose from its string and blowing helplessly through the sky.

"Help me," she gasped.

"Charlotte, hold onto me." He showed no emotion, not even relief that she'd survived. His manner was guarded, impersonal, but she was too disorientated to question this. "It takes time to adjust."

"Karl, I can't move, the room rushes away."

"That's because you're seeing the other dimension, the Crystal Ring. You must learn where to place yourself. Concentrate on me, on the room; push the Crystal Ring away. You cannot fall into it unless you intend to. You are safe."

She tried to do as he said. She let her tension go, tried to accept the glittering clarity of her senses. Leaning on his arm, she took an experimental step and the room remained solid.

"Charlotte, are you aware of what has happened?" Karl asked. "Sometimes the induction affects the memory."

"No, I remember," she said slowly. "I am like you now…" The word *vampire* didn't occur to her. "But I feel as if it happened years ago. I had such a long, strange dream. Father was in it. I thought I'd discovered all the secrets of the universe and it was so important that I told him. I was made of lead, turning into radium… but he wouldn't believe me, because that's the wrong way round, and I couldn't make him listen. It sounds ridiculous now, but it was so very real, so important."

"The visions are your mind reacting to the change," Karl said. "Everyone receives vivid impressions, each different. Don't call your experience ridiculous, Charlotte. Whatever you saw was profound."

She couldn't take her eyes off him as he spoke. This expansive, burning feeling inside her was love, transcendent love, a divine revelation.

"Walk round the room," he said. "I remember how it feels. I wanted to look at everything."

"I only want to look at you," she said.

He half smiled, but his expression was still cool, cautious. He put her away from him gently.

"If you begin to feel weak or hungry, dearest, tell me."

She walked slowly towards the window, turning like a dancer as she went.

"I feel perfect – as if I shall never feel tired or hungry again."

"That's the energy of the transformation still within you. It will fade," he said gravely.

Charlotte drew back the curtain – velvet prickling her fingers – and looked out of the window. What she saw was as shocking as her first awakening.

Oh, God, London, she thought as impressions came rushing at her, as if she'd never seen the city before. Roofs and smoke, people moving through the streets, rain falling on hat brims, distant motor horns sounding like reedy oboes... Darkness had fallen, yet nothing was hidden from her. The streetlights were diamonds brushing everything with soft colour. Shadows were velvet deep, yet she could see into them quite clearly. Far away beneath the trees she heard and saw a mouse scuffling through fallen leaves, pausing to sniff at a child's discarded mitten.

She was looking at another world. It was not hers any more. So heart-rendingly beautiful...

Karl was behind her, his hands on her shoulders.

"It's easy to lose sight of the price we pay for this," he said. "But I am not going to spare you anything. You are a vampire now."

The torrent of external impressions halted. Her mouth felt strange. As naturally as moving her lips, she could make her canine teeth lengthen into fangs. *Dear God, this can't be!* She ran her tongue over the small sharp points... so sharp that she drew blood. The taste went through her like an electric shock.

"I feel so strange," she said.

"You're feeling the thirst."

"No, it's not thirst, Karl." She turned towards him, one hand pressed over her waist. "More like happiness, but it aches."

Shaking his head a little, he drew her towards the chaise longue.

"Sit down," he said. "The first time is the worst."

"No," she said. She was beginning to tremble. Whatever he was implying she didn't want to know, she wanted to push it away. *I'm not a vampire, just... different.* "I'm not thirsty. I am all right."

Karl's hand rested on the back of her neck, hypnotically soothing. She wanted to move but couldn't, and then the door opened and Stefan came in, followed by Pierre and Niklas.

Between them, they brought a human into the room.

The dragging ache inside her flared into a corona of fire. Layers of reaction: amazement that she saw the man as *human,* a different species. He was of medium height and thin, his face gaunt, purplish shadows gouged under his eyes. His straight black hair and moustache gave him a foreign look. Charlotte stared at the man and realised with incredulity that she recognised him; he was one of Fleur's arty crowd. Pushing urgently through these superficial observations was her awareness of his blood branching through his body. He was a fruiting tree of blood...

She stood up, a faint dry groan issuing from her open mouth.

I know what I want to do and I can't...

"God help me," she whispered.

The man looked unafraid, not even dazed.

Stefan tricked him here... No, worse. He is here willingly! And the man looked straight at Charlotte and smiled, revealing white, crooked teeth.

"This is Oscar," said Stefan. "It's all right, Charlotte. He won't mind."

"That's right," Oscar agreed. He held out his wrist and she saw faint silvery fang marks. He walked towards her with a knowing glint in his eye that approached lust. "Feel free, old girl. You look so very charming."

Charlotte gaped at him.

My God, he knows! He wants it... For some reason his eagerness made her furious. And the fury swept away any clear thought and replaced it completely with thirst. He had simply become the centre, a flower to a bee.

She rushed forward to meet him, threw herself on him so savagely that his smile vanished and he cried out, "Get her off me!"

In the same moment she seemed to be watching herself from the outside, outraged in a very cool and British way. *What is that demented woman doing?*

Then her mouth filled with flesh, and from the flesh sprang honey and brandy and fire to quench the aching emptiness inside her. *Oh God... I've waited so long for this... all my life. Karl, oh please, don't let this stop.* Whatever this man was, all she felt for him now was pure, ravenous love.

The room was spiralling. The red peak of bliss seemed to

stretch forever, but after an undefined length of time she noticed that the victim was on the floor, that she was lying on top of him and he was no longer struggling...

"*Mon Dieu*, I think she's killed him." Pierre's voice was distant, as if heard on a wireless.

Karl was separating Charlotte from the source of life but she didn't resist. The sweetness ebbed slowly, gently... and she was sitting on the floor, leaning back against the chaise longue, while the whole room pulsed softly in and out like a golden heart.

"Oh, he'll be all right," Stefan said dismissively. "I bet he doesn't think you are so charming now, Charlotte."

Pierre was laughing. "My goodness, she is enthusiastic, isn't she? I think you have made her into a monster, Karl. Dr Frankenstein and Ophelia, what an unlikely pair."

"Get out, Pierre." Karl's voice was sharp. "All of you, leave us alone."

Charlotte felt the pleasure subsiding into exquisite contentment. She was sated, clear-headed. This was the first time since the transformation that she knew she was still *herself*, a rational being who understood what had happened and why. She touched her mouth, looked at her fingertips and saw blood on them. She saw the man on the floor, grinning no longer, the mauve tint below his eyes now colouring his whole face.

Stefan lifted him one-handed – as if taking a puppy by the scruff of the neck – and bundled him out of the room. Niklas followed, a door closed, and she was alone with Karl.

Then horror flooded her. She cried out, hid her face. She felt Karl's hands stroking her hair but he said nothing.

Eventually she stood and took a few steps away from him, her forearms folded across her stomach. *Such colours in my skin*, she noticed, looking down at her arms. Stolen blood bloomed through her like the sap in a pink rose.

"I was brought up not to show my feelings." Her voice was low, unsteady. "I thought that meant I wasn't allowed to *have* feelings. If I did I felt guilty. Always guilty."

She turned. Karl was watching her, very still and intent. *Why doesn't he say something?* Just watching, like a huge eye in a microscope... She felt caught in a web of tension.

"I have never experienced anything like that before," she went on. "Never. It was like being thrown off a building, I tried to save myself but I just couldn't stop. I can't ever let it happen again." Even as Charlotte spoke, she knew she was lying. The revulsion at her loss of control was nothing to the tidal waves of excitement. Yet she tried to cling to her conscience. "I can't accept this! I went out of my mind when I saw that – that man. I can't describe how terrible, how powerful it was."

"You don't need to," Karl said impassively. "The vampire instinct is strong, like a lion's instinct to hunt. If you cannot accept it, you will not survive."

"But that's the awful thing," she whispered, aghast. "I don't feel guilty. I hate myself for *not* feeling shame."

"It will pass," said Karl.

"You don't understand! It didn't feel like hunger or thirst, it was like love!"

At that, his eyes sparked. "Did I ever suggest that you would feel hatred for your victims?"

"You suggested that Ilona did."

That broke the web. That was why his eyes brooded on her, trying to judge how much she'd changed, whether she had become like his daughter. That was why he had reacted so sharply to Pierre's taunts.

For a moment she hated him for doubting.

She said, "Is this what you want to know? Ilona kills by convincing herself she hates her victims, I can do so easily because I confuse the urge with love. Does that make me better or worse than her?"

Karl stood up with vampire swiftness. Now, though, she perceived the graceful motion as quite slow. He came to her and clasped her right hand, twisting his arm around hers to draw her close.

"If you want an honest answer, I don't care!" His eyes were hard, no tenderness in him at all. "We both wanted this. Well, now we have it. Neither of us has the right to complain that it is not what we expected."

For a few seconds his words petrified her. Then she seemed to be rising above the fear, a quiet inner voice reminding her there was no need to feel helpless any more. It was a habit hard to break.

"Then believe your own words, Karl," she said gently. "I know this is as difficult for you as it is for me. Don't pretend it was only my innocence you loved, I know you better than that! I am still myself and I need your help. If you are ever hostile to me again I shall never forgive you."

He released her hand and put his arms round her.

"God, is that how I seem to you? *Liebling*, I am so sorry. I didn't know how deep my fears ran; no excuse for hurting you." He held her as he had before he took her life: with gentleness and desperation. "When I took your blood it was the most exquisite experience of my life, but it was nothing, nothing when I saw you lying there... dead. I would have sacrificed anything for you to be alive again. I was so terrified you would not come back... and almost as afraid that you *would*. But I am so glad. Just that you are still here, human, vampire, it doesn't matter. So happy, beloved." He hugged her, drew back and studied her. His eyes were gentle again, seducing her as ever. Karl, too, was still himself. "Ah, but we say too much. Let us not talk any more. Come with me."

"Where?"

"Into the Crystal Ring."

Karl took Charlotte's hand and she saw the walls dissolve. Giddiness and confusion again, she was in a world of impossibilities. Karl drew her upwards and she found herself staring at a transformed sky: clouds forming intricate, surreal landscapes. And such colours – bronze dappled with gold, swirls of palest green and turquoise, rainbow lines threading towards thunderous purple chasms thousands of feet above their heads.

Too much to take in. Nothing Karl had told her – and he'd told her so very little, after all – could have prepared her for this.

She was staring into heaven.

"Oh, but I know this!" she exclaimed, astonished that she could speak at all. Karl turned to her. Another revelation – he no longer looked human. Although hard to see clearly, he was a slender silhouette, cloaked or winged with soft fine leather and lacy membranes, with the burning face of a seraph. Proud, unfettered, subject to no law. She looked down at her own body and saw that she, too, was like him. Wild excitement seared her.

437

"We brought you here during your transformation," he said. "I wasn't sure you would remember."

"I thought it was a dream. It *is* a dream," she whispered.

Hand in hand they began to ascend the Ring. They rose through plains that rippled like sunset oceans, between copper-gold hills where vast forests sprang up only to be consumed as the cloud-hills rolled and reformed in the ether. Across this insubstantial realm they half ran and half flew, as if gravity had loosened its hold on them.

"But where are we?" Charlotte cried.

"Kristian says the mind of God," said Karl. "I don't know. It seems to be the sky of Earth, transmuted. Nothing is fixed, nothing could ever be built here. The Ring is no kingdom of immortals; we are still tied to the Earth. But learn the geography and you can travel the world more swiftly than you would believe. This realm holds dangers, too, so listen to me."

From a certain height, Charlotte could see that the flow of the landscape was not random but angled in a constant direction, like a wind current. Even the complex local disturbances were not as random as they seemed, but followed a pattern.

Like the weather systems of Earth or the storms of Jupiter? she thought.

Strange forces pulled at her. Wires of light threaded the mesosphere, seemingly full of significance.

"We use the lines to guide us," said Karl. "You will learn the contours, in time."

"Magnetism," she said, suddenly understanding. "It's the magnetic field of the Earth that we can see and feel."

As she spoke, the surface beneath her turned into cloud and she found herself tumbling through nothingness. Her euphoria ignited to panic. Karl swooped after her, caught her and brought her to rest on a lower slope.

She held onto him, gasping, "Now I believe it can be dangerous."

"The peril is not in falling," he answered. "You won't hurt yourself, even if you fall all the way to the Earth's surface. The danger is in staying here too long. And the greatest peril of all is the *Weisskalt.*"

They climbed the sides of an abyss whose substance cascaded

downwards like semi-liquid amethyst. Shades of violet flooded her eyes; pure elation carried her onwards at Karl's side between mountains of flowing glass. From the summit, Karl pointed up through layers of blue, white and silver noctilucence. Miles above, she saw a tear in the whiteness. Above the fissure a black sky blazed with huge stars.

Charlotte was half sobbing. The glory of these sights was beyond her.

"Can't we go up there?"

"The higher levels are very cold. The highest is the *Weisskalt*," Karl said. "If you went there, you might never return. I brought Ilona back but it almost killed me... not death exactly, but a hibernation so deep it might as well be death."

"I remember what you told me – about Kristian leaving vampires there as punishment." A breath of winter went through her.

"Yes. So don't be tempted by its beauty, beloved. Even the lowest layers of the Crystal Ring will drain your warmth and strength. It is too easy to linger here, bewitched, until starvation sets in. Then you'll become dormant and unable to return to Earth unless someone helps you."

"We don't have to go back yet, do we?"

"Not yet. I brought you here to rest. It is the only form of sleep we enjoy. In time we develop an instinct for how long to stay, but for now I'll watch over you and wake you when it's time to go back."

"I can't possibly sleep!" she said.

"It is not quite that. Let go, Charlotte. You will see."

At his instruction she lay down, trusting the substance of the cloud-mountain to bear her up like water. She closed her eyes but her thoughts would not cease. She turned and opened her eyes and then...

She was floating face down on an infinite ocean. A whole world lay below her, painted in ever-changing rhapsodies of colour. A trancelike state fell on her. Not unconsciousness, yet it was complete repose. She could still see and hear, but all emotions fell away and there was only the serenity of the Crystal Ring, the endless blue swirl of the atmosphere.

To Charlotte, the gleaming ridges and the smoky valleys of shadow winding between them became the convolutions of a vast brain. The strange visions of her transformation were still fresh in her mind... unfinished.

Something about human thought... every thought generating electrical activity that radiates out forever... and in this realm human thought is real, a great breathing plasma of dreams and fears... the subconscious of mankind made material so we can fly through it as if through palaces of cloud in the sky...

And here is the distillation of the two purest emotions. Fear... Time only passes in one direction. Entropy forever increases. The dead cannot come back! For them to do so is to break the ultimate law of time.

And hope. God grant us life eternal. The only way to bear the fear of annihilation is to believe in heaven. And fear makes us obedient, because we don't want to live forever in hell...

"Charlotte." Karl's voice intruded on her trance and she realised that three or four hours had passed. She wanted to stay here, floating on the soft breast of the sky... "Charlotte! Time to go back now. This is the trouble, you see. It is so tempting to linger."

Alert once more, she gasped in astonishment as the meaning of her waking vision resolved into perfect clarity.

"Oh, God, Karl!"

"What's wrong?" he said, concerned.

"Nothing – but I've so much to tell you, it's so important."

"Tell me when we're back on Earth." He stroked her head with a velvet-soft hand. "We have all the time in the world to talk." Then he kissed her, and the kiss was electric.

Karl and Charlotte were both taken by surprise, ambushed by the compelling force of their desire. He had not answered her question, "Do vampires make love to each other?" and she'd never asked again, but anxiety had remained in the back of her mind. *Will you still desire me when I am like you? Was your passion any more than sublimated need for my blood?* And it never occurred to her to ask if desire could exist within the Crystal Ring.

But as their unearthly forms tangled, fiercely devouring each other as they tumbled and floated through the ocean, she knew the answer was yes, and yes, and yes.

CHAPTER TWENTY-ONE

SHADES OF NIGHT

Karl looked across the shining river, seeing forest green and umber shading into black, a row of lights on the far bank reflected as sinuous bright snakes in the water. And beyond, the smoky silhouette of London rose against the night sky. He was content. After the wildness of the Crystal Ring, all he wanted was to rest in the prosaic arms of Earth.

Yet the Thames seemed anything but ordinary on this enchanted night. Most humans were in their beds, yet the city still murmured. Never quite silent. And these hints of life seemed to float from a great distance across the arc of night.

Karl and Charlotte sat on a bench on the embankment, watching lights rippling in the water; resting against each other, bound together in an intangible coil of rapture. Purest pleasure, to have Charlotte with him at last; yet how fragile the moment felt.

"You are such a pessimist, Karl," Charlotte said softly, laughing. "But there was no need, no need at all."

He smiled and kissed her, even more bewitched by the vampire shimmer of her face and eyes than he had been by her mortal glow.

"I am so glad you stepped through the veil," he said.

"It didn't seem a veil from the other side," she said thoughtfully. "More a chasm. But from this side... yes, like pulling back a net and seeing clearly for the first time."

"You were going to tell me something?"

"When we were in the Crystal Ring..." She trailed off. "I'll tell you later, Karl. It's too much to contemplate. I just want to be quiet now."

Karl was aware of her changing moods, from wonder and passion in the Crystal Ring, to the simple joy of walking together through this everyday yet transformed world. How delicious it had been to stroll among human crowds pouring from theatres or public houses, mingling with them while knowing that he and Charlotte were different, dangerous. Oh, a foolish amusement, yet strangely acute, and innocent. Karl loved to watch Charlotte's myriad reactions as she rediscovered the realm of mortals with vampire perceptions; a delight Ilona had denied him. The headiness of being together and free, for the first time.

Her wonder inevitably gave way to darker thoughts. Beside the river, Karl sensed her growing sombre and withdrawn. Perhaps beginning to weigh the enormity of what had happened.

After a time she asked, "How often will I feel the thirst?"

She always wanted honesty, not consolation, from him, even though he'd often used the truth to the point of cruelty: a needle to pierce illusions.

"Every night," Karl replied, "once, perhaps twice. How you choose to sate it is up to you, but I advise you not to kill outright, if you can help it. Find two or three victims and take a little from each. You can be as selective as you wish."

"I hope I should not take them indiscriminately."

"Why not?"

Charlotte looked at him in puzzlement.

"You said you try never to prey on people you know, that it was betraying them."

"Yes, but also to save myself pain. I don't want to confront the results of my own evil. Purely selfish. I've known vampires more fastidious than myself, who prey only on those who, in their eyes, deserve it. Wicked people, criminals. You can do that if it helps. But I ask, why prey only on the 'evil'? Who are we to make such distinctions, and where do we draw the line? I think it better for a vampire to be true to its nature. Still, you must choose your victims as you think fit, dearest."

Charlotte paused.

"And it will make them... insane?"

"To some degree. You won't know if they recover or not. Don't concern yourself, don't even think about it, or you'll drive *yourself* mad."

"I… I don't think I shall do that." She looked up at the clouds, her violet eyes glistening with their own vampire light.

"Or you can take the life force of mortals instead of blood, but to do that is almost certain death for the victim; not at once, but of the first trivial illness they catch. And very little pleasure for us."

"I never realised," she said, "how deeply vampires crave warmth… and touch, human touch."

"An awful thing, really. Our downfall. And Kristian, of course –" Karl stopped, cursing himself for having mentioned the name.

"Go on," said Charlotte. "What about him?"

"He insists we all strive to be like him and feed only on auras, because to take blood is a carnal sin. But then, if he didn't have his little group of sinners, he would have no one to save."

"He sounds like a pompous puritan prig."

Karl laughed. "Yes. That's precisely what he is."

Charlotte fell silent for a while.

Then she said, "What will happen if he finds us?"

"Let's pray he does not. He's not omniscient. We can go anywhere in the world we please."

"But I don't want to live as a fugitive! I don't even know that I want to leave England… not just yet."

Karl breathed out softly, wishing he could hold back the relentless flow of reality.

"If Kristian does find us, I may not be able to protect you. Not that I shan't try."

"I don't expect you to!" She raised her head and looked at him, biting her lower lip as if holding something back. She looked purely human, the nervous, passionate girl with whom he'd fallen in love. "Karl…"

"What is it?"

"I have to go back to Cambridge." She spoke hurriedly, as if unsure of his reaction.

Lead weights dragged on his heart, although he'd expected this. "Why?"

"I must speak to them – especially Father. Try to make them understand."

"Oh, Charlotte, no," he said sadly. "You want them to forgive you, but how can they? This is not something that can be forgiven. It's not even fair to ask."

"But I still love them! I can't simply leave them in pain… I thought I wouldn't care but I do. The feeling is worse than ever."

"I don't think I gave the impression that vampires are unfeeling creatures, did I? I told you this would be difficult."

"But not this bad! I didn't know it would be this bad."

Karl saw her pain boiling to the surface and knew he could do nothing to comfort her.

"You're tormenting yourself. I know how hard it is, but you must let them go."

Determination flashed in her face.

"Who are you to tell me that? You kept going back to your family, for years you said."

"Yes, and it was a terrible mistake. I am telling you to learn by what I did wrong."

"Let me make my own mistakes, then. I love them," she said, quiet and resolute. She sat forward, holding her forearms, separating herself from him. "Karl, I would quite like to be on my own for a while."

Her words gave him a jolt.

"It's too soon. You haven't learned how to use your powers. I can't let you –"

"But you can't protect me! You said as much. David and Father tried to cloister me against danger and look what happened. Pointless."

Karl's instinct was to argue, to hold her there. The thought of her walking away into the night felt like part of himself being torn away. The strangest grief, when he'd been self-sufficient for so long. But he thought, *If I let her go she will come back.*

Resisting the temptation to touch her, he said levelly, "Very well. I understand. Go and do whatever you must, Charlotte. I shall go back to Stefan. But remember, you cannot have both your family and me."

She stood up, looking stunned.

"Are you asking me to make a choice?"

"The choice was made when you became a vampire." Karl knew how heartless he sounded. He longed to take her hand, at least to kiss her before she went, but he restrained the impulse. "You cannot go back through the veil."

She went on staring at him for a moment, her amethyst eyes dark with thought. Then she drew back as if rejected, turned, and began to walk slowly away.

Karl stayed where he was, his senses and feelings drawn out after her until he could see her no more. And he told himself over and over again, *If I let her go she will come back.*

At Dr Neville's request, the following day, Elizabeth brought Madeleine home to Cambridge. Now they sat in the drawing room, while Anne and David tried to explain what had happened. Elizabeth reacted with suppressed distaste, but Madeleine was distraught.

"How could Charlotte do this to me?" she cried, and ran from the room in tears.

Anne stared after her, thinking, *Typical of Maddy to take it so personally. Is it losing Charlotte's friendship that's upset her, or is it that she's still jealous over Karl? God knows. Does it matter? The poor girl has every right to be upset. Oh, Charli...*

"What a mess," Elizabeth said tiredly. "And how has poor Henry taken all this?"

"Henry is going to leave," said Dr Neville, who was sitting at an escritoire in the corner, apart from the others. "I shan't try to stop him this time. I don't want him to go, but – he hit Charlotte. I can never forgive him for that."

"It was inexcusable, I know," said David. "But he was under extreme provocation, and von Wultendorf did a damn sight worse than strike her. I still can't believe she went with him of her own free will!"

His father did not reply. He looked grey with strain and burnt-out rage.

David went on, "He must have bewitched her. How could she love him when she'd *seen* him drinking blood, seen –"

"David, stop it!" Dr Neville's eyes were tight shut, his fists clenched. "We don't need reminding."

"Sorry, Father. I don't know. What do you think, Annie?"

"I think we should accept that she wanted to go and no one could have stopped her. Pray that she's safe and will come to her senses, the sooner the better."

"I have to agree, I'm afraid," said Elizabeth. "You might need hypnosis to find *Henry* attractive, but not Karl, I can assure you. I've always said Charlotte was a self-willed madam, no one could see it but me. She knew what she was doing."

Dr Neville struck the writing desk with his fists.

"How could she do this?" he roared. "Commit adultery with that – that… and then to run away with him. What am I going to tell people? I shan't dare show my face among my colleagues. We'll have to leave Cambridge."

"Don't overreact, George," said Elizabeth. "It's not the first scandal in history. If Henry leaves town, you can say Charlotte's gone with him."

"Why say anything at all?" said Anne. "It's no one else's business!"

"But you know what gossips people are," said Dr Neville. "Besides, I have to tell my household staff something. The Maples have been with me for years. I can't lie to them. God, the humiliation."

"For goodness' sake, is that all you can think of?" Elizabeth retorted. "It's your fault she turned out so shy and bookish. You smothered her. She was bound to rebel against it in the most dramatic manner possible."

"Are you blaming me for this?" Dr Neville turned red with anger. "I gave her everything! If it's anyone's fault, it's yours, Elizabeth. You never liked my middle girl because you couldn't turn her into a copy of yourself and I – I should never have let you loose on any of my daughters. But I trusted you, *in loco parentis*. I trusted you!"

Elizabeth gave a tight sigh. "We're not obliged to adore people, simply because we're related. The feeling was mutual, I assure you. To be frank, I didn't like Annette either, always looking down her saintly nose at my decadent ways."

"Don't you dare speak ill of Annette!"

Anne flinched at her father-in-law's anger. *Elizabeth, don't. He'll have a heart attack at this rate.*

"All I'm saying is that Annette wasn't perfect, neither am I and neither is Charlotte. You liked Karl once, remember? I believe you'd be just as furious if she'd eloped with the Prince of Wales. You simply can't bear the thought of her loving anyone except you!"

"That's absurd."

"If you'd only face the truth –"

"Oh, do stop it!" Anne said in exasperation. "What good is it to blame each other?"

Elizabeth looked away, inspecting her fingernails.

Eventually she said more mildly, "I'm sorry, George." To Anne's surprise she went to him and placed her hand on his shoulder. Even more shocking, she was struggling not to cry. "You know I'm vile when I'm upset. I don't mean it."

"No tears now," he said, awkwardly patting her hand. "You were always the strong one, Lizzie. If you break down, how can I cope?"

"We'll manage, dear. We always do, somehow." Elizabeth left the room, her chin in the air, hiding her feelings again.

When she had gone, Dr Neville sank down on an upright chair by the window and put his head in his hands.

"What is he?" he said, anguished. "A murderer, not even properly *human*. What's he done to my darling Charlotte?"

Anne went to him and put her arms around his bulky shoulders. David followed, but hung back, at a loss.

"Don't upset yourself, Father," David said. "We'll find her."

"No," Dr Neville said firmly. "You're not even to try. I made her leave, I won't beg her to come back. If she returns of her own accord – well, then I might consider forgiveness." Tears oozed between his wrinkled eyelids. "Elizabeth's right, it is my fault. I destroyed her life. Now I'm paying. Her mother, Fleur, Charlotte – God Almighty, how much more must I be punished?"

"Don't, Prof," Anne said, unable to soothe him. "You still have us."

Dr Neville nodded. Outwardly he regained control, but he looked bereft, beyond comfort.

"I had better go up and see how Madeleine is," he said. "She's my only daughter now. I've never been a proper father to her."

* * *

Alone, Charlotte did not feel lonely or vulnerable. She felt complete. The night seemed expansive, shimmering around her. She was drifting through it, completely part of it, calm, open to every sensation. The air – although misted with smoke and river smells – was deliciously fresh and cold on her skin. She walked and walked with no direction, simply floating.

At this moment she did not need Karl. She wanted no one to distract her from the strangeness, the wonder and pain of transformation. She was awe-struck, still poised between euphoria and horror, and the memory of her departure from Cambridge had taken on a white-hot vividness she had never experienced in life...

That look in Father's eyes. And Anne – how could I betray her when she stood by me throughout my wildness and selfishness, never condemned me? And Maddy... what will she feel when they tell her? God, I never knew how deep these bonds go, deeper than love. I don't care what Karl says. If I never saw them again I couldn't bear it.

Warehouses and cranes loomed against the sky; the dark bulks of cargo ships sat in the water, ugly and menacing. The darkness was alive with the creak of ropes, the slap of water, the scratching of rats. She'd wandered into an area that she would never before have dreamed of entering, by day or night. Now it no longer mattered. Even in the bleakness there were entrancing patterns. No danger could touch her, even here.

She was the danger.

As the realisation hit her, she wrapped her arms around herself.

"God," she gasped. "Oh God, what has happened to me?"

A girl on her own with no coat or hat, in the depths of night. How odd she must look, to anyone who saw her... and she sensed eyes in the shadows, following her, perhaps thinking they saw a ghost. Her normal self-consciousness had vanished. She sat down on a low concrete wall, oblivious to anything but the flowering of thought and sensation inside her.

They are thorns, these feelings. I see more clearly and feel more acutely, joy, pleasure... and sorrow. Karl didn't tell me... Oh, but didn't he say, "There are no words"? All I can see is the disappointment in Father's eyes, David's dismay... They must hate me for this.

This fact seemed perfectly, agonisingly obvious.

She said out loud, "They hate me and I cannot bear it. What am I going to do?"

Heat fell across her back like sunlight. Then a man sat down beside her, making her start. She'd felt his warmth from a distance but had failed to take notice.

"Now, pet." His voice was slurred with drink. "Bit late ter be wanderin' around on yer own, ain't it?"

His thick shabby coat stank; his eyes were narrow under the brim of a grimy cap, and his slack mouth was framed by stubble. He was threatening, repulsive. She wanted to shout, "Leave me alone!" and run for her life – yet she didn't move. That was a human reaction. With mild surprise she found that in reality, his presence simply did not matter.

"Don't be frightened, gel," he said, as if coaxing a nervous kitten. "Run away from yer 'usband? Or yer old dad?"

"Yes," she said. And to her own amazement, as if watching herself from outside, she started to cry.

"There, there, darlin'. Yer must be freezin'." He edged closer. When she didn't recoil, he grew bolder. He put a hesitant arm around her, unsure of her reaction. Beneath his caution, she sensed desire, heightened by this unexpected opportunity.

Although his coat was musty with sweat and smoke and stale beer, and his grotesque crude courtship filled her with disgust, she found her true self completely beyond these surface feelings. He was warm and human. He was not rejecting her; he wanted to hold her, to say, "Everything's all right, dear," as her own loved ones could not.

So she turned and put her arms about him, let her face slide down between his collar and the moist gritty skin. He gave a sort of shudder.

"Oh. There now, pet, no more tears."

Easy as kissing him, she nipped the flesh between her teeth, felt it break, felt the current of blood fountain gently against the roof of her mouth.

This was all the love and comfort she had wanted. Consolation for every loss, every harsh word... Fulfilment. All her pain was gone in a rush of light and energy and her heart was singing with relief, like the relief when Karl had first put his arms around her and kissed her...

But she was drifting. The man slumped against her and she came back to herself and shoved him away, repelled. Now she was on her feet, staring at his insensible bulk, overwhelmed by disgust both at him and at herself. She wanted to wash. Horrible image of Lady Macbeth, scrubbing her hands raw...

If I washed in holy water would it take this curse from me? Or the blood of the lamb, communion wine...

Charlotte turned and ran blindly, carried by the warmth of stolen blood, horror ringing though her.

Did I think I could take blood just once, as a single forgivable sin? No, it will happen again and again and...

In a cobbled lane she stopped, sensing a presence. Not the warm moist radiance of a human this time, but a jet-black hardness leaning on her mind.

A vampire.

"Karl?" she said uncertainly, looking around. In the cone of light beneath a street lamp she saw a tall broad figure slip out of the Crystal Ring into the visible world. Black hair, black clothes of the last century, the face stark white. His sheer size was intimidating, but the harsh strength of his features transfixed her. And the domineering power that poured from his eyes... not menace, but *benevolence*.

She knew at once who he was. But nothing Karl told her could have prepared her for the shock of meeting Kristian in the flesh. The dazzling awe she felt seemed to assault her from outside her, like a rain of physical blows. All her preconceptions were torn away. It was like confronting Lucifer and finding him no horned demon but an angel of light, radiating not evil but kindness, mercy, the hope of salvation. Every balm her tormented soul needed.

"Charlotte," he said. He spoke English with a rolling accent she couldn't identify. "Don't run from me. Do you know who I am?"

"Kristian," she whispered. It was all she could do not to fall to her knees.

His lips curved, a large beauty mark on his cheek rising with the smile.

"No doubt Karl told you I am a complete monster. I am not. I won't harm you. I know the spiritual pain you are suffering. So cruel of Karl to transform you then abandon you. And typical of him. Yet I don't blame him. I would have chosen you myself."

His last words slid heavily through her, like nails through flesh. She was pinned to the ground by his overpowering will.

"Don't fear me," he said gently. "You are too lovely to destroy. I suppose Karl also told you there is no God. He is wrong. Poor soul, he will return to the fold one day. But you have faith in God, don't you, Charlotte?"

"I don't know," she said, her voice almost failing.

"Ah, his paucity of spirit has infected you. But it's not too late. Let me reassure you. God exists, and He is on our side." Kristian spoke with warmth and authority that swallowed her. She wanted reassurance so desperately... "I shall answer your questions and pour balm on your wounds. Come with me, Charlotte."

"Where?"

"I'm taking you home." He made the word *home* sound so complete, so desirable. By instinct she trusted him – yet she did not trust her own instincts. She remembered everything Karl had told her about Kristian, yet she still yearned to surrender. The turmoil was tearing her apart.

"No – no I can't," she said, edging away.

His voice was warm but imperative.

"You have no choice, my child."

Warnings shrilled through her. Kristian must be the only creature left who had the power to resurrect her human fears.

I didn't understand why Karl could never escape or defeat him – until now...

She turned to run, but he caught her arm. *The Crystal Ring!* She slipped into the other-realm, but the reflex came too slow; her new abilities were still foreign, and she couldn't move fast enough. She experienced one moment of freedom – then Kristian was with her, his wolfish limbs entwining around hers.

She fought. The Ring disorientated her and she flailed like a first-time skater on ice. And now she was bound in his arms as if by steel hoops. Powerless, she felt his fangs drive into her neck, felt her strength bleeding away and a black chill spreading through her. Hideous sensation. Meanwhile the surly beauty of the Crystal Ring wheeled beneath them as they travelled.

"God allows only His immortal children here." Kristian's voice filled her head. "Look on this with awe and humility. We walk through the mind of God. Your soul is too small to appreciate how privileged and blessed you are."

When Kristian called the Crystal Ring the mind of God, she recalled her own revelation and knew he was wrong. Not that she could speak. Fear became panic at the impossibility of escape and she thought, *Oh, Karl, where are you? What will happen to us now?*

In the Ring it was hard to judge the passage of time, an hour or two, perhaps. Charlotte tried to memorise the undulating patterns of the hills as they flowed past, their colours and the distinctive flow of magnetic lines… For when she escaped, she must be able to find her way back. Then, with a vertiginous rush, they were out of the Crystal Ring and standing in a windowless stone chamber.

The change of atmosphere assaulted her senses. She felt weak, ill, her whole body crushed and bruised. And so thirsty. Kristian had taken her blood, and she burned as if he'd stolen her most precious possession.

"Welcome to Schloss Holdenstein." Kristian moved around the chamber, lighting candles and wall torches.

She stared in astonishment at a carved ebony throne on a dais, gleaming in the light of oily naked flames. The castle was like a monastery untouched for centuries. And while she was on fire with thirst and bewilderment, she became aware that the centre of her mind was cool, clear and observant. Karl had said, *"Vampires can distance themselves…"* A survival mechanism, of course.

"How long do you mean to keep me here?" she asked.

Kristian turned round, apparently surprised by her question, as intimidating as a harsh schoolmaster to a tiny child. He moved to the throne and rested his hand on the high, ornamented back.

"But this is your home now. All my flock live here."

"I am not one of your flock."

"You are now," he said with sublime confidence.

"What if I want to leave?"

"My children are free to come and go, on the understanding that they remain obedient and always return. But there is... a period of apprenticeship. Think of yourself as a novice, Charlotte."

"Like a nun?" she gasped.

Disapproval clouded his eyes and she drew back.

"A novice," he repeated, "who must earn privilege and trust. Others far stronger than you have confronted me, only to repent their pride and grievous errors. So shall it be with you. It's apparent that you must be broken before I, your master, can reforge you as an immortal should be."

A fearful vision unrolled. She knew he was capable of inflicting unnamed torments until she was reduced to begging forgiveness, confessing to any sin, all sin, promising anything... and at the end, worst of all, *loving Kristian*. Losing her mind and soul to him, believing his every word as gospel.

His presence was overwhelming, but her innate stubbornness would not let her give in. Not when she knew he was wrong. *Be scientific*, she told herself, but it was so hard under the weight of his will.

He came towards her, opening his arms, his fatherly radiance drawing her in. And her own father had rejected her...

"But join me, Charlotte," he said, his voice enthralling. "There's no need to inflict such pain on yourself when you could be received in love. Come to the Father."

"No," she whispered. "No, I won't." She made the walls dissolve and felt the metallic grains of the Crystal Ring coalescing around her.

But Kristian's fingers crushed her arm nearly to the bone as he pulled her back into the chamber.

"It seems to me, dear child, that I snatched you from that heretic Karl not one moment too soon. But no one is beyond redemption. Answer me: will you renounce your love for Karl?"

"No," she said. "Never."

He took her left hand and tugged Karl's ring from her finger. Her protest became a cry of pain as he ripped out a strand of her hair.

Then he stood back and said gravely, "Your loyalty to him is misplaced. I promise, the day is nigh when he will renounce *you*."

Thrill of terror.

"He would never do that!"

"But he will! I am telling you, child, mine is the only love you can trust! I am the Way and the Truth! Everyone else will betray you and die and rot, but *we* endure forever. God and myself."

Kristian held her shoulders, his face full of holy fervour that almost stole her reason.

"Listen to me. It is good that you've turned away from mankind and towards me. Men are vermin. Their God is false; the true Lord is not tolerant of their evil. He destroyed them in the flood and He will do so again. And we are His angels of vengeance!"

She thought incredulously, *He's mad!* But his words were strangely moving, and she could see how someone more vulnerable might embrace his ideas. To her, though, Kristian's pronouncements were stage rhetoric. He could transport her for a time, but when she left the theatre she would be herself again, unchanged.

She said, "If you destroy everyone, on whom will you feed?"

The anger of his response shook her.

"How dare you question the intentions of God? The daughter of a scientist –" he made the word sound like *satanist* "– are you not? I see the filth of that corruption is very deep in you."

Charlotte stood very still, her gaze fixed on his face, feeling that if she moved he would kill her. But she thought, *So, he hates logic?*

"Karl dabbled in your science," Kristian went on. He released his grip, to her relief. He went to sit in the ebony throne and gazed at her. "What did he learn?"

"I don't know what you mean."

"Tell me what you taught him!" The volume of his voice hurt her sensitive ears and she flinched, trembling.

"Everything we could, really. What we know of the structure of matter, the properties of elements, how to set up experiments in the lab, the principles of radioactivity. We were looking for isotopes, you see, forms of elements that –"

"Enough! This is heresy!"

"I don't know what you want me to say!" she retorted.

"Karl knows something. He's plotted against me for years."

"No. He wanted you to leave him alone, that's all."

"Don't defend him! He knows something and I want you to

tell me what it is!"

Charlotte stared at Kristian, dumbfounded. Then she thought, *He's frightened of Karl! He's frightened of science. And he's deranged, there's no reasoning with him...*

And the more he sees my fear, the more he can control me... oh, God help me find a way through this... How dare I call on God? I have only myself.

Her internal strength kept her intact. Now she let years of self-control, of veiling her inner self, come to her aid.

She said calmly, "I cannot think what Karl could have learned from us that could possibly harm any vampire."

"How, then, did he destroy the creature I made in his image?"

"I killed it," she said, staring straight into his flint-black eyes. "I killed it with ice colder than the *Weisskalt*. The double was fragile because it had no mind."

She tensed, waiting for a shout or a blow, but none came. To her frustration, Kristian plainly did not believe her. He was laughing.

"Oh, you are foolish, trying to protect Karl. Yet... if not for you, the new Karl would never have left my side. *You* drew him away to his doom. You have a lot to answer for... But it is born of naivety, not malevolence. You are so young, my daughter, and I am too harsh."

He stood and held out his hand, like a parent to a child. She suspected his sudden kindness was a trick, part of his plan to wear her down, but the change was such a relief that it was all she could do not to take the proffered hand.

"Come, I will find someone to look after you and see that you are fed." *Fed.* The word vibrated through her. "We shall talk again later."

"Then may I leave?"

Kristian's voice remained reasonable, but his pupils became thorns.

"Not yet. And if you try, I promise you will never see Karl again."

For a time, Karl walked slowly along the embankment in the direction that Charlotte had taken. He could not find her, but he didn't try too hard, knowing she wouldn't want to be found.

Eventually he returned to Stefan's flat, stepping directly through the Crystal Ring into the brilliance of the drawing room.

He was preoccupied, off his guard. The scene struck him like lightning. Niklas was standing near the window, smiling vacantly at a point on the far wall. Stefan and Pierre were seated at opposite ends of the chaise longue. And between them, his presence cloaking the room like a great dark wing, sat Kristian.

They all stared at Karl, grim-faced, as if they'd been waiting for him for hours.

A huge weight of dismay fell on Karl.

I knew he must come after us – but so soon. Less than a day we've had! Thank God Charlotte's not with me – but how can I warn her, how can I keep her away?

Stefan said, "He knows, Karl." He and Pierre were glaring at Karl. Perhaps they'd betrayed him, but he doubted it. If they had, they would surely look apologetic rather than reproachful.

Ignoring them, Karl inclined his head to Kristian.

"To what do I owe this visit?"

"Oh, many things, Karl," Kristian replied. "Many things. You don't have to ask, do you?"

"Tell me," said Karl, folding his arms.

"You destroyed the beautiful being I made in your image."

"How do you know?"

Kristian's eyes narrowed and he dug his fingers into his own throat.

"I felt it! Just as I felt the heavens shudder when *you* were slain! Only this time, there was no body to be healed."

That must mean Kristian had been to the Nevilles' house. With a sense of foreboding Karl asked, "And how did you discover this?"

"Oh, don't fret for your wretched human friends. They did not even see me. I had no inclination to touch them – not yet – but I could have done, Karl. You do not even begin to appreciate the forbearance I have shown, again and again, under the severest provocation from you!"

"You have the very patience of a saint," Karl said without inflection.

"Yes, I have." Kristian stood. His height made the room seem tiny and delicate, like a doll's house. He was out of place, as massive as a bull. "I think you are sick, Karl. To kill a creature that was so nearly *you* was like destroying yourself. Is that what you want?"

"To create the replica in the first place was sick," Karl replied. "A thing without a mind!"

"That is for me to judge! You had no right! I should punish you for that alone, but it's only one of your sins. You promised you'd come back, but you lied. Instead you create a vampire without my permission. You seduce Stefan and Pierre into helping you – even knowing that I'd punish them for it! You are the Devil, Karl."

"I thought you didn't believe in the Devil."

Kristian shouted, "Even knowing that Charlotte could not be permitted to live!"

Karl's dread was so fierce now that he battled to keep his face emotionless. He thought desperately, *How do I get him away from here before she comes back?*

Into the silence Stefan said, "We didn't tell him, Karl. He just knew."

"Stefan speaks the truth," said Kristian. "You cannot hide anything from me. You could not save Charlotte from me."

"What do you mean, *could not*?" Karl said. No hiding his horror now. "For God's sake tell me what you mean!"

"Not so aloof now, my friend? Charlotte is already at Schloss Holdenstein."

"I don't believe you."

Kristian reached into his pocket and took out a ring with a red stone. Tangled around it were strands of wavy russet hair, sparkling gold where the light caught.

"Do you believe this?"

Karl took the ring. It was the one he'd given Charlotte, without question. And her hair was unmistakable.

Their eyes were scorching him, even Niklas's. Karl felt terror, despair, rage, but he pushed down every emotion into his glacial core.

"Yes, they are hers," he said. "Is she still alive?"

"Not as far as you are concerned." Kristian's face was set, his eyes black with spite. "You have gone too far. Your human friends are going to die. Stefan and Niklas and Pierre will be taken to the *Weisskalt*. And Charlotte will love only me."

Blackness surrounded Karl. Kristian's wings closed over him, suffocating.

"What do you want of me?" he said tonelessly.

"I will make no bargains with you," Kristian cried. "Don't tell me, 'I'll do anything if only you spare them!' You told me often enough that your love cannot be bought. Well, this time I take you at your word. This is the grave you have dug for yourself. If you won't return to the fold, you shall be outcast forever – and every immortal, every human who offers you friendship, I shall strike down!"

The embittered anguish in Kristian's eyes shocked Karl. And his words shredded Karl's faint hopes of negotiation.

Then it came to him: the only answer. An idea that had been brewing since he'd been brought back to life. No, even before that. Since that night at Fleur's, when he had tried so desperately to sever himself from Charlotte and failed.

I will do this. Yes, let it begin... whether I succeed or fail, the only answer is to give in.

Kristian was a huge figure whose invisible dark wings enfolded the world. Light blazed around his head and angels sang on his shoulders.

"Are you giving up on me?" Karl said quietly, gazing at him.

"Yes!"

Karl shook his head. He let his eyes soften and allowed tears to form.

"But you never give up. Don't..."

"What? Abandon you?" Kristian laughed, a ghastly sound.

Karl moved to the window, leaned on the sill and looked out. Dawn was breaking.

"I initiated Charlotte because I could not bear this loneliness any longer. But it did not work. Once she changed, I felt nothing for her. The act was desperate and only made me realise... that nothing can fill the emptiness of this existence."

"I could have told you that. Nothing ever can, unless you embrace both God and his messenger, your master, me."

"But it's taken me all this time and my disappointment with Charlotte to make me see..."

"What, Karl?"

In the window, Karl saw reflections of Stefan and Pierre staring at him in absolute astonishment. He was about to humiliate himself in front of them, and didn't care.

"It's too hard for me to say. My pride, you know."

Then Kristian's face began to change as well.

"Pride is a sin, Karl."

"I know. And I have done nothing but sin against you since you made me. I doubt I can ever be absolved, because I cannot... Kristian, say it for me, please."

"Very well," said Kristian, moving towards him. "What is Charlotte, compared to me? She will only disappoint you, as Ilona did. I am the only one who never betrayed you. I have always been the same. From the beginning I made it clear that I wanted your dedication, and that never changes. My constant love is the only thing of which you can be certain. The world is an abyss; I am the bridge that spans it."

Kristian's words had an astonishing, unexpected effect on Karl – because everything Kristian said was true. When Karl began to weep, he was no longer forcing the tears, he actually could not stop them.

"Yes," he said. "You say it better than ever I could."

Kristian said quietly, "It is brave of you to admit as much. This could be a first step to absolution, if that is what you want."

Karl looked up, wild hope in his eyes.

"No. I deserve punishment. I won't beg for anyone's life; not Stefan's nor Pierre's, not the humans' or even Charlotte's. Whatever you choose to do is right. But if I could only..."

Kristian's hands closed on his shoulders.

"Say it, Karl."

"Let me come home with you, Father," Karl said with quiet dignity. "Give me time to think. Of course, if you won't permit me, I understand."

Kristian's eyes were wide, his mouth open.

"You would come with me, without conditions – because you *want* to?"

"Yes. I need to. However, I see no point in trying to convince you. After all, you must find it impossible to believe me."

"It is never too late to repent," Kristian breathed. His breath was as cold as a crypt. "If it's true, I shall believe you, because I always

perceive the truth. But if you want to prove yourself sincere…
Would you renounce your love for Charlotte *to her face*?"

"Of course," Karl said without hesitation.

Although Kristian tried to respond with priestly gravity, his
naked elation was painful to see.

*God Almighty, do I really mean this much to him? Or is it only
the thrill of victory?*

"Come, Karl, we'll go now. Oh, my beloved son…"

And he drew Karl away from the window, ready to enter the
Crystal Ring. Kristian's gaze was pinned to Karl and he seemed to
have forgotten everything else: the other vampires – and the Nevilles
too, Karl hoped. All that mattered to him was Karl's repentance.

Karl saw, from the blank astonishment in Pierre's and Stefan's
faces, that his change of heart had been utterly convincing.

He had even convinced himself.

Kristian had left Charlotte in the charge of a vampire named Maria,
a girl with straight dark-blonde hair, an elfin face, and the eyes of
a fanatic. She never smiled or said a word. Perhaps she'd been
instructed not to speak to Charlotte. All her questions, "How long
have you been here? Where do you come from?" went unanswered.

Maria brought a peasant woman for Charlotte. The old
woman's face was so sweet and kind that it was all Charlotte
could do to feed. She took only a few swallows, barely enough to
revive her strength, hating herself for wanting more.

"Take her away," Charlotte said, devastated. "Please let her go.
If I can't choose my own victims I won't feed."

So Maria took the woman away, and Charlotte was left alone
in a stone room, curled up on a wooden bed, watching flames
leaping in the fire grate. She knew the door wasn't locked, no
point in locking up a vampire who could walk through walls, if
she had the strength.

I might escape… but I daren't try, not yet. What will happen?

Suddenly all recent events loomed like a vast overblown
painting on the ceiling of a chapel, nightmares of horror and
ecstasy. The strangeness of her transformed body; the impossibility
of believing or accepting what she had become. She'd always been

afraid of people... now, desiring not to flee but to embrace them in the most intimate way... it all went against every layer of her nature. And yet, inside, she had a diamond-tough core that *could* accept, that was wide open to the new and impossible.

Shake off this empty-headed bewilderment, this guilt, said her inmost self. *The ecstasy you shared with Karl in the Crystal Ring, the sweetness of feeding, the intensity of it, Charlotte, the enchantment... These are the things that matter. You know it. All the rest is human detritus.*

And this was not some new vampire self speaking. It was the true voice of her soul, as it had always been. Hours went by and she spent them wandering in the garden of her thoughts, not noticing how time passed.

Then she felt a sudden presence approaching, and she looked up to see Karl entering the room. Relief and delight caught her full in the chest like a flood and she rushed to him, crying, "Oh, thank God! I thought I'd never see you again!"

There was no tenderness in Karl's face, however. He did not so much catch her in his arms as stop her, holding her away from him.

"Charlotte, I'm so sorry," he said, putting her gently aside.

Then she saw a look in his eyes that unleashed streams of foreboding.

Something's happened to him. He's changed.

"No, I'm all right," she said. "Kristian hasn't hurt me. I don't know how he found me, he just appeared and –"

"It doesn't matter."

"Don't you want to hear what happened?"

"It doesn't matter," he repeated leadenly. She felt as if he'd struck her.

"Karl, what is it?" she said, beginning to panic now.

She tried to see through his ice-cold stare to some hidden tenderness, some secret communication. It was like looking into granite.

He said, "It was all a mistake, Charlotte. I thought I had found an answer in you but I was wrong. I cannot fight Kristian any more. It's taken me all this time to see that he was right all along. I'm going with him."

"You can't!" She stared at Karl, trying to draw some response to her distress; searching for a hidden sign that he didn't mean what he was saying. There was none. Karl was firmly sealed against her, as he'd never been before.

"Is it because he threatened me?" she said.

"No. We're past all hope of bargaining, even for your life."

"Then why? You can't *want* to go with him?"

Karl let out an almost imperceptible sigh. His eyes filled with sadness, but they were remote, not seeing her. Despair scythed the ground from under her. Only a last strand of pride kept her from falling to her knees. That it should end like this, that Kristian should have his victory after all...

Yet Karl had warned her, *One of us may change*. Something had happened to him, a change of heart she could not have anticipated. Or was it that Kristian, having worn him down over the years, had finally, horribly broken him?

A small voice of reason spoke deep in her mind. Even if Karl were playacting, of course he could only convince Kristian by convincing *her*. Therefore there was no point in arguing with him. She must seem convinced – not hard at all, when Karl's words filled her with utter terror. In her heart she knew that rejecting her was the last thing he'd ever wanted. But if surrender to Kristian had become his only possible option – Oh, then, without question, he meant every word. He would do what he had to – even if it meant discarding her.

"It's my fault, isn't it?" she said. "I was your last attempt to break away from Kristian."

He looked away from her.

"Of course it is not your fault. It's all mine. I know I've treated you with unforgivable cruelty. I can only hope that one day you'll come to love Kristian as I do. Then you will understand why I must do this."

Karl was a stranger again, like the first time they'd met. Only this time his eyes were not glamorous windows to another world but blank, closed doors. She saw no way to reach him.

Oh God, he truly means this. What has Kristian done to him? She backed away as if she'd been hit in the stomach.

"Forgive me, Charlotte," said Karl.

"I can't."

His face remained as deadpan as the *doppelgänger*'s.

"I should have foreseen this. If you must return to your family, you are free to do so. You still have them."

She tried to say, "I have nothing," but no sound emerged.

And before she could protest, Karl turned and walked to the open door. She stood rooted for a moment, then ran after him.

He closed the door in her face. She heard his footsteps retreating, like hammer blows on iron. Blows raining on her heart and head.

"I have nothing," she repeated, closing her eyes. "Except myself." Then bitter tears began to flow and she hugged herself against her convulsive sobs, thinking, *If vampires are meant to be heartless why does this hurt so much?*

She felt the air shiver and looked around eagerly, her tears ceasing. *Karl?*

But it was Kristian who stood there, his pale face aglow with benevolence. She loathed him fiercely.

"My dear child, it grieves me to see you in such torment," he said. "Sometimes nothing is harder than obeying God's will. You must forgive Karl. I predicted he would renounce you, did I not? So you lose your lover – yet you'll find a greater love to replace him."

"Karl and I are allowed to love only you." Her throat ached in a spasm of grief. "Not each other. I understand."

"Good. Immortals aren't meant to couple like humans, we are intended for a greater destiny. Our devotion is to God, we are the deliverers of His holy retribution."

"I don't believe in your God," she said.

"You will, my child."

"No, I can't. I know He doesn't exist." She held his gaze, too wretched to be frightened any more. Before, she'd been afraid to tell Kristian the truth, but now there was nothing else to say.

"But I know He does."

"You're wrong! There is no God in the Crystal Ring. It's a realm created by human thoughts. *Human dreams.*"

The atmosphere rang, as if she'd shouted an obscenity in church.

Menacingly quiet, he asked, "What do you mean by this blasphemy?"

She doubted Kristian would understand, but she had to pursue her argument.

"Everything consists of energy: heat, light, matter. Even *thoughts* create electricity. The Crystal Ring is a dimension where waves of thought become material, and vampires are creatures who can physically perceive that dimension. The Ring's energy is the force that animates us! Mankind's thoughts, not God's. Without mortals we would not –"

Exist, she was about to say, when his fist lashed out and struck her. The blow lifted her off her feet and slammed her into a wall. She fell. Pain throbbed through her bones.

"Sacrilege!"

"But it's true! I had a revelation, Kristian! The Crystal Ring is the collective mind of man! Vampires exist because of human dreams, not those of God or the Devil."

He seized her. The next she knew, his long teeth were in her throat. There was nothing sensual in this violation. Kristian was incapable of sensuality. He took all pleasure and pierced it to death with his puritan guilt, poisoned everyone he touched.

Her strength faded as he went on swallowing, swallowing. His tyranny, the cold weight of him on her body and mind, everything about him disgusted her. She hoped to escape by fainting, but her consciousness clung on tenaciously. She felt every vein burning dry, endured every nuance of agony and weakness.

Now Kristian was dragging her along a dark corridor. Charlotte fought him, demented, but he was vastly stronger. He picked her up and threw her, sent her sprawling over damp flagstones. She heard a door bang shut.

Kristian had locked her in a cell.

She staggered to her feet and flung herself at the door, out of her mind with torment. Then she remembered the Crystal Ring. *Yes – try that – be calm...* But trying to enter the Ring was like throwing herself against a wall of another kind. Invisible, yet thicker than stone. She was trapped... starving.

Kristian looked at her through a grille in the door. The glint of mania in his eyes confirmed that she'd plucked a very raw nerve. That, at least, gave her a small twinge of triumph.

He shouted, "I have known many misguided immortals in my time – but none ever dared utter such evil lies! You will pay for this, Charlotte. Let us see how many days of starvation you can bear until you beg for absolution."

"Why are you frightened?" she cried, shaking the grille. "Is it because I spoke the truth? I received a revelation; you never did! You invented your vision of God to fill the void, because you can't bear to admit to the emptiness inside you!"

He brought his fists down on the door. The boom reverberated like a shell burst.

"Liar! I am the Truth! God chose me as His holy scourge of mankind!"

"How is that possible? There are millions of humans, and only a few vampires. These are delusions of grandeur, megalomania."

"But I have slain millions in my time."

His words shocked her out of her rage. She stared at him, thinking, *Does he believe such a claim?*

"How could you kill so many without being discovered?"

"I do not kill, I send souls to face their judge." His will weighed her down, bending her like a sapling beneath a ton of snow, as his words thundered over her. "I am the wings of God! I take human life silently, never soiling myself with their sweat, filth or blood. I have sucked the life force out of whole populations, all over the world. *Plague*, they call me. *Typhoid, Cholera, Black Death*. A thousand names they give me in their pitiful fear. But my true name is the Vengeance of God."

CHAPTER TWENTY-TWO

IN A WORLD THAT NEVER ENDS

Kristian stood with Karl on the castle balcony, overlooking the green folds of the gorge falling into the Rhine's beaten-silver surface. He studied Karl carefully for signs that his conversion was not genuine. Karl's eyes, normally serene – or hostile, at worst – were now troubled, and for the first time, they seemed to hide nothing. Their amber fire spoke to Kristian: *This is the hardest thing in the world for me, to swallow my pride and admit that you were right and I was wrong, but I am trying. Forgive my arrogance. Give me the guidance I need!*

"Charlotte has some strange ideas," said Kristian. "I fear I'll have to purge her of them before she can truly serve God." And he watched for Karl's reaction, the tiniest hint that Karl still secretly cared for her. He saw none.

"Deal with her as you think fit," Karl replied indifferently. "I know you'll do what's best." And he looked at Kristian with a childlike love that seemed to implore, *Save me. Lift me up, teach me.*

A wonderful contentment spread through Kristian. He could have wept.

"Now I believe you," he said, holding out his hand. In the past Karl would have rejected the gesture in silent contempt. But now he took Kristian's wrist, knelt down and bit into the vein. A single swallow of holy blood. Resting his other hand in blessing on Karl's head, Kristian felt fierce, all-encompassing love. "Oh yes, now I believe. I knew you would come back one day."

"Beloved Father," said Karl.

"I never cared about the others, you know," Kristian said tenderly. "Only you."

Karl looked up and smiled.

"What others?" he said.

Kristian lifted him to his feet and hugged him. Karl leaned his head into Kristian's shoulder, compliant surrender in every line of his body.

"It's a relief not to fight any more."

"Of course. God brought you to me, now let me bring you back to God. Let us go away from here."

"Where?"

"Anywhere, as long as it is with you," said Kristian. "We shall walk and talk together for hours, days. Forever. All the time under heaven is ours."

He led Karl into the Crystal Ring, and at nightfall they hunted together in Vienna.

"I hope your mistake with Charlotte has taught you that humans can offer us nothing," said Kristian. "In time, you will cease taking their blood and steal their life force instead. Much cleaner. You are not destroying them, but dispatching them to receive divine judgment."

Karl said nothing, only accepted this wisdom with proper humility.

Later they walked through the wild white-blue grandeur of the Alps, perhaps the nearest place to the Crystal Ring on Earth.

There Kristian closed his hand around Karl's arm and said gently, "I want you to tell me... all about Charlotte."

Karl sighed faintly, did not reply.

"I know it's difficult," Kristian continued, "but you must confess, for the good of your soul, and hers." Excitement smouldered inside him as he spoke. "I want to know everything. About the first time you drank from her. How it felt to take her life. You must confess to be absolved." His voice shook a little with anticipation... No. Purest holy fervour.

For a moment he thought Karl might revert to his old ways, and refuse. Then, to his joy, Karl responded.

"I can do better: show you all the places we walked and talked together, everything that happened. There is so much to tell you."

"Yes, yes," Kristian said eagerly. "Take me there."

"Many strange and frightening things happened to us," Karl added. "Events that made no sense. If you'd help me to understand..."

"Come, then. By God's grace, I shall give you all the answers."

It could happen, eventually, that I begin to despise Karl for his surrender, Kristian mused. *Ah, the luxury of despising him while he still adores me... but not for a very long time.* In the glow of triumph, Kristian would forgive Karl anything, go anywhere with him. In the light of Karl's beauty, Kristian's heart melted entirely from stone to honey.

Hour after hour Charlotte lay on the icy floor of the cell, her thirst a constant scream within her. She prayed for oblivion that would not come. No sleep, no reprieve from the black fire that slowly stripped her veins from her muscles, flesh from her bones. If she tried to move, the effort caused excrucation. She had no choice but to remain stretched out and gasping like a speared fish.

She prayed unashamedly – not to Kristian's dark God, but to the gentle golden presence of King's College Chapel. She prayed for Kristian to return...

But if he does I won't give in. I will never tell him he's right. I just want... want... Oh God, blood. Waking visions of blood, flooding down the walls of the cell, pouring over her in waves... but never, never a drop on her parched tongue.

Karl will come back and save me, she thought again and again. Hours went by and still he did not come.

Is this what Karl meant by hell? This is the sin, this is the punishment. My punishment for wanting this, even though he warned me... For a few desperate moments she railed against Karl. *Why do this to me, when you knew how terrible it would be? Why did you come back, why not leave me alone? Father and David were right. You are evil and you deceived me completely.*

Charlotte curled around her anguish and let out a soundless groan that went on and on. It was not sleep she craved but death. Even death itself betrayed her.

Time no longer went forwards but spread in all directions. She moved blindly through the maze of time, one way then another, but the walls were infinitely elastic and would not let her through. She had been here forever... when she was suddenly brought back to reality by five spots of acid eating through the flesh of her upper arm.

Fingertips.

Her body was so desiccated that the touch was pure agony. Looking down at her was the most beautiful female face Charlotte had ever seen; eyes glowing like Karl's in a perfect oval. Although her hair was no longer scarlet but dark and cut short, Charlotte recognised Ilona.

"Oh dear. Poor Charlotte," Ilona said mockingly. "What a state you are in."

Am I imagining this? Ilona seemed to be speaking her thoughts.

"I could have told you this would happen, that Karl would take you, use and betray you. Do you still wonder why I detest him?"

If one thing could deepen her nightmare, it was this. Ilona's eyes glittered with spite in the darkness. Then the sharp points of her teeth plunged into Charlotte's blistered throat.

She lifted Charlotte off the floor, withdrew her fangs and threw her down again with an exclamation of disgust.

"There's no blood left in you! Do you know there's no torment worse than starvation to a vampire?"

Charlotte tried to speak and found that, despite her physical distress, she was still lucid.

"I suppose Kristian sent you to torment me."

"It's amusing to gloat," said Ilona. Her Austrian accent was more marked than Karl's, her voice light and crystal sharp. "If you knew how many times Kristian has done this to me!"

Charlotte was shaken by the anger that Ilona roused in her. She felt no fear, only ice-white rage.

"You murdered my sister!" she cried, rising up to lash out with strength that came from nowhere and subsided as fast.

Ilona evaded the blow easily and laughed.

"Don't be a fool. You would kill your *own* sister if she came in now. You know how this thirst feels! It recognises no faces or names. It has no conscience!"

Charlotte stumbled back, and kept her feet by leaning against the wall. She used every shred of her will to push the thirst away.

"Don't you have a mind to control it?" she retorted. "I didn't realise how much I loved my family until this happened. *You* feel nothing but hatred."

"All this talk of love and hate," said Ilona, rolling her eyes. "You have been a vampire for all of five minutes. You are a child, you understand nothing of my feelings."

"You did not *need* to murder Fleur. You did it out of sheer viciousness. Not all vampires are like you."

"Aren't they? Those that aren't are hypocrites." Ilona folded her bone-smooth arms. "Like my father."

She moved closer, raised a hand and stroked Charlotte's hair. It was like the cupboard love of a cat whose claws may be unsheathed on a whim.

"Isn't it a nice thought, Charlotte, that all those humans who hurt you, you can now hurt in turn? You can lure them into desperate love, only to turn and mock them, destroy them. You can take revenge on the human race, over and over again."

"That is sick, Ilona. I think you are mad."

"Yes. Isn't there something romantic about a mad, sick woman who is also beautiful?" Ilona grinned in self-mockery. "Don't you want justice, Charlotte? Revenge?"

"No. I did not become a vampire for that."

"That is funny, considering you tried to kill me a few minutes ago. We are nearly all mad, dear. The awful thing for most of us is that we know it. Kristian is the only one who's insane and doesn't realise... and Karl, poor thing, is the only vampire who is sane. Or was, until he gave in to Kristian."

"I don't believe he's forsaken me. He wouldn't."

"But he has!" Ilona's face transformed with a flash of sheer pain. "You think he is so perfect. Let me give you a hint of what he's really like. I did not ask to become a vampire; he gave me no choice. He took me away from my husband, from everything I knew, and he expected me to love him for it!"

"I know," Charlotte said quietly. "He told me. But I don't believe you hate him for it, because you so obviously relish what you are."

"I am a very good vampire, it's true. He wanted me as a

vampire, so that is exactly what I gave him, to the very limit." A visible shudder passed through her, chilling for being unaffected. "So you think you know everything about me. But did he tell you about the child I lost?"

"No," Charlotte said, startled.

Ilona's misery was artless, all arrogance gone.

"When he took me away from my husband, I was expecting a child. The transformation killed it. That's what I can't forgive him for. That's why I abhor him. None of the rest. Just that."

A wave of purely mortal horror crested over Charlotte's pain.

"He – he never told me."

"No, he wouldn't," Ilona said shortly, "because he doesn't know. I never told him and I never shall."

"Why not?"

"I couldn't! The loss was too terrible to share with the one who'd caused it. And of course he would have been grief-stricken, devastated, all the human things Karl can be – but it would not have been my secret any more. It was my grief, my anger – too deep to be shared – too great to be diluted by telling *him*."

She paused at the top of a breath.

After a moment Charlotte asked, "Do you still feel grief for this now?"

"Not now." Ilona was gazing at the floor, pensive, withdrawn. "But that was where it began. This tree of bitterness, rooted in that one sorrow. He made me immortal, but he took my child, my real immortality, away..." She looked up and added softly, "You are the only person I have ever told."

Against her will, Charlotte felt sympathy for Ilona.

"Why? To make me hate Karl?"

"Just to make you realise you don't know everything." Ilona's glass-splinter smile returned, with less conviction than before. "If it makes you see Karl as he really is, so much the better. Selfish, arrogant, uncaring, guiltless – like father, like daughter."

"He knows he made a mistake with you. And he's suffered for it. He still loves you."

"No, he doesn't. He rejected me, Charlotte... because I killed your sister. All the terrible things I've done, and he never turned away from me... until I hurt *you*."

Charlotte saw through Ilona's mask then. However much she claimed to loathe Karl, his rejection had devastated her. Just as it had destroyed Charlotte.

"Where is he?" Charlotte asked.

"I don't know. He and Kristian went away together. The moment Karl relented, Kristian forgot all about me, and they've left you here to rot."

"Gone away? I don't believe it!"

"Believe it, darling." Ilona's expression was solemn, without mockery. She came to Charlotte, put a hand on her shoulder, leaned her head there too. "There is something about you, Charlotte. You defeat me. I want to be cruel to you but I can't. What's the point? I am not hurting Karl or annoying Kristian by it. They have abandoned us both."

She's speaking the truth, Charlotte thought. *Karl isn't coming back. I saw it in his eyes.* Despite the feeling that Ilona was snaring her into a bond that she did not want, Charlotte's hand crept involuntarily to caress the silky dark-red hair. And she stood frozen under Ilona's ivory-delicate hands as a sense of futility unrolled before her.

What use was taking revenge on Ilona, when Charlotte herself would feed on the brothers and sisters of others, if she had the chance? However hard she tried, she could not hate Karl's daughter. Even as Ilona stood there with venom issuing from her blood-rose mouth, there was an awful charm about her. Something of Karl.

"We've both been betrayed," said Ilona. Then, "I can't watch you suffering, while my veins are overflowing."

A barbed thrill of hunger.

"Don't mock me."

"I mean it." Ilona tipped her head to one side, curled one hand around Charlotte's head. Charlotte stared at the pale sweep of her neck. "I am giving you back your strength. Only don't drink me dry, darling."

Charlotte fell, biting so savagely that Ilona stiffened and gasped. Vampire blood burst into her parched mouth, sharp and strange. Less satisfying than human blood, yet filling her with sparkling energy. And she was ravenous. She forgot where she was and on whom she was feasting, until Ilona – with very little effort – pushed her away and held her off.

"Enough," she said.

They looked at each other. Still a trace of bitter, twisted humour in Ilona's eyes, but more than that, tenderness. Charlotte hated her and loved her. She put her arms around Ilona's neck and they held each other fiercely.

"Now, dearest," Ilona said softly, "I am going to let you out."

Karl had never expected to see this place again; the manor house in the silent woods, its stone walls dappled with age, the small leaded windows watchful. The sight arrested him with an unexpected surge of dread. Unreal, it looked, flickering as if on film. As remote as a cinematic image, yet sinister, overdrawn and under-lit in grainy monochrome.

The abandoned renovation work made the building look even more desolate. A great mistake, to interfere with its secrets. The cleared path was vanishing again under nettles and brambles. Ivy cleaved to the walls as if trying to pull them down into the embrace of the earth.

"What is this place?" asked Kristian.

Karl ascended the steps to the iron-shod front door, broke the lock easily with one hand.

"A derelict house," he said. "I came here with Charlotte. We found something in the cellars that may interest you."

A mass of cold air pushed against them as they entered the hall. Its cathedral chill enveloped them under the soaring, thickly shadowed vault of the ceiling. Karl found the stench of damp and ancient mortar shockingly familiar, evocative. He recalled trying to lull David's suspicions while his blood thirst burned. The luscious heat of Edward's blood quenching his thirst... Madeleine's terror... So much to regret, but not those hours of quietness in Charlotte's company. Then their descent into the cellar. A fathomless darkness beside which even the terrors of the *Weisskalt* paled... from which only Charlotte's sweet blood had saved him.

Did Kristian sense the atmosphere? Karl watched him carefully, but his strong face was impassive, betraying no suspicion or unease.

"I am intrigued," said Kristian. "What do you mean?"

"Don't you know?" Karl looked up into the vault, let his gaze trail downwards over the stone walls, the landing, the dust-thick stairs.

"Tell me."

"This is an ancient house," said Karl. He spoke softly, but his voice echoed. "There is a secret tunnel beneath that's even older. I believe a vampire lived there once."

Kristian turned abruptly to face him, his eyes black pits in his white face.

"A vampire?" he said sharply. "How do you know?"

"We found the bones of his victims in the tunnel. I could feel his presence, although he must have left centuries ago. Do you know who it could have been, Father? Have you ever been here before?"

Kristian folded his arms. His expression was unreadable. There was a horrible suspense in waiting for his answer.

Karl thought, *If a powerful vampire lived here in Kristian's lifetime he must have known, and may even have destroyed the creature himself. In which case he would know about the danger. What's he hiding – his knowledge, or his ignorance?*

Eventually Kristian said, "No, I have never been here. As to whether your supposed vampire was known to me, I may be able to tell if we go down and look."

Karl felt a grim thrill of reluctance and cruelty mixed. He subdued the reaction, keeping his face calm, his eyes innocent.

"This way," he said, leading Kristian into the ashen light of the kitchen. Here the builders' debris lay untouched. He noted the big square sink, lengths of pipe, timber under layers of canvas. And oil lamps.

He made to take one, but Kristian said contemptuously, "What do you want with that, when we see better by night than humans can by day?"

Karl shrugged, and left the lamp where it was. Kristian was right. A beam of light might be deceptively comforting, but it was no more protection against the tunnel than a crucifix against a vampire.

As he opened the cellar door, malodorous air reached up like clawed fingers.

God, to face this again.

The foreboding had not been so bad with Charlotte, when he'd sensed the threat but not understood it. But now he knew what waited...

With Kristian behind him, he began to descend the stairs. The walls were slimy, the miasma of centuries flowing thickly around them. Even to his acute vision, the cellar was as gloomy as a crypt. No colour anywhere. Only shades of black and grey. Again, the aura of a film, larger than life, brooding. Stacks of barrels and chests stood under the arches, their outlines blurred and thick with dirt, cobwebs roping them to the littered floor. Rats scuffled in the shadows.

Rats, insects and darkness held no horrors for Karl, who could walk cheerfully through graveyards. No, it was the memory of incinerating coldness that unsettled him. He heard no ghost voices... but their silence was worse, as if they were holding their breath. Waiting.

Now and then Karl glanced at his companion, but Kristian's face remained the same: unmoved, merely curious.

The moment he perceives danger, he will guess my intention. Why hasn't he sensed it? Could it be that in his arrogance he is deaf to what dwells here – or worse, immune? Karl made his heart a sphere of metal, dewed with ice. He could carry this out only by hardening himself and sealing away all doubts.

The big iron-bound chest that he'd dragged across to conceal the trap was still in position. Evidently Charlotte had told no one how they'd escaped, nor had they explored very thoroughly. He hauled the chest aside, grimacing as it screeched on the stone flags.

Karl paused, looking down the black stairwell. He heard the faint piping of wind across a vast subterranean distance. Darkness lapped, like a millpond that had claimed a thousand lives.

Kristian said impatiently, "Will you go first, or shall I?"

"Wait," said Karl. He let his anxiety creep into his tone. "It was very cold down there."

Kristian sneered. "A little earthly coldness never hurt us. Only the *Weisskalt* can do that."

"But this was an unearthly cold, Father."

Kristian started down the stairs.

"Not afraid, are you, Karl?"

"It was very disturbing. So much that I thought I was going to die. It's dangerous."

"Fear, Karl." Kristian's lips thinned in a smile and he shook his head indulgently. "I am surprised at you. What use have we for fear, when God Himself walks with us? Nothing can harm us. Hold onto me."

Oh, I shall hold onto you, Father, Karl thought grimly. The truth, and a childlike display of nerves – really no pretence – deceived Kristian more effectively than any lie. But foreboding coiled around him, wintry as the sullen air. *What if Kristian feels no danger because nothing here can harm him? I may well die – but there might be no hope of destroying him at all.*

Ilona took Charlotte to a room high in Schloss Holdenstein, with small windows framing views of the river gorge. Charlotte gazed out, finding it miraculous to see the outside world again after her imprisonment. She felt empty, squeezed dry of emotion, while the hunger for human blood lapped constantly through her.

There was no bed in the room, only wardrobes full of clothes, an enamel bath in front of a fire grate, and a full-length mirror.

"Why don't you bathe, while I find you something to wear?" said Ilona. "So primitive, this place. I can't stand it. I must have luxury."

"You don't live here all the time, then?" Charlotte asked.

"God, no! I have houses in Paris, Budapest, Prague... I have rich human lovers. I don't kill them until they begin to bore me. You know, we should both leave here while we have the chance."

"Where will you go?"

"I haven't decided." Ilona searched briskly through a rail of dresses. "But one thing is certain, I have had more than enough of my immortal fathers."

"You don't want to find Karl and Kristian, then?"

"They can both go to hell! Come with me, if you like. I might go to Russia, or America for a change."

Charlotte smiled. "Don't you think the Russians have enough problems, without you? Thank you, but I must go back to Cambridge."

Ilona gave her a look of exasperation.

"Oh, not your precious family again. Then I suppose you'll start looking for Karl, just to reassure yourself that he really did intend to trample your heart to pieces."

A knife of loss cut through her.

"I don't know," Charlotte said. "I can't believe he meant to reject me... but you're right, I can't forget how cold he was. If I found him and he was still the same, I couldn't bear it. I don't know what to do."

"Forget him!" Ilona pulled an armful of clothes from a cupboard and threw them on a chair. "Do you like these?" She shook out a dress of silvery crêpe de Chine and a midnight-blue coat trimmed lavishly with fur. "You know, you won't be able to enter the Crystal Ring for days. Not until you feed enough to recover your strength."

"I don't think it will take days," said Charlotte. "I can sense the Ring now... I think I could go through, if I were a little stronger."

Ilona raised her eyebrows.

"Already? To recover so fast is unusual. I wonder if Kristian has some reason to fear you."

"What reason?"

Ilona smiled thinly and shrugged.

"I've never heard him shout at anyone as he shouted at you when you denied his God. I should think the whole castle heard him."

When Charlotte had bathed and dressed, she left the castle and hunted on the hillsides above the Rhine. Feeding grew a little easier each time, as if the intensity of her need carried her beyond conscience. She felt no horror, only a distant tenderness for her victims. They were only a means to an end; to return to her family, so she could say goodbye.

Beyond that, she saw no future.

I came into this existence for Karl. Without him what's the use?

For now, the stolen life in her veins numbed her against the cruel wires of sorrow.

When Charlotte felt ready to travel, she didn't return to the castle, not even to see Ilona. There seemed no point – and if Kristian's other followers realised she was loose, she daren't risk recapture. She stepped into the Crystal Ring and, terrifying though it was on her own, she found her way home along the paths that Kristian had taken.

In Cambridge, every familiar sight was a shock, vivid and new. Delaying the confrontation, she wandered through the colleges for a time, unable to believe the soft granulation of their walls, their dignity and antiquity. She noticed some undergraduates from the Cavendish staring as they passed her on King's Parade.

"That's not Charlotte Neville, is it?" whispered one. "Never struck me she was such a beauty before." They were not seeing mere beauty, she knew, but her vampire aura, burning through their perceptions.

At last she stood outside her father's house. No sound except the soft rustle of trees against a broken sky, distant birdsong. The cream-grey walls seemed closed against her, but she sensed motes of human warmth within.

How long since I left?

No one had seen her yet. She entered the Crystal Ring briefly, passed through the walls and went up into the bedroom that had been hers.

A shock. It was like a doll's house. She was entranced by every detail, yet – just as she could never step into the dolls' world and live there – she felt disconnected. There was no sense of her mother's spirit in the room any more. No sense of her *self*.

She glimpsed her reflection in a mirror. Another shock: she looked the same. There was nothing supernatural about her. Her face appeared normal, if rather pale, almost lost between the swathe of black fur and her cloche hat.

Charlotte felt light-headed with passive, insidious horror. She thought, *I can never live here again... even if I wanted to*. She left the room and went downstairs in a trance, stopping abruptly at the bottom as Madeleine came into the hall.

Maddy looked up, jumped, and stared at her in open-mouthed astonishment.

"Charli!" she cried, rushing forward to fling her arms around Charlotte's neck. "You've come back! Oh, thank God!"

Charlotte was stunned. Her sister felt so softly pliant. The recent memory of feeding only made the pulse of her blood more poignantly enticing. She held her, staring at the creamy curve of her neck with its down of fine hair, conscious of the sweetness beneath her peach skin.

She held Madeleine away from her, shaken to the core.

"I thought you were in London, Maddy," she managed to say.

"No, Father sent for me and I've heard this awful story about you and Karl. Is it over, then? Are you all right? Come in, we're having a cup of tea. Didn't Sally take your coat?"

"I let myself in," said Charlotte, hanging up her coat and hat. "Wait – who's in the drawing room?"

"Only Father and Anne. David and Aunt Lizzie have gone back to Parkland."

That made things a little easier. Though it was her father Charlotte most dreaded facing.

"How is Father?"

Maddy shrugged. "Not awfully well, poor thing. But he'll buck up when he sees you!" Charlotte wanted a moment to steady herself, but Maddy was already opening the drawing room door, exclaiming, "Look who's here!"

Dr Neville and Anne were side by side on the sofa, drinking tea. Seeing Charlotte in the doorway they sat up and stared blankly at her. No relief in their faces, just frozen astonishment. Tension fretted the atmosphere.

Finally Anne jumped up and said, "Oh, Charli, what a shock!" Her father, stony-faced, did not utter a word.

"Now come on, tell us what happened!" said Maddy.

Charlotte could not speak.

"Don't be impatient," said Anne. "Let her sit down and have a cup of tea. You needn't say anything until you're ready, Charli."

"All went wrong, did it?" Dr Neville said gruffly. He didn't seem to expect an answer. The aura of unease that emanated from him was powerful enough to subdue even Madeleine.

Charlotte told herself, *I'm still in disgrace, of course. They don't know what to say, either.* Even Anne was reserved, if not hostile. Yet Charlotte felt such tenderness for them that their chilly welcome was unbearable.

This is a terrible mistake. Why did I come back? I can't tell them what's happened. I can't tell them a thing!

As they sat without speaking, Charlotte found herself

mesmerised by the pinkness of Maddy's mouth, the way Anne's hair curved behind her ear, the angles of their hips and knees... Seeing them as a painter would, only she did not want to paint her friend and sister, she wanted to stroke their skin and bite through and suck the life fluid out of their hearts.

God, is this how Karl used to look at us?

She pretended to drink her tea as it congealed in the cup. The idea of tasting it was more repellent than the prospect of drinking blood had once been. Even to let it touch her lips sickened her. Yet they didn't notice. Unbelievable. But then she remembered that no one – except Edward – had noticed that Karl was a vampire, either.

So now I have lost both Karl and my family too. How could I stay here, pretending to be human; not eating, not sleeping, vanishing without explanation? And the desire she felt for them... *Oh, God, tenderness, not impersonal hunger. That's the danger, that my love for them would undo me... yet I do love them. I want them to understand.*

She put down her cup and forced herself to speak.

"I can't stay. I came back to say goodbye... and that I'm sorry."

No one replied. Her father glared, his gaze cold and withering. Although her emotions were in turmoil, she felt distant from them, as Karl had suggested she would. This detachment enabled her to speak calmly, at least. As she tried to continue, she felt a familiar snow-crystal shiver in the centre of the room.

And Ilona appeared.

Madeleine gave a sharp scream and leapt up, her cup and saucer spinning across the carpet. Anne and Dr Neville froze. Charlotte was hardly less astonished. Ilona was dressed to shock: a backless gown of scarlet beaded lace, kohl around her eyes, her lips and nails painted blood red. She was a deliberate, exquisite caricature of a vamp.

Charlotte stood up, horrified. Whatever had changed between her and Ilona, she still didn't trust her.

Images of Ilona at Fleur's party...

"Excuse me for intruding," said Ilona with a venomous smile. "I need a word with Charlotte."

"What are you doing here?" Charlotte said faintly.

"You disappeared without saying *auf wiedersehen*, darling.

Your friends want to talk to you." Before Charlotte could ask what she meant, Ilona began to walk around the room, looking at each member of her family in turn. Then in mock surprise she said, "My dear, you haven't told them, have you?" She laughed and ran her fingernails down Dr Neville's lined cheek. Charlotte flinched. He didn't move a muscle, but looked mortified. "Your poor father doesn't realise."

"Don't touch them!" said Charlotte.

Madeleine and her father looked dumbfounded, but grave intelligence was flowering in Anne's eyes.

"Charlotte, who is this woman? Another of them, isn't she?"

Ilona turned as if she might attack Anne.

"Quiet!" she hissed. Charlotte watched in alarm, remembering that even Karl could not stop Ilona if she became violent. But her tone softened and she went on. "Charlotte looks well, doesn't she? Glowing, I would say. Don't you see anything strange about her?"

They looked bewildered – except Anne. She stared at Charlotte with a dark expression that cut through her. The others didn't understand, but Anne knew.

"Oh, God!" Ilona cried. "You're all so stupid! No one is less observant than a scientist, Dr Neville, as you prove. Look at me and then look at her!"

"Ilona, please don't," said Charlotte.

She continued without pity. "Your precious Charlotte is like me. She is a vampire."

Utter silence. Charlotte made her face blank and gave herself up to their stares, while falling apart inside. What was the point of denying it?

Ilona sat on the sofa arm, swinging one stockinged leg, a bright young thing at a party.

"I thought you should know. She obviously hasn't told you herself. Aren't you going to say something, darling?" she asked Charlotte. "You're not trying very hard to defend yourself."

Charlotte felt Anne's eyes burning into her. What could she do to placate Ilona? Charlotte went to her, put her hand on Ilona's bare shoulder and stroked her neck. Not the gesture of someone who felt intimidated. However odd this looked to her family, it seemed to work.

"Thank you," Charlotte said, softly bitter. "I was trying to tell them rather less brutally."

"Idiot," said Ilona with a mixture of affection and contempt. "You don't belong here. You belong with us. Stefan has a message for you; he's outside with Niklas and Pierre. Are you coming, or not?"

"Yes," Charlotte sighed with a strange sense of resignation. "If you will wait outside while I finish saying goodbye."

"Well, don't be long, or I may be forced to come back and tease you a little more." Ilona blew her a kiss and vanished. Charlotte could sense the cool flames of other vampire presences outside the house.

She made herself face her family. They looked stricken, their eyes full of incredulous horror. *They're frightened of me!*

She went to Maddy, reached out to touch her hair.

"Don't be afraid of me. It's not as bad as it seems."

Her sister jerked away, crying, "Don't touch me! Get away from me, Charli!"

Charlotte drew back, shattered by her reaction, thinking, *I could hypnotise her with this glamour until she wasn't afraid and loved me again. But it wouldn't be fair, it wouldn't be real.*

"Father," Charlotte said quietly. "Can I speak to you alone, please?"

Without a word, he stood and walked across the hall into the study. Charlotte followed, with the impression that he didn't want to do this, but could not resist her will.

Do I have this power over others now?

He sat in his desk chair but she stood, keeping her distance. In this study Karl had caught her alone and she'd lost her fear of him... as a prelude to losing everything else to him.

Do I want to step back through the veil, be human again? That was the best time. Wanting Karl, in all innocence of what I was actually asking for. Well, now I have it, with a vengeance.

Her father looked at her for a long time before he said, "It can't be true, this awful thing. Tell me it's not true."

"I'm sorry, Father. It is."

His face changed slowly as he regarded her, crumpling with fear, anger, denial.

"You're different," he said. "What's he done to my little girl? How can I get you back?"

"You can't, Father," she said softly. "I am still the same inside. But what I have become can't be reversed."

His hands curled into fists. "He's destroyed you!"

"No. I chose this. No one forced me. I wanted it."

Colour rose into his cheeks. He was shaking his head.

"*Why?*"

"Because I love Karl." She knew her words tormented him, that he couldn't bear to hear them, but she had to tell the truth. "I always loved him, even after what happened to Edward, even when I was his prisoner. Always."

"But he's evil! It's obscene. How could you do this, Charlotte? You were so blameless, innocent. He's corrupted you. Your mother would turn in her grave."

"Wouldn't you have loved Mother, whatever she did? Why must you cling to this belief that I was perfect? I never was. You are seeing the real me now. This is how I've always been inside!" She leaned towards him but he recoiled, denying her, pushing her away. The pain made her feel cruel. "You never saw Mother as she really was, either."

"How dare you! I adored her!"

"Yes, but you didn't *know* her! She wasn't perfect either. And I am not her, I never have been her."

"I don't understand what you're saying."

"Yes, you do." She knew she was hurting him but she could not stop. "Isn't this what you wanted me to be? Mother again, the saint who never existed, just a frozen image of her, captured eternally. Well, now you have that. I shall never grow old! Do you want me to stay here for you to look at forever?"

Her father was weeping, his head in his hands. She was aghast at herself, wrung out with grief... but she could not reach him. How could she comfort him with these white demonic hands that later would grasp someone else, not to console them but to feast on their blood?

Suddenly he looked old, all his vigour gone. He'd always seemed so strong. This glimpse of feebleness was unbearable.

I have done this. I've destroyed him.

"I shan't stay," she whispered. "I can't, of course. Father, don't weep. Please forgive me. I still love you."

In a voice thick with tears he said, "Get out of my house, Charlotte. As far as I am concerned I have only two daughters left; their names are Madeleine and Anne."

She went to the door, paused to look at the curved bulk of his back, the wisps of white hair straggling over his crumpled collar. Such a familiar sight... not intent on work now, but bowed down with bereavement. Only the cool centre of her soul enabled her to close the door and walk away. But all around it, human flames blazed.

Anne was in the hall, arms folded, glaring at her. Her cheeks were flushed, her eyes bright and hard. Charlotte faced her, hoping only for a word of acceptance; trying hard to ignore her enticing human heat.

"I'm leaving, Anne."

"Well, I suppose that's for the best," Anne said flatly.

"Please look after Father. I hoped we could part on good terms but he's so distraught, I can't say anything..."

"Oh, of course I'll look after him! Sweep up the mess you've left! What are friends for?"

"Anne, don't." She felt moisture gathering on her eyelashes.

"Oh, vampires cry, do they, Charlotte? Crocodile tears, I suppose."

"Why are you so bitter? You were the one person who always tried to understand and not condemn me!"

"Yes, when I thought that your good sense could win through in the end. But to do this! To deliberately become one of these – How do you expect me to be understanding? I can't even begin to adjust my mind to the enormity of it."

"Do I seem so vile to you now?" Charlotte exclaimed.

"Oh, you look and sound the same – and yet you don't. Your skin is luminous, your eyes glow. Like that woman who appeared. She killed Fleur and Clive, didn't she? The moment I saw her, I knew it was true. Yet you put your arms around her! I'm frightened of you, actually. Yet you stand there still expecting us to be friends!"

"I don't expect anything," Charlotte said quietly. "But I don't want you to hate me. I couldn't bear it. If you think I'm unfeeling, you're wrong. Emotion, pain, everything is more intense now than it ever was before."

"Oh, do you expect sympathy? You've realised that Karl's heartless charm is nothing in comparison to losing the love of your family?" Charlotte said nothing. She wouldn't give Anne the satisfaction of knowing that Karl had abandoned her. "I warned you about him from the beginning! Anyone can make a mistake in love, Charlotte, but to go on chasing it to such extremes – what did you *expect*?"

"If you're telling me I deserve this, you're right!" Charlotte drew away, beginning to detach herself from Anne, from their mutual anguish. Now Anne's eyes were full of pain while her own were tranquil. Like Karl's: a veil between the Crystal Ring and the human world. "I never meant to hurt you, or anyone... yet I have. But I shall always love you, Anne. You look on me as a demon, but do you think I could take a drop of your blood?"

Anne started, as if the thought had not occurred to her.

"I'd rather die," Charlotte went on softly. "Karl never laid a finger on anyone here – except Edward – yet he's torn this family apart and drained us of happiness. And so have I. This is what vampires do, isn't it? Tell Maddy and David I'm sorry."

Charlotte turned away, put on her coat and hat and quietly let herself out. She leaned against the front door for a few seconds, calmed by the summer air on her face, while the grief that speared her from skull to feet was so familiar that she hardly noticed it. Disaster. It all felt unfinished, to part in acrimony, without reconciliation. *They have the capacity to heal... It's me who can't change. Will I feel like this forever? Long after they've forgotten me and are nodding contentedly by their firesides, will I still be this torn, cold thing that can't die?*

She walked across the wide drive to the gate, and outside in the tree-lined street she found Pierre, Stefan, Niklas and Ilona waiting for her. Stefan put his arms around her and hugged her. It was hard to believe he'd once been so dangerous, when now he seemed so sweet. She returned the embrace, but it was not him she wanted: it was Karl.

"Why are you here?" she said dully.

"Oh, Charlotte," said Stefan. "Never try to explain yourself to humans. It takes a very special mortal to understand a vampire. We came to Schloss Holdenstein after Karl went there with Kristian. Didn't you know?"

"Should I have done? I was locked in a cell, I didn't know anything," she said, thinking, *What does this matter?*

"You'd left before we could speak to you. Karl gave me a message."

A flash of lightning in her chest.

"What message?"

Stefan lifted his shoulders.

"I don't understand it. He said, 'Tell Charlotte to remember the manner of our escape.'"

"That's all?" Her nerves were alight, numbness replaced by frustration. "What did he mean?"

"We thought you would know."

She shook her head. "But why would Karl leave me any message at all... Unless he's telling me that his surrender to Kristian was a pretence?"

"That's what we wondered," Stefan said softly.

She looked at them each in turn. Niklas apart, they seemed to expect some revelation from her. *But can I trust them? Or are they asking me to betray Karl?*

"Don't raise your hopes, *chérie*," said Pierre. "It may be his way of saying goodbye. I tell you, I have never seen Karl behave like that before. I have seen him angry, upset – I've done my share of provoking him – but I have never seen him lose his dignity. Kristian would have known if he was faking it. The moment he gave in, Kristian forgot all about punishing us. No point, if he'd won the game. Karl didn't even care what Kristian did to *you*, Ophelia."

Charlotte flinched.

"But why do you care about this? Why help me become one of you in the first place? I thought you were all loyal to Kristian!"

"Ah, trying to work out whose side we are on?" said Ilona. "No one's but our own, dear."

Stefan said, "Don't you know his favourites are the difficult ones? Look at us. None of us ever followed Kristian's dogma. We've all grown sick of having to pretend. Kristian demands love with menaces; Karl wins love simply by existing. You have that gift too, Charlotte. We believe it's time things changed."

Charlotte hung onto the words of the message, her only hope. Then she thought, *Not the manner. The* manor!

Frost crystallised in her heart. *My God, he wouldn't go there again, he wouldn't risk death, not even...*

Oh yes, he would. I know him. He would.

A flash-fire of crisis, as dazzling as sun on snow. She looked at the others, thinking, *Can I trust them? I don't know, but I must, I have no choice.*

She said guardedly, "I think I know where Karl has gone. If I'm right, he has put himself in extreme danger. Will you come with me?"

At the base of the steep narrow stairs, the domed chamber seemed smaller and more oppressive than Karl remembered. He stood beside Kristian, looking around at the dripping, encrusted walls, the drifts of soil and masonry. Countless tons of earth and stone pressed down above them. The air was thick with a cloying graveyard stench. Still no voices. The silence was a pent-up scream, as taut as a crossbow.

Opposite, the thin black tunnel wormed its way through the earth. Karl stared as if entranced. The tunnel seemed to exhale a whitish mist that trailed over his skin like fingers of liquid nitrogen.

Can't he feel it?

"This is of no great interest," said Kristian. His voice, too loud, rolled down the tunnel and awoke a faint echo. To Karl's ears the echo was a faint, anguished wail that went on and on... Kristian, though, seemed not to notice. "This way?"

He strode into the tunnel and Karl followed, walking with slow but lethal determination. Apprehension crawled around him in a cloud of ice dust. Wine jars lurked like hunch-backed, alien creatures along the walls.

"There is a barrier of debris blocking the passage," said Karl, "but there is a way through."

"Certainly there is," said Kristian. As they reached the barrels and rubbish that filled the tunnel, he didn't hesitate to put his massive shoulder to the stack. Karl knew he should stop him;

instead he simply watched, with a sense of fatalism, as the barrier creaked and swayed. If Kristian would dig his own grave...

The stack gave way suddenly and crashed down into the darkness. The vibration shook the whole tunnel. Karl sensed a voiceless, impotent anger radiating from the walls, saw a brief vision of a skeleton holding clawed hands to its own face...

Kristian stepped over the wreckage. An unwholesome chill swept to meet them, but Kristian still seemed oblivious. On the other side, he ducked under an archway into a small chamber like a monk's cell. Karl feared it might be fatal to disturb the spider's den, yet he followed, thinking, *Isn't this what I want?*

The cell shimmered with an iridescent ghost-grey light. There was the aged table riddled with woodworm, twisted stalagmites of candlewax on its surface, soot furring the low ceiling. And on the table lay the huge black book. Journal, ledger of death, Bible – whatever it was, the tome seemed the sullen heart of all the pain that haunted the tunnel.

Does Kristian feel nothing wrong, nothing at all? Karl thought incredulously. *What power can fill an immortal with such dread?*

"You did not mention this cell," said Kristian.

"I didn't come in here before," said Karl, "and I don't think we should linger."

"What is wrong with your nerves, my friend? You're behaving like a human." As Kristian moved forward to look at the book, it struck Karl how much this cell was like Kristian's own sanctum: the same austerity, just the table, chair, candles... and the Holy Book.

What was Kristian thinking? That the vampire who'd dwelled here had been a kindred spirit – or a rival?

"Don't touch it," Karl murmured.

Kristian ignored him. He touched the cover – only to snatch his fingers away as if it were red hot. The five large black prints he left in the dust were like some arcane rune to summon creatures from a lost dimension. His hand poised, he stood motionless, staring into the air. Listening.

In a mixed rush of triumph and terror, Karl thought, *At last! He hears them!*

An uncanny sound began; a harsh thin wailing, as piercing as crystal. It shrilled from the walls, the floor, from the book itself, as if every surface had soaked up the ghastly deaths, refracted and magnified them before flinging them loose. Pent-up screams arrowed from the lightless abyss of centuries, pouring out anguish, desolation, and poison-bitter grief.

And with the screams came a glacial plunge in temperature.

"Almighty God, what is this?" Kristian exclaimed. He came towards Karl, huge and pale, as if looming over a victim. "Why is it so cold?"

"You notice it now, Father?" Karl said, controlled.

Kristian pushed past him and went out into the tunnel. The multi-voiced atonal lament swelled louder, rising and falling. Karl felt the cold dropping softly over him like liquid air, scorching his hands. The tunnel became a writhing black wormhole that led into a netherworld.

"But those voices, what are they?" said Kristian.

"Ghosts, Father."

"There are no such things!" Kristian stared around him, bewildered. "It's freezing. I never felt anything like this, outside the *Weisskalt*."

"I told you, an unearthly cold... Come with me. I'll explain."

Kristian let himself be led, not realising that Karl was taking him into the heart of the peril. He rubbed his hands together, like a mortal on a winter's day.

"Godless, this place!" he exclaimed.

"That's what they thought, too, the people who died here," Karl said thinly. "Look."

They stood at the entrance to the charnel house, where hundreds of broken skeletons were piled. The air thrummed with shuddering waves of pressure, an arctic gale.

His voice low and strained, Kristian said, "There is nothing – nothing for immortals to fear in a few bones."

But these were bones heaped on bones, gleaming with sickly ochres, stained brown with age and dried blood. Screaming skulls, skeletal hands pointing in accusation. *Ah, you. You consigned us to this hell. Now you wake us to drink our revenge.* From them flowed an amorphous wave of pain, open-jawed, mindless, ravenous pain.

Kristian tried to turn away. Karl stopped him. Although he

felt his lips stiffening with frost, black fear shivering through him, he detached himself and said, "But think. All of them were slain by a single vampire. Imagine the slow accumulation of their agony in these walls." Karl's voice fell to a whisper. "Their anguish has become a vacuum. Something nature abhors… just as she abhors us."

In a ghastly way, the sudden breaking of Kristian's nerve was the most horrifying thing of all. He lurched away from Karl and ran into the darkness with his hands over his ears.

Karl raced after him, caught him, bore him down to the cold earth. Kristian tried to escape into the Crystal Ring, but Karl dragged him back. Between the two realms they hung, struggling. But the wraiths were everywhere, inescapable.

At last Karl hauled him back to Earth and pinned him there.

"What in God's name are you trying to do?" Kristian cried, writhing under him. "Karl! Let me go, we must escape!"

But Karl clung to Kristian with deathly dispassion, as if he'd become the lost souls' nemesis on their behalf. He endured the hellish suction as he felt his energy bleeding away, his limbs turning to granite. Searing polar coldness drenched him, worse than the *Weisskalt* because it was malevolent, voracious. But Kristian was weakening faster.

"Karl, help me. Don't leave me here." Kristian held one long arm outstretched in the frigid air, his face was creased with helpless pain.

Karl was staggered by his own heartlessness. *My master. My spiritual father*, he thought. *This is how I betray you. Too easy to lull your suspicions with a few soft words and vulnerable looks. Because to die with you is better than letting you live!*

"No. I won't leave you." And he wrapped his arms around Kristian and held him tight as the scorching black coldness froze them both.

It seemed to Karl that the skeletons were reassembling themselves and standing up. The energy they had reclaimed now formed luminous flesh to clothe their bones. In transparent skin and swathes of opalescent ice vapour, they walked into the tunnel and circled the two fallen vampires, pointing at them, laughing, screaming, plucking at their clothes and trampling them with clawlike feet. Gradually Karl perceived endless repetition in their motion: a hideous dance that would loop for eternity...

A revelation spilled over him. He spoke into Kristian's ear, as if the wraiths spoke through him.

"That vampire drank more than their blood. He took their life force, as you do. And in the end they turned on him and destroyed him... like this. Just as they are destroying you now."

"I need warmth, Karl." Kristian's voice was thin with anguish. "Your wrist, I must have your blood."

He began straining to fasten his teeth in Karl's flesh. Karl held him off easily, and then he thought, *Yes... that.* And he bit into Kristian's neck and began to draw the sluggish fluid out of his veins.

Like slushed ice, Kristian's blood made his teeth ache, and it was shockingly strong and sour, like a child's first taste of schnapps. And then it stung with pinpricks of fire. Karl could tolerate only a mouthful or two at a time, but he felt his own chill retreating a fraction.

"What are you doing?" Kristian whispered.

"Only what you did to all the others, Father," Karl said softly.

"You deceived me. You lied!" Kristian gave a long drawn-out groan that went through Karl like an arrow. But he could not afford pity. He observed his own ruthlessness as if from outside, amazed, horrified.

He heard his own voice saying, hard and cruel, "I never told you a word of untruth. I warned you that we might die. How does the cold feel, beloved Father? Is this how our victims suffer, do you think?"

Only then did Kristian truly accept that he'd been betrayed. Like a marble temple, he had been unassailable until an earthquake brought him crashing down. His collapse was horrific, beyond belief.

A strange reversal of their roles.

"No, you would not betray me," Kristian said through stiffening lips. "Not you, Karl. I only ever loved you. I know I hurt the others, I know I made them suffer... I was punishing them for not being *you*. A thousand times I could have tormented and destroyed you, Karl, but I did not. I never hurt you! My only sin has been to love you too much. And for that, you destroy me?"

"An ironic fate, I agree," Karl said coldly. "But we'll die together. Poetic justice."

The disembodied voices were dying away, back into the walls, back into their abyss. Sated, it seemed. Kristian seemed small and desiccated, suddenly. A black eagle, crushed and tattered. His eyes were closed, rolling a little under the lids, but he did not speak again.

Die, damn you! Karl cried to himself. Then, *One word, Kristian. One word to remind me that I am right to do this...*

"All this, for love?" he whispered. "When the simplest gesture of kindness was beyond you? Yet was it your fault you knew no better?"

Karl wept, but his tears froze. His sight was fading. Light too was energy, and the ghosts took even that. Blackness rolled in.

Now the wraiths were bearing him away into the heart of the dark cosmic machinery from which they had emerged. Karl stared into a gulf of half-seen horrors, falling towards the obscure source of terror... *that there is no rest in death...*

Bright figures came walking towards him through the slanting valley of shadows. Angels with beloved faces, come to preside sorrowfully over his fall. Sweet Ilona. Pierre, Stefan and Niklas... and dearest of all, his beloved, endlessly betrayed Charlotte.

It never occurred to Charlotte, as she led her companions through the old ice house and down into the subterranean passage, that the presences might harm them. All she could think about was Karl. When she finally considered the danger, she noticed that the tunnel was eerily quiet. No voices moaning from the inky walls, the air no colder than a winter breeze on her skin.

And there they were, twined in the darkness, like the roots of two trees that had grown together and fossilised. Karl and Kristian. Charlotte stopped, unable to stifle a cry.

Were they dead? If the supernatural void had taken Kristian's life, it could not have spared Karl.

"Karl!" she called, not daring to go any closer. Steel ropes squeezed her.

To her shock, one of the figures began to rise and come towards her. He moved stiffly, like a skeleton animated by some numinous force, spectral, terrifying. For a moment she couldn't tell which of them it was. Then she saw it was Karl, and the horror of everything almost annihilated her; the way he had rejected her, the leaden indifference in his gaze – and now this. The eldritch corpse-light in his face. She shrank away from him.

"Charlotte, help me," he said hoarsely, one hand held out to her like a frosted branch. Then he saw the others with her. His eyes moved over Stefan, Niklas, Pierre, and rested on Ilona. He spoke as if sapped of all strength, all choice, throwing himself on their uncertain loyalty. "I am not sure whether he's dead or not. I must be sure. Help me... help me to make an end of him."

Kristian's universe had contracted to a speck of blackness and he found no God at the centre. He was numbed against the frigid air that had splintered him, adrift in torpor, his life energy stolen by the dead, his blood drained by Karl.

Yet he was still alive. He saw their shapes in the darkness: Stefan and Niklas, his gilded angels; Pierre who, beneath his cynicism, adored him; his beautiful, wayward daughters, Ilona and Charlotte.

They had come to save him. If only he could call out to them, bless them...

But what was this? A dull silver line arcing through the darkness. The edge of an axe.

Karl's hands wielded the axe. Karl's eyes were fierce, mad with revulsion and cruelty. Surely the others must stop him! But they only stood and watched, gazing down as soullessly as Niklas.

The blade swept down. Kristian felt the savage wrench of pain, felt blood bubbling in the wound, choking him. Saw the insane glaze of Karl's eyes, those terrible amber eyes, as the axe fell again and again. He heard his own spinal column crack, the tendons recoiling; felt his own head bounce back a little with the blow and come to rest still staring upwards.

He gazed at his executioners. Now he realised that their eyes were full, not of love, but of twisted hatred. Had he always misread them?

Traitors, all of them. Traitors.

And he parted his lips, and saw their faces hang with absolute horror as his severed head spoke. The words came out thick and slurred.

"This – is how you love me? Even you, Ilona, Stefan? And you – Karl?"

Then the silver line came hurtling towards his forehead, and the blackness split apart and swallowed him.

They scattered and buried Kristian's body in the earth of the tunnel floor, working swiftly in charged silence. Charlotte felt removed from the horror of it, but she was trembling from head to foot. Her companions' feelings cut the air like a glass web. Not jubilation. *Grief.* It infected her too. This had to be done but no one wanted it, such a terrible thing.

At length they emerged from the ice house into the sloping mass of trees that concealed it. Night lay on the gardens of Parkland Hall. Moonlight iced the leaves. Without speaking, Stefan and Pierre shared their blood with Karl, to help revive him. And Charlotte looked on as Karl and Ilona gazed at each other, embraced briefly, almost savagely; parted again. Then Karl left them and came to Charlotte.

His face was in shadow, moonlight silvering one cheekbone and catching bronze sparks in his eyes. She had no idea what he would say, could not tell whether his eyes held love or regret. She stared at him, unable to move towards him or away. And she saw doubt in his face and realised that her thoughts were clear in her eyes.

I don't know that I can ever trust you again. I can exist without you. If you are going to reject me again, I shall reject you first!

How pale he looked. At a loss, somehow. Their positions had changed subtly: she was no longer a girl hopelessly in awe of him. Yet his beauty still brought aching tears to her throat, made everything else seem futile. That would never change. To stop loving him was impossible.

He said, "Every time we meet, it seems I have to ask for your forgiveness."

"Are you – are you asking for it now? You convinced me

completely that you no longer loved me. It wasn't even the first time! You almost destroyed me, and if it ever happened again, I'm certain I *would* be destroyed. I don't know whether I can take that risk."

"Charlotte, it almost killed me too! The only way I could lure Kristian away was to pretend that he'd won. The only way I could save those he'd threatened was to pretend I didn't care about them. And I had to convince you, because if I had not, Kristian would not have believed me either. You understand, don't you?"

He held out his hand to her. She clasped it, but didn't move any closer. How cold their fingers were. She believed him, but part of her still held back.

"Yes, I understand."

"I know what Kristian did to you, beloved, and I am so sorry. But I had to destroy him before I had any chance of saving you."

"Ilona let me out."

The ghost of a smile touched his mouth.

"I know. God, what a mess, all of this. I only sent the message in the hope that you would realise what I intended to do. I didn't expect you to come here... because I didn't think you would be able to. And I thought I should die with Kristian, you see."

"Oh God," she said, and gave in. He drew her into his arms and they clung to each other for an age. Only the soft movement of the trees around them made a sound, and then the footfalls of the other vampires – tired of waiting for them – moving away and vanishing into the Crystal Ring.

Karl and Charlotte were alone.

"Never do that to me again," she whispered. "Not for any reason."

"Dearest, there will never be any need. We may have only a few virtues, but the greatest of them is constant love."

Arms linked, they began to walk slowly through the gardens as they had once walked before, in another existence. Moonlight silvered the lawns, the fountains and statues. The shadows were jewelled with wondrous colours only vampires could perceive. This garden would always be theirs, sacred to them.

Charlotte asked, "But how long had you planned it?"

"It was in the back of my mind since we escaped from the manor, but I never made a conscious plan. I decided to take the chance only at the last minute, because I simply could see no other answer. I didn't know it would work. Kristian might have guessed, or he might have been unaffected. At best I thought we'd both die, but the ghosts took a more thorough revenge on him than on me. And I drank his blood. I think that saved me... No, *you* saved me. His blood gave me the strength to escape, but without you I would not have had the will." Karl looked up at the sky. "I did not want to kill him, Charlotte," he said quietly. "I only wanted him to leave us alone. I took no pleasure in his death."

"I know," she said.

"I loathe myself for it, in a way. He was so desperate to trust me that it was almost pathetic. But I let him trust me. Now I know how it feels to betray someone with a kiss."

"Oh, Karl, don't. It was terrible, but what choice did he give you?"

They walked on, passing the fountain where Charlotte had once sat in solitude while Madeleine's party went on without her; where she had first opened her heart to Anne and begun to fall in love with Karl. The memories were all around her, a cocoon of spun silver.

"Kristian was always lost at heart, I think," said Karl. "He never felt part of life. He had no real inner life of his own so he fed vicariously on other people's."

Charlotte said, "Did you love him?"

Karl hesitated, breathed out imperceptibly.

"I think perhaps I did. And for the reasons he gave: that he was the centre of things. Never changing. But I could not admit it to myself. By loving him I betrayed Therese, Ilona, I betrayed everything I believed in... and I think that in killing him, I was trying to bury my own guilt."

The confession shook her so much that she couldn't respond at first.

Eventually she said, "I wonder if I would love you so much, if you did not take out a knife and dissect yourself at every opportunity?"

Karl laughed. "It seems to me that vampires are no different to humans. We need a leader, but once we have one, all we want is to destroy him. Strange... but I never envisioned outliving Kristian."

"You aren't sorry, are you?"

"That I'm still alive? Still walking the Earth, at least." His hand found hers, two pale unnatural hands twisted together like white coral in the moonlight. She moved towards him and his other hand slid beneath her hair to caress her neck. "We carve a path through to what we want, in the end. All I wanted was to be with you, Charlotte. And now we have that, regardless of whom we have trampled over on our way."

"I wish I could see Anne again," Charlotte said suddenly. "I tried to explain to them... It was so painful. Worse for them than for me. It will hurt forever, won't it? All of us."

Karl made no comment, but she knew he understood. She was glad he didn't say, "I warned you."

After a while he said, "I have sometimes wondered if there is not another circle of vampires who have somehow kept themselves hidden from the rest of us, even Kristian. I wonder what knowledge lies inside the strange book we found in the tunnel."

"Do you want to go back and look?"

Karl smiled sadly. "You would, wouldn't you? No, Charlotte. Perhaps one day... but not now. I want to forget. If the book does hold any answers, at this moment I simply do not care."

Charlotte's memory leapt in a thrill of excitement.

"But Karl, I was going to tell you about the Crystal Ring! When you took me there I understood: it's made of the energy of human minds, human consciousness recreating a spiritual essence of the Earth itself; and for some reason we can perceive it as a material realm and move through it. Kristian threw me into a cell for saying that. But when I died and the Ring's energy replaced my own and transformed me, I knew, I simply *knew*. Do you believe me?"

There was a sceptical lift to Karl's mouth, but his eyes were warm. Fascinated.

"I have no reason not to. But why should the energy of that realm make us into vampires?"

"What is mankind's greatest fear?" Charlotte asked eagerly.

"Death, I suppose."

"Yes, but beyond that... the fear of the dead coming back. It's a universal terror, the ultimate violation of nature. And their greatest hope?"

"That there is life after death," Karl said, smiling.

"Yes. And the two contradict each other, but they are equally powerful. Don't you see? We are the inevitable creation of people's most powerful nightmares and dreams. Kristian wanted to destroy mankind, but he never saw that, without them, we could not exist. *They created us.*"

"Oh, Charlotte," said Karl. He kissed her mouth, then rested his head against hers. "If what you say is true, we have an answer to the question of immortality. We shall live for as long as the human race continues to fear us and desire us."

DARK UPON LIGHT

You'll find him hard to recognise
Cos he won't dress in black
He wears a suit of gold lamé
With velvet front and back
But he can touch your trembling heart
Can touch your very soul
He'll take you with him when he leaves
He'll make your dreams turn old.

He alone can read the signs
And he can read them well
But where he gets his power
There's no one here can tell
So if you're out alone at night
Be sure to take a friend
Cos it gets awful lonely
In a world that never ends...

HORSLIPS, "RIDE TO HELL"

Kristian's body lay scattered and buried, yet some essence of him was still travelling. Through darkness for a long time... and then towards a single white star that expanded as he rose towards it.

The Crystal Ring.

Though he had no physical sensation, somehow he knew he was still within his body. The Ring had drawn his remains into itself and was delivering them up as an offering to God...

Kristian lay in the *Weisskalt*, drifting under the eye of the Creator. A single blazing cold eye, focused by the dizzying walls of the aurora that soared up towards the glory, like the song of angels made visible... But he could not join them. He could not free his spirit from the frozen ruins of his body.

This is immortality.

"Did I not serve you well, O Lord?" he cried. "I have failed. I have brought you only children who turned their faces away from you. I could not make them see the truth. 'Honour thy father and thy mother,' you say... but they did not honour me! They have buried me, their creator. And it had to be Karl. The most wayward child is always the most loved... The prodigal son who never returned..."

All around him lay the bodies of other vampires – like rows of black crosses against the snow, as neat as war graves – sleeping forever in a realm that was too beautiful, too burningly cold for any creature to bear. He had condemned them to this. Now he lay among them, like some monstrous dismembered snake on the ice crust. But with a rush of passionate will, Kristian thought, *Perhaps there are others who will not fail, Lord.*

He could not even remember why he had brought them here. For disappointing him, failing him... the reasons now seemed trivial, lost.

No crime so great as the one Karl perpetrated against me.

Their bodies were not ruined. They slept, but they were not dead.

"Wake," said Kristian. His will drove him. "Take revenge. Don't let them forget me. You are my children. I command you to sleep and now I command you to wake!"

And he felt something break and fall away from him. He was relinquishing his power over them. He wanted to set them free, like a flock of dark birds to soar over the Earth. Imperfect envoys... but better than none at all.

But he was losing the battle. His tenacious immortal consciousness was slipping away at last, all the world shimmering and coalescing into a single white circle of light.

Now the eye of his creator was all he could see, blazing frigid silver. Nothing else. There was no anger within him, no pain, no sense of betrayal. No thoughts at all. Stillness.

While all around him, on the crystal-white sweep of the plain, the dark forms of his children were stretching and stirring into life.

ACKNOWLEDGEMENTS

For help with research, inspiration, encouragement and friendship: thanks to Keren Gilfoyle, Susan Charlotte Berry, Storm Constantine, Julie Parker, Anne Gay, David Gemmell, John Richard Parker, and Kathy Gale.

Special thanks to Caroline Jones and Mark Weatherall, for all their help at Selwyn College, Cambridge; and to Marlene Fleet, for "Der Doppelgänger".

Thanks also to Barry Devlin and Horslips, and to Stevie Nicks, for music that has haunted me down the years... and inspired some of the chapter titles.

ABOUT THE AUTHOR

Freda Warrington was born in Leicestershire, UK, where she now lives with her husband and mother. She has worked in medical illustration and graphic design, but her first love has always been writing. Her first novel *A Blackbird in Silver* was published in 1986, to be followed by many more, including *A Taste of Blood Wine*, *Dark Cathedral*, *The Amber Citadel*, and *The Court of the Midnight King* – a fantasy based on the life of the controversial King Richard III. As well as the *Blood Wine Sequence* for Titan Books, she writes the *Aetherial Tales* series for Tor. Her novel *Elfland* won a Romantic Times award for Best Fantasy Novel. She can be found at www.fredawarrington.com

A DANCE IN BLOOD VELVET
Freda Warrington

For the love of her vampire suitor, Karl, Charlotte has forsaken her human life. Now her only contact with people is when she hunts them down to feed. Her thirst for blood repulses her but its fulfilment brings ecstasy.

The one light in the shadows is the passion that burns between her and Karl. A love that it seems will last for eternity – until Karl's former lover, the seductively beautiful Katerina, is rescued from the Crystal Ring. For nearly fifty years she has lain, as dead, in the icy depths of the *Weisskalt*. Now she wants to reclaim her life... and Karl.

In despair, Charlotte turns to the prima ballerina Violette Lenoir, an ice maiden who only thaws when she dances. Charlotte is fascinated as she has been by no other human, longing to bring joy to the dancer. But her obsession opens the floodgates to a far darker threat than the vampires could ever have imagined. For Violette is more than human and if she succumbs to the vampire's kiss, it could unleash a new terror...

Available April 2014

THE ANNO DRACULA SERIES
Kim Newman

Anno Dracula
The Bloody Red Baron
Dracula Cha Cha Cha
Johnny Alucard

"Compulsory reading... Glorious." Neil Gaiman

"A tour de force which succeeds brilliantly." *The Times*

"A marvellous marriage of political satire, melodramatic intrigue, gothic horror and alternative history. Not to be missed." *The Independent*

"A gripping, fast-paced adventure... Great fun." *The Guardian*

"A brilliantly witty parallel-world saga... builds sure-footedly to bravura climax which entirely redefines 'Victorian values'." *Daily Telegraph*

"Politics, horror and romance are woven together in this brilliantly imagined and realised novel. Newman's prose is a delight, his attention to detail spellbinding." *Time Out*

"*Anno Dracula* is the definitive account of that post-modern species, the self-obsessed undead." *The New York Times*